Anne of Cleves

D. LAWRENCE-YOUNG

This edition published in 2018 by Sharpe Books.

ISBN-10: 1730946925
ISBN-13: 978-1730946929

DEDICATION

Although King Henry VIII had six queens, my only queen is my wife, Queen Beverley, whom I do not plan to divorce or decapitate.

TABLE OF CONTENTS

Contemporary Quotes about Anne of Cleves

"...a lady of commendable regard, courteous, gentle, a good housekeeper and very bountiful to her servants... [and never been] *"any quarrels, tale- bearings or mischievous intrigues in her court, and she was tenderly loved by all her domestics.*

"Raphael Holinshed, Chronicler. (c.1529-1580) *Chronicles of England, Scotland & Ireland (1587)*

She did "embrace virtue and gentleness wherein consists very nobility."

Thomas Elyot, diplomat & scholar (c.1490-1546) and
Thomas Becon, Protestant reformer (c.1511-1567)
The Defence of Good Women

"Everybody has nothing but good to say about the Duchess."

Baron Kaspar von Breumer, 1559.
Agent for Ferdinand, Holy Roman Emperor 1558-1564.

PROLOGUE

My name is Anne - Anne of Cleves. Once, years ago, I was the fourth wife of King Henry the Eighth but now I am dying. I am not saying this to gain your sympathy but because it is a true fact. And because of this I feel the need to tell you something about my life before I depart this earthly world.

My life has evolved around a picture, a portrait: a portrait of me. There are not many people who can say that one of the most significant events of their life was spent sitting in a spacious castle chamber and having their portrait painted by Hans Holbein, the most talented court-painter of his time. But that is exactly what happened to me.

Master Holbein the Younger was instructed by his royal master, King Henry the Eighth of England, to come over to where I lived in the Duchy of Cleves in the Rhineland and paint a likeness of me. He then had to return to England with the finished work and show it to His Majesty. In London, after studying the portrait, the king would decide whether he would marry me or not. Of course you know the king did decide to marry me but our marriage lasted for a mere six months.

Now, as I lie dying in my manor house in Cheyne Walk, Chelsea, I find myself thinking back on the different styles of life I led, that is, before and after this portrait was painted. A few days ago I made my will and bequeathed various sums of money, jewellery and other goods and chattels to all the people, both noble and base-born, who have served me so well during my life.

Fortunately for me, there has been quite a large number who were concerned about my well-being during these last two decades on this earth. Naturally, most of them were involved in my life both when I was queen and afterwards when I left the court and became known as 'the King's Sister.' But now, as I lie here on my death-bed and before I list the names of all of these kind people, I think I should tell you something of my story. Although I am now forty-two, the main part of my story began twenty years ago. It all started with the birth of a baby boy, a prince, who was destined to become King Edward VI of England, the only legitimate son of King Henry VIII.

Chapter One - A Birth and a Death

"It's boy! It's a boy!"

"The queen's had a son! – a prince!"

The joyous cries echoed down the long corridors of Hampton Court Palace to be slightly muffled by the heavy velvet cloaks and jackets of the king's lords, and by the lighter fabrics of their wives and mistresses. They had all been standing around in expectant groups for hours waiting for this piece of news. Some were leaning against the walls; others were sitting on padded benches.

"A son! A son! We have a prince at last!" Everyone there, on that chilly October morning, gave vent to their feelings of joy and relief. The king now had a son. Surely another would soon follow. At last the curse on the Tudor dynasty was broken. The nobles, the guards and the servants - in fact, the whole country - had waited for this moment. It was almost thirty years since the king had married his first wife, that Spanish princes, Catherine of Aragon. The lords, guards and court officials clapped each other on the back and their womenfolk clapped their hands and smiled. Many of the women, remembering the pains that they had experienced, also winced as they thought of their queen lying there in the shaded and heavily curtained chamber, surrounded by her midwives and other servants. No doubt she was feeling very weak and totally exhausted.

"Is he alive? Is he well? How much does he weigh?" were the questions on everyone's lips, questions that raced down the corridors of the king's rambling Thames-side palace.

"He's well, he's well. Lady Lisle says he's a bonny bouncing lad with fair hair," a young lady reported as she stepped out of the queen's chamber. "Hooray! The king has a prince at last, after all these years."

"Aye," a young page, wearing the Duke of Norfolk's colours, whispered to his friend, his hand covering his mouth.

"And only after he had two wives before this one."

"Does the king know?" a young blonde lady-in-waiting asked. "Has anyone been sent to tell him?"

"Yes, my dear. Some of his men have ridden off to Esher to tell him the good news. Fear not. If he doesn't know now, he will do so soon."

"But why is he there in Esher? I know he has another palace there, but surely he should be here, by the side of the queen."

"Oh, my dear," one of the older ladies said. "You must be new here at court and obviously don't know our King Henry."

"That's right," young Jane Westbourne bowed in respect. "I arrived here only one month ago from the country, from Derbyshire."

"Then I will tell you. His Majesty has a mortal fear of any sort of illness and the plague. The last time there was plague in London he even gave out orders that anyone who lived in London would not be allowed to come out here to the court in Hampton, whatever their rank."

"What, nobody?"

"That's right. Nobody, whether he was an important lord, a merchant or a foreign messenger from abroad. And that is why he moved out to his palace at Esher and took half the court out there with him when he heard that Queen Jane was due to give birth. He associates giving birth with illness and human frailty. And especially womanly frailty."

"But still, shouldn't he be here with her in her hour of need?"

The older, more knowledgeable woman shrugged, tapped the side of her nose and leaned over to the young lady-in-waiting. "That's men for you, and that's our king."

"But Queen Jane wasn't ill. She was just giving birth."

"I know that and you know that, my dear, but you go and try and convince His Majesty otherwise. But now I have to go," and saying that, she made off through the still crowded corridors in the direction of the Great Hall.

It was true what Lady Ashton had said. Due to his obsessive fear of illness and the plague, King Henry the Eighth had moved himself and much of his household to Wayneflete

Tower at Esher when his wife had gone into labour. He did not wish to be around when he imagined the air would be rent by the wailing and screaming of hysterical women.

There, at Esher, in the former Bishop of Winchester's red-brick palace, some ten miles south of Hampton Court, where his first wife had suffered three days of labour pains, the king made sure he passed a pleasant time with his favourites. This included hunting in the wooded hills of Surrey, playing cards and engaging in the usual gossip that was an integral part of courtly life. In order to justify his absence from his wife – "my dear sweet Jane" – in her hour of need, Henry confided in the Duke of Norfolk that he was not really far from his beloved wife. "Just a fast horse ride away," he said while maintaining that she was constantly in his mind and in his prayers all the time. "And besides, sometimes, as you know, pregnant women take it into their minds to act in a most non-regal manner and that would not reflect well on me, the country's ruler, would it?"

As Norfolk nodded his agreement, Henry continued, "And anyway, my dear Norfolk, as soon as I heard that my wife had gone into labour, I sent my messengers off to Hampton post-haste. So no-one can say that I am cut off from what is happening there."

Now that it was known that the queen had been delivered of a healthy son, masses were sung in every church, bells were rung and the Lord Mayor of London and his aldermen marched in procession from St Paul's Cathedral to Westminster Abbey. There, more bells were rung, more prayers were offered up as the Lord Mayor and all the city's highest civic officials called on the Lord to thank Him for the queen's safe delivery.

No doubt many of the more politically or dynastically-minded officials also thanked the Lord that the new child was not only healthy but a prince as well, and not a princess.

But how many of these worthy officials really thought about their Queen Jane as a person and not just as the mother of their next king? Did any of them spare her much thought? True, they knew she had retired from the rigours of courtly life some time earlier and that the king had arranged for the country's most experienced doctors and midwives to be kept close by. They also knew that the queen had suddenly developed a passion for eating quails, and so dozens of these birds were hurriedly shipped over to London from Calais and Flanders. There they were roasted and presented to the queen in order to ensure that she would remain happy and healthy.

And of course, the court being the court and noblemen being noblemen many wagers had been laid on the sex of the newborn child. Many of the lords had publicly wagered that the royal baby would be a boy, while their more wily counterparts had loudly agreed with them, but had quietly betted on a princess at the same time. But however they had wagered, all of their interest was concentrated on the magnificent chamber in the Silver Stick gallery. Some of the more superstitious court gossips were not pleased that this was the chamber where the queen had given birth. "That's where Anne Boleyn slept," they whispered as they raised their hands to hide their mouths. "And you know what happened to her. That room is cursed."

But cursed or not, the queen gave birth there. The baby seemed healthy and all of her ladies-in-waiting waited on Queen Jane hand and foot. It is true that, despite their loving care, the queen had gone into a long and painful labour. For three whole days, she had suffered, sweated and screamed. But then early in the morning on 12 October 1537 it was all over. The future heir to the throne of England had been pushed out into the waiting world outside crying lustily. He was then hastily gathered up, cleaned and handed back to his proud but exhausted mother.

"What's he to be called?" the question flew around the packed corridors once it had been established that he was well.

"Edward. He'll be called Edward and he'll be the sixth king to bear that name. That is what the king has declared. The king sent that message through this morning."

"Edward, now there's a fine name for you. I thought that the king may have decided on a Welsh name, y'know, like after his ancestors, but to be named Edward is very traditional."

"You're right there. We've had several good kings of that name," a historically minded courtier said. "Think of King Edward the First and his grandson, King Edward the Third. They were good strong kings."

"Aye, and so was Edward the Fourth. He was also a very powerful ruler."

"That's true enough, and especially with the ladies," the courtier winked. "But the second and fifth Edwards did not bring too much honour to the name, did they?"

"You are certainly right there, but the three strong ones outweigh the two weak ones, especially young Edward the Fifth. Poor lad, he wasn't allowed to live out his life, so we'll never know if he have made a good king or not."

"Well, my friend, just think on this. Today is St. Edward's Day, so that really is a good sign, isn't it?"

"You're right, but let's stop dwelling on the past and join in the festivities." Indicating that his fellow courtiers should follow him, he walked over to the open window on the second floor. "Just listen to those church bells and those fire crackers. Come, let us to church. They're going to sing a special *Te Deum* and I wouldn't want to miss these celebrations for anything."

And such celebrations there were. Important landowners and merchants distributed food and wine, free beer was handed around and bonfires were lit throughout the capital. It was impossible to walk more than a few yards without bumping into a drunken and smiling tipsy Londoner cheering the good fortune of the king and the nation.

The cry, "We have a new prince! Prince Edward!" was on everyone's lips. Even the Tower of London, that grim fortress usually associated with pain, torture, imprisonment and death could not resist in joining in the widespread feelings of joy. Its guns shot off two thousand rounds of ammunition, the sound of the exploding gunpowder mingling with the fireworks and the shouts and cries of the drunken citizenry. Ale and wine flowed like water and the capital's population sang, danced and belched. In the meanwhile, the more sober-minded bishops gathered in St. Paul's Cathedral and gave thanks to the

Lord for having safely delivered their queen of a healthy prince.

The celebrations continued until well into the night as Henry and his chief advisors made plans for the new prince's immediate future.

"When is he to be christened?"

"On Monday, on the fifteenth of October."

"Where?"

"Here, in Hampton Court, in the Chapel Royal. His Majesty does not want to have the christening at Lambeth or at any of the other palaces. He is worried that taking the young lad out of here on this grey October morning just after his birth will not be good for him."

"Ah, a really concerned father!"

"Well, wouldn't you be the same? This is his only son and you know how obsessed he is about having a male heir to succeed him."

"That's true enough. And tell me, do you know how many people he has invited to the christening?"

"Aye, four hundred."

"Is that all?"

"Yes, you know how much the king fears crowds. For him, crowds mean chaos and that's the last thing he wants. Especially now. And my wife also told me that he's given orders that all the bed-linen and clothes that the queen has used have to be carefully washed and that all the rooms, floors and walls in the prince's new apartments are to be swept and washed with soap every day."

"Isn't he exaggerating?" asked a lady-in-waiting quietly; she had joined the conversation after looking around to see if anyone else was listening.

"Probably, madam, but you know how it is with new-borns. So many of them die early and I'm sure His Majesty is scared of that happening. After all, this is his first and only son…"

"So far."

"And the king's already over forty-five years old. I tell you," he continued, also looking around carefully before adding, "and I'm not sure he is going to have another one."

"Why not?" Lady Burton asked. "Doesn't that also depend on his wife? The queen is younger than he is. She's not yet even thirty."

"Yes, I suppose you're right," he shrugged. "You women usually know better than us men about these matters but come, we'll be late for the christening. It's not every day a prince is to be christened and I'm sure it's going to be a glorious event. Can you imagine the king having it any other way, and for his first son, too?"

The courtier was right. On a raised platform beneath the magnificent vaulted ceiling in the Chapel Royal, there for all the world to see, the baby prince's three godfathers: the Archbishop of Canterbury and the Dukes of Norfolk and Suffolk stood by the gold and silver font. On the king's orders, a pan of glowing coals had been placed close by. There was to be no risk that the royal baby would catch a chill on this most important day. Huge bouquets of flowers and bowls of sweet smelling water which had been placed on both sides of the platform perfumed the air.

Before the little prince, now wrapped in a fur-trimmed mantle of cloth of gold, and under a miniature canopy of state was carried in by the Marchioness of Exeter, his four-year old half-sister, Lady Elizabeth, carried the chrism, the consecrated oil. The other ceremonial accoutrements were borne by the First Earl of Wiltshire, Thomas Boleyn, while a train of abbots, bishops and other nobles and ambassadors followed him. The end of this grand procession was brought up by the prince's nurse and midwife, his godmother and Mary, his other half-sister and the other ladies of the court, all in their traditional order of rank.

Then, in complete silence, complete that is apart from the sound of the quietly cooing baby prince, the gathered assembly stood as the archbishop christened the prince and the gentlemen at court lit their torches. As the Chapel Royal was now bathed in the flickering light, the Garter King at Arms moved to the front of the platform and in his rich baritone voice declared, "God, of His almighty and infinite grace, give and grant good life and long to the right high, right excellent, and noble Prince Edward, Duke of Cornwall and Earl of Chester, most dear and entirely beloved son to our most dread and gracious lord, King Henry the Eighth!"

Then a *Te Deum* was sung, trumpets sounded a fanfare and the newly-christened Prince Edward was taken to his joyful parents, King Henry the Eighth and Queen Jane who had been waiting all this time in their own apartments in the palace. Here the king blessed his son and then distributed alms to a small group of selected poor men and women.

And it was in this heady atmosphere of joy and pageantry that the courtiers, together with the other royal and clerical officials, guards and servants drifted back to their places in the palace to resume their usual round of duties. As they were doing so and standing in a side corridor running from the Great Hall to Hampton Court's vast kitchens, Lady Margaret of Durham was discussing the christening with her sister, Catherine.

"Now, Cat, wasn't that something? We haven't had a christening like that here for so long."

"Of course we haven't. Young Prince Edward is the first prince to be born in over twenty years. But don't you think the queen looked a little pale today? I mean, when she came out to take her child afterwards."

"But of course she did. It's not surprising considering the ordeal she went through. It wasn't an easy birth, after all."

"I know that, Margaret. But she looked so weak, and from where I stood I noticed she was positively sweating and shaking a little when she had to stand up to take the little baby. I'm telling you, she didn't look well at all, even taking into account that she'd had a long and difficult labour and delivery."

"You are wrong there, Cat. You're always exaggerating. You always look on the dark side. I am telling you, in a few days' time the queen will be up and about and everything will be as it was before. You mark my words. You'll see I'm right."

But Lady Margaret was not right. The next day the queen's temperature rose and she became more feverish. Her face

10

became more flushed and her ladies in attendance were spending all their time wiping the sweat off her face with scented cloths while trying to calm down their royal mistress at the same time. But they did not succeed. The hot and sticky queen kept kicking off all of her heavy bedcovers, groaning, and trying to pull away from the scented cloths. "When will this end? The pains in my belly and legs," she moaned and screamed. "Cannot you do anything for me? Where are the doctors? Where is my husband?" And she continued to moan and scream incessantly.

The king, of course, with his obsessive fear of illness stayed away from her chamber, but was kept informed of the situation by a steady stream of ladies and servants.

"How goes it with her? Is she still sweating? Is she still screaming?" he would ask. And the answer was always the same. "Yes, Your Majesty. Her ladies cannot seem to bring down her temperature or stop her from sweating so much."

"Then send for the doctors, the physicians," the king roared. "What am I paying them for? Just to live and eat there at the palace?"

But nothing helped. Neither the attendants' loving care and concern and nor the doctors' learned advice. Nor did prayer, medicine nor herbs help. The pale-faced and haggard queen continued to suffer for more than a week. Then on 24 October suddenly her delirious attacks ceased and she lay completely still under her heavily embroidered bedcovers.

"Has she gone?" an exhausted lady-in-waiting whispered, scared to hear the answer.

"No, not yet, Alice, but I fear she doesn't have long now. The Duke of Norfolk has sent a message to Chancellor Cromwell telling him to return to court as soon as possible. It looks as though there's going to be a lot of work for him to do. But come, let us pray and hope for the best."

But despite all their prayers, the medicine and the constant care, Queen Jane Seymour, King Henry the Eighth's third wife, after several days of pain and hysteria, quietly slipped out of this earthly world leaving her shattered husband to seek solace in his own silent chambers. Despite his fear of sickness and death, the king had come at last to her chamber to be with his wife. He had been present during the queen's last few hours trying to bring some comfort to his now silent and dying wife. He had truly loved her and although no-one could have known it then, it would be beside his third wife, Jane, the only one who had given him a son, who he would lie beside when his own time came ten years later.

Just as the christening of Prince Edward had been a magnificent occasion so too was the queen's funeral. Her embalmed body lay in state for a week in the Chapel Royal at Hampton Court, the chief mourner being Lady Mary, the prince's older half-sister. Dressed in mourning black, she and the other ladies at court had masses sung for the departed queen. Parallel with this, the Lord Mayor of London ordered twelve hundred masses to be sung throughout the City before the queen's body was transported to Windsor Castle in a long and silent procession. This included two hundred poor men all clad in black, wearing the queen's symbol, a phoenix rising from a castle.

Eighteen days after she died, and after a long ceremony, the queen was buried in a vault at Windsor Castle leaving her grieving husband to mourn for her in London at Whitehall Palace. The final requiem mass took place in St. Paul's Cathedral and the capital city's church bells tolled for a full six hours.

Jane had reigned as queen for only sixteen months and now she was gone. What would the distraught king do now?

Chapter Two - Cherchez la femme

Grey clouds and teeming rain dragged their way over from the west, blotting out the sun over London during the second week of January 1539. Rivulets of water streamed down the red-brick walls of Hampton Court Palace; and the flooded lawns and flowerbeds together with the large puddles in the courtyards reflected the threatening grey skies. As a result, the king's courtiers and officials who had to step outside did their best to avoid the puddles as they made their way from one building to another.

Everyone was complaining about the permeating damp and did their best to stay dry, wearing their heaviest clothes and sturdiest boots and shoes. But none of their efforts could lighten their feelings of depression. This was as true for the haughty aristocrats such as the Duke of Norfolk as much as it was for the lowliest servant working in the royal kitchens scouring the huge iron pots. Everyone, but everyone was suffering from the cold and the damp and that included Thomas Cromwell, the King's Chancellor and chief minister.

On this depressing January day, he was gingerly weaving his way over the slippery cobblestones in the great courtyard, hoping he would not fall into one of the many puddles that threatened to entrap and soak him. He was on his way to the king's chamber for there he had an appointment with his royal master, and this master you never kept waiting. Never.

"Come in, Thomas," the king called out as his loyal minister shook off his sopping cloak. He handed it over to a servant who left the chamber to hang it up near a fire. Henry pointed to a heavy wooden chair opposite him at the window. "I saw you dodging below in the rain and I was wondering if you'd fall, but you didn't. That was a masterful performance you put on down there. I was very impressed as I was sure you were going to slip over. But now I'll order some warm wine to take the chill out of your old bones. And some sweetmeats, too."

"Excuse me, Your Majesty, but my bones are not *that* old. A mere fifty years, that's all."

"Fifty?" the king guffawed, slapping the seated chancellor on his fat thigh. "Fifty, you say? Fifty and a few more is what I say, and what *I* say counts, does it not? And just think, I made you my chancellor six years ago and you cannot even count. Fifty! Ha!" and he slapped him again. "But come, sir, I have not summoned you here on this miserable day to discuss your mathematical skills and knowledge. No, I've called you here to talk about your finding me a new wife or, rather, about your lack of success in finding me a new wife. Now what have you got to say to me about that, eh?"

Cromwell was silent. The king had surprised him; he had not expected the question of a future queen to be the subject of their discussion. He had assumed they would be talking about some of the monasteries that had been recently dissolved.

"And by the way, Thomas, you may also remove your cap. I'll keep mine on because all I need now is to catch a cold in this wretched weather."

Cromwell took off his flat black cap and placed it on the vacant seat behind him. He knew that the king never removed his own hat in front of anyone as he did not want the world to know that he was rapidly balding. Time was working on that famous Tudor ginger hair and Henry was doing his best to deny it. The king hoped that the longish strands of hair sticking out from under his hat would give the impression that he was still the owner of a full head of thick luxurious curls, the hair that the young women had loved to run their fingers through some thirty years before.

The overweight Chancellor looked down at the floor and waited. He knew his king did not tolerate failure. In fact, as his eyes were looking down he was thinking of those men and women, proud nobles and humble servants alike, who had failed His Majesty and had paid for this with their lives.

"Come, Thomas, you are not very cheerful company on this gloomy day. Just listen to that rain outside. It hasn't been like this for months. Not since last winter." He then stretched out his heavily bejeweled hand and pushed over a plate of comfits to his chief servant. "Now let me tell you about why I have called you over."

Cromwell waited.   He was interested to hear how this conversation would develop.

Henry looked out of the window for a moment and then continued. "Thomas," he began slowly, "it's not so bad being without a wife for a while, but I must admit that fourteen months without a regular woman in my bed is not really for me. I mean I've had the odd wench from time to time but it's not the same thing, is it?"

Cromwell looked up and gave a small smile.

"And of course," the king continued, "There's this trouble with my accursed leg. It never does seem to heal and the pain is sometimes quite unbearable."

Cromwell knew what his royal master was talking about. For the past seven years the king had been suffering from ulcerous sores on his legs and six months ago he had nearly died from the bright red fistulas that had suddenly become blocked.

"God's wounds," the king swore. "Do you remember that day, Thomas? My poisoned legs nearly killed me. I could hardly speak for the pain. I had to lie there on the bed like a half-dead fish, writhing in agony, squirming and fighting for breath. I was sure I was going to die. The only thing that brought me any comfort was knowing that I now had a son to succeed me. Oh my God! The agony of it all!" The king paused for a moment as he recalled that traumatic morning. "And my clever surgeons and apothecaries," he continued. "Could they do anything? Nothing! Absolutely nothing! I could have hanged the lot of them. All they could do was to wipe a damp cloth over my forehead and tell me the pain would pass soon. Any of my servant girls could have done that. Luckily for those useless doctors the pain did pass. But I tell you, Thomas, it was the Lord's work, not theirs. But let's not talk about that now. What I want to talk to you about are my plans for my next marriage."

Cromwell looked down again. "Fear not, man," Henry laughed. "I'm not going to chop off your head yet, at least not for a while. So stop studying the floor as if it were more important than me and listen to what I have to tell you what has happened over the past year. I know you organized much of what I am going to tell you, but listen anyway."

Cromwell sat up higher in his chair and the king pulled over a sheet of paper lying on top of a pile of documents.

"Now I know that you wrote to and spoke to various European ambassadors about potential wives, did you not?"

"Yes, Sire. At the end of November '37, a month after your dear wife, Queen Jane, passed away."

"And?"

"I received an answer from John Hutton, your ambassador to the court of Mary of Hungary, the Regent of the Low Countries and…"

"And what did he say? I don't remember any of the details about that. What happened?"

"He wrote to me from Brussels where he'd been conducting a secret search to find out if there were any eligible ladies, suitable for Your Majesty and… please wait a minute, I have the report right here in my pouch." Cromwell stood up and then bent down to pull out a rolled up parchment from the leather pouch which had slipped onto the floor under his chair. "Ah, here we are," and he started reading out from the now straightened parchment record which he held out in his fleshy hands.

There is in the court waiting upon the queen, the daughter of the Lord of Breidroot, 14 years old and of goodly stature, virtuous, sad and womanly. Her mother, who is dead, was daughter to the Cardinal of Luke's sister; and the Cardinal would give her a good dote."

"Dote? What's that, Thomas?"

"It's another word for dowry, Your Majesty, but please, may I continue?"

Henry nodded his head and his chancellor continued reading.

There is the widow of the late Earl of Egmond, who repairs often unto the court. She is over forty, but does not look it.

There is also the Duchess of Milan, who is reportedly a goodly personage and of excellent beauty.

"Hmm," Henry smiled, running his tongue round his lips. "Have you any more news about her?"

"No, Sire. I just have something about this last lady, Lady Cleves. Anne of Cleves."

"Well, read on, Thomas, read on."

And Thomas did.

The Duke of Cleves has a daughter, but there is no great praise either of her personage or her beauty.

Henry was silent for a moment. Then he looked up and asked his chancellor if anything had happened to this "Duchess of Milan or that Cleves woman."

"No, not as far as I know, Sire. A month after I received this report, the French king, King Francis, wrote to his ambassador..."

"Castillion?"

"Yes, Sire. He thought it would be most beneficial if you would take a French bride as your next wife and, if I remember correctly, he recommended Madame de Longueville."

"The Marie of Guise woman?"

"Yes, Sire. So I sent an emissary, one Peter Mewtas, to France to see whether the young woman was agreeable and..."

"She wasn't."

"That is correct, Sire. When Mewtas returned to London he said that when she heard that you were a big man and that you would want a big wife, she replied that she may be a big woman but... and please excuse me, Your Majesty, but the following words are hers..."

"Yes, yes, Thomas, what did she say?" Henry asked sharply.

"She said, Your Majesty, that she might be a big woman but that she had a very little neck."

Henry exploded. "God's wounds, Thomas! Won't these people ever forget what I did to Anne Boleyn?"

Cromwell did not answer. He hid his face behind the document he had just been reading and waited for the royal storm to blow over. Fortunately it did. This was not the first time the execution of the king's second wife had been mentioned in front of him and the chancellor continued talking about Marie of Guise.

"In any event, Your Majesty," Cromwell added quietly. "The lady in question missed the opportunity to marry you for soon afterwards she married King James the Fifth of Scotland."

"Ah, that's right. I remember now. It was last year in June, was it not? By proxy, too?"

"Yes, Sire. You are right on both counts. And then he married her in person in church later on, although the exact date escapes me for the moment."

"No matter, Thomas, although I am surprised you've forgotten that one. You are normally very good at remembering such details. But tell me more. What happened to the Duchess of Milan woman?"

"Ah, Christina of Denmark, Sire. Well, John Hutton, your ambassador to the Low Countries, recommended that you marry her. He said that she was, and here I quote him, 'beauty of person and birth.' He also noted that she much resembled your dear departed Queen Jane, except that her skin was less white than hers."

"What a memory you have, Thomas. Even though you forgot that small detail about the marriage of Marie of Guise, you remembered all that about the Duchess of Milan. No wonder I made you my chancellor. How could I do without you?"

Beneath his sallow complexion, Thomas Cromwell blushed. It was not often he received such praise from His Majesty.

"Now wasn't that the woman who had two pretty dimples in her cheek and another on her chin?"

"Yes, Sire. And I see that you also have a good memory for details."

"Of course I do, Thomas. And especially when it comes to talking about marriageable women," Henry replied, wetting his thick lips again.

"And I remember, Sire, you sent Master Holbein, your court painter, over to Brussels to paint her portrait for you. If I recall, he went over there with Sir Philip Hoby, the diplomat."

"Ah, that's right, Thomas. And he said that she looked remarkably like Margaret Shelton."

"Your mistress, Sire, er, I mean your female companion," Cromwell added quickly, correcting himself and averting his gaze. He reached out to take some sweetmeats and then finished off his glass of Madeira. He then added that the diplomat had reported that the Duchess of Milan had a gentle speech and a soft face. "Just the woman for you, Sire," he concluded.

"That maybe so," Henry said, while reaching for his own glass of wine. "But nothing came of it, did it?"

"No, Sire."

"Tell me Thomas, wasn't she the one who said that if she had two heads, one of them would be at my disposal?"

Cromwell nodded and waited for another storm. This time it did not happen and again the king pushed forward the plate of comfits over to his chancellor.

"Have some of these," he said, stuffing a couple into his own mouth. "My pastry cook has certainly made a good batch of them this time. I tell you, Thomas, they are very good. Just look what they've done for me," and the king patted his ample belly and smiled. "Thomas," he said. "Never let it be said that the King of England is a small man. Not small in mind and certainly not small in body."

"Yes, Sire," and the chancellor leaned over to take some comfits from the silver platter. After a few moments of companionable munching, Henry told his chief minister to continue with his report.

"So, Your Majesty, soon after Mary of Guise had married King James, Castillion wrote to his master and enquired if there were any more French brides to be had. I remember that you thought that this was a good idea as, apart from providing you with a wife. As I remember saying at the time, it would strengthen any possible allegiance we had at the time with

France. By that I was thinking about strengthening any Anglo-French alliance which would act as a bulwark against that Catholic Emperor, Charles the Fifth."

Henry slapped his thigh and his face lit up. "Aye, that's right, Thomas. I also remember thinking that that was a brilliant idea. What a great combination that would have made." He licked his lips again. "I would have had a beautiful French wife and this country's standing in Europe would have been strengthened, especially against those bloodthirsty Spaniards."

"Yes, Sire, but nothing came of it."

"Aye, that's true, Thomas." And Henry smiled remembering what happened. "So there I was in the Great Hall here when Castillion sidled up to me and said he had a very personal message for me. 'What is it?' I asked, and he replied that since I had been sorely deceived over matters of the heart in the past, maybe I would wish to see these young French ladies first for myself.

"Just think of that one, Thomas," the king leered. "Seeing all these French ladies myself, maybe testing them out," he grinned. "Yes, I even recall the expression on Castillion's face when he joked, 'Maybe Your Grace would like to mount them one after another and keep the one you found to be best broken in.' Ha, Thomas! I would have loved to have tested these French mares, or should it be *mères*, eh? But I must admit it to you, he did succeed in shaming me for a moment when he said that to me, but then we had a round of cards and it was all over."

Cromwell did not react. Past experience had taught him when it was best to be silent. He was pleased that it had been the king who had described that potentially explosive situation and not himself.

Just as he was refilling his goblet of wine, Henry asked, "So, my chancellor, my sometimes most devious advisor, where does this leave us now? I am still without a wife and my bed is cold, especially during these wretched winter nights. But that is not my only concern. I keep thinking that if anything happens to my dear sweet Prince Edward, then I will have no heir to succeed me. I'll admit to you, Thomas, he looks so bonny and healthy now, but will he live to become Edward the Sixth? You know the old saying, don't you? 'Man proposes but God disposes.' So, Thomas, I need another wife and another son. And soon. I'm not getting any younger and I must admit that I am quite worried about this."

Cromwell looked at his royal master full in the face. "I know that, Sire, and that is why I sent two ambassadors to reopen negotiations with the Duchess of Milan two or three months ago." He sighed and held up his hands as a sign of resignation. "But as you know, Sire, she would have none of it. If you remember, she even claimed that you had poisoned Catherine of Aragon who was her great-aunt and that your second wife was quite innocently put to death. Er..." Cromwell coughed apologetically, "may I tell you what she said after that, Sire? It wasn't very flattering."

"Yes, Thomas, you may tell me, so long as it doesn't go outside these four walls," and Henry made a wide sweep of his decorated chamber.

"She said that your first wife suffered for a long time and that you had cast her out of your court and had done nothing to ease her pain."

Henry exploded. "*She* suffered? Well, what about me? Do you know what it was like to be married for over twenty years to that obstinate Spanish cow who refused to accept a divorce? Well, do you?" Henry stuck out his bearded chin and thought back on his first marriage to the daughter of King Ferdinand of Aragon. He had married her in June 1509 and after the birth of several babies who were either stillborn or who had died soon after their births, Catherine had given him a daughter, Mary. A daughter. Who wanted a daughter? What he needed was a son, and better still, several sons. For the next few years, he and Catherine had tried to produce a male heir to the throne, but their efforts had come to nought. Fifteen years after marrying his older brother's widow, Henry had ceased having sexual relations with his wife. For him it had become a complete waste of time and effort.

"Hmm," he grunted to himself. "That's when the whole

affair with trying to annul my marriage with the Pope started. For over four years I sent and received messages to Rome but it was all in vain. Yes, it took my English Archbishop Cranmer to declare my marriage to Catherine invalid, but would she accept that? No, not until her dying day. Three years later was I finally rid of her. She even signed her last letter to me, the one written on her death-bed, 'Catherine the Queen.'

"And then there was that Anne Boleyn woman." Henry was just about to continue reviewing his past history when a polite cough from his chancellor who was now standing at the window looking at the ever-widening puddles and listening to the downpour below made the king jump from the past to the present.

"My apologies, Thomas. I was just thinking about the joys of married life. Tell me, were you happy with your wife?"

"With Elizabeth? Yes, Sire," Cromwell answered, thinking of his own marriage which had ended twelve years ago with her untimely death. "Yes, Sire, I was very happy," he added, deliberately omitting to say that she had brought him three beautiful children, one of whom was a sturdy healthy son.

"Ah, women," Henry mused. "To quote that old cliché, we men cannot get on with them, and we certainly cannot get on without them, eh? But I digress. How far had we got with regards to finding me a new wife?"

"Not far, Sire," Cromwell replied, returning to the table. "And there is another problem as well that we haven't talked about."

"There always is, Thomas. What's this one?"

"It's the question of the Papal Bull, Your Majesty. That and the Holy Roman Emperor and the King of France. It seems that they have decided to join their forces to act against you and isolate this country from the European continent."

"What! Just because the Pope has revived that Bull of Excommunication which he first declared several years ago? The one he cooked up together with Emperor Charles the Fifth?"

Cromwell nodded.

"And now they think that they have me beat? Well, my dear

chancellor, they are wrong!" And with that, Henry brought his huge fist down heavily on the table. "Well, they haven't. I tell you, Thomas, there's more than one way to skin a cat. We'll get round those two crafty old men, don't you worry about that. You always have a solution to this sort of problem. What do you suggest I do now?"

Cromwell looked out of the lattice window for a moment and studied the scene below where various courtiers and servants were still scurrying about trying to avoid the puddles while keeping their heads down. He then turned back to face his king.

"Your Majesty. I have been giving this problem much thought recently, especially since our negotiations about the Duchess of Milan were unsuccessful."

"So what have you been thinking of? Out with it. I haven't given you all these high offices and baubles for nothing." He pointed to the heavy gold chain of office his chancellor was wearing. "Come on, Thomas, you have to show me you are worth such gifts."

Cromwell swallowed. He was not sure if his royal master was joking or not. He continued quietly in a matter of fact manner. "Sire, I have been thinking that the best way of opposing this Roman Catholic combination consisting of the Holy Roman Empire and the King of France together with one or two minor principalities is to strengthen some of our own current ties with the Continent."

"And how do you suggest we do that? Send over an army and hammer them like we did to the Scots at Flodden Field? Do you remember that? We had no more troubles with them afterwards. We killed over twenty-five of their earls and dukes to say nothing of an archbishop and a couple of abbots. And then…"

Cromwell held up his hand. "Oh, no, Sire, nothing like that. I was thinking how we could act against this new Treaty of Toledo which the French and the Spanish signed recently. You know, the one where they agreed to keep us out of Europe."

Henry waved his hand dismissively. "Huh, Thomas. Do you really think that the situation is as bad as that? You know what happens with most of these treaties? After all the fanfare of the signing, nothing really changes and both sides continue looking out for what is best for them. That is called politics. The art of getting the most out of the situation, and preferably at the other side's expense."

The chancellor leaned forward, took another comfit, paused and continued.

"Sire, I_was thinking that it might be a good idea if you might marry one of Europe's Protestant or Lutheran princesses or aristocratic young ladies. I know that it might mean that she'll have a slightly lower rank than that of the Duchess of Milan or of Marie of Guise but it will certainly help to balance the status quo and let the Emperor and the French think that they are not completely in charge when it comes to Europe, Sire."

Henry leaned back in his chair and put his hand to his forehead. After several minutes he straightened up. "I see," he said. "Marry a different foreign-born lady, eh? And do you have any ideas who that might be, my chancellor and royal marriage-broker?"

"Yes, Sire," Cromwell smiled. "It just so happens I do. As I said, I've been looking into this matter and I've been thinking about Ambassador Hutton's earlier reference to Lady Anne of Cleves."

"Cleves? Isn't that a small principality in the Rhineland?"

"Yes, Sire. It straddles the Rhine and is somewhat inland to the east of the Low Countries. Here, may I show you where it is on this globe."

The two men rose from the table and walked over to where an old beige coloured globe sat in its round wooden frame. Cromwell moved the great ball around slowly until Europe came round to the top. "There," he pointed. "There on either side of the River Rhine, two or three inches east of the North Sea coast."

The king did not look very impressed. He stretched himself and looked down at his still bent chancellor. "Wait a minute, Thomas. Surely this Cleves place is part of the Holy Roman Empire. They would never agree to any sort of union with me, with England."

Cromwell coughed apologetically. "It's not quite like that today, Your Majesty. It is true that this duchy – this Cleves place as you phrase it – was part of the Holy Roman Empire in the past but the duke, Duke William, recently had a quarrel with the Holy Roman Emperor, Charles the Fifth, about land rights in Guelders. My ambassadors have told me that since then, the duke has been hoping that you, as the King of England, would give him some support."

Henry slapped his thigh. "Ah, that's what he wants from me. Well, maybe he'll get it, too. Perhaps I'll be able to kill two birds with one stone and get the stone back, too if I am lucky. I'll have some influence on the Continent and get myself a new wife at the same time. That's brilliant, Thomas, sheer genius."

Again, Cromwell blushed under his sallow skin. Being praised like this twice in one day was unheard of.

"Yes, Sire," he said quietly. This arrangement could work out to be quite profitable for you and this country."

"And what do you know about the two Cleves women you mentioned earlier? Are they marriageable?"

"Yes, Sire. The duke has two sisters. Amalia and Anne. I have been told that they are both amenable young ladies. Not married and fair to look upon."

"And how old are they?"

"Amalia is about twenty-two and her sister is two years older."

"But wait a minute, Thomas. Didn't Hutton report that this Anne of Cleves was nothing special?"

"Yes, Sire, but that was just his opinion. My other emissaries have told me that she is quite a pleasant young woman. Not a striking beauty, but certainly no ugly old crone, if you get my meaning."

Henry was silent for a few moments before he asked his next question. "And are there any strings attached to these two ladies?"

"Strings, Sire?"

"Oh, you know, Thomas. Previous betrothals or contracts of

that nature. Something akin to that which Marie of Guise had with King James?"

"As far as I know, Your Majesty, both of these young ladies are – may I phrase it somewhat indelicately – ripe for plucking. There are no strings attached to them."

Henry leaned back and let out a bellow of a laugh. "Oh, Thomas, what a man you are! You spend your life carrying out delicate affairs of state for me and yet you still use the crude expressions from your youthful days in Putney. 'Ripe for plucking' indeed! Yes, Thomas, go and find out what there is to learn about these two birds. I just hope that at least one of them will be, as you say, ripe for plucking."

"Yes, Sire." And saying this, Cromwell bowed and left the chamber leaving his royal master to think about his next possible wife.

Chapter Three - Enter Anne of Cleves

My name is Anne of Cleves - at least, that is what the English call me. Here at home in the Rhineland Duchy of Cleves I am known as Anna von Jülich-Kleve-Berg. I was born in September 1515 in Düsseldorf, so that makes me twenty-four years old. My father, John, the third Duke of Cleves, was known as John the Simple - not because he was simple-minded but because he was less flamboyant than his father, my grandfather, John the Second. My grandfather was known, however, not only for his flamboyance but also for fathering sixty-three illegitimate children. It is not surprising therefore that he was also called John the Babymaker.

My mother, Maria of Jülich-Berg, had three daughters: Sybille, me and Amalia, in that order. Sybille was born in 1512 and so she is five years older than I am and Amalia was born two years after me. Sybille, with her long red hair and beautiful olive-shaped eyes was considered the beauty of the family, and I will say more about her later. We all spent our early years at Schloss Berg, a large castle near Solingen, the town famous for the manufacture of its excellent knives and swords.

Although my immediate family was not one of the most important in Europe, we did have some high-ranking and influential connections. We could trace our lineage both from the kings of England – through a daughter of Edward the First - and we were also descended from the King of France. In addition, my father was closely related to King Louis the Twelfth and my mother was connected to the kings and the nobility of the French house of Burgundy. So when I heard myself later described as a daughter belonging to a 'minor noble family from the Rhineland,' you can understand how upset that made me.

Although my father's duchy was relatively small, it was populated with hard-working folk who made it a very wealthy area. For this reason and, perhaps, due to political reasons, it was not long before my very attractive older sister, Sybille, was married. This happened thirteen years ago, in 1526. She was only fourteen at the time. She was married to John Frederick, the Elector of Saxony who was also the head of the Protestant Confederation of Germany, the 'champion of the Reformation.' This question of religion was certainly one of the reasons that my sister was seen as such an attractive 'catch.' This, combined with the fact that our duchy lay within the area of the Holy Roman Empire, meant that we were a Lutheran island within a Catholic sea.

My father believed in the teachings of the reformation and was greatly influenced by the beliefs and writings of Erasmus. My father was thus opposed to the Catholic Emperor, Charles the Fifth, and although he did not join the Schmalkaldic League, a defence union composed of ten city-states and six German Lutheran principalities, he was certainly sympathetic to their ideas and plans.

My own upbringing was quite conservative: my mother did not believe it necessary to give her daughters any education apart from some basic skills in reading and writing German. Unlike other girls of a similar standing, I was never taught any foreign languages and this was to cause me several problems later in my life.

"Mother," I asked her one day. "Why don't I have a governess who will teach me French? I've heard that other young ladies learn this language?"

"Because there's no need for that," she immediately replied. "You do not need to know any French here in Cleves and besides, French is the language of that Catholic country while here in the duchy, we believe in the Reformation."

"Well, what about learning English? I've been told it is quite similar to our own German tongue?"

"Huh!" was her reply. "And what makes you think that you'll be needing English? Are you planning to travel to England? No, my girl, a young woman's role is to learn useful skills such as needlework and homemaking, skills that will keep her future husband happy."

Despite the above answers to my questions, I believe I was my mother's favourite daughter and I was certainly very close to her. I spent much of my time in her company and we would happily sit together over our needlework where we would exchange gossip while she gave me tips about sewing and other light household chores.

When I was twelve I was betrothed to Francis, the son and heir to the Duke of Lorraine. He was two years younger than me but this betrothal was annulled eight years later in 1535. Little did I know then how much of a problem this betrothal, one in which I never saw my 'husband' even once would cause me later in life. All I remember was that I was the centre of attraction at several balls and I received a few new hats and dresses. And then, as quickly as all this had started, it was over. At first it felt like a huge anticlimax but then I became used to the idea of being betrothed without having ever seen my future partner for life.

The first time I remember hearing anything about Henry the Eighth, the King of England, was about nine years ago when I heard that he had sent some of his soldiers over to fight in the battles between the Holy Roman Emperor and the Duke of Saxony. I was told that the Duke, together with some representatives of the Schmalkaldic League had sent some ambassadors over to England to ask Henry the Eighth to help them. I recall hearing my father talk about the frequent arrivals and departures both of the English ambassador and our own, but nothing came of all this frantic political activity. Of course, as a young woman, I was not involved in any of this and when I did ask a question or two, I was silenced with, "Hush, woman, this is men's talk. It has nothing to do with you."

The next time I remember hearing of the English king was when it was proposed that his daughter, Mary, marry my brother, William. Again there was much coming and going but, in the end, nothing happened. As far as I was concerned the only thing worth mentioning was that I learned a few words and phrases in English as I helped my mother to host our English guests.

A few months were to pass before our Duchy and the King of England were linked together again and that happened just over a year ago, soon after the king's third wife, Queen Jane, had died.

This is how it came to pass.

John Hutton, one of the king's ambassadors, had been asked to write a report about young ladies who might be considered suitable wives for the newly bereaved king. Apparently my name was mentioned in this report, but it was only a few months later that I discovered that Hutton's description of me was not very flattering. He had written, 'The Duke of Cleves has a daughter, but there is no great praise either of her personage or her beauty.' What a terrible thing to say! He had never met me, but had based his report solely on malicious gossip and hearsay. Later I was told that this was because King Henry was still interested in marrying the Duchess of Milan who, according to Hutton, was 'a goodly personage and of excellent beauty.' I must admit that when I heard that despite this flattering report she had turned down the king's offer of marriage I felt very happy. Little did I realise at the time that this refusal would have a great effect on my own rather humdrum provincial life.

Then the whole situation changed in the spring of this year, in 1539. Apparently the King of England must have had a change of heart, for he sent his new ambassador, Christopher Mont, to our Duchy. He was instructed to see whether my sister, Amalia, or I would make a suitable wife for his royal master, that is, also to become the future Queen of England. My mother told me that the ambassador who, unlike most Englishmen, could speak another language - in this case, German - was instructed to discover, 'what shape, stature, proportions and complexion' Amelia and I had and what were our 'learning activities, behaviour and honest qualities.'

Again I felt somewhat insulted by this attitude but there was nothing I could do about it. I felt as if I were a prize cow or pig at a market being examined to see if I were worth the price. It seems that this ambassador had also been told to inform us that by marrying the King of England, Amalia or I would be bringing the highest and noblest honour to the Duchy of Cleves.

It was at this point in my life that I began to think seriously about being married to the English king and I began asking discreet questions about him. I must admit that the knowledge I gleaned from various sources was not very flattering. I learned that he had become estranged from his first wife, Catherine of Aragon, after fifteen years because she could not give him a son or, in fact, any children at all. I heard that he had set her aside, gave her hardly any money for herself or for her ladies-in-waiting while he amused himself with other ladies at court. It seems that he enjoyed himself mostly with a French-educated lady called Anne Boleyn whom he later married. Some people thought this was a bigamous act as he was still officially married to his first wife. However, he claimed that as he had been divorced at the time he was legally entitled to marry his second wife.

I know that my family upbringing and education had been to oppose the Pope and all that he stood for, but to go back on one's word, especially when it was about the holy state of matrimony, was for me an unpardonable sin.

Then I heard that after waiting several years to marry Anne Boleyn, the marriage did not turn out to be a happy one at all. In fact, in the end, he could not stand her and so he had her put on trial. She was accused of committing incest and treason as well as of having sexual relations with several gentlemen at court. Of course she was found guilty and the king had her taken to this fortress in London called the Tower where she was executed. But even before this, he had begun flirting with another lady at court called Jane Seymour. He must have been in love with her because the day after he had Anne Boleyn executed he became betrothed to this Jane woman.

When I asked my mother why it was so important for him to be married, she told me that the king was obsessed with having a son to succeed him. She said that the king's father, Henry the Seventh, was the first Tudor king. He had usurped the throne from King Richard the Third over fifty years earlier and had had only two sons: the present King Henry and his now dead brother, Arthur. Now, the present King Henry felt that in order to truly strengthen his reign and dynasty, he had to have another son in addition to the baby Prince Edward.

My mother also told me that he had married Jane Seymour only because she was so docile.

"Why, how was Anne Boleyn?" I asked.

"I never met her, my dear, but I heard that after the king married her, she became very noisy and petulant and that she and the king had great fights over religious matters. Apparently she tried to tell him what to do and he became very angry with her about this."

I listened carefully but I found this difficult to understand. I never remember hearing my mother telling my father or my brother when he became the duke what to do.

"And so what do we learn from this, my daughter?" my mother asked.

"Always listen to and obey your husband," I replied.

"That's right," my mother smiled and then we continued with our needlework. I did not question her but decided that my mother's opinion of Anne Boleyn was really based on hearsay and stories that she had heard from the English ambassadors and messengers who had visited our castle.

And now I hear that the English king's third marriage did not last very long either. It is true that she did give birth to a son but then she died of a fever a few days later. What a history: the first wife divorced, the second one executed and the third one dying at the young age of twenty-nine. And now my parents are considering marrying me off to this man!

And what else do I really know about this Henry? All I know is that he is a large man – 'very corpulent' – Miles Thompson, one of the English ambassador's secretaries, whispered to me, and that apart from women, what he really loves is hunting.

"What else can you tell me about him?" I asked the secretary. "Personal things, not politics or things like that. What colour is his hair? Is it brown like mine or fair like yours?"

"He has copper-coloured hair and he is quite handsome,

or..." - and here he looked around to see if anyone could overhear us as we stood in the castle courtyard – "he used to be quite handsome but now he has become very fat and has problems with his legs."

"Why? Because he is very fat?" I asked.

"No, because he suffers from these fistulas – these ulcers - which keep running and I've been told smell quite disgusting, too. And when they really hurt him, he becomes very bad-tempered and shouts at everyone in sight."

"Everyone? Even his courtiers?"

"Everyone: his courtiers, his noblemen and his servants. Only last week he shouted at me and told me that I was a flaxen-haired loon and an idiot to boot!"

I thought about this for a moment. I couldn't imagine my brother, the Duke, behaving that way. He is far too well-behaved to shout at anyone in our court. He would just give them a harsh look or a quick word and that would be the end of the matter. Then came my next question. "Can he speak German?"

"No, but he knows French, Greek and Latin, and I think he knows some Biblical Hebrew as well."

Then I asked him some more questions about the life at court in England and this is what he told me. He said that the most important man in England after the king was his chancellor or *Kanzler* as we call him here in Cleves. His name is Thomas Cromwell and he started out in life as a very simple worker. He was the son of a blacksmith and then he served as a soldier who fought in Italy and the Low Countries. Then he returned to England and he must have been quite hard-working and clever because he became the chief secretary and agent for the king's first chancellor, Cardinal Wolsey. He must have been good at his office for when Wolsey died, the king appointed Cromwell to take his place. He became Chancellor of the Exchequer and was personally responsible to the king for carrying out all kinds of royal commands.

Miles Thompson, the secretary whom I told you about earlier, said that the king made Cromwell responsible for suppressing and destroying all the monasteries in England and transferring all the wealth to the king's coffers. He also helped the king push for the Reformation of the Church and this led to both Cromwell and the king becoming very interested in the Duchy of Cleves. My brother, William, told me that the English were very keen on improving their diplomatic relationships with all sorts of duchies and states that followed the Lutheran and Protestant way of thinking. This is the situation here in Cleves and this is why the English have sent their ambassador, Nicholas Wotton, to see whether Amelia or I would make a suitable wife and queen for King Henry.

To be truthful, I do not know whether I am pleased with all this recent attention. On the one hand, I think it would be very interesting to be the Queen of England. I'm sure that it would be far more interesting than remaining here as a minor lady in a minor Rhineland duchy and I'm also sure it would be fascinating to live in the rich and exciting country that Miles described to me. Naturally I would have more dresses, jewellery and servants and I am certain that the palaces in London would be far grander than the castle I am living in here in Cleves.

But on the other hand, I would have to leave the country and the people I have known for the past twenty-four years and I would also have to leave my family. I'm not sure whether I'd miss my brother, William, very much as he is rather distant with me, especially as he loves to talk to me in a pompous and stern manner as if I were one of his underlings. I believe he thinks he should talk like this, both to me and to everyone else, as he has only recently become the duke following our father's death in February. I know that I'd miss Amalia and all the good times we had together – the games we played as small children, the secrets we told each other at night once the lights had been put out and the happy hours we spent doing our needlework in the solarium.

Of course I'd miss my dear mother even though she was quite strict with me at times. I know she was like this because of her maternal feelings of love and concern and I hope that whenever I have children, I'll look after them just as well. I know she did not want me to have a reputation as a woman of loose morals, something that I have heard about several of the French noblewomen I have heard spoken of.

But then of course there is the question of being married to a man such as King Henry the Eighth. Is he really as domineering as I have heard, or is this all an act, something put on for show? Are his courtiers and subjects really afraid of him or are these merely rumours put about by people who just love to gossip?

I know a ruler's nobles and subjects love to tell stories about their king or duke and, in fact, about anyone in the ruling family. Heavens, haven't I heard enough of such stories over the past years about my own and other ducal families here in the Rhineland? But for me, the question is, how true are the rumours and stories that I have heard about this English king?

Some things I know are facts. As I said, I know that he has had three wives; and that he has several magnificent palaces at Hampton Court, Whitehall and Greenwich and that Miles told me that the most magnificent one of all is at Nonsuch, which is in Surrey, on the southern bank of the River Thames. I also know that like us here in Cleves, he does not believe in the Roman Catholic Church and that it is very important for him that a husband and wife have the same religious beliefs.

There are also some things that I have heard about Henry that are not very pleasant to know. I have heard that he can be very cruel and unforgiving to anyone who crosses his path. Miles and another secretary told me that a few years ago when thousands of his subjects in the north of England rose up against him in what they called the Pilgrimage of Grace, he sent the Duke of Norfolk up there to suppress this uprising. Over two hundred people were hanged and that included some noblemen and churchmen. The duke then left these bodies hanging on gibbets at road junctions so everyone would know that the king would not tolerate any form of insurrection. I know that these people wanted to bring back the Roman Catholic Church, but did the king have to punish so many people in such a cruel manner? Would it not have been wiser and more statesmanlike to try and make the people see the error of their ways through persuasion and discussion in a more Christian way?

But I have also heard that the king can be very charming and generous to those he loves and respects and that he absolutely dotes on his baby son, Prince Edward. Miles said that nothing is too good for him and that all the prince's servants adore the little boy. The king, it seems, is the most perfect and loving father, visiting his son whenever he can, and if he is too busy with the affairs of state, then he sends some of his ladies-in-waiting to report back to him about his son.

I tell you, I am torn in two about the possibility of marrying this man and I really do not know what to do or think. I do not want to refuse him as the Duchess of Milan or Marie of Guise did, but I am too frightened to agree to any proposal of marriage he may offer. Of course, in the end I may not have any choice in the matter. I am a twenty-four year old noblewoman who must marry soon. If not, I will be 'left on the shelf' as the English say and *that* I certainly do not want. Oh, what shall I do? I will have to have a long talk tonight with Amalia. Maybe she will have a solution. I really hope so, for soon I must decide what to do.

Chapter Four - Plans and a Betrothal

A spring day in 1539 found King Henry and his chancellor again seated at their favourite table by the window overlooking the large square courtyard at Hampton Court Palace. The sun was shining gently, the sky was clear and blue and a few white fluffy clouds were drifting in from the west. This idyllic picture was in complete contrast to the earlier scenes of torrential rain, ever-widening puddles and flooded gardens. Two glasses of hippocras wine - a favourite of both the king and his chancellor - were to be found half-hidden among the rolled up documents and open letters on the polished wooden table.

"Your Majesty," said Cromwell as his master stood up to see better out of the window on to the courtyard below, "Please look at the signature at the foot of this document. Does it mean anything to you?"

"No, Thomas, it doesn't," replied the king almost immediately. "But come and look here," he urged his chief minister. "Here out of the window. It's a sight more interesting than one of your diplomat's scribbles. Just look at those two wenches crossing the courtyard over there...there, on the way to the kitchens. Oh, what I would give sometimes not to be king and be able to rut with wenches like that. Just take a look at the one in the brown skirt. Just look at her dukkies! Why, man, they're nearly falling out of her bodice!"

Cromwell leaned over as instructed. It was true. The king did have a great view from this window – and in more ways than one.

"Now you know why I like my work-table near the window," Henry licked his lips lasciviously. "Doesn't looking at these wenches from time to time make our work more enjoyable?"

Cromwell agreed. It was true that he also enjoyed seeing young ladies around the palace, especially since his wife,

Elizabeth, had died some twelve years earlier. However, unlike the king, if he felt the need for some intimate female company, he would send out a servant to one of the stews at Southwark, south of the river. The man would bring back one of the local harlots, the 'Winchester geese' as they were called locally, to fulfill his needs.

For a few minutes, the King of England and his chief minister lusted with their eyes and minds after the two young women below. It was only when these beautiful creatures had disappeared from view into the kitchen did the two most powerful men in the kingdom reluctantly return to their table to deal with the affairs of state.

"Thomas, this hippocras is the best I've supped for some time," Henry said, swirling the wine around in his mouth. He then wiped a few drops off his beard with the back of his hand and asked his chancellor if he could not taste the cinnamon and cloves in it.

"I certainly can, Your Majesty, but I prefer my wines to be a little less sweet,"

"Ah, Thomas, that reflects your dry personality. I, as you well know," Henry added, throwing out his chest, "prefer the richer and sweeter wines. But enough of wine and wenches - at least for the time being. Let's be serious and concentrate on the report ambassador Wotton gave you."

They pulled their chairs closer to the table and only after the king had taken yet another sweetmeat and complained about the ulcers on his left leg did they settle down to study Wotton's latest dispatch.

"First of all, Your Majesty, this diplomat has rendered us a good service while he was away in Cleves. He took Richard Berde with him and a few other good fellows and they immediately set out to obtain some portraits of the duke's two sisters, Amalia and Anne."

"And did they succeed? So far I've seen nothing."

"No, Sire. It appears that the Vice-Chancellor, a somewhat unbending cleric, one Doctor Henry Olisleger, would not allow our men to approach the two sisters closely at first. But then…" Cromwell stopped. "Ah, wait a moment, Sire, I've just had an idea. Ambassador Wotton is working in the chamber next door preparing a document for me. I think it would be best if we call him in and so we can hear at first-hand what really happened in Cleves. That would be better than me giving you a report of his report, wouldn't it?"

Henry nodded in agreement, not realizing that this was his chancellor's way of passing the blame on to someone else if, in future, if there were such a need. After having served His Majesty for over a dozen years, Cromwell knew how his royal master's mind worked, especially if any of his, Cromwell's, plans came to nothing. As the chancellor left the chamber to bring in the diplomat, Henry helped himself to another sweetmeat.

Two minutes later, Wotton was being asked to join the king and Cromwell at the table. Licking the sugar off his fat fingers, Henry asked the diplomat to report on his expedition to Cleves, adding, "And make sure you give me all the details you can about the two ladies there, Amalia and Anne. Tell me if they are beautiful, if they have pimples on their faces. Everything."

"Yes, Your Majesty," Wotton started hesitantly. It was not every day that he attended such an intimate meeting with his two masters. "We had a very slow start," he began quietly. "The Vice-Chancellor, Doctor Olisleger would not co-operate with us and…"

"Yes, yes," Henry interrupted him. "We know all that already. The chancellor has just told me about that. What I want to know is what happened next?"

"Well, not much at the beginning, Your Majesty. As I said, the Vice- Chancellor kept objecting to our requests and…"

"And then what?" the king interrupted again.

"Er… he would not allow us see the young ladies in person but offered to show us pictures of them instead."

"And did he?"

"Yes, Sire, but we told him that that was not enough."

"Very good," the king and his chancellor said in unison.

"So what did you do next, or what did *he* do?" the king asked, leaning forward.

"We told him that we wished to see the young ladies close up and that their faces should not be covered by veils or by heavy headdresses or anything of that nature."

Henry slapped his thigh. "Very good, Wotton! That's the spirit! And did he agree? Did you see them?"

"No, Sire, at least, not at first. The Vice-Chancellor became very sarcastic and said that perhaps we would wish to see them naked. Naturally we were very shocked at this response and we told him so, er...very diplomatically, of course."

"Of course," Henry said, and then asked "But did you get to see them in the end, er, not naked, of course?"

Cromwell permitted himself a half-smile as Wotton continued with his report.

"Yes, Sire, in the end. It seems that John Frederick, the Elector of Saxony, had heard of our mission and instructed the sisters' brother, Duke William, to allow us to see these young women more closely. As you doubtlessly know, Sire, William is now the Duke of Cleves, following the recent death of his father."

"Yes, yes, Wotton, I know all that," Henry said, getting up to stretch his cramped and aching leg. Then he turned to the diplomat and asked him what the result was of his seeing the two Cleves sisters.

"We found them to be quite fair and attractive, Your Majesty. Er, you must understand, looking at young ladies in order to judge their..., er, how shall I phrase it? their physical attributes is not what I do usually but..."

"Yes, yes, but get on with it, Wotton," Henry again interrupted the thin diplomat. "Well, what were they like?"

Wotton fidgeted with a piece of paper before continuing. "Well, as I have just said, Your Majesty, we found them rather fair and attractive although the older one, Anne, is probably a little taller than most women, not too tall, you understand," he added quickly, noting the slight frown on his king's forehead, "but certainly taller than your last queen."

Henry looked at Cromwell, smiled and then turned to face Wotton again.

"And her sister, Amalia? Is she also tall like her sister?"

"No, Sire." Wotton was breathing more easily now that he was half-way through his report. Cromwell had told him to expect to be more thoroughly interrogated than he was.

"Ah well, Wotton, Anne's height needs not prove to be a problem, need it? After all, I am taller than most men," and Henry straightened himself up to his full height. "And I'm sure she is not taller than me, is she?"

"Oh, no, Sire. I would say that she is about the same height as the chancellor here," he answered, looking at Cromwell, "or perhaps a mite shorter."

"Hmm," Henry grunted and then turned to face his chancellor. "Thomas, stand up and stand next to me. Now let Wotton make a comparison for the lady's height."

Cromwell stood up and moved over to the king's side. Wotton cocked his head to one side and made a mental measurement. He then assured his royal master that Anne of Cleves was about the same height as the chancellor. Henry and Cromwell both looked relieved. So far, things were going well.

"And how is she here?" Henry asked pointing to his own chest.

"What? Where, Your Majesty?" It was clear that Wotton did not understand his king's question or gestures.

"Here, Wotton, here, her dukkies, her breasts? Are they big or not?"

Wotton did not know which way to turn. He looked at the king and then he turned to the chancellor and then looked down. It was clear that he was extremely embarrassed and out of his depth. At last the red-faced diplomat looked up and faced the king. ", Excuse me, Your Majesty, I did not look that closely at the lady's er...upper anatomy. I was too busy looking at her face and trying to gain a general impression about her," he finished somewhat lamely.

"Yes, yes," the impatient king said, "but tell me, how were they? Big? Small or what?"

"I suppose they were of the usual size, Sire. I assume if they had been an abnormal size I would have taken note. That is all I can tell you about her ... er...her chest."

"Thank you, Wotton," Henry said quickly, disappointed that his diplomat could give him no more information about Anne of Cleves' physical attributes. "So tell me, if you didn't pay any attention to her body, what of her mind? Can she speak English? Did you converse with her at all?"

"Yes, Your Majesty, we did manage to talk a little, but I regret to inform you that her English - at least her spoken English - is not very good. We talked a little about the weather and about the duchy but it was clear that she had to think very carefully before she could utter a whole sentence."

"Is the English that she speaks understandable at least?" Cromwell asked.

"It is, Master Chancellor, it's just that she speaks very slowly and tends to use German words instead of English ones especially if the two are very similar."

"Give me an example of what you mean," Henry said.

"She said *gut* instead of 'good' on several occasions, Your Majesty, and she also used words such as *nacht* and *recht* instead of 'night' and 'right.'"

Henry took time to consider this before asking his next question. "But do you think she'll be able to learn English better, to speak it fluently?"

Wotton also took his time to answer before saying, "Yes, Sire, I think she may be able to improve her spoken English and become more fluent, but I doubt if she'll be able to get rid of her German accent. It's quite pronounced ..." but, seeing the expression on his king's face, he added, "but I have noticed that when people live for a length of time in a foreign country, they tend to lose their original accent, that is, it becomes less pronounced, Sire. And this opinion, if I may add, is based on listening to the French and Spanish emissaries who've come to work here in London."

"Ah, so there *is* hope?" Cromwell asked.

"Oh, certainly, Master Cromwell."

"Well, that's certainly good news to hear," Henry said, offering a sweetmeat to the diplomat. "I'm glad we've solved that problem."

"Yes, Your Majesty, but I fear we have another problem that

must be solved."

Henry whirled around and grabbed the back of the nearest chair so he wouldn't fall. "Another problem? And what's that?"

Wotton coughed apologetically. "There's the question of the betrothal, Sire."

"Of course that's a problem," Henry said impatiently. "That's why I sent you to Cleves in the first place."

"No, no, Sire. I'm referring to the Lady Anne's betrothal, her previous one. The one that Duke William and his Vice-Chancellor told us about."

Lines of anger immediately showed on the king's face. His eyebrows grew closer together and his face became even redder than normal. "Her previous betrothal?" he shouted. "Why wasn't I told anything about that? Did you know anything about this, Thomas?'

"No, not really, Sire," Cromwell muttered as he distanced himself from the king. "I must admit that I'd heard some rumour about it once, but I dismissed it as some sort of foreign gossip."

"Foreign gossip, man! What do I employ you for? To keep me informed and not to be the victim of such surprises. Now, Wotton, stop looking out of the window and pretending that you're not here, and tell me all you know about this betrothal matter. Come on, out with it, and don't hide the facts behind some sort of diplomatic babble."

Wotton returned to the table and looked at Cromwell for support. He received none. Cromwell did not wish to be involved in what he saw as another man's failure. He looked away as Wotton raised his head, faced his king and began to describe the situation.

"It was like this, Your Majesty. It seems that the young lady was previously betrothed to Francis of Lorraine a good few years ago and..."

"How long ago was 'a good few years'?" demanded Henry.

"Twelve, Sire. She was twelve years old at the time and he was a mere stripling aged ten. Nothing came of this and I suppose everyone forgot about the whole situation."

"Huh! Until now, that is," Henry said cynically.

Wotton shrugged. There was nothing else he could say. He had hoped his report would have explained the problem. It did not.

"So, Wotton, what do you mean, 'everyone forgot about it'? It looks like the duke and his wretched Doctor Olis – whatever he's called – haven't forgotten about it, have they?" Henry jutted his chin out at the unfortunate diplomat who stood facing him, his head hung low and his hands clasping and unclasping behind his back.

"No, Sire," he blurted out at length. "No, I suppose not."

"*Suppose!*" Henry shouted. "Suppose. There's no supposing to be done here. Was there a betrothal or not and, if so, is it still relevant today?"

Wotton looked down at the floor and said nothing, as did Cromwell.

"Well, man, who was this Francis of Lorraine and was this betrothal annulled? Come on, man, what happened?"

Wotton looked up again. "I can answer your first question easily, Sire. Francis of Lorraine was the son of Antoine, the Duke of Lorraine and his wife, Renée Bourbon-Montpensier. They lived…"

"Yes, yes," Henry interrupted him. "You can tell me about their lives later. For now, just tell me if this betrothal was annulled or not."

If Wotton had looked uncomfortable in his royal master's presence before, it was nothing to how he looked and felt now. He looked down at the floor, fiddled with his fingers behind his back, looked at Cromwell for support but received none. The ambassador was just left standing there, miserable and looking down at his feet. At last he said in a voice just above a whisper, "I don't really know, Your Majesty whether it was annulled or not."

"*You don't know!*" Henry flung at him. "Well who does?"

At this point Cromwell decided he could save the situation. Still keeping his distance from the other two men he said quietly, "Sire, I think that if we send another emissary to Cleves, someone more informed about such situations, we may be able to shine some light on this matter."

"Well, Thomas, who do you think we should send? And make sure he is the best man for the job." Henry then looked directly at the nervous fidgeting Wotton. "Because I'm telling you, I don't want another diplomat like Wotton coming back with an 'I don't know ' answer."

"Yes, Sire, of course, Sire," Cromwell said quickly. "I think we should send Dr. William Peter to Cleves. He's an experienced diplomat and I suggest that he insist on discussing the matter of this betrothal with Anne's mother and the Duke. Then we will know exactly what happened in the past and will therefore be able to make the right decisions as a result."

"A good idea, Thomas," and Henry smiled for the first time since Nicholas Wotton had raised the question of the betrothal. "But let us just say that if Anne is not available, maybe her sister is?"

"Yes, Sire," Wotton said, "but I believe we should first look into the question of the betrothal as your chancellor has suggested. Perhaps it is no longer valid. Besides, if I may say so, Sire, I do not think it would be good politics to marry the younger sister if the older one is available. Such things are not usually done, Sire. If you remember your Bible, even Jacob had to marry Laban's older daughter, Leah, first and then wait seven years before he could marry Rachel, the younger daughter whom he had earlier wanted to marry."

"Hmm," was Henry's only comment. He stopped pacing up and down, sat down heavily and gestured that the other two men should do so as well. All three men were silent and it became clear that the king's two officials were waiting for him to say something else. At last Henry looked at Cromwell and asked him for further details about his plan for sending Dr. William Peter to Cleves.

"Well, Your Majesty, I've been thinking about that. I suggest that not only do we send Dr. Peter and a couple of his best men over to Cleves, but we also send your court painter, Holbein, with him as well."

"Why?"

"Then he can paint a likeness of Anne of Cleves," the

chancellor answered, smiling. "But no, wait, I have an even better idea. We will tell him to paint likenesses of both the Cleves sisters and then - if necessary - you will be able to choose which one you may wish to marry."

Henry started smiling at this and Cromwell rushed on with his explanation. "This means, Sire, that if her earlier betrothal means that you cannot marry Anne, then you will certainly be able to marry her younger sister, Amalia. In this way, you will have given offence to no-one and as Ambassador Wotton has just said, no harm will have been done."

Henry smiled, but this time in full. "Thomas, you've done it again. Whenever I have a problem, you always come up with a solution. No wonder I keep you on as my chancellor even though some members of the nobility - especially the Duke of Norfolk - do not approve of my employing you. But fear not, he cannot do anything. He's all bark and no bite."

Cromwell smiled. "Thank you for your kind words, Sire, but now I suggest that the three of us arrange the details for this next expedition to Cleves. We have to make sure that Dr. Peters and his men - as well as Master Holbein - have all the necessary travel documents, you know, the laissez-passers and the rest. We also need to see that your Master of the Horse attends to the question of horses, carriages and transport in general and that one of your most eminent captains, Sire, deal with the subject of guards and soldiers."

"Thomas," Henry said, handing him a comfit. "Is there anything that you *don't* think of? Any little detail?"

"Yes, Sire. I'm just wondering whether we should also send diplomat Mont?"

"Christopher Mont? Of course you should, Thomas. After all, the man does speak German and that may ease the path through any difficult negotiations, especially with that Olisleger fellow. From what Wotton has to say about him," Henry said, looking at the diplomat who was now looking far less nervous and had stopped fidgeting. "He does seem to be rather an awkward and uncooperative person to deal with."

The three men remained at the table for the next hour going over their plans and listing all the minutiae for the forthcoming expedition. Nothing would be overlooked. The king kept reminding his two officials that his personal happiness – "and that of my kingdom, of course" – depended on the results of this journey.

On the following day Dr. Peter was commanded to come to Hampton Court. Accompanied by an assistant, he joined the king, his chancellor and Wotton at the king's table where he was given his instructions.

"Please give me a few minutes to read them, Your Majesty," the future envoy asked and the king pointed to another table on the other side of the chamber. Dr. Peter sat down and began to concentrate on the various lists and instructions that Cromwell had prepared for him. He read that he was to approach the mother of Anne and Amalia, Maria of Jülich-Berg, and 'to use all of his dexterity in this matter and to be earnest in the determination and speedy conclusion of the same.' Dr. Peter was to flatter the mother and stress how important it was for her elder daughter to marry the King of England. However, if this were not possible, then His Majesty would be more than pleased to marry Amalia instead.

After studying the detailed document carefully for ten minutes Dr. Peter rejoined the others and said that he fully understood the terms of his mission. Cromwell was pleased and smiled at him encouragingly. After all, the whole idea of the Anglo-Cleves union had been his idea and he had vested interests in its success. He knew that his royal master was not very tolerant, to say the least, of anyone who failed him. Several rotting and decapitated heads on spikes at the southern end of London Bridge confirmed this fact. Just as Cromwell was mulling over the chances of his success or failure, his somewhat morbid thoughts were interrupted by the king.

"Thomas, I think we should send Dr. Peter and Master Holbein and everyone off as soon as possible. *Tempus fugit* and remember, I'm not getting any younger."

"Most certainly, Your Majesty. I'll tell everyone to be ready to travel by the beginning of next week. We should have everything ready by then."

Urged on by an impatient king and his hard-working

chancellor, the diplomats, the court-painter together with their guards and assistants left London a few days later for the Rhineland duchy.

Using the best horses that the Master of the Horse could provide, they made good time to Dover where a specially commissioned ship stood waiting to take them over to Calais. Fortunately, the weather was favourable and they soon arrived in France. From Calais they continued through the flat, featureless Flanders countryside until they reached Antwerp. There they were hosted by a group of English wool merchants. Early next morning, the party rose and continued travelling eastward to Guelderland where they were greeted by an army of windmills whose impressive sails whirled around against the clear skies. They then journeyed further east, their horses' hooves noisily striking the cobblestones as they clattered through the small Rhineland towns and villages.

Although nothing of note happened on the journey, by the time they reached the castle at Düren in Cleves the speed of the journey with its sense of urgency had thoroughly exhausted them. As soon as they were able to excuse themselves, after being introduced to the duke, the English party left their hosts and departed to the rooms assigned to them. The social and diplomatic niceties would have to wait for the morrow.

Chapter Five - Portrait of a Lady

The next morning when Anne walked into the room set aside for Holbein to paint his portraits, she found that he had already organized himself. Anne's chair was arranged so that she would catch the best light and that now he was preparing his brushes and colours. In fact, he was so intent on mixing a crimson tint that he jumped back when Anne coughed quietly as a sign to show she had entered the room.

"Milady," he spluttered. "I did not know you were here," he said, and bowed immediately.

"That's all right," Anne said quietly. "I was just standing here and watching you. I find it fascinating to watch people work at what they are interested in. And from what I've heard about you, Master Holbein, you're certainly interested in your work."

Holbein blushed, but only for a moment. He was not sure whether Anne had noticed this as, at that moment, she was concentrating on the colours that he had prepared. She looked up and faced him, taking in his sharp brown eyes and high forehead. She noted his kindly expression and pointed to the chair to his right.

"You may be seated, Master Holbein," she said. "I do not want these meetings to be very formal."

The court-painter sat himself down as Anne continued. "Yes, Master Holbein, even though I live in this quiet area of Europe far from the centres of population such as Hamburg, Paris or Amsterdam, I am aware that you've painted some very fine portraits of Erasmus and Sir Thomas More. I must also admit that your double portrait, 'The Ambassadors,' which I like is also very well-known and appreciated."

Holbein half-rose from his seat and bowed as Anne moved another wooden chair from near the wall and sat down to face him. "But now," she said, "I believe you have a commission to paint portraits of me and my sister, Amalia for your royal

49

master."

Holbein half-bowed again and then stood up in order to move his easel. As the sun had moved since he had first organized his new studio, he decided to move Anne's chair so that the angle of the canvas would allow him to paint the portrait in a stronger light than before.

"Please, milady, could you look at me directly from where you are sitting so that I might see you more clearly?" What he saw pleased him. In front of him sat a pleasant-faced young woman who seemed to be comfortable within herself. She was not nervous as several of his other subjects had been and her smooth complexion meant that his portrait would not have to disguise any unsightly scars and marks. Her dark eyes reflected a simple honesty and she held her head up straight in an unaffected manner. He did not like the way her nun-like pale brown headdress covered all of her hair, not allowing a wisp or tendril to escape, but he had been commissioned to paint the lady in the clothes that she had chosen. He noted however, that the headdress matched the style of the front panel of her bodice and that her complexion was complemented by the red of her velvet sleeves.

Above all, despite her aristocratic gown and sparkling jewellery, the lady projected an air of modesty. Perhaps the small cross worn just below her collar helped to give that impression. This portrait with its jeweled cross and two simple chains at her breast would certainly find favour with the king. Holbein knew that his master was looking for a quiet and modest wife to replace his 'dear Jane.' He did not want another forceful or argumentative woman like Anne Boleyn to share his kingdom and his bed.

Holbein's thoughts were suddenly interrupted when Anne asked, "Will you be painting a single portrait of each of us, or a double portrait which will include both me and Amalia?"

"I will be painting two separate portraits, milady. First I will paint yours and then I will paint your sister's. I also hope, if I have enough time, to paint some pictures of this castle and the surrounding scenery. It is so different from what I'm used to in London or where I used to live in Basel."

"In Basel?" Anne said. "I didn't know that. I thought you were originally from the Low Countries or from the Rhineland. Certainly not Switzerland."

"No, milady. I was born in Augsburg, a small town near Munich, but then I moved to London and Basel looking for commissions."

"And I understand you were very successful there."

"Yes, milady," he answered, picking up a short bristled brush. "And now I work for His Majesty, King Henry, as his court painter."

Anne was just about to say something when Holbein said, "If it please you, milady, I would like to start working now as I hope to catch the sunlight before those clouds to the west move over here."

Anne nodded and Holbein asked her to stand in such a position that the light from the window lit up her face.

"And what about my clothing and headdress?" Anne asked. "Will they be good enough for your portrait? Are they of the right colour and style?"

"Fear not, milady. I will deal with that question later. First of all I wish to make a sketch of you and then I will concentrate on the details later."

Anne nodded and moved to where Holbein had told her to stand. For the next twenty minutes she did her best not to move and not talk to him as he sketched the outline features of his portrait - the one that would be known hundreds of years later as the iconic portrait of Henry the Eighth's fourth wife.

The only time the painter said anything was when Anne developed a cramp in her right leg and she had to bend down and rub and shake it vigorously. "Please do not move, milady. I am trying to make the basic sketch for the final portrait. As you know, His Majesty wishes me to paint the best likeness of you as is possible."

Anne gave her leg one last shake and resumed her position directly looking at the painter. She stood up straight, her head held straight and held her hands together just below her waist. Some time passed before Holbein spoke again. "I think you may now rest awhile, milady," he said, stopping to stretch his back. "I also need to drink something. Is it possible for me to have a beaker of ale?"

Feeling somewhat relieved that she was allowed to move, Anne left the room to tell a servant to bring a tray of drinks and sweet pastries.

"And in the meanwhile, Master Holbein," Anne said on returning, "while we're having this little rest, please tell me something more about yourself. I always like to know something about the people with whom I work. All I know about you is that you are an excellent court painter and that you can speak English and German. I'm pleased about this last point because my own English is not very good and I was worried that I wouldn't be able to talk much with you. Do you ever have the opportunity to speak German in the king's court today?"

Holbein shook his head. "Hardly any, milady. There is almost no-one there who speaks the language. Sometimes I talk to Christopher Mont, the diplomat, or he asks me about a word or phrase but no, I speak very little of my mother-tongue today in England. And of course, milady, you must remember, the English do not like to learn or speak foreign languages. They are convinced that their language is *the* language. If they had their way, the whole world would speak English. But come, I've been talking enough. I've come here to paint your portrait, not to talk about me." And wiping some paint off his hands with a rag, he asked Anne to return to where she had been standing before. The light on her face was just right and he was anxious to begin.

He worked without speaking for the next ten minutes and then stopped to clean a couple of brushes. Anne took the opportunity to ask him to tell her more about himself.

"As I told you, milady, I was born in Augsburg near Munich. My father was a painter as well as a draughtsman and my brother Ambrosius was also a painter."

"Ah, a family of painters."

"That's right, and so too was my father's brother, Sigmund. We all worked in our family workshop in Augsburg. Then in 1515, my brother and I moved to Basel where we worked as journeymen and practised more of our art…"

"And craft."

"Yes, milady, I suppose you could call it a craft as well. We were apprenticed to Herr Hans Herbster who was the most famous painter in Basel at the time. Not only did we learn more about our profession, but we also worked as designers of wood- and-metal cuts. We did this for a local printer. It was during this period that we were invited by a preacher called Oswald Myconius to illustrate the margins of Erasmus' essay, *The Praise of Folly*. Have you heard of it?"

Anne shook her head. She was not well read and she certainly had not studied Erasmus' work on the Protestant Reformation. She asked Holbein to continue.

"I think we must have pleased him because shortly afterwards we began to receive many commissions. These included painting murals in Lucerne as well as decorating large wall panels in rich merchants' houses. And at the same time I also began studying the works of Andrea Mantegna, an Italian painter who was very good at engraving and painting frescoes. Then I moved back from Lucerne to Basel where I got married."

"To whom?"

"To Elsbeth Shmid, milady, a widow who was then running her late husband's business. But come, I'm talking too much and not painting enough. If I don't finish my work in time, my master will chop off my head."

Anne held her hands up to her face. "Would he really do that?"

"No, milady, at least, I hope not, but I must continue, so please ask your questions later." He took up his brush again and continued with his work for another half-hour during which they hardly exchanged a word. Occasionally he asked Anne to move a hand or leg slightly, but that was all. Then, just as he was about to start mixing some colours to reflect the tone of Anne's cheek, the room grew dark.

Muttering an oath in German, he looked out of the window and saw that a bank of dark grey clouds had moved in, covering the sun.

"Milady," he said turning to face his subject, "I see that we'll have to stop for a little while until those clouds move away."

"Oh, good! So now you can tell me about your wife, your Elsbeth Shmid."

Holbein smiled. "Yes, milady, as you wish. Well, as I told you, her late husband was in business. He had a tannery and was very successful. My wife is a few years older than me and we had a son in addition to the son she'd had from her first marriage. Then we had a second son and my life was going very well."

"And isn't it now?" Anne asked. She took a sweetmeat from a plate and offered one to the painter.

"Oh yes, milady. Certainly. I'm very happy to work at the king's court. I meet and speak to so many interesting people there."

"So tell me, how did you get there from Switzerland?"

"Oh, that was a piece of luck. I became quite friendly with the scholar, Erasmus, and he commissioned me to paint one or two portraits of him. These I did using oil paint and tempera."

"What is tempera? I know what oil paint is."

"Tempera is a form of paint which the artist makes by mixing the pigment with a liquid such as egg yolk. This sort of paint dries much more quickly than oil paint and it's a very old way of making colours. Even the ancient Egyptians used it. But to get back to Erasmus, he liked my work so much that he told all his influential friends and I started to become well-known. Then in 1524 I moved to France – to the court of King Francis."

"And did you learn to speak French there as well as paint?"

"*Oui, Madame, je parle le français pas mal maintenant.*"

Anne looked at him quizzically. It was clear that she had not understood him.

"I speak French quite well now." Holbein translated.

"I don't know many languages," Anne admitted. "In addition to my German, I know a little English and I suppose that if I do ever go and live in England, I'll have to learn to speak it better, especially after what you said about the English and what they think of foreign languages."

Holbein smiled and then turned to look out of the window at the sky, but the clouds were still blocking out the sun.

"But please continue, Master Holbein. Your life and travels are so much more interesting than my own life here."

Holbein nodded and continued.

"Well, again I have to thank my good friend, Erasmus. He recommended me to his friend, Sir Thomas More, the cleric who was a friend of King Henry."

"Wasn't he executed?"

"Yes, milady." Holbein was quiet for a minute as he thought of how the king's friend had stood up to his royal master and had paid for this with his head. Then Holbein looked up and saw that Anne was waiting for him to continue. For her, Sir Thomas More was just the name of a foreign courtier and advisor.

"So on Erasmus' recommendation, I moved to England and spent two or three years there painting portraits. I painted several of Sir Thomas and his family as well as of other clerics, such as the Archbishop of Canterbury, William Warham. I enjoyed myself in England but then I had to return to Basel, otherwise I would have lost my Swiss citizenship. Of course my wife and children were very happy to see me again and while I was there, I painted a portrait of them as well."

"But didn't you return to England again?"

"Yes, milady. Again I was very lucky. Thomas Cromwell, an important man who was and still is the king's chief minister commissioned me to paint a portrait of himself. And after that, several other important people wanted me to paint their portraits, too. I really enjoyed this but the portrait I really enjoyed painting was the double one that you talked about earlier."

"'The Ambassadors'?"

Holbein nodded. "I see that you've heard about me and my work."

Anne smiled and Holbein continued.

"This portrait is of two important men: Jean de Dinteville, an ambassador, and Georges de Selve. He was the Bishop of

Lavaur. I used both oil paint and tempera and I painted this portrait on a piece of oakwood."

"Not canvas, like you're using for me?"

"No, milady. But now, let me look outside and see what is happening with these clouds." They both walked over to the window and saw that most of the clouds had moved away from the sun. However, there were still a few more moving in from the west. Holbein frowned slightly because he wanted to continue but Anne was quite pleased as she was very happy chatting to the painter. He was someone new in her life and, with his descriptions of the outside world he was quite different from the people she usually met in Cleves.

"Tell me, master painter, I heard that you also painted one or two portraits of the king's second wife, Anne Boleyn."

"Yes, milady, that is true, but I believe the king had them all destroyed after she was executed. I am not sure, but that is what I was told."

Anne was silent for a moment. This King Henry had had his wife and one of his best friends and closest advisors executed and now maybe she would become his wife. She shuddered at the thought. Holbein noticed this.

"Are you cold, milady? I could close the window, if you wish."

"No, it's all right," and Anne decided to change the topic of their conversation. She looked up. "Do you paint only portraits? Don't you paint pictures of nature – of flowers and scenery?"

Holbein turned back to face Anne. He had been happily smelling the scented air outside the castle walls. The sweet smell here was completely different from the heavy and polluted air that he often smelt in London.

"I'm sorry, what did you ask me, milady? Ah yes, do I paint pictures of nature? Sometimes I paint pictures of flowers and trees and the like but to be honest, I prefer painting portraits. They're far more interesting. The human face is so much more fascinating than say a tulip or a marigold, wouldn't you say?"

Anne nodded in agreement and brushed a stray wisp of hair back into place under her headdress. "And now you are going to paint my portrait."

"Yes, milady, if the sun and clouds outside will let me." He walked over to the window and looked out. He then turned round and asked Anne to move back to her original position. He then asked her to make a few small changes in how she was standing, took up his brushes, moved his easel a little and started working again.

"Now, milady, if you will cast your eyes down a little for a few minutes that will give me just the right expression of modesty I wish to capture. Here, let me adjust your headdress a little. Ah, that's perfect. I am sure the king will be delighted with this portrait." He then made a few slight adjustments to the magnificent red gown, with its decorated gold bands and pearls and then stood back to admire the result. "Ah, that is just so, milady. Now I must concentrate before any more clouds come along."

He rapidly sketched in some more lines and then took up his brush and began stroking some paint onto the canvas which was now beginning to take on a life of itself. While Anne was watching him out of the corner of her lowered eyes, he alternately mixed his colours and then looked up at her as he continued working. Occasionally, he looked outside up at the sky but from what he could see, he would have a sufficient amount of time before the light would again be overcome by the clouds.

For a week the two of them met in this room every day except one when the overcast sky prevented the artist from obtaining the light he wished to exploit. Despite this delay, however, the portrait was almost finished a few days after that. He then spent another few days when the bright sunlight was not essential for him to add some of the finer details of her jewellery and the embroidery on her dress and headdress. When all of this was completed he asked Anne and her family to come and take a look at the finished portrait.

As usual, Anne's brother, the Duke was very short with his appreciation.

"Yes, it does you fine, Anne. I'm sure the king will like it. And now," he said, turning to leave, "I have some work to do," and saying that he left the room.

Anne's mother and sister were more forthcoming. "It's beautiful," Amalia said, clearly quite impressed by what she saw. "You look so calm, so poised."

"Yes, and so modest," her mother added. "I'm sure the King of England won't be able to refuse to marry you."

Holbein breathed a quiet sigh of relief. It seemed that he had been able to capture Anne's air of modesty despite the richly embroidered clothes she had been wearing.

"And I love the way Master Holbein has brought out the colour of your face and also the gold colouring of your jewellery," her mother added. She turned to the painter. "Oh, Master Holbein, the necklaces look so real I feel that I can pick them up and touch them. You know, take them off my daughter's neck and put them on my own."

Holbein smiled his thanks and felt very pleased. More than once he had heard his subjects and their families say that he was so skilled at making his portraits look so real, so close to life.

"And, Anne," Amalia said, stepping up close to examine the portrait. "Just look how finely Master Holbein has painted the veil on your headdress. It makes you look so delicate. I just hope," she said looking at the painter, "you will paint such a good portrait of me. I will wear my dark blue velvet gown with its gold trimmings and I'll wear my dark blue embroidered headdress and shoes to match. And mother, may I wear that lovely string of pearls you have? That will really complete the picture."

"Of course you may, my dear," Julia answered and then she turned again to Anne and the portrait.

"Oh, my darling daughter," she said, wiping her eyes and pulling Anne closer to her. "You look so lovely. I'll be so sad and miss you if His Majesty decides to take you for his wife."

Holbein smiled from where he was standing to the side. It was a good feeling to have one's work appreciated. It is true that he had felt the pressure to complete the portrait quickly but he felt that he had painted a true likeness. That is what he was known for and that is what his royal master had demanded. He was pleased with his work and the effect that it had on Anne and her family. Now he was looking forward to painting a portrait of her younger sister as well. On hearing that she was planning to wear her dark blue and gold gown he was already thinking of the pigments and brushes he would use. Yes, it was good to have your work admired especially when he knew how important it would be for his royal master, the ever-demanding King of England, King Henry the Eighth.

Chapter Six - Negotiations

To his surprise, Holbein did not enjoy painting the portrait of Amalia as much as he had that of her older sister. When he saw she would not or could not stand for more than a minute or two without fidgeting, he decided to paint her sitting down. He arranged for her to sit in a carved wooden chair next to a decorated table. The chair had padded armrests and that made it easier for the young lady to sit still. The table bore a vase of flowers that complemented her auburn hair and dark blue gown. But Holbein soon discovered she could not sit still for long even in this position. To solve the problem he asked her to hold her brown and white fluffy pet dog on her lap. When the dog began to squirm around on her lap, Holbein gave her a heavy book to hold instead.

But that did not help either. And when her long delicate fingers were still, then her mouth was not. Unlike her older sister who knew when to keep quiet, Amalia did not. Perhaps, Holbein thought, her ceaseless stream of questions was a result of having been brought up in this small duchy, in such confined surroundings; maybe that was why Amalia felt that she had to ask the painter about London, Paris and Basel.

"Which city is the grandest?"

"They are all grand, milady, but I think London is the grandest."

"Which country has the most handsome men?"

"They can be found everywhere, milady."

"So tell me, which country has the prettiest women?"

"Pretty women are also to be found everywhere."

"And the most fashionably dressed?"

"Also all over, milady."

"Are we ladies in Cleves dressed more fashionably that the ladies in London?"

Holbein thought for a moment before answering. "For Cleves they are fashionably dressed and the same may be said for the ladies in London," was his diplomatic answer.

In truth, Holbein found Amalia to be much less interesting and more superficial than her older sister. When he talked to her during their breaks over the next two weeks, he found her questions irritating and that her stubbornly held opinions on people and places were not based on facts or experience, but merely on hearsay and emotions. This was not the case with Anne. Anne wanted to learn more about life. She wanted to know more about the world outside the duchy and was very pleased when the painter added to her store of English vocabulary or corrected some of her grammatical mistakes in English.

The result was that although the ducal family praised Holbein's second portrait as much as the first one, he himself was not pleased with it. To be truthful, he felt he had not captured the younger daughter's superficial and more vacuous nature. However, he was not allowed the time to dwell on comparing the two sisters and their portraits. As soon as he had finished and the paint was dry on Amalia's portrait, the two paintings were very carefully wrapped and, accompanied by their painter, were sent to England, to his royal master at Hampton Court.

*   *   *   *   *   *   *

It was a pleasant sunny end-of-summer day when the king sent for Cromwell, the Duke of Norfolk and the Earl of Oxford to come to his chamber at Hampton Court. They were to view the two portraits which had been set up on easels near the window. This was where Holbein had advised the king that the natural light would do them the most justice.

After the four men had settled down in their chairs, the king stood up, and with his feet spread apart in his characteristic manner, addressed them. "Gentlemen, you know what you're here for. I'd like to hear your honest opinions about these two portraits that Master Holbein has painted. I'd like you to tell me the truth, the honest truth and not the version of the truth that you think I'd like to hear. Fear not," he added, seeing the

Earl of Oxford momentarily wince. "If your opinion differs from mine, I'll not send you to the Tower, at least, not this time. I've spent some time looking at these two portraits and have already reached my own conclusions. You are all married men of the world and know what women are like. So gentlemen, let us proceed."

The three men stirred uneasily in their seats. They looked at one another and then at the king. They knew that they would be telling him something personal. Something more personal than whom to appoint for a certain post or which fortress needed its defences reinforcing. Oxford suddenly showed great interest in the decorated ceiling while his brother duke swallowed and decided to study the floor between his shoes. Only Cromwell sat calmly, maybe because he, more than anyone else, had sat here for so many hours in the past with his royal master. Henry sat down and started drumming his fingers impatiently on the table next to him.

"Well, gentlemen, I am waiting," he said at last. "Come now, have you all been suddenly afflicted with the disease of dumbness?"

Cromwell coughed and started speaking in an unusually apologetic tone. "Your Majesty, you must realize that I am not an expert on artistic matters and nor am I a great man with the ladies," he began, "but I would like to say that..." and he looked at the two dukes who were pleased that the chancellor had taken the lead in this problematic discussion. "That, er...," Cromwell continued, wiping a few beads of sweat off his forehead with the back of his hand, "that, er, in my opinion, the picture of..."

"Yes, come on, Thomas, out with it," Henry cut in impatiently. "I've promised not to send you to the Tower. You are among friends here."

Cromwell looked out of the corner of his eye at Norfolk and knew this was certainly not true. The Reformation-minded chancellor had had several vicious arguments with the Catholic duke. He also knew that Norfolk was permanently jealous that he, the son of a Putney blacksmith and merchant, had much more influence over the king than he, Norfolk, had ever had.

"I think, Sire," Cromwell said slowly, "that the portrait of the older sister, of Anne of Cleves, shows a woman to be more suitable to be your wife."

Henry smiled encouragingly and the chancellor continued. "And not only that, Sire, that is in terms of what we can see on these canvasses, and from a brief talk I have had with Master Holbein as well as from this note from your envoy, they confirm my own humble opinion about the lady. Here, please allow me to read it to you. It is about her suitability in marrying you in relation to that question of the earlier betrothal to…"

"Yes, yes, Thomas, read the report," the king interrupted him again.

Cromwell stood up, reached for his pouch and pulled out a piece of paper and began to read.

I find the Council willing enough to publish and manifest to the world, that by any covenants made by the old Duke of Cleves and the Duke of Lorraine, my Lady Anne is not bound; but ever hath been and yet is at her free liberty to marry wherever she will.

The king smiled, said nothing and then pointed to the Duke of Norfolk. "Come, sir, you are the country's leading duke, what is your considered opinion?"

Norfolk, who had noticed that the king had smiled twice when the older sister had been referred to, and despite what he thought about the king's chancellor, said that he fully agreed with Cromwell. He was also aware that if he said that he preferred the younger sister to be the king's next wife and the country's next queen, he would not be incarcerated in the Tower. However, he also knew very well that His Majesty had a long memory, especially when it came to holding grudges against anyone. Past experience had taught him that the king did not suffer opinions that differed from his own.

"Sire," he continued in a louder and more confident tone that belied his true feelings. "After studying this lively portrait I think that the older sister seems to be a far more suitable woman, a more mature woman to be your future queen and helpmeet."

Henry smiled for the third time during that fateful meeting. "And you, sir," the king asked, nodding his head in Oxford's direction, "What do you think?"

Oxford, who was as devious as his brother aristocrat, especially when it came to placating his royal master, unhesitatingly gave his opinion. "I agree with my fellow duke and your chancellor, Sire. The younger sister seems to be too young for you, perhaps not sufficiently mature for a mind such as yours." He smiled briefly and then quickly reached over to pick up his glass of red wine.

"Are you implying, my good Earl of Oxford, that I am old?" the king asked, jutting out his bearded chin.

Oxford lowered his head so as not to face His Majesty. "Oh, no, Sire. It is just that I think that a ruler of your stature and intellect would not be happy with a wife who is, er, how shall I phrase this...?"

"Carefully, Oxford, carefully."

"Yes, Sire, er, with a wife who perhaps maybe a trifle empty-headed, er, that is, much less intellectual than your royal self." He paused, looked at the king, and on receiving no clear reaction, continued. "The portrait of the older sister, of the lady Anne, Your Majesty, seems to me to be, and please remember that I, too, am no expert in the world of art and of portraits ... um , the portrait of Lady Anne seems to show that she is more thoughtful, Sire, more considerate, er, more..."

"Enough, Oxford," Henry said raising his pudgy bejewelled hand. "I understand what you are saying. There's no need to treat me like a slow schoolboy who cannot learn his lessons."

Oxford sank back in his chair and concentrated on the glass of wine he was holding. Now he and the other two men waited for their royal master to say what was on his mind.

Henry stood up and walked slowly around the seated group. Although his ulcerous leg was sending sharp pains though his body, he enjoyed the feeling of power he had over these three men, his most senior advisors. It did not take much effort on his part to notice that as he passed by the two noblemen they cringed slightly, though had they been told this, they both would have denied it most vehemently.

"So, gentlemen," Henry said after settling down again in his chair and placing his leg in a position where he hoped it would be less painful. "This is what I've decided." He paused to look at the three men carefully, noting Norfolk's facial twitch, Oxford's expressionless grey eyes and Cromwell's sharp features. "I've decided to take the Lady Anne to be my next wife and queen." Each of the three advisors breathed a silent sigh of relief. Their royal master had agreed with their opinions. The king continued. "As such, I'll be instructing my envoys - probably Wotton and Mont - to return to Cleves in order to have a marriage contract drawn up by the lady's brother, the duchy's ruler, Duke William of Cleves."

Cromwell and the noblemen smiled. This important meeting was going well.

Henry then indicated that he had more to say. "And if you gentlemen are interested in my reasons for choosing the Lady Anne over her sister, Amalia, then yes, the question of age and probably maturity is indeed relevant." Henry walked over to stand next to Holbein's portrait of Anne. "While I think that both portraits show two very comely women, I think that lady Anne seems to display a more gentle disposition than her sister. Yes," he said as he closely examined the features on Anne's portrait. "Yes, a disposition more like my deceased queen, Queen Jane, that is, and perhaps a little like my first wife before she became so hard-headed and stubborn. I must admit, I like the expression of her eyes, soft and forgiving, and her face is unblemished, without any unseemly marks or scars. Master Holbein has assured me that what you see here today, gentlemen, is how the lady really looks. He says that here," and he pointed at Anne's portrait, complete with sleepy eyelids, "that he has painted a truly faithful likeness of the lady."

"Your Majesty," Cromwell said. "I am sure he has. If you remember the portrait of..." and then he stopped himself as he was about to remind his king about his friend, Sir Thomas

More.

"Yes, Thomas, you were saying?" Henry said, looking directly at his chancellor.

"Yes, Sire, I was just about to comment on that portrait that we call 'The Ambassadors' and how closely Master Holbein depicted their features. If you recall, it was a most detailed and exact likeness of Jean de Dintville and the Bishop Georges de Selve. I was most impressed, Sire and, I believe, so were you. I remember that you noted how well Master Holbein contrasted the light and shadows in this work."

"Thomas, I did not realize that you were such an accomplished critic of the arts," Henry said, raising his eyebrows. "I'd always thought of you more as a dealer in money, property and power."

"Thank you for the compliment, Your Majesty," Cromwell said, looking down for a moment. "But over the years, especially since I started working for you, Sire, I have come to learn to appreciate some of the finer aspects of life here at court."

Henry smiled. "Oh, what a flatterer you are, Thomas. But just remember, there is a limit you know of how much flattery that even I can take. But, for now," he said clapping his hands, "let's return to the business at hand. We're here to discuss and plan the business of my next, and hopefully the last of my marriages."

At the end of the following week a contract was signed in Düsseldorf and then towards the end of September 1539 the Duke of Cleves dispatched several envoys to Henry's court. They were led by the duchy's Vice-Chancellor Olisleger and Francis Burchard, the Vice-Chancellor of Saxony.

It was a warm, muggy day when the delegation was shown into the king's chambers. They were greeted by the king himself, who was wearing a dark, bejewelled hat and a maroon jacket trimmed with gold and seeded pearls. Standing to the side was a more modestly dressed Cromwell in his customary loose black garb. Nicholas Wotton and Christopher Mont were wearing dark blue and dark grey robes respectively; the only jewellery that they wore consisted of the finely engraved gold clasps which closed their gowns.

After they had all taken their places around the long oval table, the king, with Cromwell to the right and Wotton and Mont to the left faced the two foreign vice-chancellors in order to open the negotiations.

"Now you gentlemen know what I want," Henry said after everyone had shaken hands and gone through the usual pleasantries. "My question to you is what do you want in exchange?"

Olisleger looked at Burchard who gave him a brief nod, muttered something in German and then said, "Your Majesty, we understand that you are interested in marrying the Duke of Cleves' older sister, Lady Anne..."

"Yes, yes," Henry said impatiently. "We all know all that. The question is, what price will I have to pay for this?"

"Ah, we are coming to that," Olisleger replied quietly, looking straight at the king and noting the blotchy skin and the ostentatious jewellery. "We would wish to discuss several points such as the future queen's income in this country and..."

"Yes, and..."

"And, Your Majesty, the size of her dowry and the amount she will receive if, God forbid, if you or," and here Olisleger continued with lowered eyes, "if her brother, Duke William, should die before she does."

"You mean a pension of some sort?" Cromwell asked.

"Yes, sir. That is correct."

Olisleger then sat back in his chair, looked at Burchard for support and wondered if he had asked for too much. He knew that since the English king had recently dissolved the country's monasteries, his exchequer was not short of money. He was aware, however, that the overweight monarch - despite his great wealth - had a mean streak.

Henry looked at the Vice-Chancellors of Cleves and Saxony and fiddled with the ring on his fat finger then turned to look at Cromwell. "Thomas, you can continue from here. You are more familiar with these financial matters, but just don't give away half of my kingdom for this woman," he half-smiled. "If you do, it is you who will end up paying the bill."

Cromwell tried to smile in return and then turned quickly to face his foreign visitors. "My lords," he began. "First of all, please let me hear how much you were thinking of in terms of a dowry. Also, please take into account that Lady Anne will be marrying my king and that you will not wish to appear to be either mean or grasping in the eyes of Europe."

"That is all well and good," Olisleger replied looking to Burchard for support, "but you must remember that the Duke of Cleves is, how do you say it in English? *weniger reichlich*, er, less affluent than His Majesty." He looked around and pointed to the richly decorated walls and ceiling. "I mean, look at this palace, this chamber. I fear we cannot match this in our humble duchy."

"No, no, of course you cannot," Henry said rather grandly. "But what can you do? I cannot be seen to be buying a wife, as it were, on the cheap."

"Of course, Your Majesty. Therefore I suggest the Lady Anne's dowry shall be something in the region of seventy thousand florins and…"

"*Seventy thousand florins!*" Henry exploded. "Is that all? Come, gentlemen, we are talking about my future wife who will also be the Queen of England. Seventy thousand florins for her dowry is more suitable for a serving wench or the like."

"Surely, Your Majesty," Burchard said, looking up. "Are you not exaggerating a little? Seventy thousand for a wench?"

"Perhaps," Henry acceded, "but please note, there is no way we will agree on seventy thousand florins." He then turned to Cromwell and indicated that he should continue with the negotiations.

"Gentlemen," Cromwell smiled. "I am sure that my king was thinking more in terms of one hundred and twenty thousand florins," he said, wondering how this sum would be received.

He did not have to wait long for his answer. "One hundred and twenty thousand for the lady's dowry!" Olisleger gasped. "I am very sorry, sir, but that sum is impossible, quite impossible. As I have just said, my duke is not as rich as your king and such a sum would bankrupt us all."

From the way he was saying it and from the way in which Burchard was nodding vigorously in agreement, Cromwell saw that Duke William's Vice-Chancellor was not protesting in vain. He really meant what he said.

"Come," Cromwell said in a quiet voice. "Tell me how much your duchy can afford. I know you paid a dowry of one hundred and ten thousand florins when Lady Anne's older sister, Lady Sybille, married the Elector of Saxony some twelve years ago."

"Oh, no, sir. I must tell you, you are mistaken. That dowry was fixed at one hundred thousand florins. I remember, I was involved in the…"

"Ah," Cromwell interrupted. "Then your duchy could afford that sum then. And now? And please remember, Lady Anne will be marrying," and here Cromwell looked to his left, "the King of England, King Henry the Eighth, not a mere Elector of Saxony."

Henry patted his chancellor on the back. This meeting was now moving as he had wished. Burchard swallowed and decided not to make a point of Cromwell referring to his master as 'a mere Elector.'

"Well," he began, "seeing as we wish Lady Anne to appear as important as her sister, and if Vice-Chancellor Olisleger agrees, we will also agree to one hundred thousand florins." Olisleger nodded but it was obvious to all that he was not happy with this arrangement. Burchard continued, "But, Your Majesty, it must be understood, this is our final offer. We will not be able to pay one florin more."

"Agreed!" Henry said, striking the table. "Now let us seal this with a glass of hippocras."

"Excuse me, Your Majesty," Cromwell said after having drained his goblet, "but now we must work out how this dowry is to be paid, to be transferred from Cleves to London."

Henry looked at his chancellor. "In cash, of course, Thomas. What else? We are not Arabian nomads who deal in camels, are we?"

"No, no, Sire. That's not what I meant. I meant how many payments?"

A second, but briefer round of discussion continued. Twenty minutes later it was concluded that despite the initial protestations of ducal poverty, the dowry would be paid in two installments: forty thousand florins would be paid on the wedding day and the remainder would be sent to London within twelve months after that.

After another break for a meal both sides returned to the king's chamber for a further round of negotiations. At first, Olisleger and Burchard wanted to delay this for a day or two, but after Wotton and Mont had informed them that His Majesty was quite impatient to conclude this stage of the proceedings, the two vice-chancellors agreed. They accompanied their English counterparts back to the king's chamber and Henry instructed Cromwell to continue.

"And now," Cromwell said, unrolling a document in front of him, "we must be harshly practical and discuss the eventuality that if His Majesty should predecease the Lady Anne, who of course will then be his happily wedded wife, what her financial situation will be. These dower rights will naturally be arranged for a fixed sum per annum. The question is: how much will that sum be?"

Perhaps because none of the advisors present really wished to talk about the king's demise, especially in his presence, the solution to the problem was quickly found. In the event of Henry dying before his wife, she was to receive fifteen thousand florins annually and be allowed to retain all her gold and silver plate.

"And if my lady wishes to return to Cleves in the sad event of His Majesty passing on, would that be allowed?" asked Burchard.

Cromwell turned to the king who nodded approval. Wotton then asked Cromwell to dictate the agreed terms and then he recorded them all in his neatest writing on a large piece of parchment.

It was almost sunset by the time this meeting was over as Henry stood up to indicate that he had had enough for the day. He winced as the ulcer on his left leg sent a stabbing pain through the lower half of his body and he reached out for the back of a chair for support.

"Well, gentlemen, I think we've have concluded today's affairs satisfactorily," he said after the pain had subsided. "As my chancellor has said, we'll have the final marriage contract drawn up and signed in the next few days. I'd like it to be signed and witnessed either here in London or at my castle in Windsor. Are there any objections?"

There were none. Everyone around the table nodded or murmured in agreement and it was decided to meet at Cromwell's chambers on the following morning. There they would arrange all the final details for Anne's journey to London: the route, the costs and which attendants, servants and jewellery she would be bringing with her. "Jewellery, that is," Cromwell added, "that befits such a lady, the daughter of such noble parents and the intended bride of so great a king."

Late that night, after dismissing all his servants, and sitting in his private chamber with only his brother-in-law, Charles Brandon, the Duke of Suffolk, for company, Henry decided to review the day's events. After taking a glass of mulled wine for a nightcap, he invited the duke to have a close look at the portrait of Anne of Cleves. Placing a burning torch on each side of the painting, Henry told Brandon to scrutinise Holbein's portrait critically.

"Come, Charles, look at this picture carefully and tell me what you truly think. Am I right in wishing to marry her or am I about to place my head in another noose like I did with Anne Boleyn?"

Brandon was silent. He was thinking and appraising the portrait.

"I will admit," the king continued, "that she certainly looks more docile than that Boleyn woman. She looks more like Jane, I think, that is, in terms of temperament, but do I need so much activity now at my age? After all, I am well over fifty and I know that all the major activities of hunting and even warfare are more or less over for me, especially with this cursed leg of mine. So tell me, am I doing right in saying I will marry this woman?"

Brandon stepped back a little, cocked his head to one side

and looked at the painting carefully. Despite the flickering light, he noticed the downcast eyes and the plain face in contrast to the rich red velvet and the gold trimmings. He noted the quality and size of the pearls and of the other jewels and then he looked again at the face below the heavy Dutch-style nun-like headdress which covered her hair completely.

"Sir," he said at length, "in my eyes she looks most modest, virtuous and demure, almost to a fault. She certainly looks very different in character from your second wife, if I may add, and she has a certain dignity which cannot be denied." He hesitated for a moment and looked at his brother-in-law who told him to continue.

"She certainly shows distinct breeding, sir, and I think she will prove to be a fine wife and queen. I must say this from just looking at this portrait, and I think your Master Holbein has painted a fine portrait here. It is true that she does not seem to have the sparkle and zest of Anne Boleyn but, as you said, who needs these qualities at your time of life? This woman," he added, looking at the portrait, "will give you what you want: peace and quiet. You don't need another nagging wife like your second one or a stubborn one like your first."

"By Jove, Charles, you are right," Henry said, taking his eyes off the portrait. "I knew I could count on your opinion. Come, let's have another goblet of wine and drink to a long, happy and trouble-free marriage. Don't you agree that after all these years and three marriages that I deserve the peace and quiet you have just spoken about? Here, let us drink a toast to the future Queen of England."

"Aye," the king's brother-in-law added, "And to her future husband."

Chapter Seven - Farewell to Cleves

With his foot on a low footstool, the king was sitting in his chamber reading a theological treatise. Suddenly there was a loud, insistent knocking on the door and a few moments later he found himself facing the flushed face of his chancellor. He was carrying a large map.

"What is it, Thomas?" Henry asked. "You look worried. Have you discovered that the Lady Anne has the pox? And why are you holding that map?"

"No, Sire, it's…" Cromwell answered, still panting heavily.

"Not another uprising in the north? Where is it now? York? Doncaster? Newcastle?"

"No, Sire, it's nothing like that. It's just a question of bringing your future wife to England."

The king looked up at Cromwell's concerned face. Now that he had found a wife, had successfully negotiated all the details about her dowry and had been assured that there were no problems regarding her past betrothal, what else could go wrong?

"Tell me, Thomas, and be quick about it. I know you are much involved with this marriage. Have all your plans come to nought?"

"No, Sire, well I hope not, Sire," Cromwell bowed. "It's just that there are problems in how your lady will make her journey from Cleves to London."

"What do you mean *how?* By horse and carriage, of course. And a ship to cross the Channel. How do you expect her to arrive here – to grow wings and fly?"

"No, Sire, I didn't mean "how" like that. I meant, which route should she take?"

"Why, what's the problem? The shortest one, of course. Surely there are roads from Cleves to the coast. Didn't Wotton, Mont and Master Holbein all make the same journey?"

"Yes, Sire, there are good roads as far as I understand," Cromwell answered, nervously rolling and unrolling the map which was still in his hands. "The problem is, Sire, which route should she take from Cleves to the coast?"

Henry lifted up his hand. "First of all, Thomas, pray sit down and stop playing with that wretched map. Now please explain yourself. You are talking in riddles."

Cromwell took a deep breath, lifted his heavy body into the padded chair and unrolled the map on the table. He then showed it to the king.

"This is the situation, Sire. There are two possible routes that the Lady Anne can take. The most direct one is to travel overland from her castle at Cleves through the Low Countries to our English enclave at Calais," he said, tracing his finger along the route on the map. "From Calais she will be able to take a ship to Dover and then proceed to London."

"And the other route?"

"That the Lady Anne should travel from Cleves through the Guelderland, which is here," Cromwell said, pointing out the area on the map. "This area should not present a problem as it is in the domain of her brother, the duke. Then she should be secretly smuggled across the Zuyder See in the Low Countries. There she would board an English ship and that will bring her to Dover or possibly, she could continue sailing up the Thames to London."

Cromwell stepped back from the map and sat down.

"But, Thomas, I do not see the problem. Surely it would be better to take the first route you suggested, the one through Calais. It is English territory and no harm should befall her there. After all, she won't be travelling on her own. She'll be escorted by guards and the like."

"I know that, Sire, but the problem is that much of the Low Countries is ruled by Queen Mary of Hungary and..."

"Ah, I see what you mean. She is the sister of Charles, the Holy Roman Emperor, and you are concerned that they will not give Lady Anne and her party a safe-conduct pass."

"Exactly, Your Majesty. Especially as the Duke of Cleves, and therefore his immediate family are said to lean toward

Lutheran beliefs as opposed to the Catholic ones of Queen Mary."

Henry was silent for a few minutes while his chancellor fiddled with a quill pen on the table. At last Henry looked up.

"Thomas, what do you know about this Zuyder See route? Is it safe in terms of navigation? Are there any dangerous shoals and sandbanks there? Don't Dutch pirates ply their so-called trade in this area?"

Cromwell thought carefully before answering this last question. After all, he was talking about bringing his king's future wife over to England and nothing should go wrong. The price of failure was not even to be considered.

"I think," he said slowly, "there may be a certain amount of danger in this area, Sire, and that is why I have given orders to dispatch, secretly, of course, two experienced shipmasters, er, I have their names here," and he stopped to pull a list out of his pouch. "Ah, here we are, Masters Richard Couche and John Arborough. They'll see if this area is navigable and, if it is, then they'll produce a pilot's chart. This will then be given to the captain of the fleet who will bring the Lady Anne here to England."

"Ah, Thomas. As usual you think of everything. What would I do without you?" Henry smiled at his chancellor and then looked at him directly. "So, as far as you can see, the choice is this: either taking the shorter route and risk not receiving a safe-conduct pass through the Low Countries or travelling a longer route safely overland but risk having problems in the area of the Zuyder See?"

"Yes, Sire. And of course, there is another problem which affects both of the routes I have suggested. It is the question of the weather."

"The weather?"

"Yes, Sire. This journey or rather the Channel crossing will be made during the winter and you can understand what that means?"

"Storms at sea?"

"Yes, Sire, that and the exposure to the elements that might adversely affect the Lady Anne's health and beauty."

"So, Thomas, I understand you prefer the shorter Calais crossing, for that would mean less time at sea, especially if the weather's bad?"

Cromwell nodded. "And that is why the Council and I would be happy if you could write a personal letter to the Holy Roman Emperor, asking him for a special safe-conduct pass for the Lady Anne and her party." He paused, looked at his king and continued. "We feel, Sire, that if *you* wrote this letter, as the king of this country, as opposed to the Council writing it, it would carry more weight. Then of course, if this request is granted, the route through Calais would be much shorter and safer."

What Cromwell did not say to his royal master was that he, his chancellor, did not wish to become too involved in the international European political scene. If he wrote the necessary request and it was turned down, then he, Cromwell would be blamed for any future problems, but if His Majesty's request was refused, then he and not Cromwell would be held responsible. Cromwell had never allowed himself to forget how the king at the beginning of his reign had had two of his chief ministers, Richard Empson and Edmund Dudley, executed for having angered His Majesty.

Despite his reluctance to correspond with the Holy Roman Emperor, Henry did write to him and was happily surprised to promptly receive a positive reply to his request. The following letter was then sent to Queen Mary of Hungary and the safety of the Cleves travelling party was assured.

Begging you, most excellent Princess, Our dearest and most beloved sister and good cousin, that, taking into consideration the purport of the Emperor's letter, as well Our own desire, as expressed in Our last letter – you may be pleased, for the personal security and comfort of the said Lady Anne and suite, to add to her passport such full orders and favourable commendations as may be required and it is in your power to give since such is, as We can see, the good intention of our said brother, the Emperor.

The next stage was that Henry ordered that ten of his ships were to make ready to bring his bride from Calais to Dover and that all the towns between Dover and London where Anne would rest overnight or pause for refreshment during the day should arrange suitable processions and festivities.

"Which towns are you thinking of, Your Majesty?" Cromwell asked the king one rainy November evening as they were sitting in his chamber. A map of the south of England was spread out on the table between them.

"Here, Thomas" and Henry leaned over the table. "Dover, Deal, Canterbury, Sittingbourne and Rochester."

"Hmm, a journey of about seventy miles, Sire. I'm sure she will be extremely exhausted after making her way from Cleves to Calais and from there to Dover."

Henry smiled. The recent news that his future wife was to be given a safe-conduct pass and that his chief minister was doing his best to ensure that she would be given the best possible reception filled him with pride and joy.

"So, Thomas, the man with all the answers, what will her first vision of English territory be? It will be Calais, of course. Now what's to be arranged there in her honour?"

"Fear not, Your Majesty. I've sent orders to have the roads and town walls repaired. Your residence there is to have its gutters replaced and all the cracked and broken windows are to be repaired. I've also seen to it that the royal emblems over the Lentern Gate are to be repainted and gilded so that they may appear as they were when they were originally commissioned."

Henry smiled appreciatively and Cromwell continued. "In addition, Sire, all the furniture, curtains and carpets are to be replaced where necessary and various parts of the flooring are to be similarly repaired. I can show you a list of what has been done and what still needs to be done." He passed a list over and Henry smiled at him again.

"Thomas, you have surpassed yourself. Well done."

Cromwell smiled but wondered why could his king not praise him so in front of the other advisors, especially the earls, lords and dukes? They all thought he was nothing but a jumped-up servant, the son of a poor artisan who had risen too far and too fast. And at their expense as well. Many, he thought would be very happy to see him fall or, if not actually fall, taken down a peg or two. He had heard all of them from time to time whisper behind his back or stop whispering the moment he entered the Council chamber.

"Huh! Son of a blacksmith, or the like and now the king's chancellor! And telling *us* what to do."

"What were he and his father doing when we first fought for the king or his father? Probably working in his father's smithy no doubt or grubbing for money."

"That's right. Just like Cardinal Wolsey who came before him. Another jumped-up trader turned chancellor."

"Aye, but look what happened to him. Where's he now?"

Yes, Cromwell had heard it all. His sombre thoughts were suddenly cut short by his king's urgent voice.

"Thomas, who d'you think should first greet the Lady Anne? Have you given any thought to that?"

"Yes, Sire. I have written to Lord Lisle, your resident-deputy of Calais. In addition to receiving instructions to make the town look as beautiful and well-cared for as possible, he and several other nobles have been charged to pay the lady their respects in your name."

"I see. And which nobles are to do this?"

"Sire, I do not have the complete list with me, but I know that Lord William Howard, the Duke of Norfolk's brother, and Sir Francis Bryan will be on hand."

"Very good, Thomas, and I presume you've arranged for a yeoman guard of honour to be present?"

"Of course, Sire. Here, I've a copy of the instructions that I've sent to Lord Lisle. Let me read you some of them."

Taking a folded page from his pocket, Cromwell began to read:

...in their best array, to meet and receive her Grace at her Entry into the English pale and, after their due reverence and salutations made to her, they shall conduct her and her train to the town, making all honest and friendly semblance and

entertainment, whereby they may perceive themselves most heartily welcome.

And as for your yeomen guard, Sire, there will be two hundred of them, all wearing coats of blue and red - the colours of the royal arms of England."

Henry clapped his hands. "Excellent, Thomas. I 'm most impressed, and I hope that Lady Anne will be as well. Now, just before you go, do make sure that by tomorrow morning I have a complete list of my courtiers who'll be on hand to greet the lady. That is, both at Calais and also here in England, at all the towns you mentioned earlier."

"Yes, Sire." Cromwell bowed and hurried out. If the king said he wanted something by tomorrow morning, then it would be delivered tomorrow morning. Past experience had taught him that one did not keep His Majesty waiting. And since Henry had set his sights on marrying Lady Anne of Cleves in the very near future, it had become even more urgent to have her brought over to England as quickly as possible.

*   *   *   *   *   *   *   *
*

If the plans for the forthcoming royal meeting and wedding were taking place at a furious pace in London, then the same could be said for what was happening in Cleves.

From the moment Anne's family received the letter saying that she had been selected to become King Henry's fourth wife and the Queen of England, the mood in Cleves changed from anxiety and anticipation to a frenzy of bustle and activity. This frantic atmosphere was heightened when a second letter of personal congratulations was received, this one being signed by none other than Thomas Cromwell, Chancellor of England.

"Look, it's from the king's chief minister," an English-speaking official told Anne. "He is wishing you all the best and assures you that everything will be done to make you happy in your new country."

Anne looked at her mother, who was trying her hardest to

hide her feelings over her being parted from her daughter soon, perhaps even forever.

"Come over here, my dear, and sit next to me," she said giving Anne an affectionate hug. "Now," she continued, wiping her eyes, "let us look through your robes and gowns once again to see which you should take with you and which may need repairing. We don't want the English to think that just because you come from a small duchy, we're poor and don't how to dress in style."

"But mother, Amalia and I went through all my clothes, even my underclothes yesterday. None of those that I wish to take with me need repairing. I'm quite sure of that."

"Annele," said Julia, hugging her daughter again. "Your sister is not as thorough as I am. Now let's go up to your room and we'll look through your trousseau again." Of course, Duchess Julia's sharp eyes found a small tear in the sleeve of a green velvet gown. She held the gown up and Anne could just about see the light peeking through the small hole.

"You see, my love, what would've happened if you'd worn this gown to a ball in London? What would people have said, eh? Don't you remember all the spiteful remarks people made here last Christmas when one of the ladies wore a gown with a small tear at the back? What was her name? She was a cousin to the Elector. Oh, never mind. But that's what the people here - at least the women - gossiped about for a good week. We don't want that happening to you, now do we?"

And then there were the horses to be examined and the carriages and wagons to be inspected. One carriage was found to have an ill-fitting door while two of the wagons which were to carry Anne's trousseau and other supplies had loose wheels which needed to be changed. Several of the guards' uniforms were handed over to the seamstresses to have various holes, tears and trimmings repaired while the horses were taken to the castle blacksmith to have their shoes examined or changed if necessary. In addition, several servants were given the task of examining all the reins and were also told to polish all the horse buckles and brasses.

"I do hope it'll be a sunny day for Lady Anne's journey," the chief blacksmith said, looking up at the pale wintry sky. "Not just because of the journey, but I want the carriages and horses to look their best, especially after all the work we've done."

And while all this frantic activity was taking place, Anne would take herself off from time to time and sit down with Mistress Gilmyn. Cromwell had sent this English gentlewoman over to Cleves to instruct Anne in the ways of England and to try and improve the future Queen of England's command of the English tongue.

"Please remember, milady, that the English do not put all their verbs at the end of their sentences - especially in the past tense as you do in German. Therefore, please do not say, 'I have the horse not seen' but 'I have not seen the horse.' Do you understand? This is very important."

Anne nodded. To her this did not seem to be a major problem.

"And also please remember that English is perhaps easier than German. In my language we have only one word for your *der, die* and *das*. And it is *the*. This means that *der Tisch* and *die Tür* in German simply become '*the* table' and '*the* door' in English."

Again Anne nodded and promised to remember these rudimentary grammatical rules.

"And of course," Mistress Gilmyn continued, "the same must be said for the English word, *a*. In German you have *ein, eine* and *einer*, whereas in English we just say *a* before words when we mean *one*. We have *a* man, *a* woman, *a* child. But do not worry, we will continue with those words and some others tomorrow."

Anne nodded and said she would try and remember but, in truth, she had other and, for her, more pressing thoughts on her mind. She was thinking about her imminent marriage and the reasons it was so important to her and to everyone else. She had been told why this marriage and its success were so important for her brother, Duke William, and the duchy of Cleves. Vice-Chancellor Olisleger had given her a long and boring lecture on the political and religious ramifications of this new personal and international union and why it must not fail. At the same time Anne was also aware of her future groom's reputation.

One did not become a thrice-married king without word of it spreading around the continent, especially as many of the European crowned heads and other aristocrats were connected by marriage themselves within a large and extended family group.

Anne knew of Henry's reputation. He had had three wives already. The first had been cast aside after fifteen years of marriage and then left to live an isolated life far away from court and her daughter for the rest of her life. The second wife he had had executed after she had been tried for treason after being queen for only three years. Ironically, Anne half-smiled to herself, Henry had declared that he had really loved her, even to the end. Her end, that is. To prove this, he'd had a professional swordsman brought over especially from France to execute her rather than allow an ignorant English axeman to butcher her on the block! This was a sign of love? And the third wife had not had much more luck either. She had died a few days after giving birth to her first child. True, the baby had been the much desired and hoped-for son, but that did not help his poor mother in any way.

In addition, Anne had heard malicious tales that the king had more or less abandoned his third wife while she was suffering as he could not bear to be near her while she was suffering so much pain. Were all these stories true, or were they just nasty gossip? How could he have rejected his first wife after fifteen years? How could he have had his second wife executed, even by a professional swordsman? And how could he have deserted his third wife in her greatest hour of need? Wasn't a husband supposed to support his wife in sickness and in health? Anne could not understand how her husband-to-be had acted as he had. What sort of man was he and how would he treat *her*? Would she be got rid of if, for whatever reason, she failed to please him? And if so, how? Exile? Execution? It didn't bear thinking about.

It is true that Henry and his kingdom were far richer and larger than her brother, the duke, and his Rhineland duchy, but were money and lands everything? Here, she had everything she knew and loved. Her mother and sister lived here, and her brother, even if he did not show too much affection and warmth, was kind enough and protected her. She loved the old castle at Düren and the surrounding countryside. She loved the local people and her servants and they all loved her in return. Would life be like this in England? How would she be treated there? Would the English people like her or would they treat her as a foreigner who was there only because King Henry had decided it to be so? Time would tell. Until then she would have to wait.

At last the great day for farewells arrived. One could feel the tension in the atmosphere that always accompanies the beginning of an important expedition. The horses stamped their feet impatiently on the large flagstones, the reins jingled in the air and the newly-polished horse brasses sparkled in the sun. Masters were giving and servants were receiving orders. Everyone was bustling about moving boxes and trunks from here to there as well as carrying out the last-minute preparations that somehow had been forgotten in the mounting excitement and activity. Packages of all sizes and shapes were wedged in between larger ones in the supply wagons, or were pushed through the windows of the carriages for the passengers to carry on their knees or to be placed on the floor. Ropes were tightened for the hundredth time; knots were untied and retied; hats and bonnets were straightened and the accompanying guards were inspected yet again. Everyone was moving about frantically. Major officials gave orders to minor officials. Minor officials gave orders to the servants and the only one who remained calm was Anne of Cleves herself, the lady in the eye of this storm of activity.

Anne stood by the door of her carriage with Mistress Gilmyn trying to absorb the fact that this massive undertaking was being carried out for her sake, Anne of Cleves, the sister of Duke William and the future Queen of England.

After much shouting and the giving of more orders and counter-orders, the train of wagons, carriages and guards was lined up in the castle courtyard. The servants were assembled and Anne, accompanied by Mistress Gilwyn and Lady Keteler, who had just arrived from England to act as another aide and travelling companion settled down in the duke's own carriage. Another twelve ladies and gentlemen had been chosen to accompany Anne on her first journey beyond the boundaries of her native Cleves. They all settled down comfortably in the carriages that were to travel immediately in front of and behind the more luxurious vehicle of their mistress. The Duke of Cleves may have claimed in his negotiations with King Henry that he was poor, but he did not wish to show any outward signs of poverty as his sister travelled west, especially on this most important of journeys.

In addition, John Frederick, the Elector of Saxony supplied thirteen trumpeters to proclaim the arrival of the entourage as it passed through all the towns en route. The train was also to include Vice-Chancellor Olisleger and the Earls of Overstein and Nuennare. Anne's young cousin, Count von Waldeck also travelled with her and, in all, over two hundred and sixty people were to accompany Anne on her historic journey to Calais.

When the noise and bustle were over, when all the knots and ropes had been adjusted for the last time and all the horses made ready, a certain quiet and semblance of order settled over the courtyard. Her brother, Duke William, left his place at the upper storey window from where he had been watching the last minute preparations and came down to stand at the top of the flight of the castle steps. There, with his wife, his mother, Julia and Amalia by his side they all waved their final farewells. Eyes were wiped, last minute, hugs and instructions were exchanged and everyone wished Anne well in her new land and rôle in life. It was with great reluctance that Anne finally climbed into her carriage. She did her best to smile as she wiped back the tears from her eyes and waved her white handkerchief to her family and to those who would not be travelling with her. Then the duke raised his hand as a sign to the leading horseman and the long train with its carriages, wagons, mounted guards and foot soldiers made its way under the portcullis and out of the courtyard in the direction of

Calais. Anne's historic journey had begun – the result of an English king, far away over the sea having chosen her to be his fourth queen. And all because he had been so impressed by her portrait.

Chapter Eight - Calais

Despite King Henry's impatience to meet his new bride, the long train of carriages and wagons did not and could not hurry their way over the gently undulating Rhineland plain. Due to its sheer length and the number of people involved, this long column of horsemen and vehicles covered only five miles each day. It was not until 3 December 1539 that it finally rumbled into Antwerp, the crowds along the sides of the streets waving as it passed.

This old town on the River Scheldt had seen much action since it had first been established over eight hundred years earlier. Norsemen had attacked it a few times before capturing the town and then burning it down to the ground. It was then rebuilt and turned into a German frontier town, a town built to defend the area from various Flemish counts and other nobles.

Then a more peaceful era came into being and the town grew and developed. It joined the important Hanseatic League, and its role as a commercial centre grew. This happened also because Bruges, its rival sister-city to the west began to decline as its port silted up. As a result, all the major guilds began transferring their offices and their trading centres to Antwerp. Because of its position on the eastern bank of the wide river Scheldt, Antwerp did not suffer from the silting problem.

By the time Anne's long line of carriages and wagons arrived in the city centre, over one thousand merchants had settled there. Each of them had built a fine house and each one had tried to outdo his neighbour in terms of architecture and style. These houses represented the major trading nations of Europe, but the finest one was said to be owned by Sir Thomas Gresham.

"Just look at that house," Anne said to Mistress Gilmyn, pointing out of her carriage window. "It's almost as big as our castle back in Düren."

"Aye, milady. It belongs to Sir Thomas Gresham, an English merchant and banker and whose father is, I believe, the Lord Mayor of London."

Anne was suitably impressed and continued looking at the other rich buildings, gaping and gawping like a peasant who had come to town for the first time in her life. Later, Mistress Gilmyn told her that over two hundred thousand people lived in Antwerp and that hundreds of ships bearing spices, sugar, silk, gold, wine and grain sailed in and out of the port every year.

This was the first great city that Anne was to see before she made her own triumphant entry into the city of London. Not that her entry into Antwerp was not a triumph. It was. Thousands of the city's citizens, both rich and poor, came out to see the long ducal train and wave to the happy bride-to-be. She demurely accepted their cheers and blessings as she sat by her carriage window. Even the well-travelled Nicholas Wotton was heard to remark that he had never seen so many people gathered to receive a visitor to this town – "No, not even for a king or an emperor," he said.

The train of carriages and wagons slowly made its way through the twisting streets, passed the magnificent cathedral of Notre Dame with its high, delicate spire and then continued on to pass the Steen, the old castle near the riverside.

That night the affluent English colony of merchants and traders in Antwerp arranged a splendid reception to be held in Anne's honour, Despite her concern that she would not live up to the occasion, her natural warm personality and humility ensured she was well-acclaimed by one and all to be the future wife of the King of England. It was the first of these occasions and Anne had no reason to feel embarrassed or uncomfortable. She carried off the evening well and everyone present blessed and praised her.

Two days later, after a couple of the carriages had undergone some repairs, the wagons were repacked and the whole train set off for Bruges via Bever, Stecken and Tokkyn. Although the city fathers of Bruges were aware of their city's gradual decline, this did not prevent them from displaying the grandeur of its most important buildings which included the beautifully proportioned Hôtel de Ville and the Halles market with its imposing 13th century square tower as well as the white-fronted Bequinage, set in its fine and well-trimmed gardens.

As in Antwerp, Anne and her entourage were greeted by the city's mayor and his officers. Many of the townspeople had taken time off from work to cheer the progress of her train as it made its way past the churches of St.Boniface, St Sauver and Notre Dame. The train then continued on to the town hall – an inspiring building which boasted many tall perpendicular windows set below a roof bearing several spires and turrets.

But Anne and her retinue could not spend much time here among these picturesque and historic surroundings. Henry was impatient to see his future wife. So after staying for one more day in Bruges the long train left on the morrow travelling in a westerly direction to Dambrugh, Nieuwpoort and Dunkirk. Though much smaller, these Flemish cities mirrored the affluence and magnificence of Antwerp and Bruges. With her limited knowledge, Anne wondered how London, the city of her future husband, would be able to excel what she had seen so far.

"Is London really so grand, as grand as this?" Anne asked Nicholas Wotton who was sitting next to her.

"Yes, milady. It certainly is. Just wait until you see the king's palace at Hampton Court or his other palace at Nonsuch," he boasted. "They make these town halls look like farmer's barns in comparison. And as for the River Thames and London Bridge, Antwerp cannot even begin to compete."

The journey continued slowly on its way without anything special happening. The only untoward incident which marred the general feeling of joy and expectation occurred at Dunkirk. Here a Catholic priest preached a sermon which several members of Anne's train considered seditious. William Fitzwilliam, the Earl of Southampton, who had been dispatched by the king to act as a liaison, heard of this but did nothing about it. On his return to England he assured His Majesty that the cleric's words 'did not pose any danger or hazard' but he did admit that the sermon had been 'full of unfitting words.'

If this minor incident had cast a rather gloomy feeling on Anne and her attendants, this was dispelled on 10 December when they entered the coastal town and sea port of Gravelines. As they passed the sea-wall, Anne asked for her carriage to be brought to a halt. This was the first time that she had seen the sea.

"It's so big," she said to Mistress Gilmyn. "I just cannot believe that there is so much water in the world."

"It may be big, milady, but at this time of the year it is also very cold."

"Yes, and very windy, too." Anne replied as she and her ladies held on to their headdresses. "I can see that by the size of the waves. But tell me, isn't the sea supposed to be blue? In all the pictures we had at home, the sea was always blue. Here it's dark grey."

"Ah, milady, that's because those pictures were painted on a sunny day in the summer. Then the sea looks blue. It takes its colour from the sky. Now it's grey and overcast, and that's why the sea looks like it is today."

Anne thought about this for a moment, pulled her cloak around her even more tightly and then asked Mistress Gilmyn whether they could sail over to England if there were waves on the sea.

"There are always waves on the sea, milady. The question is, how high they are. If they're high, that means there's a storm and so we'll have to wait. If they're lower and more gentle, then it'll be safe for us to sail from Calais to Dover. It all depends on the winds."

"But don't we need strong winds for the sails?"

"Yes, milady, but if they are too strong they'll blow the ship over."

"I see. So we need winds that are not too strong, so as not to make a storm and not to blow our ship over but they must be strong enough to move our ship on. Oh, I'm learning so much these days. Something new every day."

"Aye, milady, and what *I* am learning," said Mistress

Gilmyn, "is if we don't return to our carriage now, these winds will give us a chill. You cannot afford to catch a cold, and besides, everyone is waiting for you."

Anne nodded and together with Mistress Gilmyn, returned to the carriage, both of them holding onto their hats with one hand while with the other they drew their cloaks more closely around themselves. Once inside the carriage, they arranged the thick travelling blankets across their laps and soon the train rumbled off over the cobbled roads into the centre of Gravelines.

"Who are all those people?" Anne asked a few minutes later as a large crowd which had gathered in front of the carriage separated like the biblical Red Sea to let them through.

Wotton looked up from the document he had been studying and stuck his head out of the window. "They're some of the local nobles and their families and servants who've come here to greet you, milady. I recognize one or two faces, but that's all. I also think that there are quite a few other townsfolk come to join them."

"I believe you're right, sir," Lady Lisle agreed. "I also recognize some of the people out there." As wife of the resident-deputy of Calais, she had been asked to accompany Anne on the last stage of her journey, the stage that would include Anne's triumphant entry into the city of Calais itself.

"And after Gravelines we'll soon be arriving in Calais?" Anne asked.

"Yes, milady, it's only about a dozen miles west of here along the coast."

"And is Calais the only English town in France?"

"Yes, milady. I can see that you're beginning to become very excited about this. This seeing your first English town. Believe me, it'll be well worth this long journey. My husband has seen to it that the town has been cleaned up in your honour and that you'll be able to have there anything you desire."

A few miles later Anne's eyes lit up as she noticed the decorations strung along the sides of the road and that the retainers were wearing a livery of a different colour and style.

Cromwell, acting in His Majesty's name, had spared no

effort in making Anne's first contact with England impressive and memorable, even if this did take place on the other side of the English Channel. As her carriage drew to a halt on the outskirts of the town, Lord Lisle, the highest ranking local official, received her with deep bows, kind words and gracious smiles. Then the Earl of Southampton, the High Admiral of England, accompanied by thirty gentlemen of the King's Household followed suit. These included Sir Thomas Seymour, Sir Francis Bryan and many other gentlemen. They were all dressed in blue velvet and crimson satin and the overall effect achieved Cromwell's aim of deeply moving the somewhat naïve Lady Anne. This powerful, colourful vision was heightened further when Anne noticed that behind the blue and red clad nobles, two hundred yeomen had also appeared. Each one was clad in the same matching blue and red livery.

Fortunately the threatening grey clouds overhead withheld their rain and the colourful parade passed beneath the recently repaired and decorated Lentern gate. From here they continued to see where His Majesty's ships lay in shelter alongside the harbour walls.

"Am I to sail in one of these?" Anne asked, looking at the ships close up for the first time in her life.

"Yes, milady," Lady Lisle replied. "We'll sail to England in a few days when we know how the weather is. In the meanwhile, we'll spend the next few days here in Calais. I'm sure you'll be very happy here."

"I'm already very happy, "Anne smiled. "When I see how much care you've taken over this journey, I cannot be anything else."

Then, as Anne and her retinue were about to enter the town they were startled to hear a sudden cannonade which echoed and reverberated around them.

"What's happening?" she asked, crouching down in her carriage, her hands clapped to her ears. "Is someone attacking us?"

"Oh, no, my dear" Lady Lisle smiled. "It's a salute. The ships are firing their guns - a salute in your honour. Look out there in the harbour. You can still see the smoke from the ship's cannons."

Anne straightened herself and looked out of the window. Sure enough, a cloud of black smoke was drifting slowly over the town from the ships. As she continued looking she could make out a party of sailors cheering her as they spotted her carriage near the sea wall.

"So is this how the English honour me?" she asked Lady Lisle. "With noise and smoke? Will it be like this in London, too?"

"Probably, milady, but even more so. King Henry is not known as someone who does things in a quiet and mean way. But come, dry your eyes and put your bonnet back on properly. I see it fell off when you ducked down for cover."

Feeling a little foolish, for Anne saw that she had been the only one who had reacted as she had done, she adjusted her bonnet and made herself comfortable again. Then her carriage and some of the train made its way to the Exchequer, the king's official house in Calais. There she and her entourage were to eat and rest after their long slow lumbering journey from Cleves.

As before, it became clear that Cromwell had spared no expense in entertaining his king's wife-to-be. In the freshly painted and decorated building, everything that Anne could possibly wish for was on hand: from food to entertainment, from comfortable rooms to willing and helpful servants.

That afternoon jousts were held in her honour and later that evening a huge banquet was also arranged to honour the king's future queen. That night when all the nobles and their servants and attendants had retired, it was generally felt that the Lady Anne had made a good impression on everyone present. Perhaps they mistook her shyness, her lack of pushing herself forward in case she committed a *faux pas*, as a sign of modesty, but that only increased their approval of their monarch's choice of a future partner.

Now all that remained was for Anne to bid farewell to the part of her retinue that was to return to Cleves, and then board one of the royal ships that had been sent out from London. But this was not to be.

The following day, Vice-Chancellor Olisleger, the Earl of Overstein and the Duke of Saxony's marshal, Sir John Dulzike, were informed that owing to the high winds and stormy weather Lady Anne would not be able to cross the Channel for the next few days.

"But fear not, gentlemen," Lord Lisle and the Earl of Southampton said, trying to calm their impatient guests. "We've arranged that several of our men who are knowledgeable about the ways of the sea will maintain a continuous watch on the situation. As soon as we have a suitable wind, we'll set sail. So please try and contain your impatience and you'll see that all will be well in the end."

In the meanwhile, Lord Lisle and the Earl of Southampton laid on more banquets and entertainment for their guests to while away the time.

"You, know, perhaps this delay is not so bad," Anne smiled at Mistress Gilmyn. "It's giving me more time to improve my English and also to practise playing the game of cards I've heard that King Henry loves to play."

"Do you mean 'Cent,' milady?"

"Yes, I've started learning how to play it and I'd like to play several rounds with you and Lady Lisle. After all, haven't you been telling me that it'll be important for me to keep my husband happy?"

Despite Anne's limited schooling and her lack of sophistication in comparison with the English ladies accompanying her to London, Anne learned the rules of the game very quickly. Soon she was holding her own against the various noblewomen playing against her; and at the same time they noticed how her English was improving. Of course she could not rid herself of her German accent, but now that she was talking English all the time she was speaking much more fluently.

All seemed to be going well until, quite unexpectedly, she caused a minor furor. The Lady Anne committed a serious breach in social and courtly convention.

They had been waiting for several days in Calais when Lady

Lisle came rushing into her mistress' chamber on the top floor of the Exchequer. Anne was busy standing by her open window listening to and smelling the choppy grey sea below. She was wondering when she would be able to set sail when Lady Lisle addressed her.

"Please excuse me, milady, but you cannot invite the Earl of Southampton and several of his fellow lords over to your chamber for a meal."

"Why not?"

"Why not? Because it is not done, milady."

"What does it mean, 'it is not done'? They have shown me every kindness while I have been here and now I wish to show them I appreciate this."

"Milady, in London, where I believe our court is much larger than the one you are used to back in Cleves, it is not done that queens and princesses invite noblemen to sup with them in their chambers." Lady Lisle put a reassuring hand on Anne's shoulder. "I'm sorry," she added, "but it's simply not the custom."

"*Aber warum nicht*, er, why not?" asked Anne, forgetting her English for a moment.

Lady Lisle shrugged. "Why not? I don't know the reasons for this. Perhaps there aren't any. All I know is that a young princess or member of the royal family cannot do what you have done. Some malicious people would start spreading rumours. Yes," she concluded, "that's probably the reason."

Anne was silent for a few minutes while she absorbed this information. Then she looked up and smiled at Lady Lisle. "But we're not in London yet. We're still in France."

"Yes, milady, but Calais is the English part of France. It's just like being in London."

Anne was silent as she thought about this. Then smiling again she faced Lady Lisle. "I know what we'll do. I'll invite several of the lords to come to my chamber to eat - and you and your husband will come along as well. In that way, I'll not be the only lady there. And yes, we can invite Mistress Gilmyn as well. She's been so kind and helpful since I first met her in Cleves."

Lady Lisle did not reply but curtseyed and hurried off to consult her husband. She did not want to cause a stir, especially with the king about his future wife.

"But that's against the rules of the court," Lord Lisle said.

"I know that, my dear, but Lady Anne has persuaded me that as we're not in England and not in London, it should be perfectly all right. She said that this was done in Cleves and as we've not yet crossed the Channel there should be no objection to her doing the same thing here."

Lady Lisle waited for her husband's reaction. When he did not say anything, she continued.

"Besides, she's such a sweet lady and has borne herself so well. And also, if I'm there, together with Mistress Gilmyn and some other women, I cannot see what harm will be done."

"Hmm, maybe you're right, my dear. Yes, perhaps it is a good idea after all. It will give us a better opportunity to see what Lady Anne is like if we dine with her in a smaller group. I mean that is not how we've been dining with her up to now, what with these large banquets."

Lady Lisle smiled. Her husband was usually right on such matters.

He continued. "You know, my dear, and don't tell anyone that I said this, but I feel that Lady Anne seems a little livelier than the king's last wife. She's interested in everything that's going on around her and everyone seems to be very happy to serve her. Apart from her German accent and those unfashionable German style gowns that she wears, I quite like the lady. And I'll tell you something else. She's no fool. She may appear to be naïve but she's definitely no fool."

Lady Lisle smiled at her husband again. "My dear, I didn't know you noticed things such as dresses and gowns, but yes, you're right about her gowns. And as for those headdresses, she'll have to change them. I know for a start that His Majesty favours the French style, you know, the hats and bonnets that Anne Boleyn wore."

"Sssh, my dear. Don't let anyone hear you say anything like that if you wish to keep your pretty head on your pretty shoulders."

"All right, then," she smiled. "Headdresses as worn by Queen Jane."

Now it was Lord Lisle's turn to smile. "That's better, and safer, too. Now let's see who Lady Anne can invite to her chambers tonight."

In the end, despite the fears raised by Lord and Lady Lisle, the meal passed off very well. After a few slightly embarrassing moments at the beginning, the honoured guests who included the Lords Grey, Hastings, Howard and Talbot as well as Messrs Bryan, Knevet and Seymour together with their wives and Cromwell's own son, Gregory, all enjoyed the meal and the evening. Polite and gentle jokes were exchanged, the food and wine were praised and so too was Lady Anne's rapidly improving English. The result was that the Earl of Southampton sent a message to his king saying that his future wife and queen 'was like a princess.' Henry could not have hoped for anything better. Lady Lisle, who was to echo the earl's remarks, wrote to her daughter that Lady Anne 'is so good and gentle to serve and to please.'

However, if Henry had entertained any hopes of spending his first Christmas with his new wife, the high seas in the Channel dashed them to pieces. Reports on the winds and waves were delivered every day to the parties both in London and in Calais. Fifteen days were to pass before Anne could finally leave the cosy atmosphere of the Exchequer and board ship for England. However, at the same time she was feeling homesick for Cleves. This feeling was strengthened when a packet of letters arrived from the duchy bit had not contained any personal missives for her.

Finally, on 27 December 1539 the hoped-for trumpet blast was sounded. The men designated to 'lie outside the walls and give immediate notice of fair weather' recognized a break in the storms. Acting on instructions, they blew long, loud blasts on their trumpets as their signal that the crossing could now take place. Immediately the last minute packing was carried out, and among cheers and waving handkerchiefs Anne was escorted to the king's ship that would take her to England, to her husband and to a whole new way of life. Ropes were cast off, last minute boxes and supplies were hoisted aboard, and the ship, accompanied by a royal convoy of fifty other ships started sailing out of the safety of the harbour.

Surprisingly perhaps, considering that Anne had never set foot on a ship before, it did not take her long to become used to its swaying motion as it ploughed its way north over the Channel. Soon, unlike several of her attendant ladies who either stayed below deck or who had climbed up on to the foc'sle to vomit, Anne moved about confidently.

She walked from one side of the deck to the other and watched the coast of France recede and then strained to catch her first glimpse of England. She became used to the sound of the heavily flapping sails, the slapping of the waves against the wooden hull and the sound of the wind as it whistled through the ship's rigging.

"When will we reach England?" she asked the captain standing next to her at the rail overlooking the bow.

The tanned, brawny man who had been specially chosen for this mission looked at his pale-faced passenger. "Very soon, milady, that is, if these winds allow us. But you can never tell here in these parts of the Channel, so I'm afraid you'll just have to be patient."

Four hours later when Anne asked the same question, the captain had a more definite answer to give her. "You see those lights over there, there to the right? Well those belong to the new castle the king has built at Deal, a small town up the coast near Dover. If everything goes according to plan, we'll be landing near there although at the moment I cannot tell you exactly when that will be."

"A new castle? I hope His Majesty didn't build it especially for me."

"Oh, no, milady. The king's had about thirty such castles – he called them Device Forts – built all around the south coast to protect the country from invasion. The castle that you can just about see from here is one of them. Personally I think the king was right. Did you know that when Julius Caesar invaded England, he landed at Deal, so I'm not surprised that His Majesty had a castle built there."

Anne held on to her hat and smiled up at him. "Ah, but this time we come in peace."

"Very true, milady. But now I have work to do, so please excuse me," and bowing, he left his chief passenger to continue staring ahead, trying to make out the details of the approaching English coastline.

Even when the murky grey clouds to the west had hidden the sun and the weak daylight had turned to a threateningly dark evening, and despite a few calls from Mistress Gilmyn and her other attendants to join the other ladies below, Anne remained on deck for the remainder of the voyage. "I must see as much of this as I can," she thought." I doubt if I'll ever travel again by ship. I must make the most of this."

Half an hour after thinking this and after a voyage of several hours over the choppy grey seas, she landed that evening near Deal on the south coast.

What were her thoughts as the white cliffs of Dover loomed up out of the dark sea? What would life with her new husband be like? She had heard so many stories about him, and some of them were - to be frank - quite frightening. As she stood on the deck holding on to a rope she asked herself these questions over and over again. These questions and others had been continuously on her mind since she had first been informed that she was to marry England's eighth king named Henry. At first they had seemed somewhat vague, somewhat distant. She was in Cleves and he was far over the sea in London, but now they all seemed so immediate.

Now, looking ahead over the ship's prow, she could see that she was approaching his country. Within half an hour she would be standing on dry land, on England. A mere seventy miles away from the king. From then on, she would not be Lady Anne of Cleves, the sister of Duke William, the ruler of a small and not very important Rhineland duchy. No, soon she would be 'for better, for worse, for richer, for poorer,' Her Majesty, Queen Anne, the wife of King Henry the Eighth of England.

Chapter Nine - A Meeting in Rochester

It was late in the evening when Anne and her party were allowed to walk down the gangplank and step foot for the first time on English soil. Surrounded by torch-bearing attendants, she was escorted to the castle and, in the flickering light, made her way up the ramp and over the moat to the main entrance. It was too dark for her to notice but had she looked up at the building she would have seen that the rounded keep in its centre was surrounded by six rounded bastions and that they too, in turn were surrounded by rounded and fortified structures. And topping this imposing castle was a large red and white flag of England, flapping proudly and loudly in the wind.

Anne, however, was not destined to stop for long at Deal. After being given time to refresh themselves, she and her attendants set off for Dover, just a few miles to the south. Fortunately the weather was good and even though it was late December, Anne and her retinue which now included several nobles and important clerics who had ridden down from London, rode slowly along the cliff tops to Dover – 'the Key to England.'

Unlike the newly-built fortifications at Deal, Dover Castle was three hundred years old and its massive square towers and defensive walls seemed to cover much of the land overlooking the nearby high chalk cliff tops. It was not the first time that royalty had stayed at the castle. King Henry II had improved its fortifications; his son, King John, had fought his would-be usurper, the French king Louis VIII here, and three hundred years later Henry VIII had given orders that the fortifications were to be further reinforced. Now the future Queen of England was to spend the night there.

Early the next morning, Anne was awoken in her chamber by an urgent knocking on the door. Getting out of bed quickly, she found Mistress Gilmyn standing there in a heavy travelling coat, shivering in the cold morning air.

"Milady, the weather has turned during the night."

"Turned?"

"Yes, milady. It is now raining heavily and it doesn't look as if it will stop soon. Everybody wants to know if we're to wait here today and maybe tomorrow - or are we to continue on to Canterbury?"

Going back to her room to take her own travelling coat, Anne stepped out to where she could see the dark clouds scudding in from the west. The roofs of the castle's outbuildings were glistening in the rain and now she was aware of the sounds of flowing water as the overflowing gutters poured their contents onto the flagged floors below.

"What does the Duke of Suffolk say? Have you asked him?"

"Yes, milady. He says that if you've no objection, he'd prefer to travel on to Canterbury today. He says it's only fifteen miles to the north of here."

Anne thought for a moment. Travelling in the rain was certainly not enjoyable, especially for her attendants and horsemen who, unlike her, would be outside her carriage riding and walking in the wind and the rain. On the other hand, the storms in the Channel had already delayed their arrival in London by two weeks and she had heard that her future husband was very anxious to meet her.

"I think that we should leave here today," she said after a short pause. "Please tell the duke that after I've had breakfast and said my prayers I'll be ready. And maybe," she smiled hopefully, "it will have stopped raining by then."

Mistress Gilmyn bobbed a curtsey. "I do hope so, milady," she said and pulling up her hood she hurried off to deliver Anne's decision to the duke.

But the hopes of Anne and Mistress Gilmyn were not realized. The heavy rain continued during the day and the drenched entourage made its way to Canterbury along the old Roman road. It came to a halt at Barham Down, just five miles south of their destination. There, within the shelter of the parish church they were made welcome by Thomas Cranmer, the Archbishop of Canterbury, together with several other

100

bishops and gentlemen. After being allowed to rest and warm their chilled bones for a while, Anne's retinue, now enlarged by that of the archbishop continued on its way to Canterbury. In the early evening, they all entered the city which would be forever associated with the murder of Thomas à Beckett nearly four hundred years earlier. The ceaseless downpour cut the welcoming ceremonies to a minimum, and Anne and her closest attendants were rushed over to St. Augustine's Abbey where they were to stay the night.

After Anne and her ladies had changed out of their soaking travelling clothes into warmer and drier ones, she asked to meet her ladies all together in the nave of the abbey.

"Hmm," she said looking around and noticing some of the broken masonry. "I was told that this cathedral was one of the biggest and finest in England."

"Excuse me, milady," Mistress Gilmyn whispered. "We're not in the cathedral itself. We are in St. Augustine's Abbey."

"*Ach so*, so why are some of the walls all smashed up?"

"Because, milady," the Duchess of Suffolk whispered to her. "His Majesty had the abbey dissolved recently and then it was broken up."

"*Dissolved*? What is this *dissolved*?"

"It means that the king and the chancellor gave orders for their officers to come here and destroy this and other church buildings."

From Anne's expression, it was clear that she did not understand. Lady Suffolk continued with her whispered explanation. "The king's men came, chased away all the nuns and the priests, broke up the buildings and sold off all the lands and church property. This included all the gold and the silver and the holy books. Then they gave all the money to the king."

Anne looked troubled. She remembered vaguely having heard something about this in Cleves but had not paid much attention to it.

"But why?" Anne asked, looking at the remains of what had obviously been a beautiful stained glass window. "This church must have looked so wonderful then."

The duchess did not wish to become involved in a long explanation that would have had to include the controversial issues of religion and politics, especially as this would have to be given to the king's future wife and queen. "Let's just say, milady, that the king was and still is against the Roman Catholic Church and so he's had many of its buildings destroyed," she shrugged.

Anne could not understand this but seeing the expression on the duchess' face, she decided that she had asked enough questions. Then she and her ladies retired for an hour before going to the refectory for a warm meal.

If the evening meal at Dover had been highly appreciated, then the one here at Canterbury was even more so. What could be better than feasting on beef and poultry cooked in fine sauces followed by a variety of sweetmeats and sugary comfits? All of these delicacies were accompanied by sweet, mellow wines. In fact, so far, apart from the weather, Cromwell's detailed planning had gone so well that the Duke of Suffolk and Thomas Cheney wrote to the chancellor recording that

The mayor and citizens received her with torchlight and a good peal of guns. In her chamber there were forty or fifty gentlewomen in gentle bonnets to see her, all which she took very joyously, and was so glad to see the king's subjects resorting so lovingly to her that she forgot all the foul weather and was very merry at supper.

Back at Hampton Court, Cromwell hurried to show this report to the king who, on reading it, clapped his chancellor on the back.

"Thomas, we're going to have a wedding and a marriage like we've never had before. Despite my aching leg, I can feel it in my bones. I tell you, this Anne of Cleves will be just the right wife and queen for me."

Cromwell smiled. He knew how important it was to keep his impetuous king and master happy.

"This lady, I tell you, she'll be like no other. Oh, I am so impatient to see her; to hold her in my arms. Thomas, just look at that portrait. Look at that smile, that face. Don't you agree with me when I say I'm the luckiest man alive?"

Cromwell smiled again and then saying he still had much work to do, he bowed hurriedly and left the chamber. There were still many points to check regarding Anne's journey and her entrance to London. If the reports concerning Anne's arrivals and overnight stops at Dover and Canterbury were anything to go by, how much more successful would her arrival be when she reached London?

In the meanwhile, some forty miles east of the capital, Anne's train was making its slow and sopping wet way from Canterbury to Rochester via Sittingbourne. The teeming rain continued unabated.

"Is that Rochester?" Anne asked as she pointed at a large square tower in the distance from her carriage window.

"Yes, milady," replied the Duchess of Suffolk. "That tower is Rochester castle. It is very big and it overlooks the whole area. I believe it's one of the oldest castles in England."

Anne looked at her, interested.

The duchess continued. "Yes, it is well over four hundred and fifty years old. William the Conqueror built it."

Anne looked suitably impressed, and the duchess who felt it was part of her duty to educate her queen-to-be as much as possible, continued with her explanations. "And can you see that huge building next to it? The one with the towers pointing up to the sky? Well, that's the cathedral. It's not as big as the one you saw in Canterbury and it's not quite as old, but it's older than the castle. My husband told me that it's about nine hundred years old."

Anne looked even more impressed. The duchess continued,

"We'll be spending our time at the Bishop's Palace where I've been told that His Majesty has gone to great expense to make our stay here as comfortable as possible."

Anne closed the curtains of the carriage as the rain was beginning to wet their clothes. "Oh, I do hope so. At least we've been able to travel within this carriage. But think of my poor attendants and guards. Those poor people must be soaked through and through. And cold. But tell me, why are we stopping here?"

She opened the curtain a fraction and looked out. "Who are those men over there? There must be at least one hundred of them, and they're all on horses."

"I believe they belong to the Lord of Norfolk, milady. I recognize their livery. He's come with a company of his men to escort us into the town. I suggest that you close the curtain before we get soaked like the men outside and sit back and wait. Let's try and enjoy what's left of this journey."

*   *   *   *   *   *   *

While Anne was making a favourable impression on her future subjects, her husband-to-be was burning with impatience to see her. Despite his bad leg, he kept pacing up and down, back and forth, as he kept passing the easel bearing her portrait.

"I must see her, Thomas, I must. Just look at her, her eyes, her face, her figure. She looks so demure, so gentle. How can I go wrong with this woman?"

Cromwell was silent as his king continued pacing up and down.

"Just look how she stands there. Just look how she holds herself. Oh, Thomas, what a wife she will be for me! What a queen she will be for England! Oh, Thomas. And the sons she will give me. Just think of that. Brothers for young Prince Edward. What could be better, eh?"

Cromwell smiled again. His plans were going so well. All the reports he had received so far were glowing with their praise of the lady. He looked at Sir Anthony Browne, another member of the king's Privy Council, and one of His Majesty's closest confidants.

"I tell you, gentlemen," said Henry, stopping his endless pacing to look at the portrait once more. "I really feel like riding down to Rochester to see her. I just cannot wait until she reaches London."

"Your Majesty," Cromwell said, stepping forward. "Do you

think that that is a good idea? Think of your leg. Think of this weather. Please look outside, Sire. The rain may have eased off a little, but it's certainly not the weather for long rides for this time of day. Can you not contain your impatience?"

He looked at Sir Anthony for support.

"Your Majesty," Sir Anthony said. "Much as I appreciate your desire to see the lady, I agree with your chancellor that perhaps it would be best if you wait another day or so."

The king whirled round on his advisors, his voice rising. "Listen, you two. You two are free men; you are free to be with whatever women you want. I am not. Everyone looks at me all the time. If I were to pinch a serving wench on her behind, the whole court would know about it within half an hour. That is not the case with you. When you do anything to a woman, no-one pays any attention. That is not so with me. I want a woman! I want a wife! And I want her now!" And he brought his fat hand flat down hard on the table. "My mind is made up. We will go and surprise her at Rochester. Are you game, Sir Anthony?"

"Yes, Sire." Past experience had taught this Privy Councillor when to agree and when to disagree with his king. Now was the time to agree.

"You, Thomas, will remain here to see to the final arrangements for Lady Anne's official entrance into London and I will go with Sir Anthony and a few others to Rochester today."

"But, Sire," Cromwell protested. "Is this such a good idea? I realise that you are so impatient to meet the lady, but should you really do so before all the plans for doing so have been properly worked out?"

"Of course it is, Thomas. You may be my learned chancellor, but as the son of a Putney blacksmith or whatever, you obviously have little knowledge of romantic love or tradition, has he, Sir Anthony?"

Sir Anthony smiled a little and Cromwell fidgeted uncomfortably. He hated being reminded of his simple background, especially in front of the king's noblemen.

"Did you not know, Thomas, that kings and princes have

always been known to see their lady-loves, their brides, before their wedding?"

Cromwell shook his head and looked first at the king and then at Sir Anthony. This aspect of the royal tradition was new to him. Henry warmed up to his theme. "Yes, Thomas, the first king who did this was Louis the Second, the King of Naples and Sicily. He disguised himself as a simple knight and set off to see Yolande, his bride-to-be. She was the daughter of King Juan the First of Aragon. Isn't that so, Sir Anthony?"

The knightly courtier nodded in agreement and Cromwell continued to look uncomfortable. Despite his many years of service to the king, he had never before heard of this tradition.

"And what about the former King Henry, Sire, King Henry the Sixth?" Sir Anthony asked. "Wasn't he supposed to have met his wife, Margaret of Anjou, secretly before his wedding?"

"Exactly, Sir Anthony. I've also heard that story," Henry smiled and turned to face his chancellor. "So you see, Thomas, there *is* a precedent for my impatience, and right royal ones at that. And I'm sure that if you look further into this you will find some more examples."

"That's true, Sire," Sir Anthony said. "I can think of another one. About seventy years ago the Duke of Milan pretended to be his own brother, the Duke of Bari. And as such, he secretly met his bride, Bona of Savoy."

Henry slapped his thigh. "You see, Thomas, I *am* right. I will go in secret to Rochester and surprise my bride. Sir Anthony will come with and we'll ask a few more fellows to join us. Oh, this will certainly be a surprise for my lady. Just you wait till I return, Thomas. You'll hear all about it. I'm telling you, this is going to be quite a meeting, and all in the romantic tradition, to boot."

Two hours later, the king, Sir Anthony and several of his closest friends set out for Rochester. Luckily the rain had stopped but the road was muddy and they had to ride very carefully. By the time they had covered the thirty miles to their destination, they were all spattered with mud and it was difficult to see who was king and who was not.

Henry wasted no time when he arrived at the Bishop's Palace. Quickly dismounting from his sweating horse, he strode into the palace as energetically as his painful leg would allow and, surrounded by his five companions, demanded to know where the Lady Anne was staying in the building.

The attendant recognised none of the dishevelled men in their muddy cloaks. All he recognised was their air of authority. Therefore, he did not hesitate to point the way up to the chamber from where Anne and her ladies were watching a bull-baiting spectacle in the courtyard below. Anne, intent on watching this new form of sport for the first time, only half-turned round to see the half dozen men enter the room. She then turned back to watch the angry dogs below, snarling and biting frenziedly at the maddened black bull.

This was too much for the love-sick monarch. Pushing his noblemen aside, he strode over to where Anne was leaning out of the window. Putting his damp arms around her waist, he planted a heavy kiss on her upturned and surprised lips. Her face said it all.

"*Was ist los?* What is happening?" she gasped, pushing the heavy king off her. She wiped the disgusting royal saliva off her lips with the back of her hand. "Who is this man? What does he want?" she cried. And looking dismissively at her attacker, she hurried and half-hid behind two of her ladies standing by the window. They were watching the bull fight below. The maddened creature had just gored two of the howling dogs below in the belly and the sounds of the wounded beasts carried up to the ladies' room.

Henry stumbled back causing a sharp burst of pain to shoot up from his throbbing leg. *This* was the woman he had been dreaming of ever since he had clapped eyes on Holbein's portrait? *This* was the princess he had been dreaming about in bed? This creature, who was more interested in the fate of an angry bull than in him, King Henry the Eighth of England, her future husband? It was unthinkable. Nay, impossible. She was taller than he had supposed, and those clothes, those heavy German-style clothes! What had he been thinking of when he had agreed to marry this woman? What could he do about it now?

He looked at Sir Anthony who was standing at the other end of the room. This courtier, just like the others, averted his gaze. No help was coming from any of them.

Did not she recognise me? Henry asked himself. Do I look just like an upstart courtier? What had gone wrong here? I am the king, Henry kept repeating to himself. King Henry the Eighth of England. Doesn't she know that? Why didn't she recognise me?

Spinning round to face the door, his cloak whirling around his broad shoulders, the angry and insulted monarch stamped out of the room closely followed by his band of nobles.

"Did you see that?" he spluttered outside to no-one in particular. "She didn't even recognise me! Me, the King of England! There I was, as large as life and she ignored me. No! She rejected me. Pushed me off like some meddlesome fly! Get me out of here. Get me away from all this!"

Continuing to mutter something about this disastrous adventure, Henry gathered his men around him. They clattered down the stairs to the stables where they had left their horses ready to return to London. "I rushed here 'to nourish love' – and see what's happened," he growled to himself. A farce, an insult. His New Year's romantic mission had turned into the worst snub he had ever suffered. It was an unmitigated disaster, however it was judged. And to him of all people, the King of England!

Meanwhile, upstairs in the chamber where it had all happened, other thoughts and accusations were now swirling around like thick smoke as Anne and her ladies began to realise what had just happened.

"Why didn't you tell me that he was the king?" Anne asked Lady Lisle, accusingly.

"We didn't have the time, milady," replied Lady Lisle, unhappily fidgeting with her sleeves. "It all happened so quickly."

"I tried to tell you it was the king," the Duchess of Suffolk said, "but…"

"But, what?" Anne demanded, sounding angry for once.

"Didn't you see what he did to me?"

"Yes, milady, but as Lady Lisle has just said, we had no time. As you saw for yourself, he just burst into the room without any warning." The duchess shrugged her shoulders and held up her hands in a gesture of helplessness. "There was nothing we could do. Absolutely nothing. Please believe us."

Anne shrugged her shoulders with the same helpless gesture. Her ladies were right. There had been no time or warning that the king was on his way. There had been nothing that they could do. The harm had been done. Was this huge and sweating man with his small mean eyes and blotchy skin to be her husband? His face was fat and flabby, his hands were enormous. Was she destined to spend the rest of her life with this forceful monster?

And not just that, but to be his wife and share his bed and have children by him. It was too much, she thought as the tears welled up in her eyes. Why did I agree to marry him? Why couldn't I have stayed back at home in Cleves? It is true that life there was indeed slower and without all the excitement that I've had over the past few weeks, but at least I knew where I was and what was in store for me without any surprises like this. Even my strict brother, the duke, behaved better than this king had.

Anne turned away from her ladies and looked out at the gory spectacle below. The bull was lying there panting out its life on the bloody red flagstones, oozing blood from several gaping wounds to its belly and its flanks. Two of the dogs were lying in their own pools of blood and intestines and a third one was yelping and licking piteously at the place where its hind leg should have been.

But Anne saw none of this. Her eyes were clouded over with tears which then ran down her cheeks. All she could do was think about what had just happened to her. What would happen now? What would happen in the future? Will I have to marry him now? She thought. Will he still want to marry me after I failed to recognise him and show him any respect? What will my brother say? All the plans and negotiations – have they come to nought? Will I be sent home, a disgrace to my family and my country? And I had been told that the king was so handsome, so dashing and how lucky I was to be his next wife. And yet all I saw and felt was this huge man with his fat slobbering lips.

Downstairs, in a small room near the stables, an angry and frustrated King of England was also having thoughts about his country and his future marriage. But this time, his pacing up and down the room was not born of impatience, but of anger. White-hot anger.

"What do I do now?" he shouted at his courtiers facing him in a semi-circle. "How do I get out of this?" None of them dared to look at him. They either looked down at the muddy floor or up at the decorated ceiling. They fiddled with the rings on their fingers or fidgeted with their sleeves or any button that happened to be at hand. Not one of them had an answer, or if he did, he did not dare say it. A heavy and tense silence answered the king's questions.

Finally Sir Anthony could stand it no longer. "Your Majesty," he began quietly. "Perhaps this was just some sort of a mistake. Perhaps, because we were all dressed the same, she did not recognize you. Look, Sire, we're all wearing the same colour cloaks." And he pointed to his and the king's to prove his point.

"But I'm the king," Henry said, loudly and slowly. "I am bigger than all of you. Everyone knows that I'm a big man. Everyone. She should have recognised that."

"Your Majesty," Lord Russell continued, trying to pacify his sovereign. "We know this but the lady comes from abroad, from a small duchy. Maybe she was never told how big you are."

That was the wrong thing to say.

"What?" Henry roared. "Don't they know about me in that Cleves place? Have not they heard of me? Am I just a simple peasant living here in England? Oh, just you wait, Master Cromwell. You got me into this and you will get me out of this, or by Jesus Christ and all His saints you will pay for this."

On hearing this, a silent and collective sigh of relief was felt by the group of courtiers. None of them liked the king's chief minister. To them, despite his official role and newly acquired titles, he was still the son of a south London blacksmith – an upstart who had wormed his way into the king's confidence at their own expense. Now he would pay. The king had just said that his chancellor was responsible for what had just happened. They conveniently forgot that once, when this marriage proposal had been first broached in the Privy Council, they had been the first to support it. They had all told their king that this was the best thing that he could do.

"Yes, Your Majesty," they had said, smiling. "This Lady Anne of Cleves will be a much better wife for you than Mary of Guise."

"And yes, Your Majesty, she will be a far better choice than Christina of Denmark, Charles the Fifth's young niece."

"That's very true, Sire. This Lady Anne is older. That means she'll be more mature. She'll be much more suitable for you, Sire."

But now this was the past and it was as if it had nothing to do with them. Their problem was now staring them in the face - how could they keep their sovereign lord happy? The despised and mighty chancellor would pay the price for this. Even the king had said so. Just now. Master Thomas Cromwell, the Chancellor of England, in his perennial black coat would be laid low just like the black bull whose torn and bloody carcass was now being dragged away outside, over the wet, slippery flagstones.

The king looked at his men. He knew what they thought of his chancellor and they knew he wanted revenge. This whole plan had begun to unravel at the edges and someone would have to pay. They did not know or care who it was, so long as it was not one of them. So who better than the chancellor they thought and, without thinking, Sir Anthony and Lord Russell fingered their necks.

"Come, I have decided," Henry said, now in a calmer voice. They looked up. What now? "We'll leave here at first light for London. We'll make for Greenwich and take my barge from there, and then I'll decide what must be done. In the meanwhile, Sir Anthony, you'll make sure that the Lady Anne receives my present of furs and sables. These she must have. Never let it be reported that the King of England went to meet his bride empty-handed. Never let it be said that I am mean and vengeful."

The king turned to Lord Russell. "Go and see about the arrangements for our staying here the night. Go now."

Russell bowed and quickly left to find a steward. He was relieved to have a reason to leave the room.

"Now all of you go. I wish to remain here on my own for a while. We'll meet again when Lord Russell has arranged our stay for the night."

As quickly as possible, the remaining courtiers muttered, "Good night, Sire" and filed out of the room leaving their still angry but now subdued king pacing the room wondering how he would solve this new marital problem.

The next day, after a fast ride to Greenwich as he had planned, the king and his men sailed up the Thames back to London. Facing his men on the royal barge, Henry tried to justify his outburst from the previous night.

"Whom should I have trusted? I'm telling you, she looked nothing like that portrait that Master Holbein painted. Nothing. I'm now so ashamed that I praised her the way I did. Oh what a fool I was. What a fool. And gentlemen, I must tell you, I like her not. Not at all. Nothing!"

Chapter Ten - A Decision is Reached

By the time Henry had reached his palace at Greenwich his temper was as black as pitch. His head was aching, his breathing was laboured and his leg was throbbing painfully. After stepping down from the royal barge onto the pier, he entered the palace, changed his muddy clothes and had the marks of the previous night's insult washed off of himself. At least, the external aspects of it. Inside, he was still seething. Then, after ordering something to eat and drink he called for his inner circle of advisors, that is, the men who had ridden down with him to Rochester, to join him in his chamber. "And make sure you bring Master Cromwell with you," he ordered the captain of the guard. "I wish to see him immediately."

The captain in his splendid Tudor livery of green and white decorated with the Tudor red and white rose whirled round and left to fulfill his royal master's orders. He wondered why the king's chief minister had been called 'Master Cromwell' this time and not 'my chancellor' as the king was wont to call him. The captain shrugged his shoulders and thought that it was not his problem. His task was to carry out His Majesty's orders and that was that. What lay behind these orders or what led up to them was not his business. Perhaps the chancellor had mislaid an important document or forgotten to attend a certain meeting. 'All I know is this: I think I 'm better being in Master John Stock's shoes today, the captain of the king's guard, rather than in Master Cromwell's. Hmmm, it doesn't look as though His Majesty is very pleased with his chancellor.' And thinking thus, Captain Stock took four of his men and they started off down the long corridor in the direction of the chancellor's chambers.

Ten minutes later, Thomas Cromwell, the Chancellor of England, wearing his customary black gown and flat black cap was being ushered into the royal presence. Normally he would have walked this route unescorted, unless he happened to be carrying an important document or something else of great value. But now he was wondering as he stood at the open door why he had been escorted to His Majesty's chamber when he had not been asked to bring anything at all. He looked around at the other advisors sitting there trying to learn from their faces what the reason was for this hurriedly called meeting, but their blank expressions gave nothing away. Not one of them greeted him, even officially. It was most unsettling.

Cromwell stood there, searching in his mind for a reason for this meeting. How had the meeting gone with Lady Anne? Was His Majesty pleased with what he had seen and heard at Rochester? He certainly did not look happy. Had the lady fulfilled his expectations? Full of foreboding, Cromwell scanned the Privy Councillors' faces again. They gave nothing away, that is, those who even bothered to look up at him. All of this was very strange. Usually it was he, Cromwell, who was the first to know what was happening in the royal circle. After all, it was he, Cromwell, the Chancellor, who usually initiated much of what was planned here at Greenwich or at any of the other royal palaces.

He was just about to ask a question when the king pointed to him. "Thomas Cromwell," he heard as the king's harsh voice cut through his thoughts. "Sit down there," and he pointed a fat bejeweled finger at his bewildered minister and the chair he was to sit in at the far end of the table. Sir Anthony Browne allowed a slight smirk to cross his face as did Lord Russell when they observed Cromwell's obvious discomfort. This was a scene they had not witnessed before however many times they had sat here in this chamber for special meetings with the king. Usually it was Cromwell who would sit at the king's right hand and be treated in the friendliest of terms. He would have all the necessary documents at hand, or the suggestions and recommendations which His Majesty would generally accept. More than once, Henry would clap his chancellor on the back or lay his hand on his chancellor's arm and everyone present would see that Thomas Cromwell was a power in the kingdom. This was not the scene now, if only because Sir Anthony Browne was the advisor now sitting where the chancellor was accustomed to sit.

As the worried and curious chancellor took his place, he could not help wondering why, apart from what was happening to him, why this meeting had been called so hurriedly in the first place. Cromwell looked around the table. Why were there no sweetmeats and why was there no goblet of wine on the table in front of him? All the others had been thus served. After all, these refreshments were a regular occurrence at these closed meetings with the king. Why haven't I been so honoured? What have I done wrong? What has happened? Cromwell kept asking himself.

He was not allowed to remain in the dark for long. As soon as he had sat down his royal master declared the meeting open.

"Tell me, Cromwell, answer me this," the king asked, jutting out his chin and pointing to the unfortunate man. The questions then began to pound into the shocked chancellor like heavyweight punches. "How do you like this woman? This Lady Anne of Cleves. Do you find her personable? Fair? Beautiful? Do you think she is as the reports say she is – especially those reports made to me? I pray you, sir, tell me the truth and only the truth."

Cromwell looked around the polished table vainly for some sort of support. He found none. He knew he was not liked by the lords sitting there, especially by the Duke of Norfolk, but perhaps, he hoped, at least one of them might have given him some sign of support.

Looking directly at his king, he replied, his lips trembling a little, "I take her not for fair, Your Majesty, but to be, er, of a brownish complexion. Why, Sire, how did you find her? As Master Holbein had painted her likeness?"

The king half-rose and then sat down again heavily. His leg had given him a violent twinge and this did not help him keep his temper under control. "Sir," he said looking straight at his chancellor through his small eyes, "She was nothing so well as she was spoken of. And, I tell you, sir, if I had known then what I know today, she would not have been allowed to step foot in my kingdom."

Now Cromwell understood what the situation was about, but he still did not know whether the king's anger and disappointment was due to his betrothed lady's looks, or her manner, or both. He did not have much time to dwell on this problem because his royal master was addressing him again.

"Cromwell," Henry smacked his hand down on the table. "I want a remedy to this situation. I want a solution. A good one. And I want it now." This time it was the king's turn to look around the table for support and unlike his chancellor, he got it. Just by looking at his councilors and how they nodded in his direction, Henry knew that his chancellor was isolated. "You got me into this and now, by Jesus Christ and all His saints you will get me out of it." The councilors smiled. All the blame had been thrust onto the head of the king's despised chancellor.

"Come, sir," Henry demanded. "What remedy do you have?"

"Remedy, Sire," Cromwell repeated playing for time. "I have none at this moment. Please give me time to think of a solution. I'm sure I will have one by the morrow."

This was the wrong answer. This was not what the angry king wished to hear. He wanted a remedy now. Here and now. Cromwell squirmed in his seat.

He had worked with the king long enough to know that he, his most faithful advisor, the man who had guided him through the thickets of the 'king's great matter' – the divorce from his first wife, Catherine of Aragon, and his subsequent marriage to Anne Boleyn – was the most troubling situation he had experienced so far. He had survived that and doubtless, once his royal master had cooled down, he, the ever-faithful and hard-working chancellor would survive this 'matter,' too.

As the other councillors looked at him and then back to their king, Cromwell looked up. Hoping he was wearing a winsome smile, he leaned forward over the table.

"Your Majesty," he said at length. "Perhaps we could annul this marital arrangement in one or both of the following ways."

All eyes were now concentrated on the chancellor. He continued, slowly and hesitantly at first but gathering speed as he outlined the new plan his agile brain had just dreamed up.

"Sire, perhaps we could insist on receiving an official confirmation from the Lady Anne's brother, the Duke of Cleves, which states in no uncertain terms that he authorises Your Majesty to conclude the legalities of this forthcoming marriage and…"

"Yes, and what else?" Henry asked aggressively.

"Don't you see, Your Majesty, if that fails, we'll be able to say that since we haven't received any written and official evidence that the Lady Anne's previous betrothal several years ago was never officially annulled, we may conclude," and here Cromwell allowed himself to smile a little, "that the lady is still formally betrothed to the Duke of Lorraine's son. Therefore, as a result you'll be able to say that you most sincerely regret you will not be able to marry her."

There was silence in the room as the king and the other councilors considered this latest idea. All you could hear was the chirping of a few birds on the window-sill. Cromwell looked around the table and noted for the first time since he had been escorted into the room that some of the lords were allowing themselves to smile or nod their heads in support of this idea. Would it get him off the hook? Would this plan work? Even the king's face looked less red and aggressive. Henry fiddled with one of the rings on his pudgy fingers. From Cromwell's experience, this was a sure sign that he was still nervous but that he was considering his chancellor's latest suggestion.

"Maybe you have found a solution," Henry said slowly. "But if so, we'll have to do something about this quickly. Tell me, Cromwell, are there any of the lady's German retinue here?"

"In London, Sire?"

"Yes, of course in London," the king answered testily. "Where else?"

"No, Your Majesty," Sir Anthony said, the first person other than the king and his chancellor to have spoken since this meeting had started. "Some of them are due to arrive here at the palace later this afternoon, that is, if the weather permits."

"I see," Henry said. "So when they arrive, no matter what the hour is, have them sent to me immediately and then we'll see if the chancellor's suggestions may be carried out. In the meanwhile, does anyone else have any other ideas?"

The king looked around but no-one present had any other solution or idea to offer. "In that case, I wish to rest and do not wish to be disturbed until any of Lady Anne's retinue arrives."

He got up, and leaning heavily on his silver-topped walking stick, left the room leaving his advisors sitting around the table to plan and speculate about what would happen next. They did not have much time. Four hours later, a somewhat rested but not restful monarch was back in the same seat in the same room. He faced his advisors and at the same time faced several of Anne's advisors who had just been ushered into the king's chamber.

Fortunately, three of them could speak a passable if somewhat heavily accented English so that there were no problems of communication. After a round of introductions and explanations of their official roles, they were asked if they could produce any documents relating to the duke's permission for his sister's marriage to the king.

"*Nein*, er, no Your Majesty. We do not have any such *Dokumente*, er, documents here with us in England."

"And," the Duke of Norfolk asked, "do you have any other papers or documents relating to the annulment of Lady Anne's previous betrothal to the Duke of Lorraine's son?"

The ducal representatives immediately went into a huddle and after much head-shaking and gesticulating, the oldest looking one shook his head from side to side and turned to look at the Duke of Norfolk. "*Nein, Ihre Lordshaft*, Your Lordship. We do not have any documents about that, either."

"*Ja, ja,*" a thin-faced representative added in better English. "We know that the question of the betrothal to the French Duke's son was *annulliert*, er, annulled, cancelled twelve years ago. *Ja*, it was in 1527," he said shaking his head positively. "And I must say, *Ihre Lordshaft*, if such a document exists, I doubt if we will be able to find it in the near future."

"*Ja, das ist richtig*," the first representative nodded. "And as for the other documents which belong to our lord, the Duke of Cleves, we do not have them here either."

Then seeing the expressions of deep disappointment on everyone's faces, especially the king's, the most senior of the Cleves' delegation turned towards Henry, who was nervously drumming his fingers on the table before him and said, "*Ihre Erhabenheit*, Your Majesty, we could send to Cleves for these papers, these documents and hope that they will be found there."

Henry looked at Sir Anthony and the Duke of Norfolk. "What do you think? Surely this would take some time, no?"

"Yes, Sire," the duke replied. "And all it would do, I believe, is to postpone matters. Your Majesty, if you want my honest opinion as one of your principal advisors, and this is also the advice of all of us here," he added quickly, "is that you have no choice other than to marry the Lady Anne."

The king looked at him hard in the face and the duke instinctively leaned back in his chair. Then Henry studied the faces of his advisors, one by one, as his eyes swept around the table. He knew that they had been discussing this situation while he had been resting and that the duke had merely expressed their collective opinion. The room was tense and silent. Henry knew that the time had come to make a decision. It had to come now. He leaned forward in his chair and the rest of the assembly waited.

Suddenly one of the Cleves' delegation had a coughing fit and they all waited until he had recovered. Henry leaned forward again.

"This is my decision," he said quietly. "We will proceed with this wedding as though nothing has gone wrong. All of you will carry out the allotted tasks for which you have been appointed. And please remember, not one word, not one word I say about this meeting must ever be allowed to become public. Is that understood?"

All the heads in that quiet room, English and Clevian, aristocrat and gentleman adviser nodded in agreement.

"I do not want to hear any gossip and whispering on the morrow about what happened in here today. If I find out that someone has whispered something to his wife or mistress or whoever, they will feel the fullness of my wrath. Have I made myself clear?"

From the rapid   nodding of heads, it was obvious that everyone present understood His Majesty's instructions.

"Good, then you may all leave me now and proceed with your duties."

As they rose to leave Henry raised his hand. "Wait. All of you may leave, except Master Cromwell. I wish to talk to him in private. Thank you."

The heavy door closed shut and Cromwell was left there alone at the far end of the table facing his royal master. Never had he felt so unsure of himself in the king's presence. Henry raised his hand and pointed to a space next to him on the floor to his left.

"Master Cromwell, stand here. You need not bother sitting down. You will not be here for long."

Cromwell's agile brain immediately began to analyse those instructions. What did the phrase, 'for long' mean? Remaining in this room or remaining in this life? He had never had to consider such a situation in the past, at least, not seriously. But now he was in a completely different situation. He knew that apart from a small clique of close friends he had no-one important whom he could call on for support. He had to think quickly. He decided that he would appeal to this king through the political aspect of this situation and play down any of the personal details with regards to his king and his future wife.

On receiving a sign from the king that he had permission to talk, Cromwell began. "Your Majesty," he began slowly. "Despite any doubts that you may have this moment concerning your marriage to the Lady Anne of Cleves, I'm fully convinced that in the end, this marriage can only bring great benefit to you and this country, to your great realm, Sire."

He waited for a reaction and on receiving none, continued. "If we alienate the Duke of Cleves and the Rhineland area in general, Sire, we here in England, will be left standing alone, with no European friends and allies."

Henry looked at him straight in the eye. What Cromwell had just described was the situation that he himself had imagined. Noting his interest, an encouraged chancellor continued. "Sire, if this is indeed the situation, the situation that I've just described, we'll be left facing both France and the Holy Roman Empire. They would then feel bold enough to forget their earlier differences of opinion and perhaps initiate a joint venture – an invasion of our shores, Sire. That is of course a situation that we cannot allow to happen."

The king nodded in agreement. What his chancellor had just said made sense. Every word of it was true. Henry knew this himself, but he was pleased to have his experienced chancellor confirm his opinion. Whatever Henry thought of Cromwell regarding his disappointment with the Lady Anne, he was able to recognize his chief minister's wide experience and shrewd brain. For this, he was head and shoulders above all the other advisors who had been sitting in this room several minutes earlier.

"In addition, Sire," Cromwell added, anxious to press home his advantage. "We cannot send the Lady Anne back to her home in Cleves unmarried."

Henry looked at Cromwell full in the face. This was a new aspect to the situation.

"Why not?"

"Because, Your Majesty, apart from it being seen abroad as a case of very bad manners, and from this court as well, it will also be perceived that the lady has been wronged as someone who has done no wrong at all."

"No wrong at all? Please explain yourself."

"Sire, from what I understand, and please remember that I was not in Rochester at the time, it appears that she had acted most rudely towards your person. She acted, how shall I say it delicately? - in a manner that was most disrespectful to your royal presence."

Cromwell looked at the king to see how he was taking this. Henry said nothing but just flicked his fingers indicating that the chancellor should continue with his explanation of the Rochester situation.

"Your Majesty, if the lady is sent home in disgrace, for this is how it will be understood abroad, the rest of Europe will consider this, er, please permit me to say this, Sire, - the rest of Europe will consider this to be a most unchivalrous act. She will be rejected by any future suitor, Sire and…"

"That, Master Cromwell, is not and will not be my problem."

"I know that, Sire, but her brother, the duke, may become so incensed by this situation, that he may consider declaring war on this realm. I honestly do not think that what I've just described will necessarily come to pass but, if it does, there is a possibility that he may be supported by either France or the Holy Roman Empire or indeed both of them. This, you realize is a situation that we must never allow, especially as these two powers would love to have an excuse to attack us here in England."

"But, Thomas," Henry said, forgetting he was still angry with his chancellor. "We both know that the duke does not support the Roman Catholic Church. Why should he be supported by the French and the Holy Roman Empire?"

"Because, Sire, I was thinking of the old maxim – the enemy of my enemy is my friend. The Duke may be willing to swallow his differences with these two major powers in order to have revenge on you, Sire."

As the king was busily digesting his chancellor's interpretation of future political events, Cromwell decided to add another argument to support his case.

"Sire, if indeed we do send the lady home, this country (he did not dare say 'you') will be seen as a country whose word, whose promises and agreements, are worth nothing and are ones that are broken just like that," and he flicked his fingers to reinforce his argument.

Henry nodded. His chancellor was right. All he needed was for the major powers in Europe to combine their forces against him. He did not want to spend more money on reinforcing his coastal defences or to lay out more money on equipping his local militias. Henry knew well enough that wars cost money and that the outcome was not always sure. Cromwell's interpretation of the situation, both in terms of international politics and also with reference to the king's personal aspects confirmed his own opinion. Yes, as usual, his pragmatic chancellor had cut to the heart of the matter. Everything must be done to prevent a war with Europe. But just as he was thinking this, he also began seeing himself in a self-pitying way. Why did I allow myself to become involved with this woman and this petty dukedom? he thought and was thinking on these lines when he became aware of Cromwell's voice again.

"And of course, Your Majesty, there is always the question of the Auld Alliance. You know, Sire, if France should attack us from the south, then the Scots may also feel that they should join in." Cromwell paused for a moment and then continued. "As you no doubt may recall, Sire, the Scottish King James the Fifth, married his French wife, Mary of Guise, just over a year ago. And the carrying out of the military side of that Auld Alliance would be the worst situation of all." Cromwell stopped to allow his royal master absorb what he was saying. "Yes, Sire, that would even be worse than having both of the European powers attacking us in the south."

Cromwell stopped and stepped back a step.

"Sire, I know you told your council that you have decided to marry the lady, but what I'm trying to do is this. I'm hoping to give you good reason for doing so. I do not wish you to feel that you are putting your head in a noose. I'm just asking you to take everything relevant into consideration and be convinced of the wisdom of that decision. Too much depends on this decision and I'm sure you will not allow an, how shall I phrase it, Sire? – an unwise decision to be taken. In all, Your Majesty, I'm sure the recent embarrassing situation in Rochester will be allowed to pass unnoted and forgotten, especially as very few people were present when it occurred."

Cromwell permitted himself a small smile. Past experience had taught him to know when he had succeeded in convincing his royal master over a certain plan or argument. Now he waited for His Majesty's reaction.

"You are right, Thomas. You usually are. But do not think that you can escape scot-free with all your plans and reasons. Although I said I'll marry this Cleves woman, I'm certainly not feeling very happy about it. And," he added, wagging a finger at his chancellor as an angry teacher does to an errant pupil, "I'm certainly not pleased with you for having got me involved in this situation in the first place. Despite what you've just told me and despite what I said to the council earlier, I'm still thinking that if there is a way that I can get out of this situation, and one that will not imperil my kingdom, I will carry it out. Do you understand?"

Cromwell shifted uncomfortably on his legs. "Yes, Your Majesty, I do."

"Then you should remember to be very careful in the future, for I'll not look kindly on any similar plans to these. Is that clear?'

"Yes, Sire."

"You are dismissed," and Henry heaved himself up, turned his back on his chancellor and pointed to the door.

It was a very worried man who left the king's chamber that morning. Was it a coincidence, he thought, that just as he turned the corridor to walk to his own office, there through an open window he could make out the four square towers of the Tower of London on the nearby horizon?

And so, as the king commanded, the wedding arrangements which had already been organized were now given further impetus. The royal officials and servants moved to carry out their latest orders for His Majesty's first official meeting with his fourth wife. This was to be in the New Year on 3 January 1540.

And while all this frantic activity was being carried out in London, Anne and her party were leaving Rochester and were making their way to the capital. First they passed through Gravesend and then continued for an overnight stay at Dartford. The queen-to-be was now only fourteen miles from London and her new husband.

As she sat in her carriage, between waving to the cheering

crowds who had gathered along the way and who were oblivious of what lay behind the scene, Anne could not help but wonder what her reception would be like in London. Was her first meeting with the king just a temporary setback? Was her husband-to-be really such a gross fellow and would she be able to calm him down if he were still angry with her?

She had absolutely no idea how he would greet her and what she would be expected to do. All she knew as she left the Dominican priory in Dartford the next day was that she would have to act as demurely and as submissively as possible. As she and her retinue made its inexorable way west, she hoped and prayed that the royal storm she had witnessed in Rochester was just that, a passing storm in an otherwise calm sea. Only time would tell.

Chapter Eleven - A Glorious Procession and a Last Minute Meeting

If Cromwell thought that fate, Holbein and various high officials and councillors, both English and Clevean, had betrayed him, then at least the weather on the morning of 3 January 1540 was on his side. The sun had risen over the capital and burned away many of the clouds by the time hundreds of people had started swarming to where the king would officially first meet his fourth wife. The air was crisp and cold where the magnificent pavilions and tents had been pitched at Blackheath at the foot of Shooter's Hill.

The tents, prepared for Anne and her retinue, had been warmed and perfumed. They stood near a special pathway that had been cleared so that a royal route led them from the tented encampment straight to the gate of Greenwich Park. Cromwell had indeed thought of every detail which would make this meeting as successful as possible.

On each side of the processional route, merchants, English, Italian and Spanish, together with members from the city council and aldermen, had gathered round ready to cheer their new queen. This crowd was made larger and more impressive by the presence of several knights and fifty pensioners, all wearing their gold chains of office over their rich velvet uniforms. And if all this were not enough, then Cromwell had arranged that the king's men, together with those of his own retinue and those of the Duke of Southampton and other nobles, would also be present. Many of these showy figures were mounted on their richly caparisoned horses. On the outer edge of this magnificent scene the people of London were also there to cheer on their king's new wife.

At twelve o'clock Anne and her retinue appeared after completing the last part of their route from Dartford. The Londoners were immediately impressed by her.

"'Ere, Tom, she looks nice, don't she? All smiling. But

who's that with her? Yes, them on those two fine horses?"

"The first one? 'im on the left? That's the Duke of Norfolk. Don't you recognise 'is skinny face? And the one next to 'im is the Duke of Suffolk."

"And is that the Archbishop of Canterbury behind him?"

Tom craned his head and stood on tiptoe. "That's right, 'im and all those other bishops and lords. But ssh, be quiet, I'm trying to hear what the Earl of Rutland's saying. That's 'im, standing next to Sir Thomas Dennis and Doctor Daye."

"I can't hear 'im. What's 'e saying?"

Tom put his hand to his ear and strained to listen to what was being said. "Sorry, mate. I don't know. I can't hear 'im that well. But I can just about 'ear that 'e's saying something in Latin, at least, it sounds like church language. I suppose 'e's saying something like welcome to London or England or somethin' like that. All I can make out is the word *bene.*"

"Here look, there's that foreign looking feller, yes, 'im in the funny hat. 'e's replying to 'im. Is he also speaking Latin?"

"Yes, I think so, but 'e's turned 'is back on me so I can't 'ear 'im properly either."

"Ooh, look over there. Just look at those ladies. Aren't they dressed nice? I bet their clothes must be worth a fortune – all that gold cloth and jewels and stuff."

"Yeah, you're right. You know who any of 'em are?"

Harry raised himself as high as he could on his toes. "Yes, I can recognize some of them. That one over there is Lady Frances Dorset and she's standing next to Lady Margaret Douglas. They're the king's nieces."

"And isn't that the Duchess of Richmond standing behind them – the one with the low-cut bodice?"

"Yes, that's right. She really does look something, doesn't she, in that gown?"

"Aye, she does that. By the way, 'ow do you know who all these people are?

I can recognize only one or two of them."

"Don't you remember, Tom, I used to work at the gardens at Hampton Court. Was there for nigh on five years. Saw nearly all of these lords and ladies then. But I must say, 'is Majesty has really laid it on for 'is new wife this time. 'e never did as much as this for the others."

"Look, look! There's the Lady Anne again. She's getting out of her carriage. She looks all right, don't she?"

"Yes, but isn't she wearing funny clothes? All bundled up, like. They look foreign, not English at all. I mean, not like our English ladies."

"Yeah, come to think of it, you're right. Look at her 'at. It's a bit strange. It's like a cowl with bits stuck on it hanging off the sides. I think our English 'ats are prettier."

"So do I. By the way, Tom, I wonder what 'is Majesty will think of 'er clothes. I know my Alice wouldn't like them. Too heavy, she'd say. Not that we can afford to buy anything like them, of course."

"Neither can we. My Jane would agree with you there. But look, she's kissing all the king's ladies now. Must be thanking 'em for looking after 'er. But I must say, even despite her clothes, she does look pretty, don't she? I think," and here Tom lowered his voice, "I think she looks prettier than the king's last one, that Queen Jane, don't you?"

Harry nodded in agreement.

"Can you see what she's doing now?"

"No, not now," Harry said, moving his head from side to side. "She's just gone into one of those tents. That big one over there. I suppose they'll be giving 'er some cakes and wine, or something like that."

"Probably. I tell you, 'arry. I wish I'd brought something to eat and drink, myself. My stomach's rumbling something awful. Let's see if we can find ourselves a meat-pie and a bottle of ale."

While Tom and Harry were setting out on their mission, the king was setting out from Greenwich Palace to meet his future. He rode through the park, his entourage led by his richly-dressed court officials, all in purple velvet and all mounted on magnificent horses, their caparisons blowing gently in the January breeze. Then the king followed. His clothes, too, were of purple velvet, embellished with shining jewellery and gold buttons, deep red rubies and sparkling diamonds. His hat and sword belt were similarly adorned. If he had intended to present a picture of power and wealth, he certainly succeeded.

The captains of the guard, Sir Anthony Wingfield and Sir Anthony Browne, rode next to him. They, too, were dressed in their finest cloaks and gowns and their horses were also brightly caparisoned. By the time this cavalcade had reached the tent where Anne and her ladies were resting, Tom and Harry had returned, each clutching a meat pie and a bottle of ale. This time Harry's wife, Alice, was with them.

"Look, Alice. The Lady Anne is coming out of 'er tent to meet 'im, the king, I mean. Can you see 'er gown? It's pretty even if it does look a bit strange. Don't you think so?"

Alice nodded. "Yes, and I like that coronet thing she's wearing on top of her hat. All black and pearls. It certainly makes 'er hat look better. Not so heavy looking. I wouldn't mind having a coronet like that and I'm sure your Jane wouldn't either," she said, nodding her head at Tom.

Tom raised his head. "Look, you two. Lady Anne's getting on 'er horse now and riding towards the king."

"And some of her footmen are going with her. Look, they're all together now."

"Yes, and can you see that 'is Majesty has taken off 'is 'at to her. I must say, 'e don't 'ave much hair, does 'e?"

"No, he doesn't," Alice giggled and then clapped her hand over Tom's mouth. "Keep your voice down, Tom," she whispered. "There's guards everywhere. But it's true, you don't often see him without his hat on, do you?"

"Aye, you're right, there, my dear. But can you hear what they're saying to each other?"

"No, Harry. We're too far away, but it's true what you said about her gown. It doesn't look very English, does it?" Alice cocked her head to one side to have a better look. "I think it's more Dutch style, but it matches her bonnet even though it's not like the Frenchie ones that all the rich ladies like wearing. Now if I were a lady at court..."

But Tom and Harry were not to find out what Alice's courtly aspirations were for her words were suddenly drowned out by a blast of trumpets. The king and his new lady were making their way through the lines of the assembled lords, ladies and important churchmen. Then, at a given signal, all of the king's company mounted their horses or entered their carriages and set off for Greenwich Palace. As they did so, Tom, Harry and Alice, together with hundreds of Londoners walked alongside doing their best to keep up with the mounted horsemen and the glittering carriages.

"Say, 'arry," said Tom suddenly, pointing in the direction of the procession. "Why is that carriage over there empty? Look, there's no-one in it. I'm prepared to jump inside it."

"I'm sure you are, my friend, but don't."

"Why not?"

"Because I just heard the bloke behind me say it was a present from the king to Lady Anne, and I don't think she'd be very 'appy to see Master Tom Tomkins riding in it, do you?"

"No, I suppose not. But don't you think our English soldiers look better than the Lady Anne's? I don't like their black uniforms very much. They look kind of threatening."

Harry and Alice nodded in agreement and said that the king's men-at-arms looked far more regal than the Clevean ones. "But I suppose," Harry added, "when you come from a little place like Cleves, you've got to make your soldiers look fierce or otherwise everyone will attack you."

"Hey, stop a minute, you two," Alice said, tugging at her husband's sleeve. "Everyone's come to a halt."

"Why? What's happened?"

"Look, the king and Lady Anne and the others are all listening to those people over there. Can't you see?" Alice said pointing to the head of the procession. "There's a choir over there of some sort. Look, all those churchmen and children. Listen. They're singing hymns, I think. I must say, they do sound good from 'ere, even though I can't 'ear the words properly. Can you?"

Tom and Harry shook their heads and while they were doing so, there was some more serious shaking of heads taking place just less than half a mile away in his chamber at Greenwich Palace. Thomas Cromwell was having a final meeting with some of his most loyal officials. Urged on by his insistent tone they were still trying to work out a diplomatic way of annulling the imminent wedding. Was there nothing they could do to save their king?

"Is there no evidence of a pre-nuptial contract with the Duke of Lorraine's son?" Cromwell kept asking as he paced his office, his body bent forward, his hands clenched behind his back.

"No, sir. We've studied every document, every piece of paper we have. There's absolutely nothing here which can prevent His Majesty from marrying the Lady Anne."

The chancellor stopped his pacing up and down long enough to ask his next question. "And have you spoken to Chancellor Olisleger and Ambassador Hochsteden again?"

"Yes, sir. We spent over two hours with them yesterday going over the whole situation."

Cromwell sat down. He was still not completely sure that the king would indeed marry the Lady Anne and, as a result, he could not help but wonder how he had got himself into this situation. He knew that it was not really his fault, but would His Majesty see it that way? He doubted it. But he did not doubt how His Majesty would react. It did not bear thinking about. Lesser men than I have paid very heavily for displeasing his royal master, Cromwell thought. Some paid with their purses and the less fortunate ones paid with their heads. The chancellor rubbed his neck. Maybe I should have listened to my father after all and stayed on as a soldier abroad. Ah well, it's too late now. Now I've got to do something about my king and this woman because if I cannot find an answer soon…

Cromwell was brought out of his morbid thoughts by a polite cough from one of his older officials. He was standing at the chancellor's elbow with a rolled up document in his hand. "Sir? What do we do now?"

"Haven't you found *any* faults, *any* legal loopholes that might render our contract with the Duke of Cleves null and void?" the desperate Cromwell asked yet again.

"No, sir. It's all exactly as it should be. There's nothing wrong with it at all. Nothing," a tall cadaverous-looking official said, looking up from the table.

"That's true, sir," the other black-coated official added. "While you were working on the arrangements for the procession and the wedding, we read and reread all the documents one hundred times to see if there were any such loopholes."

"And were there any? Even a small one?"

"No, sir. There's not even a jot out of place."

Cromwell's shoulders slumped even lower and he cast his eyes over the document strewn desk. "Then that means we have no choice," he said quietly. "The king will have to go through with it. But don't any of you ever dare to mention what we did in this office today. Because if you do and I hear that word has got out, you will have me to deal with. Is that clear?"

The four black-coated officials nodded their heads vigorously. Just as Cromwell knew his master and king, so these men knew their master and chancellor.

Cromwell shrugged again in resignation. "Well, let's hope she gives him a son, and quickly." He then held his hands as if in prayer. "For if not, I do not want to think of my own future."

"Fear not, sir. She seems to be a lusty lady," the fattest official said. "I'm sure that once His Majesty and the lady are left together in private they'll both do their duty. You'll see. This time next year we'll be sitting here laughing and working out the details of a royal christening. Just you wait."

Keeping this in mind as some sort of cold comfort, Cromwell hurried off to make his report to the king. He had done his best and now everything depended on His Majesty 'doing his duty' as one of his most senior officials had phrased it.

In the meanwhile, the royal procession had reached the courtyard at Greenwich Palace. Just as Tom, Harry and Alice were about to push their way through the crowds to the front, the sound of a powerful explosion rent the air.

"What was that?" gasped Alice her hands to her ears.

"It was the cannon, my dear," Harry explained. "Those over

there. Can't you see them? They've just fired a salute for the king and 'is wife. My, that was loud. My ears are still ringing."

"So's mine," said Tom, removing his own hands from the side of his head. "But she's not 'is wife yet, y'know."

"Well, it's too late for 'im to get out of it," Harry said, unknowingly echoing the words of the chancellor's officials. "He won't be able to wriggle out of this one, will 'e? But, then why should 'e want to? Especially after all this." And he swept his arms over the large crowds, the still-smoking cannon and the decorated courtyard.

"Ssh, be quiet, you two," Alice hissed. "Look, the king's holding 'er. Oooh look. He's giving 'er a kiss. Oh, I do love weddings, don't you?"

"Er, of course I do, my dear," smiled Harry. "Where else can you get your 'ands on all that free ale? But look," he said, craning his neck. "Where are they going now? They're walking off over there, there to the right. I wonder why?"

"Aye, and she's taken 'is arm."

"Ah, don't they look nice and 'appy?" Alice said, wiping a tear off her cheek. "I'm telling you, I do so love weddings," she repeated. "There's nothing like a couple about to be married, be they rich or poor. Ooh, I do 'ope it all works out well. But why shouldn't it? It's time we had another queen on the throne and hopefully, one for more than a couple of years. So all I can say is good luck to them both." And she blew a kiss in the direction where she had just seen her king kiss his future wife.

Just a few hundred feet away, the king's chancellor, now alone in his office, was still pacing up and down echoing Alice's sentiments. Oh let this marriage work, he said to himself as he looked out of the window on the joyous scene below. If not...well, I don't dare think about that. It just doesn't bear thinking about.

Chapter Twelve - *"I like her not!"*

Cromwell was lucky. The fine weather that had greeted the king's first official meeting with his wife-to-be continued until their wedding day. Tuesday, 6 January,

1540 dawned bright, clear and crisp as the king and his retinue entered the gallery next to the hall where the ceremony was to take place. The king looked magnificent. He was wearing a rich gown of cloth of gold, trimmed with black fur and decorated with silver flowers. In addition, his satin coat was fastened with large diamond clasps which sparkled in the morning sun.

Clad in such a grand style on his imposing frame, and topped with an equally impressive fur-trimmed hat whose jewels shone in all directions, King Henry the Eighth indeed looked like the majestic ruler he set out to be. But all of this was for external show. Within himself, the glittering king was not at all happy. If he could have found any cause, great or small, to annul this forthcoming marriage to 'that Cleves woman,' as he had recently described Lady Anne to his chancellor, he would have gladly done so. Pointing his finger at Cromwell, he indicated that his chief minister should leave where he was sitting at his favourite window seat and sit next to him. Cromwell hurried over. What now? he thought. An hour earlier he had left the top Clevean officials, Olisleger and Hochsteden, poring over some documents, together with Sir Anthony Browne and the Duke of Norfolk. Had they, he prayed, found any reason to cancel the wedding before it was too late?

Henry crooked his finger to show that he wished him to sit even closer to him. "Listen, Thomas, and listen well," he whispered conspiratorially into his chancellor's ear. "If it were not to satisfy the world and my realm, I would not go through with what I must do this day for any earthly thing."

Cromwell said nothing. It was the safest reaction.

"Now, where is the woman and why are we waiting here?" the king hissed quietly to his chancellor. "I thought you said she'd be here by now."

At that moment, in another room, the woman in question, together with some of her Clevian and English attendants were making the final adjustments to her wedding gown.

"Milady, please stand still for a minute. I'm trying to sew on this button."

"Lady Anne, please allow me to fasten this belt."

"Yes, and let me close this collar. If you keep moving, I cannot do so."

"Please turn your back to me, Lady Anne. I haven't yet finished brushing your hair. It is so long and I must say, the colour really matches this cloth of gold."

"But isn't my hair supposed to be curled up inside my cap?" Anne asked.

"Oh, no, milady. For your first and, we hope, your only marriage, tradition says that you must wear it loose, down your back."

Anne looked at her attendant quizzically. "Why?"

"This style is said to symbolise your virginity, milady."

Anne did not look impressed with this answer but said nothing.

"Please lower your head, milady so I can put on your coronet. There, it must be straight and fit tightly so let me pin it on securely. We don't want it falling off in the middle of the ceremony now, do we?" asked the maternal Lady Suffolk as though she were talking to a small child.

"May I see what I look like now?" Anne asked a few minutes later. "Does anyone have a mirror here?"

One of her Clevean attendants produced a jeweled mirror and Anne studied her reflection critically in the polished metal surface. She liked what she saw. Staring back at her was a woman wearing a splendid long-sleeved gown in the heavy German style. On her head she was wearing a gold coronet, while large jewels sparkled around her neck and waist. Fortunately, she was so busy admiring what she saw that she did not hear one of her English attendants whisper that although the Lady Anne did indeed look very impressive, the German style with its many layers and heavy skirts certainly looked much less delicate than the French style that the king liked. The king would have been the last one present to admit it but it had been Anne Boleyn, his second wife, who, with her French upbringing, had introduced the elegant and lighter French styles into his court and made them the fashion of the day.

Just as Anne was returning the mirror, one of the king's messengers appeared at the door. Mistress Gilmyn asked him what he wanted.

"His Majesty would like to know when the Lady Anne will be ready."

"Very soon, young man. Now go and tell the king she'll be out within a few minutes."

And so she was. Several minutes later, the door of her dressing-room opened and Anne, accompanied by Lord Wirich of Dhun, Lord Overstein and John Dolzig, the Saxonian envoy, led the procession of ladies to the palace where the wedding was to take place. The stout Henry Bourchier, Earl of Essex, who had arrived late, then took up his position at the front of the procession and he, together with the three Clevean nobles, led Lady Anne, now walking slowly and demurely to meet her husband-to-be. On entering the hall Anne's retinue stepped aside and the king took his place on her right hand side. Apart from a brief glimpse, neither of them looked at each other or smiled.

Just as they were both standing there, their eyes determinedly fixed ahead, Archbishop Cranmer intoned the traditional question whether they were at liberty to be wed. First he asked the king. "Have you come to this solemn occasion with deceitful intentions?"

"No," muttered Henry.

"Lady Anne. I must ask you the same question. Have you come to this solemn occasion with deceitful intentions?"

"*Nein*, er, no," she answered quietly.

"In that case," continued the archbishop in his deep voice, "I must warn you in the name of the Father, the Son and the Holy

Ghost that if you know of any impediment to this union, you must immediately declare it now."

Still looking straight ahead at the decorated wall behind the archbishop both Henry and Anne replied in the negative as soon as he had said the words. Then Cranmer turned to face the assembled lords and ladies. "You, who are here today to witness this union between this man and this woman, do any of you know, in the name of the Father, the Son and the Holy Ghost of any legal objection to this union? If you do, then I charge you to reveal such an objection immediately."

No-one moved. The only sound to be heard was the slight rustle of several of the ladies' gowns as they turned around in vain to see if such an objection had been raised. Then the archbishop turned to face the royal couple again. "Henry Tudor, King of England, wilt thou have this woman to be thy wedded wife, to live together under God's ordnance in the holy state of matrimony? Wilt thou love her, comfort her, honour and keep her in sickness and in health; and in forsaking all others, keep thee only unto her, so long as ye both shall live?"

No-one seated in the front row looked more intently at the king at this point than Thomas Cromwell, the Chancellor of England as his royal master cast his eyes around for a second as if he were looking for an escape. No, there was nothing more that either the king or his faithful chief minister could do to change this situation. Then looking straight ahead, Henry answered in a quiet or, possibly, resigned voice, "I will."

Then, on hearing these same words of affirmation repeated by Lady Anne in a subdued tone, Henry slipped the wedding ring on to his wife's finger. The ring bore the words 'God send me well to keep.' Henry was now a king and a husband – 'for better or for worse' - to his fourth wife, Anne of Cleves. This was the lady who would be known to posterity by her dignified portrait showing her pleasant face, in her heavy Dutch style cowl and gown, standing there looking smiling at her portrait painter, Master Hans Holbein, the Younger.

"Where are they going now?" one of the Duke of Suffolk's pages asked his friend.

"To the chamber to the right, to hear the Mass of the Trinity," his friend Guy answered. "And look, George, the king's holding her hand."

"Well, of course he is. That's the way it should be, isn't it? Don't you ever hold hands with your Margaret?"

Guy blushed and turned away for a moment. "I didn't know you knew about that."

"How could I not know? Haven't you learned yet that there are no secrets at court? Everyone knows everyone else's business here."

Guy Harrison had arrived at court only a few months earlier from Trowbridge, Wiltshire. His family had close connections with the powerful Wiltshire Seymour family, and he now saw that indeed he had a lot to learn if he were to make his way in the world.

"So now, do we just have to wait here?" he asked.

"Yes, Guy, but it won't be for long. My lord, the Duke of Suffolk, will be escorting the Lady Anne…"

"Queen Anne, you mean."

"Aye, that's right. They'll be escorting Queen Anne to her privy chamber and later we'll all be going to the wedding feast."

"Well, Richard, I hope the food's hot this time. That's the trouble with all these palaces. The kitchens are so far away from the halls that by the time the food gets to us, it's cold."

"Oh, stop complaining. You can always go back to Trowbridge if you want. Me, I prefer eating roast duck and capons - even if they are cold - to the bread and pottage we used to eat all the time back in Lincoln."

"I suppose you're right, Richard. So let's go and find our places in the Great Hall."

"Aye, and don't forget that after the meal there's going to be a special masque. I overheard my mother talking about it with the Duchess of Norfolk."

"Do you know what it's going to be about?"

Richard shrugged his shoulders. "The usual things, I reckon, Guy. Something taken from the Bible or about love and chastity. At least, that's what my mother said."

"You mean something like they had last year in memory of Queen Jane? Just after I arrived here?"

Richard looked around and put his finger to his lips. "Sssh, Guy, don't talk about her so loudly. The king is now married to Queen Anne. You don't want everyone overhearing you, do you? Come, let's go. All this waiting about has made me hungry."

And the two young men set off in the direction of the Great Hall. After pushing their way through the throng of well-dressed lords, ladies and court officials, Richard and Guy found their places towards the lower end of the table and waited.

"How many courses do you think there'll be?"

"Oh, about ten, I suppose. You know, soup, fish, swan, capon, meat and stuff like that."

Richard was right. But in addition to his list there was also roast goose, partridge and pheasant as well as rabbit. And then came the fruit and a wide variety of pastries. All of this was washed down with wine and ale. It was several hours later that the king rose, belched and took the hand of his newly wedded wife and left the banqueting hall. Accompanied by his closest advisors, the royal couple then made their way to the king's private chamber.

There everyone stepped back from the bed as a priest stepped forward to intone a blessing over it. "O Lord God, watch over your servants as they sleep in this bed and protect them from all demonic dreams." Then after adding a few words against infertility and impotence and sprinkling a few drops of holy water on the royal couple, he bowed and indicated that the assembled company should now leave the chamber. They should allow His Majesty and his queen to fulfill their duties as man and wife with no further interference.

For a full five minutes after everyone had departed, Henry and Anne lay there stiffly parallel and silent in the wide royal bed. Each one lay there, stretched out, alert, hardly breathing, not touching and waiting for the other to make the first move. At last Henry could stand it no longer. Slowly rolling his vast body over to her he began to move his hands about under his wife's fine shift. Anne lay there frozen. She did not and could not move a muscle. Nothing like this had ever happened to her before. Her mother had not told her what to expect on her wedding night.

Henry's hands were hot and sweaty. What should she do now? What's he doing to me? she thought. As she looked up in the candlelit chamber she could see the faint outline of the carved angels on the ceiling, but here below on earth she could feel the king's sweaty hands reaching up to her breasts and pinching her nipples. But his fat fingers were there for only a few seconds as he slid his hands down over her stomach and down to her smooth thighs. Pushing her legs apart, he briefly felt in the moist place between them and then rapidly withdrew his hand. He then rolled back over and muttered "Good night" and soon snored himself into a noisy, dreamless sleep.

Anne lay awake for some time afterwards. Is this what married life was about? she asked herself. Was it about *this* that the village girls who worked in the castle at Cleves used to giggle about, especially after one of their number had been married? It was really too puzzling for her. Was this the romance that all the troubadours and poets had described? This grunting and groping? Before falling into a troubled sleep, she too rolled over, turned her back on her husband and muttered a short prayer as her mother had instructed her to. Her last thought that night was that she'd discuss the whole situation with several of her closest ladies-in-waiting on the morrow.

Early the next morning an apprehensive Cromwell was summoned for a special audience with his royal master. Entering the king's private chamber, he saw him sitting in a well-cushioned chair, his oozing, ulcerous leg resting on a footstool. His face told the whole story.

"Good morning, Your Majesty. I hope that..." he began lightly, fearing the worst.

"It is not, Thomas! It is *not* a good morning and I did *not* have a good night!"

"Why, Sire, how does Your Majesty like the queen?"

"I don't," Henry shot back at his shocked chancellor. "I did not like her before our wedding and now I like her even less. She is nothing fair, and evil smells float about her body. Her breasts are soft and I'm not really sure from the other parts of her body that I touched that she is indeed a maid, despite what you or her brother or even the woman herself may claim. I tell you that I found her so unpleasant, Thomas, that I had no appetite for her and left her as I found her. If she were a virgin beforehand, she is still one now. If she wasn't, and I think that is quite possible, then surely she is not one now."

Even if this were the answer that Cromwell had half-expected, he was taken aback at the vehemence with which the words were was shot at him. The chancellor was already seeing the future. Did this mean that His Majesty had already made up his mind to rid himself of his fourth wife? And if so, how could this be done? By divorce? By annulment? And what would this mean for England and her relationship with the Protestant countries on the other side of the Channel? And, the Chancellor suddenly thought, feeling beads of sweat breaking out on his brow as his hands grew cold and clammy, what does all this mean for me? And was His Majesty's disappointing and frustrating night merely the result of 'first night nerves' or was this to be a permanent situation – permanent that is until a solution could be found? And if so, Cromwell's brain raced ahead, what form of solution would that take?

Keeping his head bowed low, the chancellor waited a few more minutes pretending to study the chamber's dark oak panelling.

"Surely," he began slowly. "As married men, Your Majesty, both you and I well know that sometimes the, er, how shall I phrase it? er, the act of love does not always occur as we would wish. Sometimes, Your Majesty, the reactions…"

"*Sometimes, nothing, sir!*" Henry hurled at Thomas. "There was nothing. Nothing I tell you. No act of love and no reactions! Nothing. Her flabby breasts and belly did nothing for me. It is true that her skin was soft, but I tell you, it felt soft like an old woman's: soft and wrinkled. She could do nothing for me. Absolutely nothing! And if all of that weren't bad enough, just listening to her speak was torture to my ears. That heavy German accent and the way she pronounces her words. Yes, I know English is not her native language, but to hear her say 'Good night' which sounds more like *Goote nacht* is not the way to make me feel lusty or anything close to such feelings - feelings that should exist between a man and his wife in bed. And that is especially so when it's their wedding night, no?"

For once, Cromwell was speechless. He did not know what to say. He had suspected that something like this might take place - but not to this degree.

"She lay there, Thomas," Henry continued, "lay there like a wooden post and I did as well. She could not rouse me at all. I've never ever felt like this with any other woman, royal or not. And you know - maybe better than most men in this court - that I do not act like a simpering youth when I'm in bed. Even my first wife was able to do more for me and she was much older than this…this Clevean cow."

Cromwell slowly raised his head. He was not used to conversations like this – and certainly not with his royal master.

"Perhaps, Sire," he began gently, trying to placate his red-faced king, "perhaps the queen was a trifle nervous. After all, she'd had a long day and you were, it must be said, the first man she had lain with. Perhaps her mother had not given her sufficient instruction on how to behave and…"

"What do you mean, 'sufficient instruction?" Henry asked. "That woman hasn't received any instruction at all! Nothing, I tell you. And not only did she just lie there, but I tell you, she smelt as well!"

"Smelt, Your Majesty?"

"Yes, Thomas, smelt. Are you completely deaf this morning? Do I have to spell it all out for you? That woman smelt. Under all those gowns and petticoats, that woman smells. Maybe to her Clevean folks she looks beautiful, but underneath it all, I tell you, she is far from that. She is fat and flabby, and she smells!"

Cromwell opened his mouth to say something when Henry barked at him, "You may leave me now. But just remember what I said before. You got me into this, Master Chancellor, and you will get me out of it. I cannot continue my life with that woman at my side. So start thinking, Thomas, and start thinking very, very quickly. Now go!"

As the chastened chancellor bowed and left the chamber his neck began to itch. Was this an omen? he asked himself as he hurried along the long corridor to his office. No, surely not. One does not execute the king's chief minister for mistakes such as this. For treason, yes. For inciting rebellion or religious subversion, yes, but surely not because the king's new wife is fat and smelly and he likes her not. But as the day passed, Cromwell began feeling less and less sure of himself. All around him in the halls and corridors of the palace he could hear the whispering and giggling as word of the king's disastrous nuptial night spread around like an overflowing pool of water.

In his usual thorough way, Cromwell decided to discover exactly what was happening. He knew that no-one would tell him directly as he was seen to be too close an adviser to the king for that. Early that afternoon he called his secretary over to his office and wasted no time in giving him his instructions.

"Find out what all this whispering is about and give me your report by seven o'clock this evening."

"Yes, sir," and, in his attempt to escape his master's nervous anger, the secretary almost ran out of the office.

Seven o'clock that evening found the pale-faced secretary, standing ramrod straight in front of his master's desk.

"Well, man, out with it!" Now it was Cromwell's turn to bark at his underling. "Tell me, what's all the whispering about?"

"It's about the queen, sir."

"Yes, I know that. What about her?"

"The courtiers are saying, sir, that the king couldn't er, couldn't get…"

"I see. And …?"

"And they say that they just lay there together in bed, sir, doing nothing."

"And just how do they know of this? And is it true or not?" Cromwell added quickly.

The secretary looked about as if someone else might be in the room listening. "They say, sir, that the king himself told some of his lords about, er, what happened last night and that he even told his physician, Doctor Butts, about it."

"Oh, he did, did he? Well go and fetch Doctor Butts and bring him here immediately. I wish to have a word or two with the good doctor."

"But, sir, I believe he is eating or with his family now."

"I don't care, man. Just bring him to me as soon as you can. I will be waiting here for him. Now go."

The secretary scuttled off and ten minutes later a worried-looking royal physician was facing the king's chief minister who, if the truth be told, was far more worried than the trembling doctor who faced him across the desk.

"Doctor Butts," the chancellor started immediately without any of the usual small talk. "What did His Majesty tell you about his wife, that is, about their activities last night?"

"Well, sir, he said that he enjoyed the feast and that the food, especially the capons were ..."

"Stop playing with me, man," Cromwell thumped his fist on the table, forgetting the doctor's honourable title. "You know exactly what I'm talking about and it's not about eating capons. Now tell me what he said to you."

Butts looked around. He could not believe how he had just been addressed. He had never been treated like this before. He had heard that the king's chief minister could be coarse but he had never experienced this himself. "Sir, surely you of all people must know that what passes between me and my patients. That professional bond is confidential. And if that patient happens to be His Majesty, then that bond becomes even more sacred. Sir, I cannot..."

"*Cannot, nothing*!" Cromwell exploded. His nerves were wearing very thin by now. He walked around the table and thrust his hot face right up to the doctor's. "Tell me what His

Majesty said or it will be the worse for you. You know that I 'm the chancellor and if you don't wish to find yourself in the Tower you'd better give me what I want, and now!"

Butts saw that he had no choice. Physician-patient confidentiality was one thing, but being on the wrong side of the chancellor and ending up in the Tower was another. He shrugged. If the king had already told half of his court about what had happened or, rather, what had not happened that night in the royal bed, he reasoned, then surely I can divulge this information to His Majesty's chief minister.

"Sir," he began. "His Majesty reported to me that he found the queen's body offensive and as such, she was unable to provoke any, er, how shall I say it...?"

"Anyway you like, Doctor, just say it."

"Yes, sir. The queen could not provoke His Majesty to, er, to perform the act of love. When I tried to explain to him that this may have been due to a case of nerves or tiredness, he strongly denied this and claimed that he had then experienced two wet dreams that night."

Cromwell sat down and then faced the nervous doctor again. "And did he say anything else?"

"Yes, sir. He said it was clear that he was not ignorant about the act of love and that neither was he impotent. He said that the birth of his four children had proved that - especially as his son had been born less than three years earlier."

"Wait a minute, Doctor. *Four* children you said?"

"Yes, sir. Prince Edward, two princesses and the illegitimate Henry Fitzroy."

"Ah, yes, I'd forgotten about him. So what else did the king say to you?"

"He said, sir, that if this woman is to be his wife, then he'll not be able to have any more children for the good of the realm. That is all, sir. All I can add is that His Majesty is a very unhappy man."

"Yes, I know all that," Cromwell added gruffly. "And tell me, did he say anything about my rôle in any of this?"

"Oh no, sir. He just said he felt very disappointed. 'Disappointed and cheated' were the exact words he said."

Butts looked up. The storm seemed to have passed. The chancellor was now pacing around his large desk quietly, drumming his fingers on its smooth polished surface.

"May I go now, sir? My wife is waiting for me and I also have to pay a visit to the Duchess of Suffolk. But," he added, feeling a little more confident. "Fear not, sir. If you wish I'll come and see you and the king tomorrow together with Doctor Chambers and we'll see if we can find a way to solve this little problem."

A weary and an even more worried Cromwell dismissed the black-gowned physician with a casual wave of his hand and walked slowly back to his chair. He sat down heavily and began to think what he could do about this new and troublesome situation.

Doctor Butts was as good as his word. The next day, together with the chancellor and his colleague, Doctor Chambers, they were ushered into His Majesty's presence.

"We've been discussing your situation, Your Majesty," Doctor Butts began in his most calming tone. "We both feel that there's nothing for you to be afraid of. From our experience," and here the royal doctor looked at his colleague for support, "we feel that this is a passing affliction that occurs to more married men than who would admit to it during their first few nights of married life and…"

"Yes, but Doctor Butts, I've been married before. Three times."

"Yes, Sire. We know that, Sire," Doctor Chambers took over. "But this young woman is clearly inexperienced and new to the whole situation of the marital bed. Therefore, Your Majesty, we suggest the following solution. You should not force yourself on her and that you should regard this present period as, one might say, a period of initial ignorance on the queen's part."

"Yes, Sire," Butts added, trying to sound encouraging. "Let's say that this is merely a temporary period which under your expert tuition will surely come to an end soon. If both of you refrain from carrying out any major activity at night and just act tenderly towards one another, then we're sure that this problem will solve itself."

"That's true, Sire," Chambers nodded. "Another idea may be to sleep in separate beds for a few nights and just visit each other from time to time, but of course," he added quickly, seeing the king's face, "we leave this decision up to you."

Nodding his head, the king dismissed the two doctors and turned to face his still anxious chancellor.

"Master Cromwell," he began. "I'm still not happy and even though my two doctors have described my situation as temporary and one that can be cured, I'm not completely convinced. I therefore suggest that you return to your office and as I said yesterday, start thinking of a way to get me out of the mess that you've got me into. I expect you to come up with a solution very quickly. You normally do on most occasions, so let's hope that your brain can think of one this time as well. Now please leave me as I wish to have a rest."

As his royal master had commanded, Cromwell started thinking how he could save His Majesty and also himself. If the king were telling everyone at court what had happened, he thought, then it was clear that he did not see himself to blame. After all, few men, especially His Majesty, would admit to their lack of success in the marital bed or in any bed, in fact. And yet here he was, telling half of his court about his inability to perform the most basic act of love with his new wife. If it did not bode well for the king, it certainly did not bode well for the king's chief minister who, all along, had urged his master to marry this woman. In all, Cromwell concluded, the whole situation looked quite desperate for the three main people involved: the king, his wife, and most of all, for himself.

But then a brief smile crossed Cromwell's face. Perhaps he had just thought of a solution, after all. Couldn't Master Holbein be blamed for any of this? After all, hadn't he painted the flattering portrait that had lured His Majesty into this marital trap? Perhaps this is where a solution was to be found. Hmm, Cromwell said to himself as he stood up to leave his office. I've been through difficult times before and solved all sorts of problems in the past for His Majesty, I don't see how I cannot find a way of solving this problem as well.

Chapter Thirteen - Intimate Conversations

Just as the king had had some intimate conversations with Cromwell and several other close advisers, both medical and courtly, in the week following his disastrous nuptial night, so too did his wife hold similar conversations with her ladies-in-waiting.

Taking the new queen aside in an arbour in the palace grounds, Lady Rutland and Lady Rochford, Anne Boleyn's sister-in-law, asked her if she were still a maid.

"Still a maid?" Anne replied, her eyes childishly bright and innocent.

Lady Rutland coughed quietly. "Your Majesty," she asked quietly, deliberately keeping her English simple. "Do you lie in bed with your husband, His Majesty, all night?"

"Yes, of course I do. Isn't that what wives are supposed to do? I lie there every night. When he comes to bed he kisses me and takes me by the hand and says, 'Goodnight, sweetheart.'"

"Yes, and?"

Anne smiled. "And then in the morning he kisses me again and says, 'Did you sleep well, darling?' Why, isn't that enough? He's very sweet to me now. On the first night of our marriage I think he was very tired and angry, but now that has passed. Isn't that good? *Ja?*"

Lady Rutland looked at Lady Rochford and raised her eyebrows slightly before turning again to the queen.

"But, Your Majesty, does he er… touch you?"

"Touch me? *Ja.* We hold hands and sometimes he kisses me on the cheek. Here," and Anne pointed to her soft cheeks.

Lady Rochford decided she would have to be more specific. "No, Your Majesty. What I meant was, does His Majesty touch your private parts?"

"My private parts?"

"Yes, Your Majesty. Down here, between your legs. And here," she said pointing to her own bodice-covered breasts and her lower body.

Anne looked somewhat shocked. "Oh, no, milady. He touched me on those places only on our first night in bed. It was not nice. So since then he just holds my hands instead." And she bent down to pick some daisies.

"And he doesn't do anything else?" a mystified Lady Rutland asked. "Does he tell you to touch him, say, under the covers, under his night shift?"

"Touch him? Touch him where?" an equally mystified looking Anne asked.

"His legs, his belly, his prick."

"Oh, no, of course not, Lady Rutland. Why should I want to touch him down there?"

"But, Your Majesty," Lady Rutland asked, "What did your mother tell you about wedding nights and husbands?"

"My mother? *Nichts*. She told me nothing about such things. She just told me to make sure my husband is happy with me and that it was my duty to obey him in all things. That's all."

"Didn't she say anything else?" asked an exasperated Lady Rutland.

"Oh, no, milady," replied Anne, shaking her head. "She taught me how to sew, how to embroider, how to repair holes and tears in clothes and useful things like that. She also taught me to read poetry and how to write letters and also a little about numbers," she finished brightly, thinking of the happy days she had experienced at home in Cleves at her mother's side. Then, the talk of husbands had always referred to tall handsome men who were gallant and brave. Not fat ageing men who walked around with a stick and whose ulcerous legs smelt disgusting.

"And nothing about men, husbands and bed?"

"No, Lady Rutland," Anne replied, sharply returning to the present. "Why?"

"Because, Your Majesty, if you continue like this with the king, you'll never give him a son, and after all is said and done, that's what he wants most from you. A son, even two."

"But he already has one, Prince Edward."

"That's true, Your Majesty," Lady Rochford agreed. "But he

wants another one. One son is not enough – especially for this king."

"*Ach so*, now I am beginning to understand. But now, if you don't mind, I want to go inside. It's getting cold out here in the garden."

"Yes, Your Majesty, but if we can talk about one more thing out here just before we go in, it will be very good. You see, no-one can overhear us out here."

Anne looked around her and saw no-one else was there. "*Ja*, what is it you want to say to me?"

"Lady Rutland and I have been discussing between ourselves how you can keep the king happy and we decided it would be a very good idea if you could change your style of clothes. We fear His Majesty doesn't like your clothes."

"Not like my clothes? Why not? Are they *nicht elegant und modisch*, er, not elegant and fashionable? Are they not fine enough for him? Feel this material. It was very expensive and my mother chose it most carefully." And she held up her gown for Lady Rutland to feel the rich and heavy fabric.

"No, Your Majesty, it's not a question of the quality of the fabric. It's the style he does not like. Here in the English court we ladies prefer to wear the French style, clothes like we are wearing now. Like these hoods we are wearing."

"Yes, look, milady," Lady Rutland added. "These French five-pointed hoods are just what His Majesty likes and…"

"That's right," Lady Rochford interrupted. "And these low-cut gowns that show off more of our shoulders and the tops of our breasts." And smiling, she gently laid the queen's hand on the soft exposed part of her full bosom. "*This* is what the king likes to see."

"Aye, and so do all the other men at court," Lady Rutland smiled. "And touch them if they can, too."

"*Ach so*, and this will help me with the king?"

Lady Rochford nodded. "Knowing the king the way we do, it'll certainly be better if you dress more as we do. That'll make him very pleased with you."

"Aye, to say nothing of the other men at court as well," Lady Rutland murmured. "But let's go inside now. I can see that

Her Majesty is shivering a little and so am I. The men may like to look at our breasts but in this weather only half covering them can be rather chilly. So let's go in and warm ourselves by the fire."

But none of this well-intentioned advice helped. Although over the coming weeks, Anne shed her heavy Dutch-style headdresses and gowns for the lighter French style, when it came to matters of the flesh, the situation between the king and his wife did not improve. And not even after the chancellor had had a serious *tête-à-tête* with the Earl of Rutland, the queen's lord chamberlain.

"Come, sir," Cromwell had begun as the two of them were seated in the chancellor's well-appointed office sipping some spiced wine. "We must find some means to persuade the queen to be more compatible with His Majesty. The safety and the security of our kingdom rests on this to a large degree, don't you agree?"

Rutland nodded. He had already heard quite a lot about the king's marital situation both from his own wife and from the various stories that were circulating quite freely around the court.

"As you'll admit, my lord, this present situation cannot be allowed to continue indefinitely," Cromwell continued. "His Majesty's been married for over three months now and I understand that there's no improvement in the situation. I tell you, my lord, you must find a way, that is, between you and your wife to counsel the queen to use, er, how shall I say this? – to use all pleasantness to the king. Remember, my lord, His Majesty must have another son. One is not enough. Our Prince Edward might be a very bonny and healthy lad now, but who can tell? Who knows what will happen in the future? Even princes and princesses with all the best love and care in the world have been known to die at an early age. Think, my lord, think of what happened to the king's own brother and sisters: Edmund, Katherine and Elizabeth. They all died early."

Rutland nodded in agreement. He was fully aware of what was at stake.

However, unfortunately for Cromwell, the Earl of Rutland

felt that he could not approach the queen on this subject and when he spoke of it with his wife a few days later, she could not help him. Then the next day Lady Rutland had an idea. "My lord," she said as they sat down together in the privacy of their comfortable solarium. "I know what I'll do. I shall ask Mrs. Loew to advise Her Majesty."

"Who? The German woman who's been allowed to remain in England with the queen?"

"Yes, my dear. She seems to have the queen's ear. I've seen them more than once in a huddle discussing various matters. Of course, they were talking in German so I don't know what they were talking about but it does seem that Her Majesty likes · to discuss all sorts of matters with her. In fact, I'd even go as far as to say that this Mrs. Loew is her favourite, that is, among her German ladies."

"So try your best, my love, and let me know what happens."

But nothing happened. When Lady Rutland asked Mrs. Loew to come and see her a few days later she asked her if she and the queen had discussed the queen's nocturnal activities in the royal bed. Mrs. Loew's normally placid pale face turned bright red.

"*Nein, nein,* er, oh, no, Your Ladyship. Of course not," she spluttered. "My Lady Anne would never talk to me about things like that. All she'll tell me is that she and the king wish each other "Good night" and give each other a gentle kiss on the cheek before going to sleep."

"Can you not talk to her again and…"

"Oh, no, certainly not, Lady Rutland. My lady will not hear of such matters. And besides, such topics are not easy for me to talk about and especially with Her Majesty. Back home in Cleves we would never…"

"Yes, yes, I understand," Lady Rutland nodded quickly. "You may go now. Perhaps I will speak to you later about this."

To be honest, Lady Rutland understood the situation in which she had placed Mrs. Loew and so she decided not to pursue the matter any further with her. That night, with a heavy heart she reported her lack of success to her husband.

He, in turn repeated this information to an increasingly nervous chancellor.

"And are you sure there's no other way of getting any more information out of these women?" Cromwell asked, finishing his goblet of wine without offering any to his informant.

Rutland shook his head. "I think we've done everything that we can possibly do, sir. I've come to the conclusion that we'll just have to let nature take its course. I mean, how long can a husband and wife lie together in bed without anything happening? Can you seriously imagine the king allowing a woman to share his bed night after night without his lusty nature getting the better of him? It's just not possible. Fear not, Master Chancellor," Rutland added as he stood up to leave Cromwell's office, "Something must happen. Otherwise, it just doesn't bear thinking about."

"Well, let's hope and pray you're right there, sir. Because if you're wrong, I... well, I just don't want to think about it. So, good day to you, sir," and Rutland left, leaving an increasingly frustrated chancellor sitting at his desk contemplating a not very happy vision of the future.

Chapter Fourteen - Cromwell is Surprised

Cromwell's vision of the future certainly did not include the following meeting which occurred two weeks later. The chancellor had been in a foul mood: either barking orders at everyone or being deliberately kind and considerate and speaking gently to anyone with whom he had dealings. He was behaving like a ship which had lost its bearings and did not know in which direction it was heading. So it came as a complete surprise to him when his royal master asked him to come and see him in his chamber to be greeted as he had been in the past, the past that is, before the Lady Anne had appeared on the scene.

"Ah, do come in, my Earl of Essex," Henry welcomed him. "Do draw up a seat and come and sit beside me like you used to in the past."

"Earl of Essex, Sire, I..."

"No, no, Thomas," Henry smiled, holding up his hand. "Please lay these protestations aside. I have seen it fit to promote you and grant you the title held by the late holder of this title, Henry Bouchier. As no doubt you know, he died a couple of weeks ago when he broke his neck falling off his horse. Naturally I was very sad to hear about this accident but I've decided to keep this old title alive. Therefore, soon you will proceed from here to the Council chamber where you'll hear your full title read out together with all the honours that go with it. That is what I wish to tell you for the present." He paused and then added before his chancellor could say anything. "You may go now as I'm about to dine with Her Majesty."

"But, Your Majesty," Cromwell began. "I do not..."

"No, no, Thomas, fear not and please be the first to accept my congratulations. You look a little surprised. Do not think of your king as an ungrateful monarch who knows only how to chop heads off disobedient subjects or cast other unhappy souls into the Tower."

"Oh, no, Sire, I just…"

"No, no, Thomas. I've said quite enough. Now please make your way to the Council. They are there waiting for you." And seeing that he would learn no more from His Majesty about his sudden and unexpected promotion, Cromwell hurried off. Imagine his surprise when as the guards opened the Council chamber doors and ushered him in, all the members surrounding the long oval table stood up as one man and bowed to him. Cromwell was amazed. Nothing like this had happened to him before. He was aware that most of the men there despised him and thought he was nothing but a presumptuous upstart. They tolerated him only because of his close relationship to the king. And yet here they were, these same councillors now bowing down to him in great deference. It did not make any sense. Cromwell's mind raced ahead. What was behind all this? Had this anything to do with the king's marriage? Had His Majesty resolved his differences with the queen his wife, now his wife of three months' standing?

As the heavy silence continued in that long and lavishly decorated hall, and all of the councillors stood up straight, the Garter King of Arms banged his silver-knobbed staff on the floor. "Thomas Cromwell, Chancellor of England," he proclaimed in a loud voice. "I am bid by his gracious majesty, King Henry the Eighth of England, to inform you and all the other assembled magnates gathered here that from today, the eighteenth of April, 1540, you are now to be known to us all," and here he paused in order to let the power of his words sink in, "the Earl of Essex, Viceregent and High Chamberlain of England, Chancellor of the Exchequer, and Justice of the Forests beyond Trent."

Cromwell stood there, stunned. All this, and for me? Now? And after all what His Majesty had told him about his marriage? Surely it was not possible. Now he was only one degree lower than a duke. To prevent himself from shaking he gripped the top of the chair in front of him and humbly lowered his eyes. He did this, in fact, so that no-one would notice the shocked expression that covered his face. Then in order to hide his feelings further, he sat down and busied himself with signing a few documents lying on the table in front of him. By the time he had finished, he signalled that all the councillors should sit and take their places. He made a short speech thanking them for granting him these great honours and then, in his usual business-like manner, said that the Council should proceed with the business of the day.

That night, at a celebratory ball at Greenwich Palace, the recently promoted Earl of Essex was in for another surprise.

"Who's that young lady over there?" he asked his secretary. "The one who's been fawning all over His Majesty all evening?"

"Why, don't you know. Sir? That's Catherine Howard."

"What, one of the Duke of Howard's brood?"

"Yes, sir. To be exact, she's the daughter of Lord Edmund Howard and Mistress Joyce Culpepper."

"And what's she doing here, that is, apart from trying to gain the king's attention?"

"Her uncle, the duke, brought her to court recently to be a lady-in-waiting for Her Majesty, sir."

Cromwell thought about this for a minute. How could this latest move by one of his fiercest opponents on the Council affect him? He knew from past experience that Thomas Howard, 3rd Duke of Norfolk, was a bitter enemy, was jealous of his power and did little to hide his great dislike of the king's chief minister. Whenever he had the opportunity to foil any of my ideas at the Council, Cromwell thought, he did not hesitate to do so. And now the duke's niece had been brought to court to worm her way into the king's heart. Would that also mean that she would try and worm her way into the king's bed as well? From the way she was caressing His Majesty's thigh, it certainly looked like it.

Suddenly Cromwell turned to his secretary again. "Tell me, why haven't I seen her here before? Is this the first time she's been here?"

"Oh no, sir. She's been here several times in the past but perhaps you didn't notice her because you've been so busy of late. As we both know, sir, you've been very concerned about His Majesty and his problems with the queen."

Cromwell grunted and took a couple of sweetmeats from a passing servant. "Yes, that may be so, young man. Indeed, I have been very busy recently dealing with that problem, but I must tell you I don't like the way Mistress Howard is behaving over there. If I didn't know any better, I'd say she is flirting with His Majesty – and in the presence of his wife, too."

"But, sir," the secretary said. "I'm not sure that you're right in what you're saying. After all, it was Her Majesty who agreed that young Catherine come here tonight, so surely everything must be in order?"

"I'm not sure, Master Secretary. Just look how she's showing herself to the king. That bodice seems very low-cut to me. And I'm no expert in the latest fashions."

"I agree with you, sir, but my wife tells me that that style is the latest fashion and that any woman at court who doesn't want to be thought of as old-fashioned is now wearing those low-cut bodices like the young Catherine Howard girl."

"Humph! That may be so, but would your wife put her hand on the king's knee - if not higher - like Howard's niece is doing now? I mean, just look at her! She's practically fondling his codpiece!"

"Yes, sir, I can see that. And as for my wife, I can assure you that she is an honourable woman and would certainly not offend His Majesty."

Cromwell nodded in agreement, but before they could discuss Catherine Howard's behaviour any further, a servant entered and signalled that he had a note for the chancellor. Cromwell opened it quickly and read that the king wanted him to attend a private and urgent meeting on the morrow in his chamber.

"Ah, please enter," Henry beamed the next morning as Cromwell stepped into his master's chamber. "Please enter, my new Vice-regent and Earl of Essex. Hmm, maybe I'll make you a duke next time. Now where would you like to be a duke of? Cumberland? Cambridge? Surrey? Oh, well, we'll see." Henry pointed to a chair for Cromwell and, as in the past, the pair of them sat down next to the table. "Now, Thomas, take some of these delicious comfits and tell me how your new title sits on you? Well, I hope."

"Oh, certainly, Your Majesty, but I fear that several of your lords are less than happy with my promotion."

"Just ignore them, Thomas," and Henry waved his hand dismissively. "They'll get used to it in time. They always do. Just think what they'll say when I make you a duke, eh?" Henry leaned over to grab a fistful of comfits and then sank back into his chair. "Now let me tell you why I've called this meeting. I have two important matters that need your attention and both of them are to do with my forthcoming divorce."

The king could not have shattered Cromwell's feeling of well-being any more dramatically. "Divorce, Sire? Now?" he said, spluttering a few comfits over the table.

"Yes, Thomas. Divorce."

"Sire, I know you are less than pleased with the queen - but divorce? If I may say so, Sire, you have been married to the queen for only four or five months."

"I am fully aware of that but it's been four or five months too long. Surely, you of all people must be able to see that the present situation cannot be allowed to continue."

And before Cromwell could say a word, the king continued. "Thomas, I have given this matter some very serious consideration over these past few weeks, so listen very carefully. There are two sides to this divorce: one political and one personal. First, the political one. Since you first made overtures to the Duchy of Cleves last year, the whole political situation in Europe has changed. That being so, I now understand that I have nothing to gain politically by being married to this woman. In other words, this alliance with Cleves is worthless."

"How so, Your Majesty?" Thomas asked, noting that the king had said that he, Thomas, had made the overtures a year ago.

"How so, Thomas? That's easily explained. I assume that you've seen that the Emperor Charles the Fifth may be trying to take over the Rhineland area. This area includes Cleves and

Guelderland, and it looks as though he intends to do this by force of arms."

Cromwell nodded and quickly arrived at the obvious conclusion. "And so, Your Majesty, if that were indeed to happen, we would have to send an army over to Cleves in order to support the queen's brother."

"Exactly, Thomas. My goodness, it never took you long to see what was happening, did it? Here, take some more comfits."

Cromwell did so and the king continued. "Now, not only do I not want to commit an English army to a war which will not directly benefit my country, I also don't want to spend all that money on such a venture either."

The chancellor nodded in agreement.

"Thomas, you and I did not dissolve all those monasteries and abbeys just to pay for a war, did we? No, of course not," and Henry brought his fist hard down on the table as he said so. "Now I'll tell you about my personal reasons I want this divorce."

"No, Sire, there is really no need," Cromwell said quickly. He had already learned about his master's reasons through his domestic snoops and spies. Besides, he did not wish to become even more involved with the king's marital problems. Now that he believed or, rather, he hoped that he had steered clear of them, he definitely did not wish to become involved with his royal master's problems once again. The trauma that he had undergone at the beginning of the present marriage was enough to ensure that he would not repeat the folly of becoming so deeply involved with his royal master's private life again.

In a brief but vivid moment, he recalled what had happened to Cardinal Wolsey, the previous chancellor and his mentor. The cardinal had become involved with His Majesty and his desire to divorce his first wife, Catherine of Aragon. When he had failed to bring this about, Cromwell remembered, the past chancellor had been summoned to London but perhaps fortunately for him, he had suddenly died on the way. Could such a situation happen to me? Cromwell thought. Suddenly dying or even being executed simply because His Majesty wanted a divorce?

The chancellor's grim thoughts were interrupted by Henry's voice. "Yes, Thomas, there is a need for me to tell you about the queen. I want you to fully understand the situation I am now in." The king leaned forward conspiratorially as though he wanted nobody else to hear what he had to say. "While it is true, Thomas, that the queen is a gentle, kind and sweet lady, we are not compatible in bed. As you know, I find her body fat and flabby and that she also gives off noxious odours. All this prevents me from fulfilling my royal duties. I know *I* am able to father a son or two, for I've done so already, haven't I?"

"Yes, Your Majesty."

"But I cannot do so with this woman. It is just impossible. And besides, I don't think she knows what she's supposed to do in bed either. I've heard through some of her ladies that she told them that her mother had never given her any instruction about such matters. Did you know that, Thomas?"

"No, Sire." was the quiet answer.

"And so, as my chief minister, you will see that I have no choice. I must divorce this woman and have a new wife who will give me sons. My son, Prince Edward, is not enough. For the continuation of the Tudor dynasty I must have at least one more son. Is that asking for so much?"

"No, Your Majesty. I fully understand your need for another son or two, but I feel I must ask you, how will this look abroad – divorcing the queen after only a few months of married life?"

"Thomas, I must now admit I do not care how this will look abroad. I believe I'm strong enough to be above such gossip and European tittle-tattle. For there is another point to be considered, as well. I am now almost fifty years old and who knows how much longer, er, the sap will still be flowing; the fires will still be burning in my loins, eh?"

Henry looked hard at his chief minister who realized now it was just a question of time before Anne of Cleves would join the list of the king's previous three wives. The other question, Cromwell asked himself, was how this was to come about? An annulment? An execution? A death by natural or unnatural means? It was clear that his royal master was determined. Anne had to go. All that remained was to see how this business would be brought about and how much he, Thomas Cromwell, would be involved.

Cromwell then fired another shot. If this one failed, then he knew that the price of failure could be his own execution.

"Your Majesty," he began slowly. "Suppose we let it be known abroad, especially in the queen's duchy of Cleves, that after a few initial problems with your wife, everything is now going well and you are more than happy that you married the lady."

"But of course, Thomas. That is exactly what we are going to do. We're not going to let them hear otherwise. Therefore I'll continue to appear in public with my queen and soon, when we have a big jousting festival to celebrate May Day, she will be there standing at my side as the good and dutiful wife and queen. But, Thomas, remember, my true feelings towards this lady are to be kept a secret – a secret that is known only by me, you and a few members of the Council. Is that understood?"

Cromwell nodded, even though he knew that this secret was well-known by more people than the king had just mentioned. But now his sharp brain was racing ahead and he was already planning how to bring about the royal couple's inevitable divorce in the quickest and quietest way possible. And not only that. He had to devise a scheme that he, the newly-appointed vice-regent and chancellor, the instigator of this marriage, would not also fall once the divorce was finalized. But Cromwell still had one last question to ask. After hesitating for several moments he asked, "Your Majesty, is young Catherine Howard involved in anything we have just been discussing?"

Henry's face lit up for a moment as he thought of the pretty Howard girl and how she had caressed him the night before. Smiling at the memory, he faced his long-serving chief minister.

"Master Cromwell, the Duke of Howard's niece has nothing

to do with any of this. She's completely irrelevant to my plans so you may forget all about her. Your task, may I remind you, is to obtain a divorce from my wife. And the sooner the better. That is all. Let me deal with everything else." And from the tone of his master's voice, Cromwell knew that this meeting had come to an end. He took one more comfit, bowed and made his way out.

As he closed the heavy door behind him he could not help wondering how many more intimate meetings with the king he would be having in the future.

Chapter Fifteen - Cromwell is shocked

The next day Henry called his Council together for a meeting. He was about to address them from a standing position but as he rose he winced as a white-hot needle of pain shot through his leg and he resumed his seat. "My lords and other members of this council," he began in a quiet and pious tone. "I have recently been informed that what I have been told about the lack of a pre-nuptial agreement between my wife and the Duke of Lorraine's son is not true. That information was not correct. Such a document does exist."

He then looked around the table and everyone present looked as shocked as they knew they must. It would not have been wise to do otherwise.

The king continued. "I have called you here to inform you of this new situation and also to tell you that since I have learned about this I have been wrestling with my conscience about what to do. For as you surely must realize, on hearing this, that I, your king and sovereign, am married to a woman who has already been promised; has been betrothed to another. And, as you must realize, this obstacle to my marriage to Queen Anne has given me no peace of mind and no rest. I am sure you all understand what this means, both for me and for the country I serve."

They all nodded. They all understood. The king was looking to them for their support in ending his latest marriage. There was no other way of understanding His Majesty's announcement. Since first hearing that their king was not happy with his fourth wife, they all knew it was merely a matter of time before they would be summoned to help him rid himself of the lady. It was only a question of how and when.

Wincing again and leaning heavily on the table, Henry stood up and faced his council. "I will leave you now and await your careful response." He then took his silver-topped stick and walked slowly and painfully out of the council chamber.

The expected answer did not take long in coming. By the early afternoon his Council told him they understood his problem and fully sympathized with their ruler's unenviable situation.

A few days after this council meeting Cromwell sought out a meeting with Thomas Wriothesley, the Earl of Southampton, one of the king's closest advisors. He was feeling desperate and was looking for help from wherever he could find it.

"My lord," Cromwell said, slightly bowing. "May I speak honestly and openly with you for I am feeling sorely troubled about His Majesty's marriage."

"You're not the only one," the earl replied, "but probably not as troubled as His Majesty himself."

"Of that I am in no doubt, but since I was responsible for His Majesty's involvement with this woman, I'm now charged with getting him out of this marriage."

The earl said nothing but indicated that Cromwell should continue.

"The king does not like the queen. This we all know. In fact, he has never liked her since he first set eyes on her a few months ago. I also believe she's still as much a maid as she was when she first came to England."

"Yes, sir, I've also heard this. This news is not new," the earl commented as he took a sweetmeat without offering one to Cromwell. "So what do you plan to do about this situation?"

"I'm not sure yet. I was hoping that you might have an idea."

"I don't and as far as I'm concerned this is your problem. All I know is this: the rest of the Council and I are expecting you to find a solution very quickly because we were not for this marriage and we do not wish to be tainted with it now. Is that understood?"

Cromwell nodded, bowed and left the room. He could see quite clearly that the earl and the other Council members could not be counted for support. He would have to find the solution on his own.

The May Day celebrations came and went. The king and his wife stood there together, waved and smiled, and an outsider would naturally have assumed that all was well. Of course this was not so. May turned into June and a solution had not been found. The king continued to smile and to appear kind and loving to his wife but in the privacy of his chamber he continued to berate his Earl of Essex for not succeeding in finding a way to bring this marriage to an end.

Ten days into June found Queen Anne, despite the grey skies and threat of rain, walking in the palace gardens with the Earl of Rutland and his wife. Just as they were about to change the subject of their conversation from discussing the queen's new wardrobe to what else she could do to please her husband, a messenger appeared. He was wearing the Duke of Norfolk's colours and it was clear that he had rushed over to the garden with his news. Quickly bowing, he stopped to catch his breath.

"Slowly, lad," the earl said. "Surely your message cannot be that important. We're not at war with France or Spain, are we?"

"No, my lord," he panted. "It's about the chancellor, er, the Earl of Essex."

"You mean, Master Cromwell?"

"Yes, my lord."

"So tell us, what happened to the Earl of Essex," Lady Rutland said, forgetting herself and pushing herself in front of the queen. "Is he dead?"

"No, milady. But he will be soon."

"Why? What do you mean?"

"Well, you know milady, that when the wind blows a gentleman's hat off, any other gentleman who is nearby, doffs his own hat as a sign of respect?"

"Yes. Please continue."

"Well, my lord," the messenger said, now facing the earl. "When the wind blew the chancellor's hat off this morning, none of the other gentlemen present did so. He looked around and said that it must have been a strange wind to blow his hat off and yet leave all their own hats on."

"And then what happened? Did the other gentlemen then doff their hats?"

"No, milady. They just ignored him and went into dinner."

"Strange," the earl remarked. "But not necessarily deadly."

"Ah, but I'm not sure of that, my lord," the messenger said. "For during the meal no-one spoke to the Earl of Essex, not even about affairs of state. I was standing at the side watching and it was as if he were not there at all. They ignored him completely. I tell you, my lord, I've never seen anything like it before."

"And did they kill him afterwards?" the queen asked, not used to English customs and politics.

"Oh, no, Your Majesty," the messenger bowed. "After the meal was over they all walked over to the council chamber to deal with the affairs of state."

"Including the chancellor?"

"No, my lord. He waited outside as usual in order to receive some of the day's petitioners."

"And did any of them stab him, or do anything like that?"

"Oh, no, milady. Nothing like that happened. No, I think what happened may have been even worse than that."

"*Warum? Was ist passiert?* Er, what happened?" the queen asked, momentarily forgetting her English.

The duke's messenger bowed again. "The chancellor then entered the council chamber but when he did so, none of the lords stood up. They merely looked at him and remained seated."

"Is that very strange?" Anne asked the earl.

"Yes, Your Majesty. The newly promoted Earl of Essex is the most important member of the Council and by tradition all the other members stand up when he enters or leaves." He then turned to face the messenger and asked, "And so what happened next?"

"The earl remained very calm, my lord, and just said that the lords must have been in a great hurry to take their places and he began to walk over to his seat at the top end of the table. But he never got there."

"Why not?"

"Because the Duke of Norfolk, my master, called out, 'Cromwell, do not sit there! That is no place for you! Traitors do not sit among gentlemen.'"

Rutland looked straight at the messenger's face and then holding a thin finger under the young man's chin, demanded, "This is not gossip? Are you sure that this is what he said? Now tell me true, for I know your master cannot abide the Earl of Essex."

"Yes, yes, my lord, every word I'm telling you is Bible true. You know I would not lie to you."

The earl ignored this last comment and told the young man to complete his report.

"Well, after this, my lord, Cromwell, I mean the Earl of Essex faced my master and told him he was no traitor. He was about to say something else when Sir Anthony Wingfield, the Captain of the Guard, walked into the chamber with six of his men and arrested him."

"Didn't anyone do or say anything?" Lady Rutland asked.

"Yes, milady. The earl asked on what grounds he was being arrested and Sir Anthony laughed and said that he'd learn that somewhere else. Then the chancellor protested that he demanded to see the king but either Sir Anthony or the Duke of Norfolk, one of them, I cannot remember exactly who, replied that this was not an appropriate time and that he must accompany them to the Tower."

"Cromwell? To the Tower? Oh, how are the mighty fallen," the Earl of Rutland said half-aloud. "And was he indeed taken to the Tower?"

"Yes, my lord, but not before he had torn his hat off and hurled it to the floor. I'm telling you, the minister acted like a fox surrounded by the hounds. When he saw that there was no-one there who'd support him, he cried out, 'This, then, is the reward for all my services?' Nobody said anything and so he called out to anyone who'd listen, 'On your consciences, I ask you, am I a traitor?' And then all pandemonium broke out, my lord, there in the Council chamber."

"What happened?" the queen asked. She had understood most of this report and now wanted to know more about this powerful man who had arranged her wedding. "Did they kill him then?"

"Oh, no, Your Majesty," the messenger answered. "We

don't do things like that in this country. Some of the councillors shouted that the earl was a traitor and others started shouting all sorts of things and beating the table with their fists. I'm telling you, I've never witnessed a scene or heard such a noise in a Council meeting. Then the noise died down a little and one of the councillors, I don't know who it was, cried out from the back of the chamber, 'Let him be judged by the bloody laws he has made. Under them many an innocent word has become treason.'"

"And did they take him out after that?"

"Yes, Your Majesty, but not before he had pulled his hands away from the guards and pointed to all of the members present. Then he said that he had never wished to offend anyone there, but if they were to treat him like this, he renounced all his claims to pardon. He also said that he hoped the king wouldn't let him languish for a long time in prison."

No-one said anything for a moment. They were all thinking how suddenly the king's most powerful minister had been laid so low. And so suddenly.

"And what happened after that?" Lady Rutland asked, fearing what she would be told but still wanting to hear more.

"As Sir Anthony and his men turned to escort the earl out of the chamber, the Duke of Norfolk stepped forward. 'Stop!' he shouted to the captain. 'Traitors must not wear the Order of the Garter,' and he ripped the order off from the earl's his neck and one or two of the other members, including the Earl of Southampton, ripped the other insignia off from the earl's gown as well. I am telling you, my lord, in the end I must admit I was feeling quite sorry for Cromwell. I don't like him, but it must have been most humiliating to be attacked like that and especially by those who were supposed to be under his authority. And, if I may say so, sir, the chancellor had once thought that the Earl of Southampton was his friend."

"And then what happened?"

"They took him to the Tower, Your Majesty."

"Tell me, young man, before you go, how did the other members of the Council act? Were they *all* against the Minister, or did some of them step forward to protest?"

"Oh, no, my lord. No-one came forward to protest. Most of them cheered and some of them shouted, 'Revenge' and things like that. A few clapped and cheered but, as I said, no-one supported him. And after Sir Anthony had taken him out of the chamber, many of the members came over to my master and clapped him on the back or shook his hand. Especially the Catholic lords. 'Well done!' they kept saying to the duke. They said he'd done a good job and they were very happy he'd dared to stand up to the king's chancellor."

"Well, I'm not really surprised," said Rutland. "To me it smacks of Catholic revenge, especially after what he'd done to their abbeys and monasteries a few years ago."

"And what'll happen to him now?" the queen asked, looking at her chamberlain. "How long will he be in your *Gefängnis*, er, your prison?"

"I cannot tell you that, Your Majesty. That'll be for the king and perhaps my master, the duke to decide. But I can tell you this. After Cromwell was taken out of the chamber through the back door, some of the members were calling for a Bill of Attainder to be drawn up against him."

"What is this Bill of Attainder?" Anne asked, stumbling over this new legal term.

"Your Majesty," Rutland explained. "It's a bill, a law passed in parliament against an accused man. If he's found guilty, then he can lose his titles, his property and even his life."

"So that means the parliament can kill him?"

"That's right, Your Majesty, but the king has to give the final order; to sign the death warrant."

Anne was silent. She never remembered her father or her brother doing such a thing. She knew that they had sent robbers and other criminals to be locked up, but they had never ordered anyone to be killed.

As they were standing there, the messenger started fidgeting. "Excuse me, my lord, may I go now? I've delivered my message and now I must return to the duke."

"Yes, you may go, but take a word of advice from me. In future, do not express your opinion to anyone who you don't know well. That's a way of making enemies in the future."

It was clear that the messenger did not understand. "What do you mean, my lord?"

"Do not say whether you like someone as a lord or not, like you said about Cromwell. It's not always a good idea, especially in these times."

"Yes, my lord, I'll remember that." And so saying, he turned and quickly left the garden to report back to the now exultant Duke of Norfolk.

"May we sit down on that bench over there?" Lady Rutland asked, looking at the queen. "That news has quite shocked me and I must sit down for a few minutes."

"*Ja, ja,*" Anne said and they all moved over to sit on the bench in the sun.

"What will happen to him now?" the queen asked. "How long will he be in the Tower?"

"I cannot tell you that, Your Majesty. It all depends on your husband and parliament. He could be there for a very short time or he could rot there for years. There are no laws about this."

Again Anne was silent and then asked, "But what has he done to make the king and the Duke of Norfolk so angry? After all, he was the king's chief minister, wasn't he?"

Rutland shrugged. Even though he had a shrewd idea of what lay behind Cromwell's arrest, he was not willing to voice his opinion to the queen. "I don't know exactly, Your Majesty. You will have to ask your husband yourself. But you know, my dear," he said, turning to his wife, "there is a certain irony here. For from what that young messenger said, it was Cromwell himself who brought in this law allowing people to be arrested as he himself was. But leaving that aside, it looks as though he is finished. I wonder who'll take his place now - one person or several? For after all, Cromwell as Chancellor certainly filled many rôles for His Majesty."

"Yes, that's true," Lady Rutland said. "But you know, even though I didn't particularly care for the man - I mean, he was somewhat rough and uncouth and he always used to dress in those dreary black caps and gowns - he did carry out a lot of good work for the king. And I'm sure His Majesty could always count on him for his support. I'm not sure that that could be said for many of his other ministers and advisers."

Rutland nodded slightly in agreement. He did not want to say too much in the presence of the queen. One never knew what she might say to her husband in the privacy of their chamber.

"But tell me, my dear," Lady Rutland said to her husband. "If the Duke of Norfolk arrested the chancellor, he must've known that the king would support him, don't you think?"

"Of course. So what's your question?"

"If the king was planning to send him to the Tower, then why did he recently promote him to be the vice-regent and also give him all those other honours?"

Rutland looked around and saw that the queen had moved away and was busy looking at some flowers behind some of the taller rose bushes. Keeping his voice low and pulling his wife next to him he said, "I think our king likes playing with people. Do you remember how he entertained Robert Aske?"

"The leader of the Pilgrimage of Grace rebellion?"

"Yes, before he imprisoned and executed him? Then that's what I think he's doing to Cromwell. Raising him up and then cutting him down, but hush now, not another word. Her Majesty is coming back."

A minute after the queen had rejoined them she suddenly sneezed and pulled her shawl more closely around her shoulders. "I'm feeling rather cold. I'd like to go inside."

Silently, they walked back across the lawn to the palace. All of them were thinking about the sudden turn of events and how it might affect them personally.

Chapter Sixteen - *Annulment*

While an ousted and most apprehensive chancellor was languishing in the Tower, thinking about his probable execution, events were moving very quickly in other parts of London.

At the beginning of June 1540, the king could be seen in his barge on the river being rowed to Lambeth where he would be entertained by Catherine Howard. His daily journeys down the Thames did not go unobserved by his curious subjects.

"Wonder where 'e goes every day, Ned? I tell you, it's about this time every evening 'e passes this spot by London Bridge."

"Don't you know, Tom? He goes to visit that Howard girl at Lambeth Palace."

"Do you mean 'e's doing with this queen what 'e did with his first one?"

"Meaning?"

"Meaning 'e sent Catherine of Aragon away so's 'e could be with Anne Boleyn."

"That's right, Tom. Except that this time it's not Catherine of Aragon, but Catherine Howard."

"Catherine Howard? But she's only fifteen years old, or so they say."

"So what? You know our king likes 'em young. Our present queen was half his age when he married her back in January."

"Yes, I know that, Ned, but my wife told me that 'e was going to Lambeth so's 'e could pay 'is respects to the Dowager Duchess of Norfolk."

"Oh, Tom, you and your wife are really green. If you believe that, you'll believe anything. No, my friend, our king has already had enough of his present wife and is looking for elsewhere to sow his oats."

"So those rumours are true what I 'eard, y'know, about the king not sleeping with 'is wife?"

"Of course they're true. But come on, Tom. Let's be off to

the 'Dog and Duck.' Standing 'ere and gossiping 'as made me quite thirsty."

Another person who was thirsty that evening was the queen herself. Not for a bottle of cheap ale, but for information. A few miles up the river at Richmond, she was trying very hard to understand the new situation in which she had found herself.

"Lady Browne," asked Anne, pacing up and down clasping and unclasping her hands . "I don't understand why we had to leave the king's palace at Hampton Court and move to Richmond? this one. He told me when I asked him that it was because of the plague but I find that very hard to believe. There isn't any plague in London, is there?"

"No, Your Majesty," Lady Browne shrugged and looked to Lady Rutland and Lady Edgecombe for a satisfactory answer, but they both just shrugged and looked away.

"And," Anne continued, biting into an apple. "If there is a plague in London, why is my husband still there? Everyone knows that he's scared of the plague. Look how he protects young Edward. One of my servants told me yesterday that once His Majesty even moved to Windsor when there were only a few vague rumours of the plague. *Ach so*, I don't understand that man or what he's doing, at all. Do you?"

"No, Your Majesty," lied Lady Rutland, "All I know is that you and your household have been moved here to Richmond and…"

"Is it because of Catherine Howard?" asked Anne, to the surprise and discomfort of her three ladies.

This was the last question they wanted to hear. They knew the answer, but how do you tell a newly-married queen, a lady whom they had learned to love and respect over the past few months, that her husband had already cast her aside in favour of a younger and more vivacious woman? They had even heard their royal master referring to Catherine Howard as 'a rose without a thorn.'

"Your Majesty," Lady Edgecombe said, laying a hand on the queen's shoulder. "Sometimes men feel the need to be separated from their wives for a while and that may be the reason we've seen sent here to Richmond. I wouldn't be surprised if we're all called back in a week or two."

"Lady Edgecombe is right, Your Majesty. I don't know if you have this saying in Cleves but here in England we say, 'Absence makes the heart grow fonder.'"

"Ja, back home in Cleves we say *Durch die ferne wächst die Liebe*. Not being there makes your heart want more."

Lady Browne smiled at Anne. "That's right, Your Majesty. I know that when my husband has had to go away on various missions for the king, and sometimes for well over a month at a time, when he comes back, he is much more loving than before he left." And her eyes sparkled as she remembered the last time, just a week earlier when they had spent nearly three whole days in bed making up for lost time. Oh, the passion of it all! Oh, the fun and the heat! It had been almost worth not having him around for three weeks. And now he was so gentle and considerate. Maybe, she thought mischievously for a second, I should ask His Majesty to send him away on another mission. Not for too long, just for two or three weeks.

Lady Browne's delicious thoughts were suddenly shattered as she became aware of the queen speaking German.

"*Aus den Augen, aus dem Sinn*."

"Pardon me, Your Majesty, did you say something?"

"Yes, Lady Browne. In Cleves we also say, 'Not in the eyes, not in the brain'."

"Ah, you mean, 'Out of sight, out of mind.' Yes, we say that here, too. But I'm sure that is not what His Majesty is thinking of. No, he probably wants some peace and quiet, that is, without us ladies about, to plan what he wants to do about the questions of religion and..."

"What to do about France and Spain," Lady Edgecombe added. "So yes, Your Majesty, I wouldn't be too worried that we've been sent here to Richmond. And besides, this palace is very comfortable and the gardens here are so pretty."

Anne cocked her head to one side and considered what her ladies had just told her. Then she said, "That's all true, ladies, but remember, you've all been married for several years, I've been married only since January, just five months. Not even half of a year."

"That's true," Lady Rutland replied quickly. "But remember, just as we women are all different, the same may be said of our menfolk. They are all different, too."

Anne did not look convinced and started pacing up and down again. "But are you sure the king hasn't sent us here because he wants to get rid of me? I know he's not pleased with me in bed and now maybe he wants to do with me what he did to his first wives: chop of their heads or just send me away. I tell you, I don't know what is happening, truly I don't." And she began to dab at her eyes with a handkerchief as the tears began to flow down her cheeks.

Lady Browne was the first to react. She walked quickly over to the queen and held her face gently in her hands. "Please, Your Majesty, please don't cry. I'm sure the king will come to visit you here soon or call you back to court. He's probably thinking about what he should be doing about the French king or the Holy Roman Emperor and he doesn't want us women about. Come, let's continue with our embroidery."

"Yes, Your Majesty," added Lady Rutland, . "Please show us how you sew those little red and yellow flowers and make them look so real."

A few days later, at the end of June, the Earl of Rutland returned to Anne's palace at Richmond to organize the proceedings for His Majesty's forthcoming divorce. He found his queen inspecting the flower beds in the palace grounds. After acknowledging his presence, she handed him a knife and asked him which colour roses he preferred: the red or the pink.

"The red ones, Your Majesty. They are of a much more positive shade."

"Oh, my lord, there I must disagree with you," she smiled. "I find the pink ones are so much more gentle and suitable for a queen's palace. So please, can you cut me off a few, but please be careful of the thorns. Thank you. But I'm sure you have not ridden over from London just to answer my questions about the colour of flowers in the garden."

"That's true, Your Majesty," smiled Rutland. . "I've come

here to tell you that His Majesty would like you to know that he would do everything that should be seen as right according to the law of God."

"Excuse me, my lord," asked Anne, looking puzzled. "But what does it mean 'according to the law of God'? What is he going to do?"

"It means, Your Majesty, that to use your husband's words, he must discharge his conscience and yours in order to maintain the peace of the realm."

"And does this mean that he wishes to use my past betrothal to the Duke of Lorraine's son as a reason to divorce me?"

Rutland made a small bow. "Yes, Your Majesty. That's what the king told me yesterday. He said that he has reached this decision in order to keep his lords and the whole country content."

Anne smiled cynically. She realized now that her husband would use any excuse to divorce her. Perhaps this one would be the safest one for her, especially as it did not hint at any treasonous action. She knew that the official reasons for Anne Boleyn's execution included treason, incest and adultery. Anne realized that she could not be charged with these last two crimes, but she did not want His Majesty to have any excuse for invoking a charge of treason.

"Tell me," she said a few moments later. "What will happen now? It's clear that my husband really wants to get rid of me at any price but what'll happen to me? Will I have to leave this palace, to leave England and return to Cleves?"

Rutland looked uncomfortable. He could not answer that question. "I'm sorry, Your Majesty, I have no idea. All I know is that the king is going to meet with his advisor tomorrow in order to discuss this matter. Please believe me, Your Majesty, that when I say I do not know what will be the result of this meeting and that is the Lord's truth. All I know is that your husband wants this divorce to be carried out as quickly and as quietly as possible."

"I'm sure of that," Anne nodded and then added, "Because of Catherine Howard?"

Rutland started fidgeting. He had not known how much his

queen had known of her husband's flirting with the Duke of Norfolk's niece. He coughed apologetically. "Er, that was not mentioned, Your Majesty. All I was told was that you and the king were no longer living as man and wife and therefore it would be best for both of you if this divorce were carried out as speedily as possible."

"*Ach so*," Anne said. "And so he'll get his advisors to agree to this?"

"Yes, Your Majesty. And now, if you'll excuse me, I must leave now if I'm to catch the tide back to Greenwich." Rutland then looked around cautiously to check that he was not being overheard before continuing. "But please let me say, Your Majesty, I must say I'm truly sorry about what has happened. To have come here from a foreign country and to learn our ways and then to be divorced, this is truly a... a very sad and unfortunate situation."

"Thank you, my lord. That is very kind of you." And this time it was Anne's turn to make a small bow. "I must tell you that the support I have received from you and your dear wife these past few weeks has been most appreciated. Please tell her that."

Rutland nodded and turned to leave when Anne said, "Before you go, my lord, please remember to keep me informed about the king's plans. Sometimes I feel so cut off here in Richmond when all sorts of things are happening behind my back. As it is, it's very hard hearing all these reports, especially when they are not in my own language. Sometimes, you know, one of my German ladies has to translate them for me."

"I'm sure that's true, Your Majesty, but please permit me to say that your English has really improved in the time you've spent here in England. You're now speaking it most fluently."

Anne blushed. She was not used to receiving compliments from English noblemen. "It's most kind of you to say so, my lord. But you should go now or you'll miss your boat. I just hope to see you or one of your messengers soon."

The earl bowed and hurried away leaving the queen wondering what the results of the forthcoming divorce would be. Where will I be this time next year? she thought. Will I be still be in England and, if so, where? In London? In Richmond? Or will the king send me away with hardly any money to a distant castle such as Kimbolton as he did with his first wife? But then, I may not be in this country at all. I might be back in Cleves with my family. Do I want that? No, I'm not sure I do any more. Life there was so quiet, even boring. Here I have my ladies, fine clothes and entertainment. And what will my rank be? If I am not the queen, what will I be? A duchess? A marchioness? What? But whatever I do and whatever happens to me, I will do anything I have to in order to stop myself being pushed aside and abandoned in a country house or castle with no money or support.

The next day went as the king had planned. The lords were assembled and presented a petition to the king asking him to have the legality of his marriage to Lady Anne of Cleves investigated. On receiving His Majesty's permission, this would be carried out by a clerical and legal convocation of twelve clergymen and lawyers. Included among the charges they were to look into would be the question of examining the queen to see if she had any chance of bearing children, especially a son.

Under the king's orders, the convocation's experts produced a solution to his problem within three days.

"Your Majesty," their spokesman said, rising from his chair and facing the king at the next Council meeting. "After much thought and deliberation, we have indeed arrived at a solution to your problem," he began pompously, aware that all eyes were upon him, "and this is our conclusion. If the son of the Duke of Lorraine had stood by his alleged prenuptial contract and we have not found or received any evidence of this contract being annulled, then your marriage to the Lady Anne of Cleves earlier this year is null and void."

Hearing this, His Majesty smiled and indicated that the red-gowned spokesman should continue. He did.

"If, however, Your Majesty is married to the queen in name only, then the Church, the holy institution that we all believe in and which guides our thoughts and actions throughout our lives, has the power to annul this union, especially if, as claimed by Your Majesty, you were espoused against your will."

Henry smiled again. He was hearing what he had intended to hear. Sitting higher in his chair, he thanked the spokesman for 'his kind words and learned opinion' and continued. "Members of this Council, please believe me when I say that I have no other aim but for the glory of God, the welfare of my realm and the triumph of truth." As he said this, he knew that the European political situation had changed in the past six months. He knew that owing to the current political situation on the continent, Charles the Fifth, the Holy Roman Emperor would not argue with him. He also knew that the queen's brother in Cleves would not be able to count on the Emperor's support if he decided to declare war on England in order to defend the honour of his sister and his country.

So while the king's divorce was being discussed by his loyal clergymen, his House of Lords had come to a similar conclusion.

"Your Majesty," they informed him later that morning. "We have agreed to the dissolution of your marriage to the queen, and we base our answer on three very sound reasons," their spokesman declared. "The first one is based on your wife's probable prenuptial contract to the son of the Duke of Lorraine. The second concerns your clear lack of consent to this marriage and lastly, the state of non-consummation of this marriage renders the whole situation completely null and void."

An hour after hearing this Henry summoned his closest advisors to meet him in the chamber where until recently he had held so many meetings and private conversations with Chancellor Cromwell. After they had sat down around the oval table, the king opened the meeting.

Trying not to smile too broadly, Henry began. "My lords, we now have a solution to my marital problems, a solution which also carries the blessings of our holy Church and which allows me to divorce my wife, the queen. The question before us now is this: what shall be done with her? Shall she be permitted to remain here in London or in Richmond or shall we send her off to a distant part of the country, say to Cambridge or even Lincoln, so that she will not be able to have any influence over what happens here in London? However, if you think that these suggestions are not acceptable, then would it be a good idea if we dispatched her back to her home in Cleves where her brother, the duke, will be able to do whatever he wishes to with her? There she will be with her own family and they will be responsible for her. She may even find herself a husband there and if so, may I be permitted to add, that if that does happen, she will have to improve her bedtime behaviour."

This last remark was followed by a round of laughter and smiles before the king raised his hand showing that he had not yet completed his speech.

"If, indeed, she is either sent home or remains here within the boundaries of our realm, we must be sure that her brother, the duke, will not cause us any problems knowing that he will receive no support from the Holy Roman Emperor. This is excellent as we do not wish to waste any of our country's money on a foolish war; a war fought for the honour of a woman. If you remember your Classics, my lords, when the ancient Greeks fought for the honour of Helen of Troy, then the results were most unsatisfactory, especially for the Trojans. So therefore, my lords, what are your suggestions on how to conclude this sad affair?"

Since the king's advisors had already discussed the situation before the meeting, it did not take them long to reach their discussion. Three hours later, the Earl of Rutland found himself facing a nervous queen telling her about the Council's decision.

"Your Majesty," he started after assuring her that she would not be imprisoned or executed. "This is what has been decided. We hope you will agree to the terms of this settlement because both His Majesty and the lords think that they are very generous and beneficent."

"Beneficent? For whom?"

Rutland smiled. "For you both, Your Majesty. Both for you and His Majesty."

Anne did not look convinced but indicated that her chamberlain should continue with his report.

"First of all, Your Majesty, you will be granted four thousand pounds…"

"Is that all?"

"Yes, Your Majesty, not four thousand pounds in total but four thousand pounds *per year*. In addition, you'll be given the manor here at Richmond and also another at Bletchingley."

"Excuse me, my lord, but where is this Bletchingley?" Anne asked, thinking of how Catherine of Aragon had been sent far away from court.

"It's a manor in Surrey, Your Majesty, not too many miles away from here."

"And is it a nice place or is it an old castle?"

"I've never been there, Your Majesty, but I was told that it's a pleasant place and fit for one of your rank. Do you wish to know anything else?"

"So that is what I am to receive: two manors and four thousand pounds a year?"

"Oh, no, Your Majesty, there is much more." He pulled out a piece of paper from his pouch and, after scanning it, told the queen that the king had also decided to grant her Hever Castle.

"Hever Castle? Wasn't that the castle owned by the king's second wife's family, the Boleyns?"

"Yes, Your Majesty, but when her father died a few years ago it became the property of the king. Now he wishes to give it to you."

Anne considered what Rutland had told her. Three pieces of property and a very good annual allowance. It was certainly more than what she had thought she would receive. And not only that, but the manors and castle were not too far away from London. Maybe in time she would be allowed to visit the court and the capital city. She looked at Rutland.

"Ah yes, I nearly forgot to tell you," he continued. "The manors in question are very profitable and each one makes over five hundred pounds per year. This, His Majesty has decided is money that will remain in your hands. His Majesty neither wants nor needs it."

"Please tell His Majesty that he has been very generous with me. Be sure to tell him that I appreciate this."

Rutland bowed. "I most certainly will. I'm sure he'll be very pleased to hear that. And His Majesty said that you may also keep your two favourite ladies from Cleves here in England: mistresses, Gertrude and Katherine."

Anne clapped her hands and her face lit up. "Oh, I am happy. I was thinking that I would have to send them back home and I know they would not like that. They love serving me and they have grown to like the English ways, especially Katherine. She really loves her new style of clothes, you know, the gowns and the French headdresses. She's like me. Gertrude is not so keen on them but she enjoys living here and is working hard to improve her English. Oh, that *is* good news, my lord."

"There is still a little more, Your Majesty."

"More?"

"Yes, Your Majesty. The king also told me to inform you that you may also keep your personal cook, Schoulenburg, the one you brought over from Cleves with you."

Anne clapped her hands again with joy and her eyes sparkled. "Oh, good, then she won't have to teach Gertrude how to make those *kleine Kuchen* and *Gebäck,* those little cakes and pastries that His Majesty and I love so much. Hmm, I'll even be able to send some over to him in the future,"

"Certainly, Your Majesty. But before I go, there is one last thing I was told to tell you."

What? More? Anne thought. What more could the king give her? He had given her money and property, allowed her to keep her three favourite servants, what more could there be? Ah, but perhaps she would receive all of this only on condition that she fulfilled certain conditions that her chamberlain was about to tell her.

"Yes, my lord," she asked quietly. "What else does His Majesty want?"

Rutland bowed. "It's very simple, Your Majesty. From now on the king has declared that if you agree to the above conditions, you will officially be known as the King's Sister."

Anne knitted her brows. She had never heard of this title. She knew that His Majesty had two sisters who were alive, but what was the meaning of this new title, The King's Sister – *Die Schwester der Königen*?

She turned to face the earl. "My lord, "I've never heard of this title before. I know that His Majesty has two sisters. There is the older one is, Margaret, who was married to King James the Fifth of Scotland and who is now married to Lord Methven, and there is his younger sister, Mary, who was married to King Louis the Twelfth of France and is now married to the king's brother-in-law, the Duke of Suffolk. So how can I become the king's sister? What does this mean?"

"This is an honorary title, Your Majesty. As the King's Sister, you will have precedence over all the other ladies at court, that is, apart from a new queen, if His Majesty decides to marry again and of course, as well as the two princesses, Mary and Elizabeth. And the king instructed me that I must tell you that there will always be a place reserved for you at court."

Anne was silent as she absorbed this new information. Things were getting better and better, far better in fact than she had ever imagined. And just as she was thinking about this, she heard the earl give a quiet cough.

"Excuse me, Your Majesty, I have some more good news for you."

"More?"

"Yes, Your Majesty. The settlement that I've just told you about will also allow you to keep all of your furnishings and your plate."

Anne felt she had to sit down. Her head was swimming with all this unexpected news. She could hardly believe what Rutland was telling her, and just as she was trying to absorb all this she heard her chamberlain tapping quietly on the table to gain her attention. She looked up.

"And there is even more, Your Majesty. The king said that since he does not wish to see you come to court in future poorly dressed and looking like a beggar, he and the Council have decided that you may keep all of your gowns, pearls and other jewels."

Anne could hardly believe her ears. Not only was she not about to be cast out from court, poor and isolated, but now she would have more personal wealth, property and jewellery than she had ever owned in her life. And not only that, but she would be allowed to stay in England, keep her servants, be permitted to come to court and also be known as the King's Sister. Just as she was thinking of how her life had changed, she heard her chamberlain's gentle voice again.

"And, Your Majesty, if I may play with words, to crown it all, His Majesty in his generosity has asked me to give you this gift of five hundred marks." And saying this, he took a leather pouch from his satchel and bowing down, he handed it over to the newly-created King's Sister.

"My lord," Anne said at length. "You and His Majesty have been most kind and generous to me. Please give me a day to consider all that you have told me and discuss it with my ladies. Please remember, this document is in a foreign language for me and so I'll have to read it very carefully and have it translated by one of my ladies from Cleves. After that, if everything is as you say it is, I'll give you my answer tomorrow. Is that acceptable?"

Rutland bowed and saying he would forward the queen's message to the king, he left for Greenwich. He sensed that the queen would agree to the terms of the settlement and that the king's second divorce would proceed much faster and more smoothly than the previous one – the infamous 'king's matter' concerning Anne Boleyn – which had caused a storm throughout the kingdom some thirteen years earlier.

Chapter Seventeen - The Annulment Finalised

Anne was as good as her word. Later that day after consulting her ladies and using them to help her with her English, she informed the king that she formally acknowledged the dissolution of her marriage. After writing that she had put her faith in God and loved and trusted the king, she added:

So now being ascertained how the same clergy have given their judgement and
sentence, I acknowledge hereby to accept and approve the same wholly and
entirely putting myself , for my state and condition , to your highness' goodness and pleasure; most humbly beseeching Your Majesty that, though it be determined the pretended matrimony between us is void and is of none effect, whereby I neither can nor will repute myself your Grace's wife.

She finished off saying, that she was still his humble servant and thanked His Majesty for taking her to be his sister. She signed it, 'Your Majesty's humble sister and servant, Anne, the daughter of Cleves' as a way of confirming her new status at court.

As fast as the king's couriers could ride and as fast as his oarsmen could row the royal barge eastward along the Thames, Anne's letter of confirmation arrived at Greenwich in record time.

The speedy reply and positive tone of Anne's letter surprised the king. Does she wish to divorce *me*, Henry the Eighth, the King of England, so quickly? he thought after he had read it. And for a moment, his inflated ego and the image of himself as the handsome and powerful ruler was seriously punctured. But just then, a sharp stab of pain from his infected leg reminded him of his age and infirmity. But then, he thought, I now have the pretty Catherine Howard. She is far more enticing than Lady Anne. However, despite his thoughts about his latest mistress, Henry began his reply to Anne's letter, 'Right dear and right entirely beloved sister'

We take your wise and honourable proceedings therein in most thankful part,
as it is done in respect of God and His trust, and, continuing your conformity,
you shall find in us a perfect friend, content to repute you as our dearest
sister.

He then confirmed the conditions of the agreement and that his parliament would also agree with all the details concerning the divorce.

After receiving this, Anne felt that it would be her duty, and in her best interests, to write to her brother in Cleves explaining to him what had happened to her over the past three months.

"But how shall I tell him?" she asked Lady Rutland. "The last time he saw me was about eight months ago when I left Cleves to become the Queen of England. Now I'll have to tell him that my marriage has been annulled but that I wish to remain here in England. If I don't, I won't be able to receive the manors in Richmond, Bletchingly and Hever."

Nevertheless and again helped by her ladies, she wrote to her brother, addressing him as 'My dear and well-beloved brother' before telling him about 'the matter of marriage between His Majesty and me.' She told him about the divorce and then informed him 'that my body remaineth in the integrity which I brought it into this realm' and that His Majesty was to 'adopt me for his sister.'

After penning the above, Anne returned her wedding ring to the king. "Please give this to His Majesty," she instructed the king's messenger. "I believe it is to be broken up as a ring as it means nothing and now has no value."

That evening as she was sitting in the palace gardens in

Richmond discussing her affairs with her ladies, Sir Anthony Brown appeared. He made his way over the lawn to the small group of ladies and bowed to Anne.

Anne smiled. "Sir Anthony, there is no need to bow down in front of me any longer. I am no longer your queen."

"I know that, Your Maj... er, milady, but you are the king's sister."

"Very true. I must get used to my new title and position. I must say, it is very strange that - within less than one year - I've been the sister to the Duke of Cleves, the Queen of England and now I am a sister to the King of England." She smiled to herself for a moment and then asked Sir Anthony why he had come to see her.

"I've come to tell you that today your marriage to the king was formally annulled by a special Act of Parliament and that the king's Privy Council petitioned His Majesty to remarry."

"To Catherine Howard?"

Sir Anthony said nothing. Instead he pulled a small piece of parchment out of his pouch. "Milady," he began, and then stopped. "Allow me to read you the words that are written here. Here, the Privy Council petitioned His Majesty to

frame his most noble heart to the love and favour of some noble
personage to be joined with him in lawful matrimony, by whom His
Majesty might have more store of fruit and succession to the comfort
of his realm.

"*Ach so*, but it doesn't say that this woman is to be Catherine Howard, does it?

"No, milady, but I'm sure that that is the king's intention. Isn't that the case?" Lady Browne asked her husband.

Sir Anthony was more diplomatic and was unwilling to commit himself with words. He merely nodded in agreement. The king's infatuation with the young woman was no secret. How could it be when he was known to take the royal barge to her Lambeth home most nights, and that when she was with him in the palace he would allow her to caress him in front of all the court while he stroked her hair, neck and back in return?

Then Sir Anthony faced Anne again. "Milady, there is one more thing you must do in order to complete the annulment. In a few days, Sir Thomas Wriothesley, the Clerk of the Signet, will come here to disband your household. He'll arrange for you to change your servants for new ones who will be approved by the Privy Council."

Anne nodded and asked if she would have to give up all of her servants apart from those she knew about.

"No, milady, only those whose names are written on this list."

Anne was not looking forward to this but realised that she had no choice. Her servants had been good to her but now most of them would have to leave and return to their former service at Greenwich Palace. There, she thought, they'll probably have to serve the king's fifth wife, Mistress Catherine Howard.

Two days later, and aided by the king's advisors Anne, with mixed feelings completed the letter to her brother describing everything that had happened to her. Then a copy of this was made and sent to the suspicious king who thought that maybe his divorced wife had accepted the divorce so quickly because she had a far more devious plan in mind. When Henry read his copy of the letter, he saw that his fears had been completely unfounded and that there would be no international repercussions as a result of the new situation.

That night the king showed his copy of the letter to Sir Thomas Wriothesley.

"Just look at this. Do you realise what it means? It means that I have my divorce and the whole affair took less than one week to complete. Now compare that to the struggle I had with my first wife or with the problems I had with Anne Boleyn. One week with this Anne of Cleves. That's all. No fuss, no feminine tantrums and no blood. And now I'm a free man and can do what I want. Do you understand what that means?"

Both men nodded. They both knew that what His Majesty wanted, His Majesty usually obtained. And in this case it was a young woman called Catherine Howard.

"Here, Sir Thomas, have some of this spiced wine. It's very good. Come on, drink up. We have some exciting times ahead."

The same night while the king was celebrating his luck with Sir Thomas Wriothesley, two other devious men were also sitting down, drinking and discussing the affairs of state or, rather, affairs of the heart. His Majesty's heart. They were Thomas Howard, the Duke of Norfolk, and Stephen Gardiner, the Bishop of Winchester.

"Here, please sit here," the duke said, indicating an intricately carved wooden chair. "I've instructed my servants that we're not to be disturbed for the next two hours, that is, unless war breaks out or the mobs start rioting again."

Gardiner smiled his peculiarly crooked smile. This is how he liked his meetings - with as few people present as possible, and only those who were truly involved in any business that he was trying to bring to fruition.

"And now," Norfolk continued, "may I offer you a glass of this fine Madeira. It is excellent and was first recommended to me by His Majesty last week."

The bishop drew his cassock about him and sat down before leaning towards his host on the other side of the table.

"To His Majesty," he said, raising his glass.

"And to the True Church," Norfolk replied.

"Well, your Grace, it looks as though we've succeeded," Gardiner said, reaching out for a little cake topped with marchpane.

"Succeeded? With what?" the ever-suspicious of Norfolk asked.

"With your niece, of course. Young Catherine. Now the king can have her, can marry her and, in this way, we'll be able to push our plans forward for the Catholic Church."

"Aye, the *Roman* Catholic Church, not the one that His Majesty has devised."

Norfolk smiled in agreement and thought of how he had

190

used his light-headed niece to capture the king's heart. "Do you remember how we invited the king to dinner, here in Southwark in March, and how I arranged for Catherine to dance in front of the king? There he was, sitting next to the queen and I was wondering if he would fall for our Catherine. But when she came in wearing that low-cut gown and then bent down low just in front of him to pick up the kerchief that she had dropped…"

"Accidentally."

"Of course and when I saw the expression on his face, I knew that we'd caught him. You should've seen him. His lips were wet and slobbering and his eyes were almost falling out of their sockets. I'm telling you and I would hate to think what was happening inside his codpiece. He was like a bull in heat. And all of that happening right under the nose of his wife."

"Yes, I remember you telling me that. Those were the exact words you used at the time, *a bull in heat.*"

If the bishop's smile could be described as crooked, then the duke's was even more so. He thought back again to that fateful night. "And do you know what? The king didn't even look at his wife at all when he asked my niece if she'd be so kind as to sit at his feet. It was as though he weren't married to her at all. It looked very clear to me that his wife counted for nothing."

"Oh, I think that's exactly how he was feeling. This divorce which has just been approved was really just a formality. I've been informed that he hadn't lain with her for weeks, months perhaps. More or less since he married her."

Norfolk tried to keep his face straight when he heard this.

"My lord bishop," he said pompously. "I am quite shocked. Such words of gossip coming from a man of the cloth, a bishop, and the Bishop of Winchester, to boot. I thought you men of the cloth were supposed to think celestial thoughts and be above such earthly prattle."

"Come, come, Norfolk. You should know me better than that by now. We've worked together for some time now, haven't we? And besides," he said stuffing another marchpane topped cake into his mouth, "how can I, as a man of the cloth, to use your words, have such lofty thoughts if I do not know what is happening down here on earth? Surely, if all my thoughts were based on the heavenly world, I would have nothing to compare them with, now would I?"

Norfolk nodded and filled his guest's glass with some more Madeira. "Perhaps you are right there," he continued, refilling his own glass. "But I'll leave the world of theology and philosophy to you. I prefer dealing with what's happening down here in my world, the world of the court and politics. And," he added, "by the way, I think we were most fortunate that the plan to use my niece has worked out so well."

"Fortunate? Why?"

"Oh, I see the wine has gone to your muddled head." Norfolk laughed. "So please allow me to unmuddle you. My plan has killed two - perhaps three - birds with one stone and I believe we may even receive the stone back for further use."

"Three birds? Two aren't enough?"

"No, my religious friend. Not in this case. So let me enlighten you. First," he said, holding up his thin index finger, "we now have the opportunity to advance the Roman Catholic Church."

"Two?"

"By enticing the king with my niece, I have become even closer to His Majesty, especially now that Thomas Cromwell has been removed from the Privy Council, probably forever. I'm telling you, we will not have to worry about him trying to further the Lutheran or Protestant cause any longer."

"O, how are the mighty fallen," Gardiner said piously, raising his hands in prayer. "Norfolk, if it were true for Saul and Jonathan, then it is certainly true for Thomas Cromwell."

Norfolk grimaced. "Yes, you are probably right there, and I cannot say that I am very sad about that either."

"And what was the possible third bird you mentioned?"

"Well, according to my spies at court, His Majesty is becoming more and more infatuated with my niece and rumours of marriage have been whispered abroad. If that were to happen, and I don't see why it shouldn't, then we will really have the ear of the king for anything we want - your religious affairs and my more earthly ones." Norfolk rubbed his hands gleefully. "I'm telling you, Stephen, now that the Lady Anne and Cromwell are no longer with us, the world is ours."

"And there's no chance of the Lady Anne having any say in what happens at court?"

"Absolutely none. First of all, she won't be living there. She'll be at Richmond or Bletchingly or somewhere else and also, can you see His Majesty listening to her once he has my Catherine? Remember, he hardly took the Lady Anne into consideration when she was queen. So do you think he will listen to her now that she's well out of the way?"

"But she *is* the 'king's sister,' isn't she?"

"Huh, an empty title, Stephen. Simply devised to keep everyone happy. It's never existed before, I doubt if it'll ever exist again and, in any case, as a title it carries no weight. No, fear not, my friend, Lady Anne of Cleves will not disturb us. She has her money, clothes and title and that's the end of that. Now take one of these sugared fruits. They are quite delicious."

For a few minutes there was silence in that dark oak paneled chamber, a silence gently disturbed as the two men, the duke and the prelate, munched on sugared fruits and drank their Madeira. Then the duke slapped his thigh and smiled.

"I've just been imagining our king and my niece together. He's interested in discussing religious topics, hunting and having a good time and she's interested in clothes, jewellery and having a good time."

"Ah, so there *is* a common field between them."

"Oh, there most certainly is. Having a good time. Although she won't be able to join in his discussions on religion and hunting. I mean, she can just about read and write. He'll keep her happy with clothes and baubles and the like and my light-headed niece will be just the one to keep His Majesty's mind off that disgusting stinking leg of his. She'll be both a real tonic for him and the key to the kingdom for us."

The bishop smiled at the thought and then looked at the Duke. "Norfolk," he said putting his empty glass on the table, "this whole situation, especially with your niece and Cromwell has made me think. Life is like a see-saw."

"How so?"

"It's quite simple really. Until recently, Cromwell was high up, even higher than you in many ways, if I may say, but look where he is now."

"Low down; rotting in the Tower."

"Exactly. And where was your niece?"

"Hidden away at the Dowager's Palace in Lambeth."

"And now where is she going to be? If we have our way, at the top - next to the king. Now do you see why I say life is like a see-saw? It's not only your individual situation, it is also how you are in relation to those who surround you. Don't you agree?"

Norfolk nodded. The bishop was right. So just let me make sure that I remain at the top, he thought. Life at the bottom, that is, in a dungeon in the Tower, is certainly not for me. He gave a slight shudder at the thought and quickly drained the rest of his glass of Madeira.

And as for the Duke of Norfolk's prediction, it came true. In a private ceremony conducted by Bishop Bonner, Henry quickly married his fifth wife but kept it a secret for ten days. He wanted time to enjoy his latest catch without being disturbed by the daily routine at court. Now he could savour his wife for the first time since Queen Jane had become pregnant with Prince Edward in the winter of 1537, over three and a half years earlier.

Chapter Eighteen - The End of Cromwell

Late one afternoon as Anne, Lady Browne and Lady Rutland were sitting in the solarium sewing, there was a knock on the door and Sir Anthony Browne and Lord Rutland entered the solarium. From their dusty boots and dishevelled hair it was clear that they had ridden over to Richmond from London very quickly. After a brief bow to the 'King's sister' the two men quickly kissed their wives and then stood back to face the three women.

"Lady Anne, ladies," Sir Anthony said. "We've just come from court with the latest news."

"Is it about me?" asked Anne immediately, holding her head between her hands.

"No, milady. It's about the king's past chancellor, the Earl of Essex."

"Do you mean, Thomas Cromwell," Lady Rutland asked.

"Yes, my dear. I do."

"What's happened to him?"

"Nothing yet, but the question is, what *is* going to happen to him?"

Lady Rutland looked at her husband and drew her long forefinger across her white throat.

"Yes, my dear. It certainly looks as if he's going to be executed. Parliament passed a Bill of Attainder against him this morning."

"On what grounds?"

"On the grounds, Lady Browne, that as a man whom the king had raised from a 'very base and low degree,' and whom His Majesty had 'enriched with manifold gifts' he is now a traitor and a heretic."

"And that is not all," Sir Anthony added. "He has also been charged with being false and corrupt and of being 'a deceiver and circumventor' of His Majesty's reign. This, to quote the Bill, had been proved by many 'personages of great honour, worship and discretion.'"

The ladies stood there dumbfounded. How had such a mighty man been brought so low and so quickly? It was frightening. Surely, Lady Rutland thought to herself, if this could happen to the all-powerful Thomas Cromwell, Earl of Essex, vice-regent and chancellor, then the same could just as easily happen to her husband or to any other lord who served His Majesty. Easier, in fact, because they had none of the authority that Cromwell had wielded until recently. Suddenly she was aware of Sir Anthony's words cutting into her thoughts.

"And the irony of this is that much of Cromwell's undoing was caused by himself."

"What do you mean, my lord?'

"I mean, milady, that Cromwell when he was chancellor or, as the Bill says, 'of his own authority and office,' had arranged for 'persons apprehended upon suspicion of treason' to be tried and arrested" Sir Anthony explained.

"Yes, and there was also the financial side to his crimes," added Rutland.

"Why, did he take bribes? Was he corrupt?"

"Lady Browne, that is only part of it," Rutland continued. "After making sure that certain devious souls had crossed his grasping palms with silver he granted export licences for the export of money, beans, beer, leather, horses and all manner of goods. And all this was done without His Majesty's knowledge."

Sir Anthony nodded and then added another crime to the already grim and fatal list. "In addition the Bill charged him on the grounds of *scandalum magnatum.*"

"What's that? It sounds like Latin."

"It is, milady. In plain English it means he has been rude and oppressive to the king's nobles."

"And for this you die?" Anne asked, holding her hands to her mouth.

"Yes, milady," Rutland replied. "Especially if the king in question is King Henry the Eighth and you've also angered the Duke of Norfolk and Cardinal Pole, the country's two leading

Catholics."

"That's right," Sir Anthony added. "Cardinal Pole called Cromwell a 'messenger from Satan.' That means that Cromwell won't be expecting any Christian mercy from the cardinal, will he?"

"That's right," Rutland said. "And also when he was chancellor, he had many of Cardinal Pole's family executed or imprisoned."

"And what did Cromwell do when he heard about this Bill of Attainder?" Lady Browne asked.

"He sent a letter to the king from the Tower."

"No doubt he wrote to the king asking for mercy and reminding him of all he'd done for him in the past," Lady Browne remarked.

"Aye," her husband added. "But I don't think he'll be receiving much mercy now. If I remember correctly, His Majesty is not known for changing his mind once he's decided that someone, noble or base born, has acted against him."

"And do you know exactly what he wrote?" Lady Browne asked. "Did you see this letter?"

"Yes, my dear. We saw it at the Council meeting this morning. Cromwell wrote that the king had been most bountiful to him, had acted like a father and that if he, Cromwell, had offended His Majesty, then he had not done so willfully."

"I doubt if that'll help him," Lady Rutland commented and the rest of them nodded their heads. There were a few moments of silence and then, for the first time that morning, they became aware of the light breeze outside, and of the birds chirping in the palace gardens. Now in that light room in the queen's new palace, everyone present thought about what had happened. They all knew that it did not pay to cross the king's path. They also knew that the real reason that Cromwell was now rotting in the Tower was because his arch rival and enemy, the Duke of Norfolk, had exploited his royal master's displeasure over his marriage to Anne of Cleves. However, since the woman in question was now sitting there with them, they could hardly discuss this aspect of the chancellor's fall in her presence.

Then Anne raised her head and looked at the others. "But won't there be a trial? I heard that if anyone breaks the law in this country, then he can have a trial. I remember my brother, the duke, telling me this and about something called Magna Carta." Then she turned to Sir Anthony. "Tell me, sir, didn't anyone say a good word for the chancellor this morning? After all, it was he who brought the king and me together."

"That is true, milady," Sir Anthony replied, looking slightly uncomfortable. "Archbishop Cranmer did try to say something in Cromwell's defence and he even sent a letter to the king."

"Did he read it?"

"Yes and he told us what the archbishop had written. He said that Cromwell had served the king with much wisdom, faithfulness and diligence and if previous kings had had such dutiful servants about them, then they would have been much happier. He also added that the king does not know whom he can trust today and suggested that His Majesty should beware of several other councillors. He didn't mention their names specifically but hinted that such men included the Duke of Norfolk and Stephen Gardiner, the Bishop of Winchester."

"But this is so sad," Anne said. "I doubt if my brother, who is known to be a hard man, would have a man killed just like that. He would probably put him in the dungeons or make him pay a lot of money. No," she added, shaking her head. "He wouldn't cut his head off. Cannot the king do that as well, make Cromwell pay a lot of money instead?"

"I suppose he can, milady, but I doubt whether he will," Rutland said. "From what I know about His Majesty he'll probably spare Cromwell's life as long as he is useful and then he'll have his head cut off."

Rutland's prediction came true. First the king plundered his former chancellor's mansion at Austin Friars and carted away fourteen thousand pounds worth of gold and silver-gilt plate. This he had transferred to the king's jewel house, but only after exploiting Cromwell's knowledge of the law to have his fourth marriage finally dissolved. Then once these acts had been completed Henry signed the warrant for his fallen minister's execution.

The actual execution did not take place until 28 July but in the meanwhile Cromwell wrote several letters to his past master pleading for forgiveness. To the 'most bountiful prince to me that ever was king to his subject and more like a dear father' the king's most important prisoner wrote:

What labours pains and travails I have taken according to my most bounden duty, God also knows, for if it were in my power, as it is God's to make Your Majesty to live ever young and prosperous, God knows I would....If it had been or were in my power to make Your Majesty so puissant as all the world should be compelled to obey you, Christ knows I would.

But none of this helped. On 28 July, Thomas Cromwell, the king's past Earl of Essex and Chancellor of the Exchequer, was led to the straw-covered wooden scaffold. It had been erected on Tower Hill, and there Cromwell addressed his last words to the bloodthirsty hordes who had come to see him die there:

Good people, I am come here to die and not to purge myself as some may think that I will. For if I should do so, I would be a wretch and a miserable man.

And as he started his last appeal to the crowds, Sir Anthony Browne whispered to the Earl of Rutland that even now, the king's past chancellor was not short of words.

"You are right, but listen to what he's saying now. Something about him not being a Lutheran. Listen."

Many have slandered me and reported that I have been a bearer and supporter of those who maintained evil opinions, which is untrue. But I confess that as God, by His Holy Spirit, instructs us in the truth, so the devil is ready to seduce us – and I have been seduced. Bear witness that I die in the Catholic faith of the Holy Church.

"Humph," Rutland grunted. "I doubt if Norfolk or Gardiner will believe that one. They're absolutely sure that he is the devil incarnate."

"You're right, but listen. Is he going to say something about the king and his marriage? For after all, that is what has brought him to this sorry end."

Rutland shrugged and said, "Listen, I think he's finishing his speech off now."

I confess I am justly condemned and I urge you, gentlemen, study to preserve the good you possess and never let pride or greed prevail in you. Serve your king, who is one of the best in the world, and who knows best how to reward his subjects.

"Well, I hope I get a better reward than that," Sir Anthony said, pointing at the block where Cromwell was now laying his head. "I didn't like the man but I hope he doesn't suffer. You know, Rutland, isn't that executioner a little young for the job? He's new, isn't he? He looks as though he's not had much experience."

Unfortunately for Cromwell, Sir Anthony's opinion was borne out by fact. After looking at his executioner, Cromwell raised his eyes for the last time to heaven and said, "Father, into your hands I commend my spirit." Then he took one last look at the crowds before asking the axeman to remove his head with one blow. It was not to be. Gurrea was no expert, and it took three painful chops to remove Cromwell's head which then fell onto the bloody straw below. Of the most important reasons given for the chancellor's untimely demise, the main one was that his royal master had not liked his wife and queen, Anne of Cleves.

Chapter Nineteen - The Rise of Catherine Howard

I am free – free for the first time in over a year not to think about a future marriage or actually being married. Free since my mother first told me that master Holbein was coming over to Cleves to paint my portrait for the King of England. And what a year it's been! So many things have happened. My portrait was painted, I travelled to England, I married the king and then I was divorced. Since then I've spent most of my time living here at Richmond Palace being waited on hand and foot. So now I'm probably the richest unmarried woman in England. I have three large, profitable estates and manors, an annual income of at least four thousand pounds, cupboards full of clothes and shoes, boxes of jewellery as well as ladies-in-waiting, servants and a very good staff to work in my kitchen. Apart from the queen and the two princesses, I am the highest ranking woman in this country – me, Anne of Cleves, a marchioness and most important of all, the King's sister. What an unbelievable situation! I can hardly believe it. From being the sister of a minor Rhineland duke to being a woman in my position, this has all happened within a year and a half!

But I fear there's also been a dark side to all of my good fortune. Yesterday Lady Edgecombe told me that Thomas Cromwell, the old chancellor, was executed at the Tower and that three Lutheran clerics were also burned at the stake. Lady Edgecombe said that they'd been burned in order to prove that Cromwell had supported churchmen who had opposed His Majesty's religious views and so they had to die. I didn't know these men but I did know the king's chancellor quite well.

I know he was the man who had suggested that I should come to England and for that I am now grateful, even though I was not at the time. I also know that most of the court didn't like him; in fact, many people there were frightened of him and his power but, in the end, I saw that his power did him no good. I must admit that I did not like him either. He was a tough and grasping man and would stop at nothing to achieve his ends - which were usually to get what he wanted for the king. But eventually his enemies, probably with the king's blessing, banded together under the Duke of Norfolk, brought him down and had him executed. The excuse they used for this was the failure of my marriage to His Majesty.

Then later in the day I heard that three more clerics were burned at the stake -again because they were connected in some other way to the chancellor. One of them was the chaplain to Catherine of Aragon, the king's first wife. The second was the tutor to her daughter, Princess Mary, and the third was an unknown cleric who had written to the king in defence of Catherine of Aragon's Roman Catholic views many years ago.

When I heard this I thought that His Majesty was a very strange man. Not only did he burn Lutherans, but he also burned Roman Catholics, the men who opposed the Lutheran way of thinking. I think the only reason he did this was because the Roman Catholics also differed from the king's own religion, the new *English* Catholic way of thought, his new Church of England. These last three deaths also showed that His Majesty has a very long and vengeful memory. It has been after all, almost ten years now since he banished his first wife and daughter from court.

Now that I know how full of spite the king can be, I hope I've made the right decision to stay here in England and not return to Cleves. I know that my brother would not be happy to see me again, but at least I wouldn't be executed on my return. I just hope and pray that the king won't change his mind, and take back all that he's given me and then treat me as he treated his first wife. Poor thing, she was forced to live in poverty and banished to a gloomy castle far away from London.

All I know now is that I'll have to be very careful and make sure that I keep the king happy and give him no cause for complaint or suspicion. I know that sometimes in the past he made some terrible decisions, terrible that is, for the people who later suffered because of them. More than once Lady

Rutland and Lady Edgecombe have told me that His Majesty used to boast about how he was at the beginning of his reign some thirty years ago. They told me how he used to be so handsome and active, a dashing ruler with a head of thick auburn hair. He was a man whom all the ladies at court loved to be with, either dancing with him or sitting next to him in the banqueting halls.

Now, not many of them would wish to do so and I fully understand them. Of course I cannot say this to anyone as this would be considered treason, but he is so fat and heavy and his face is so red and ugly. His eyes are like pig's eyes, half-hidden in the folds of flesh on his face and he does smell so. No, not all of him, but when you're near him you can smell the pus that seeps out from the bandages on his legs. Sometimes another woman or I used to tie them up for him in an effort to relieve his pain. But then he would shake his legs and the bandages would work themselves loose and we would all have to pretend we weren't suffering from the noxious smells that had escaped once again.

One woman who seems to be prepared to stay with him these days is young Catherine Howard. She was brought into my household, pushed in might be a better way of saying it, by her uncle, the Duke of Norfolk. At first I thought that she'd been given her position just because she was a very pretty and cheerful young girl who'd make me happy as well. For if you remember, for the first three months after my wedding I wasn't very happy because I didn't understand what His Majesty wanted from me and it was then that Mistress Howard joined my household. Then later, when my English started to improve, I learned that the duke had pushed her into my household so that he could use his niece as an excuse for him to be closer to the king.

I must admit that I think the duke's plan has worked very well. It is very rare today to see His Majesty in court without seeing this young woman next to him. She attends all the banquets, masques and dances and when the king cannot dance because of his painful legs, he tells one of his men to dance with her and then sits there gazing at her just as a proud father would look at his beautiful and clever daughter.

And then when she's not dancing, she and the king always seem to be touching and caressing each other. He loves to stroke her smooth skin and is always running his fat hands over the back of her neck and her shoulders. Once, when he thought no-one was looking, I saw him slip his hand down the front of her bodice and fondle her breasts. She didn't say anything or push his hand away, but just smiled up at him as if she were enjoying this. How she did so, I don't know. But it was only when he saw that one of the ladies-in-waiting was looking at him that he quickly pulled out his hand like a small boy caught trying to steal sugared almonds from his mother's kitchen.

And then, yesterday morning I heard some more news about the king and Mistress Howard. An hour ago when I was in the garden picking some roses, my servant Kathryn came up to me. Even though we used to talk to each other in German she still looked around to see that no-one could overhear us. She told me that she had just arrived from the court where she'd heard from one of the servants that the king had married Catherine Howard.

"Married? *Already?*" I found it hard to believe. "My divorce was finalized only two weeks ago."

"I know that, milady, and they're saying in court that His Majesty married her on the same day that Cromwell was executed, but that it's been kept a secret until now."

"Why? Surely he's allowed to marry whom he likes, isn't he?"

"Yes, milady, but the people at court say he wanted some time to be with her alone, so very few people knew about it. And those who did were sworn to silence."

"And where did this marriage take place?"

"At Oatlands, milady."

I smiled. "That's ironic. His Majesty had that old palace rebuilt for me, but now he's using it for his new wife."

Now it was Kathryn's turn to smile and we continued talking in German. These English are so bad at learning foreign languages. Some of the more cultured ones at court can speak

French and Italian while the scholars know Greek and Latin and perhaps a little biblical Hebrew, but most of the court can speak only English. At times like this I'm very happy that I know German and it's pleased me that the king has allowed me to keep my two Clevean servants. This also means that I will not forget my mother-tongue.

"So is the Duke of Norfolk pleased now? He always used to walk around with such a bitter face, as if he's been forced to swallow a glass of vinegar."

"That's true, milady. But now I haven't seen him smile so much as I have this past week. Some people have remarked on this and said they didn't know whether it was because the king had married his niece or because he'd got rid of Cromwell at last."

"Probably both," I said. "But now, I suppose, Norfolk will be wanting to advance his plans for the Roman Catholics as well."

"I'm sure you're right, milady, for I often see him whispering and talking to the Bishop of Winchester, to Stephen Gardiner. Once, when I was walking along one of the corridors in the palace, I overheard them talking about how they'd start making problems for Archbishop Cranmer."

"Didn't they see you?"

"They probably did, but you know how these lords and bishops tend to ignore us servants - as though we're invisible - unless they want something? They just carried on talking as if I weren't there and I continued on my way."

I couldn't understand why these two men would want to cause problems for the archbishop or how they could even do so unless it was all over the question of religion: Catholic or Reform. Archbishop Cranmer was one of the most powerful men in the country but I had no doubt that they would try at least to limit his power even if they couldn't topple him completely. I knew that the duke and the bishop were two of the most devious men in the kingdom. If Norfolk had succeeded in getting rid of Thomas Cromwell after he'd been in power for almost ten years, I supposed he'd also try and do the same to Archbishop Cranmer. I just wondered when and how it would happen.

In the meanwhile I continued to enjoy my new life at Richmond as the King's Sister. As time passed, this magnificent building became my favourite residence and I loved strolling around its great parks and gardens with my friends and courtiers or eating with them in the huge, lavishly decorated banqueting rooms. Sometimes I would watch my friends play tennis in the special courts and, at other times if the weather was fine, I'd go for a ride on the Thames in my barge. There I would glide along the river, pass the green river banks, dangle my fingers in the water and throw crumbs of food to the swans which always seemed to be there. Now I understood why the courtiers and messengers who came to see me at Richmond usually preferred to come by boat if possible. It was a much more relaxing way of travelling than riding over the bumpy roads in a jolting carriage.

I must admit, however, that after a couple of months at Richmond I found I did miss the court and all its hustle and frenetic activity. And so when at the end of 1540 I received an invitation from the king to come to Hampton Court at the beginning of January, I was very pleased to accept it.

At first, it was a little strange to be back there and I noticed that the courtiers and servants did not quite know how to relate to me. I was neither royalty nor the wife of a lord, a duke or an earl. I was the King's Sister. It was as such that I saw everyone defer to me and this I admit, I found rather pleasing. What did trouble me, however, was the thought of how the new queen would receive me. Our rôles had been reversed. When I had been queen, Catherine had been one of my youngest ladies-in-waiting, but now that she was queen, I had to defer to her, even though I wasn't a lady-in-waiting and was eight years older than her.

Apart from the question of how I'd be received at court after an absence of six months, there was the question of which presents I should take with me for the king. After all, what do you bring to a man who has everything, and if he does not have it, then he can have it whenever he wants? In the end, after much thought I sent him two magnificent horses, each one caparisoned in a rich purple velvet cloth.

Then on 3 January 1541 I presented myself at court. At first there were some problems of protocol: how would the young queen formally receive me? Who was to curtsey first? Were our presents to be exchanged publicly before the whole court or was this to be done privately in her chamber? What did the courtly rules of etiquette demand in connection with my meeting the king? What should I call him and what would he call me? Should I curtsey and or should I give him a sisterly kiss? And if so, where? On his cheek or on his lips?

Before setting off for the palace I heard from one of my servants that Queen Catherine was a trifle nervous about seeing me again, especially as we would both be in our new rôles. Later I found out that she'd had a hurried consultation with Chancellor Audley, the new Earl of Essex who, as Cromwell's successor, was now acting as head of the royal household.

However, despite all our fears, all went ahead very smoothly. I entered the queen's presence and immediately made a low curtsey and wished Her Majesty well. I must say that my past lady-in-waiting also played her part well and asked me to rise immediately and to come and sit next to her. To my joy, she received me most kindly and showed me much favour and courtesy. I then looked around for His Majesty but saw he was not present. I believe he wanted to see how his new queen and I would get along with one another before he appeared. Then once he saw that we were having a pleasant conversation, he made his own entrance and greeted me with all courtesy and friendship.

Perhaps my gift of two horses helped because he immediately greeted me with a low bow and then kissed and embraced me. We three then retired to a private chamber and partook of a most enjoyable supper while, in the background, some beautiful lute, viola and recorder music was being played.

His Majesty was very interested in what I was doing with my life now that I was no longer his wife and he asked me many questions. Then he said he was feeling tired and wished to retire for the night. Before leaving he said that we two women, 'his wife and his past wife' as he phrased it, should remain in the chamber and continue talking and 'gossiping as you women know how best to do.' Then the queen and I returned to the main hall where after dancing with each other, we danced with several gentlemen of the court.

The following day the queen, seeing that she'd got on so well with me presented me with two lap dogs and a beautiful jewelled ring. I thought this was very gracious of her and thanked her most sincerely.

I stayed at the palace for one more day and then returned to Richmond. However, before I left, the king gave me another present, an annual rent of one thousand ducats. This of course made me very happy, not only because of the money, but also because it showed that His Majesty still thought kindly of me and wished me well in my future. Even though our married life had been short and unsuccessful, it was clear that my new title as the King's Sister meant something more than mere words. All in all, I considered that my first visit to see my past husband and his new wife had been a success.

Perhaps one of the reasons for this success was that none of us spoke about politics or religion. Catherine was a member of the powerful Norfolk Roman Catholic clan, while I'd been brought up to be much less staunch in my beliefs and the king's religious beliefs had not yet been clearly defined. Nevertheless, despite our differences, especially between Catherine and myself, when it came to talking about clothes, shoes and jewellery, we found we had lots to talk about. And of course this included gossiping about various members of the king's court: what they were doing and who they were doing it with. The queen kept telling me how much her new husband had showered her with jewellery and fine clothes, and I told her that I had noticed this. I also said that she looked very happy to be his wife.

I told her that whenever I met her when I'd been at court she had seemed to be wearing a new gown or a different cluster of jewels to decorate it. I joked I'd never seen so many different rubies, diamonds and amethysts. She laughed and said that she'd had to change her clothes and jewels so often as the king had given her so many. She said that he had insisted on seeing her try them out in front of him and all of his courtiers. As she said this, she drew me to her, kissed me and said that she'd not worn so many different gowns and jewels just to show she'd received more from the king than I had. I told her that I believed her and we laughed together and hugged and kissed each other again.

However, soon after I returned to Richmond, I was to hear some truly disturbing news about the queen's conduct at court, news that would shake the royal family and cause even more heads to roll, either into the bloody basket on Tower Hill or at the hanging tree at Tyburn.

Chapter Twenty - The Fall of Catherine Howard

Just three months after my successful visit to court, Lady Rutland approached me as I was sitting in the warm sunshine in the garden. I was trying to understand some English love poetry. Lady Edgecombe had recommended some of Sir Thomas Wyatt's poems since they were easy to understand and he tended to use simple vocabulary.

Farewell, Love, I read. *And all thy laws forever,*
Thy baited hooks shall tangle me no more;
Senec and Plato call me from thy lore,
To perfect wealth my wit for to endeavour.

I was just trying to work out who or what 'Senec' was when Lady Rutland suddenly appeared at my right hand and asked if she might disturb me.

"Yes," I said, and then added, "What is it, milady? You look most troubled."

"I am, but I'm pleased to see you are following Lady Edgecombe's advice. She loves poetry, especially the poets of today, such as Sir Thomas Wyatt and Henry Howard."

"Who? The Earl of Surrey?"

"Yes, milady, but I haven't come to talk about poetry; there's something far more serious."

"What, my family? My mother? My sisters? My brother?"

"No, no, milady. It's about the queen."

"Has she lost her baby?"

"No. milady. I think that it's something far worse than that. In fact she's done something and might lose her head for it."

"What do you mean?" I asked. None of this was making sense. I had thought that the king and new his wife were deeply in love.

"Well, it's like this, milady. Do you remember about one month ago when the king cancelled all the banquets and masques at court because of his bad leg?"

"Of course I do. I was about to go to London when I received a message not to."

"Well, during that period, my dear, when there were no activities at court, the queen became very friendly with a young man called Thomas Culpepper."

"What do you mean 'very friendly' with him?"

"They…"

"Wait a minute, Lady Rutland. Aren't the queen and Thomas Culpepper cousins?"

"Yes, milady, but according to the stories we've been hearing these last few days at court, the queen had become quite bored while the king was indisposed; you know, no dances, no reason to wear all her new gowns and jewellery and so she began to see Master Culpepper in secret. And," Lady Rutland continued, "if that weren't bad enough, they asked Lady Rochford to arrange these meetings."

"But that's not so bad," I shrugged. "It may not be very wise. Everyone knows at court that Lady Rochford is a true gossip. She can't keep a secret like a leaking bucket can't hold water."

"I know that, my dear, and so do you, but it's clear that those two, the queen and Culpepper, did not."

"And how many of these secret meetings did they have?"

"I don't know exactly, milady, but I know that they continued even when the king set out on his Northern progress – you know, when the whole court set out for Yorkshire and the north."

"But surely the queen has been sleeping with the king, hasn't she?"

"Perhaps, milady, but as Culpepper is a trusted member of the king's household he could get very close to the queen as well." She sighed and looked at me sadly as if she knew what would happen. "I suppose they carried on with their affair while His Majesty was busy with his own affairs, I mean the affairs of state."

"And does the king know about all this?"

"I don't think so, milady. But if he doesn't know now, it

won't take long before he does. You know what gossip is like at court. You need only one lord to look more than once at a lady and tongues start wagging nineteen to the dozen. It can't be long before His Majesty knows and when that happens I don't want to be at court on that day, or even that week. I'm telling you, my dear, the king will be so angry that anything can and probably will happen."

I sat there dreading to think what could happen and I saw that Lady Rutland was thinking along the same lines. "Oh, poor, stupid Catherine Howard," she said at last in a whisper as she gathered her gown around her ready to leave. "Don't these young girls ever learn? Just show them a few diamonds or give them a pretty gown or two and they surrender their honour without a thought for the future. Oh, I'm so glad I wasn't brought up like that. But enough of that," she said trying to shake these gloomy thoughts from her head. "I must go now but I promise I'll let you know if anything else happens. But you must promise me, in return, not to tell anyone what I've just told you - not even in German to your Kathryn or Gertrude."

I nodded my head and she bowed low and left, leaving me to my thoughts and Sir Thomas Wyatt's poem about *Farewell, love.*

That night as I lay in bed I couldn't help thinking about the king and his young wife. If this story is true, my light-hearted queen, I thought, you'll not be so light-hearted much longer. If you, as His Majesty's 'rose without a thorn' hurt the king with one of your thorns, I would certainly not like to be in your dainty shoes when he finds any blood on his royal fingers.

For the next two days all I could think about was Catherine Howard and her foolish ways. I could understand the exciting feelings of power and plenty that came with being close to the king - but being so close to this king, together with his stinking leg was, to use an English understatement, not a very pleasant experience. And to be the king's wife and then be caught with another man had to be the worst experience of all.

The first person who gave me more detailed information about what had passed between the queen and Thomas

Culpepper was Alice Skipton, one of my best friends at court, an intelligent woman and one on whom I knew I could rely on. She sent me a sealed letter with a royal messenger who had to return to London. It arrived sometime after the progress had arrived in York where most of the court, and especially the king, were extremely annoyed that the Scottish king, James the Fifth, had refused to meet King Henry.

My dearest Anne, she wrote.

I hope you will not mind but I will write this letter in simple English as I know that although you can now speak English quite well, you told me earlier you still have problems reading the language and sometimes do not understand all the words. When you read this letter you will understand why I do not want you to ask anyone about any of the words in it. I will also be pleased if you burn this letter when you have finished reading it and not talk about it with anyone.

As you know, we set out from London on this Progress and from the beginning we had many problems. The heavy rain made it very difficult for all of our carriages to move and many of them became stuck in the mud -especially on the open roads between the towns. However, we did succeed, finally in reaching York although we arrived there much later than the king had wanted. His Majesty had planned to meet the King of Scotland but, in the end, even though he had promised to come down to York from Edinburgh, he never arrived. Some of the people on the Progress said that King James was afraid to meet our king, but whatever the reason, Henry was furious and shouted at everyone for a few days afterwards.

But now I must tell you about Queen Catherine. While we were on the move, Thomas Culpepper, a good-looking young man, was frequently seen in the queen's company. Naturally a lot of people gossiped about this but of course this did not include me. According to the usual rumours that are part of our courtly life, he used to visit the queen at night when she was staying at Lincoln, Pontefract or here at York. One of the stories I heard was that he was almost caught in her bedchamber by Sir Anthony Denny who, as you know, is one of

His Majesty's most trusted advisers. (You first met him soon after you arrived in England.) He had come to the queen's chamber to ask her about some travel arrangements, but she was inside with Culpepper. Fortunately for both of them, the door was locked on the inside so either he hid under the bed or else he managed to climb out of a window and thus he was not seen there.

And so, my dearest friend, I am telling you this so that you should know what is happening at court even though you are not here with us. As is customary, the Catholics and the Protestants are fighting over who will have more influence with the king and that is the reason that whatever the queen does or whatever happens to her in the future - whether it be very good or very bad - it will be of great import for everyone.

I leave you as your dearest friend and remind you to burn this letter when you have finished reading it. I hope you are in the best of health.

Alice Sk.

After reading this letter I immediately threw it into the fire and again felt very worried about what could happen to the queen. Even though she was the Duke of Norfolk's niece I knew that because of her natural innocence and trust in people, she was very naïve in the ways of the court. I also knew that if the king heard about this story, his fury would be frightening and probably deadly.

After a few days, I managed to push this matter to the back of my mind and began to think about my wardrobe. Which gowns would I keep; which ones would I have repaired for the winter and which ones would I get rid of or give to some of my friends? These they could wear as they were or use the material to make new gowns for themselves.

I grew more aware of the approach of winter as the autumn leaves fell on the lawns at Richmond. The days were growing colder and shorter and I felt this even more than some of my friends as, by nature, I am a 'summer' person. I am so fond of the long, bright summer days and, most of all, I really enjoy the long summer evenings when I can sit outside until late with my ladies. Then we can embroider, read or just gossip as we watch the sun go down with its deepening orange light reflected on the River Thames.

And thus it was, as I was sitting outside in the gardens on a pleasant September evening that I heard footsteps running towards me from behind. I put down my sewing and looked around and was most surprised to see Alice Skipton moving as fast as her elegant shoes would allow.

"Alice, Alice, what are you doing here?" I asked, noticing that she was not smiling her usual smile. "Is anything wrong?"

"Yes, milady," she said as she bent forward to kiss me on the cheek. "Much is wrong."

"With you?"

"No, milady, with the queen."

"Has he…?"

"Yes, milady. According to a couple of my friends at court, Archbishop Cranmer has found out about the queen's affairs."

"Affairs?"

"Yes, milady, with Thomas Culpepper and with one or two other men."

I could not say anything for a few minutes. I sat there in complete shock and held my head in my hands. Then I looked up at Alice who was also shaking in fear with the thought of what would probably happen.

"But Archbishop Cranmer?" I asked. "How did he find out? He's such a mild fellow. I'm surprised that her uncle, the duke, and Bishop Gardiner haven't had him removed from office or eaten him up."

She leant forward and held my hand. "No, milady, this is no time for jokes. This is a very serious matter. Let me catch my breath and I'll tell you what I know."

I waited a few minutes and then I poured her a glass of wine and slid a plate of sweet cakes over to her which she started nibbling. We sat there for a little more in friendly silence as she finished her wine and then she began.

"First of all, milady, there are two parts to my story," she said quietly. "The good part and the bad part."

"So tell me the good part first," I said. "Bad news can always wait."

Alice gave a small, almost imperceptible smile. "The good part is that the king doesn't know the bad part."

"And the bad part is?"

"The bad part is the continuation of what I wrote to you in that letter from York when we were on the progress. Much more has happened since then."

"What? More details or more people?"

"Both, milady." Alice took my hands and held them in her own warm hands. Then she looked at me straight with her sharp dark eyes. I knew this woman was no fool and anything she told me would be reliable information. "So listen carefully, my dearest Anne and I'll tell you all I know - but," and here she looked around, "you must not tell anyone else, not a soul, And not even your Kathryn or Gertrude even in German, because they may accidentally tell someone in English. Do you understand?"

I nodded.

"So this is what I know. It seems that while the king and the court were away on the progress a man called John Lascelles came to speak to Archbishop Cranmer. He told him things that he'd heard about the queen's past life, that is, when she was a young girl living in Lambeth with her step-grandmother Agnes, at the Duchess of Norfolk's house."

"What did she do there that was so bad?" I asked, wondering what terrible things a young girl of about thirteen could do.

"It seems," Alice continued, now talking in a conspiratorial whisper even though nobody could hear what we were saying, "that while the queen was growing up in this house, she'd had some sexual affairs with at least two young men there. One of them was with her music teacher, Henry Mannox, and the other was with Francis Dereham who was the secretary to the duchess."

"But surely the duchess must've been living there to see that young Catherine behaved herself?"

"No, milady, and that's part of the problem. According to the various stories I've heard, Catherine and Dereham became so friendly that they called each other 'husband' and wife' and he even trusted her to look after one hundred pounds for him when he had to go to Ireland on the king's business."

"So, even supposing that these stories are true, Alice, how did this John Lascelles get to know about them? Surely they would have made sure that nobody knew about them."

Alice shook her head sadly from side to side. "No, my dearest Anne, it wasn't like that at all. In those days, the Duchess spent little time in her Lambeth house and so all the young people there – and there were more of them, not just Catherine and her own young men – took advantage of her absence. One of them was called Mary Lascelles…"

"John's sister?"

"Yes, and she told Archbishop Cranmer all about the queen's past with Mannox and Dereham."

"So why did he report all this to Archbishop Cranmer? What would he get out of it? Surely it had nothing to do with him?"

For an answer Alice looked at me and held out the small gold crucifix she wore around her neck. "It was because of this, milady. Religion. John Lascelles, who it seems isn't a very nice man is also a very fervent Protestant. As you know, the Howards are Catholics, Roman Catholics, and they are not happy with what the king has done to their Church over the past few years. So I think that the reason for Lascelles' tale-bearing is that he wishes to cause as many problems as he can for the Howards. And this includes blackening their name in the eyes of the king."

"And so he has," I said in a resigned tone. "Or if he hasn't done so yet, he will do so soon. Oh, Alice, if His Majesty hears of this, I'm sure there'll be trouble. When I was married to him I saw things like this on several occasions and when they happened someone was always hurt. Oh, my poor Catherine. What has she done? And what will happen to her?"

Silently, we both sat there in the garden. All you could hear were the birds chirping in the trees and the distant sounds from the river. Each of us was thinking about the worst that could happen to the young queen and to the others if the king got to hear of this sordid story.

"Tell me, Alice," I said, looking up after some time. "When Catherine and Dereham called each other 'husband' and 'wife,' was this just a childish game for fun or were they really betrothed to each other? And do you know if they had signed any form of nuptial or pre-nuptial contract?"

She shrugged. "I don't know. I suppose you're thinking of the situation you had with the Duke of Lorraine's son many years ago?"

I nodded and immediately thought of my own past experience. "You know," I said, "if there was a contract, of any sort between them, it means that..." and I could not bring myself to finish off the sentence as I held my hands to my mouth.

"Yes, my dearest Anne, you are right," said Alice, completing my sentence. "It would mean that, in the eyes of the Church, our king is a bigamist." She paused to let the words sink in. "Can you imagine that – our King Henry, the ruler of our country, the king who has been five-times married – is a bigamist? I wonder what the archbishop will do? What will he say? If he doesn't report it, he'll be damning his soul forever, and if he does report it, then the chances are that Catherine will be imprisoned or even die for it."

"No, no, Alice, the king won't kill her for that. I know he'll be furious and shout and box a few people's ears and maybe throw a few people into the Tower, but I'm sure he won't kill her. After all, he's too much in love with her. Just look at all the clothes and other gifts he's given her."

Alice did not look convinced. "I hope you're right, my dear. You lived with him for six months and you should know."

"I'm not sure that I really did live with him but I just hope that however angry he becomes, he'll do the Christian thing and forgive her afterwards."

"Amen," said Alice and kissed the crucifix around her neck.

I heard no more news about the queen for a week or so, that is until Alice came over to see me again at Richmond Palace. At the time I was sitting next to a window trying to catch the afternoon light doing some embroidery with Lady Rutland and Lady Edgecombe when Alice was ushered into the room. After greeting the two ladies, she said that she wished to talk to me privately and so, excusing ourselves, we went out to the same place in the garden where we had sat earlier and knew that we could not be overheard.

"Listen, my dear," she began as soon as we had sat down. "I'll not waste any time but just tell you the latest news." She stopped for a moment, breathed deeply and said, "Archbishop Cranmer has reported what he's heard about the queen to the king."

"He has?" My mouth was open and I was in shock. Even though I'd hoped and prayed that this would never happen, it had. I could already foresee the results of the archbishop's words. But would they really happen?

"Yes, Anne, the archbishop went to see His Majesty at Hampton Court. He went on the king's special day of thanksgiving, you know, when the king attended a special service to thank God for the joy his latest marriage had brought him. I heard that the archbishop had written a report about what he'd learned from John Lascelles and his sister and then he presented it to the king after the service.

"But that's terrible, Anne. To learn all this just after he'd been praising the Lord for giving him such a good marriage at last." I stopped for a moment and imagined a furious Henry reading the report as his chief cleric waited in the background.

"And what did the king say? What did he do?"

"He just sat there, as if he'd been struck dumb. I'm telling you, milady, this report was completely unexpected. It was like a thunderbolt. A friend of mine who happened to be there at the time, but for obvious reasons I won't tell you her name, told me that she saw the king just sit there, bent over with his head in his hands for a full five minutes without moving. He was in complete shock. Then he called the archbishop over to him and asked him why he'd written this report instead of telling him personally."

"What was his answer?"

"He said that this report was so damning that he didn't have the heart to tell it to the king in spoken words, but that he'd had to write it down instead."

"So what did the king do next?" I asked, even though I was afraid to hear the answer.

"My friend said that she was very surprised at what the king did next. He told the archbishop that he didn't really believe this report and that much of it was clearly based on hearsay. He told Cranmer to investigate these 'nasty rumours' as he called them, more thoroughly. His actual words were, 'You are not to desist until you have got to the bottom of the pot.'"

"And then?"

"Then after the archbishop had left, the king gave orders that Her Majesty was to be confined to her rooms with Lady Rochford until he'd learned the truth. 'For the good of the realm,' he said, 'I will stay apart from the queen until I know what has happened.'"

"And what happened to the queen?" I asked, imagining the poor girl, frightened out of her mind and locked away from the bright lights and excitement of the court.

"Oh, my dear Anne. She was in a state of shock - just like the king had been earlier. His guards came over to her rooms while she was practising some new dance steps with her ladies and they sent all the ladies away without any explanation. The captain of the guard said that this is what His Majesty had ordered and that the ladies should leave immediately. Once the queen was on her own she asked why but they would not or could not give her an answer. They just left her there and posted a guard to stand there by the door."

"How long was she left on her own?"

"A few days."

"Oh, the poor girl," I said. "She must've been so scared. Just thinking about her makes me feel so frightened for her. Poor little Catherine suddenly locked up without knowing why. Alone and without her friends. Just with that Lady Rochford who is *not* the best person to have with you in time of need. Oh my poor little girl," I repeated and started to weep. In my mind I was imagining that bright young woman caged up like a small bird banging its wings on the sides of its cage, aching to find the open skies and freedom.

Then I noticed that Alice was also quietly weeping and after dabbing her eyes with a handkerchief she continued. "Then the archbishop again questioned John Lascelles and he repeated the same story that he'd told him earlier. And then, to make matters worse, the archbishop learned that the queen had taken Dereham back again into her household after she was married to the king."

"But why?" I couldn't believe that she had been so foolish.

"It seems, milady, that Dereham and a few of the other young people she used to know at Lambeth kept pestering her for favours. They kept saying that unless she helped them gain positions at court, they'd start spreading stories about how she used to spend her days, or rather her nights, at the duchess' house at Lambeth."

I listened to this explanation quietly as Alice continued.

"Then as I said, the archbishop returned to the king and told him that his earlier report was true. The queen had betrayed him and had committed adultery."

This was the news that I hoped I would never hear. If I had sat there without moving earlier when Alice had first told me her news, now I sat there like a rock. I was completely stunned. Bigamy. Adultery. It was too much. I'm not sure I even blinked my eyes. I was only brought out of my shock when a twig fell from the tree above me and fell onto my face. I shook my head, brushed the twig away and faced Alice.

"Tell me, has anything happened to her family as well? Have they been questioned or taken to the Tower?"

"I don't know, Anne. All I know is that most of them have abandoned her although, to my surprise, the duke - who more or less pushed her into the king's bed - did try and comfort his niece a little when she became hysterical, but I'm sure he had reasons for that."

"Yes, you're probably right. He never does anything unless he thinks he'll gain by it," I said. "Perhaps he was trying to calm her down so she wouldn't say anything against him. *That's* the sort of help she'd get from him."

"I'm sure you're right, milady. I'm thinking of the time before you came to court of how much help the Duke of Norfolk gave his other niece, Anne Boleyn. He didn't lift a finger to help her. In fact, he was in charge of her trial and did nothing to save her. He couldn't get rid of her quickly enough."

She stopped talking for a minute as she thought back to those grim days some five years earlier.

Alice dabbed her eyes again and continued. "So now that I've heard about how the queen is behaving at the moment, I am not really surprised. I heard she was crying all the time and that she was refusing to eat. My friend said that she was acting like a mad woman and she kept talking about ending up on the block."

"But that's terrible, Alice. It can't be true. She's so young and she's such a sweet and innocent little thing."

"I know that, my dear, and you know that, but will His Majesty think like that? I doubt it very much. All I know is that she and Lady Rochford both began to act hysterically: crying and calling out for the king to come so they could explain what'd happened to them."

"And of course he did not come."

"Of course not, my dear. You should know him by now. If there are any problems in the palace, especially ones involving women, he does his best to keep away and let someone else deal with them. In fact, the only time the queen did see him was just as he was at prayer at the Chapel Royal. She managed to push her way past her guards to go and plead with him but then the guards pulled her back."

"And did the king do anything?"

"Yes. He just looked at her for a moment and then turned away."

"So what's going to happen next?" I asked.

Alice shrugged. "I don't know. All I know is that Thomas Culpepper and Francis Dereham have been arrested and taken to the Tower to be questioned."

"You mean tortured."

Alice nodded and then told me that she'd heard that they were going to be put on trial soon at the Guildhall at the beginning of December.

"So, Alice, where is the queen now? Is she still at Hampton Court?"

"No, my dear. She's been taken to Syon House and I heard

that while she was there she admitted to a lot of the stories about her past to the duke. Perhaps she thought that if she tells the truth, things will go better with her."

"Perhaps," I said, but I was not convinced as I thought of my pretty lady-in-waiting of the past, my poor little Catherine trapped and abandoned and left to the mercies of her furious husband and his scheming duke.

Alice stood up to leave and so did I. We both had tears in our eyes, not for ourselves, but for our queen who had reigned for only a little over a year, and now we feared she would soon be paying the highest price for her earlier sexual affairs. If the young men in her life had been taken to the Tower, then she would have no chance to save herself. Everyone who could rid themselves of her in order to save their own skins would do so.

Alice and I hugged each other silently and then she slipped away through a side door. I hurried back to my ladies and apologized in her name saying that she had to catch the tide and return to court immediately for personal reasons.

The next part of this story I heard from Lady Browne and Lady Rutland. The queen's past affairs with Dereham and Culpepper were no longer secrets to be whispered in gardens or in silent chambers. It was on a grey and rainy day in mid-December 1541 when my ladies and I met in my chamber at Richmond. Originally I had invited them over for a meal and a day of female gossip, but immediately after sitting down, they told me their grim news.

"I suppose," Lady Browne began, "that you've heard about what happened to the queen's two lovers, Dereham and Culpepepper?"

"A little," I said. "I heard that they were both executed yesterday."

"Yes, at Tyburn. Dereham was hanged, drawn and quartered but Culpepper was luckier."

"Luckier?"

"Yes," Lady Rutland added. "Because of his family's past connections and his past service to His Majesty, he was beheaded instead."

I sat there quietly. To be killed, to have your life brutally taken from you just because you'd slept with a young girl whom you didn't know at the time was destined to become the queen and wife of the most important man in England seemed to be terribly unfair. And just as I was thinking this, Lady Browne tapped me on my forearm.

"And there's more, milady. The queen's aunts, the Dowager Duchess of Norfolk and Lady William Howard and Lady Bridgewater have also been arrested and sentenced to life imprisonment and all their possessions have been transferred to the royal coffers."

"That's right," Lady Rutland said. "And they've also arrested some of the queen's past friends who used to live with her at Lambeth as well as Lady Rochford. They've all been taken to the Tower and are to be questioned."

"And what about the queen herself?" I asked.

They both shrugged. They did not know.

"All I can say," Lady Browne said, "is that His Majesty cannot or will not believe she's guilty. But she is still a prisoner at Syon House and it's rumoured that the king himself wants to talk to her."

Later I heard that there was some truth to these rumours. The king had invited his queen to attend a special session of parliament so that she could defend her good name. She refused however, and told His Majesty's delegation that she would prefer to submit herself to the king's mercy. I heard that she had made such a good impression on His Majesty's ministers that they returned to Syon House and asked her, even begged her to come and defend herself in parliament. Again she refused and so the Privy Council petitioned the king that a Bill of Attainder be passed for him to sign. Henry agreed to sign it and so the Bill was prepared for him, but when the moment came for him to actually sign it, he refused and withheld his signature. Then when I heard this, I felt happier than I had for quite some days. I hoped it meant that the queen's life would be spared after all. Unfortunately, this was not to be. The Privy Council got around this problem by attaching the Great Seal to the Bill and writing *Le Roi le veut* – The king wills it – on the Bill itself. Then the Bill was read out to both houses of parliament and so it became law. So with or without his signature the queen and Lady Rochford were both condemned to death.

This happened at the beginning of February 1542. On 10 February the queen was transported in a closed barge from Syon House to the Tower. I was told that now she knew she was going to die she began to act more calmly and seemed quite resigned to her fate.

The tragic end of this story happened three days later. Although many of the king's courtiers were present at the Tower, I did not attend and so, as usual, I learned what had happened there though my chamberlain, the Earl of Rutland and his wife.

"Poor Catherine," Lady Rutland said, and started to weep as she recalled the previous day's grim scene. "She looked so small and frail standing there next to all the lords and guards and the axeman. Sir John Gage, the Constable of the Tower, guided her to the scaffold and told her that if she wished to say anything, then this was the time to do so."

"And did she say anything?"

"Yes, milady," Lord Rutland replied. "She said that all the people should look upon her as an example of one who had led an ungodly life and that she prayed for her husband and that she deserved to die for her heinous sins."

"Did she really say that?" I asked. I found it hard to believe that a young lady such as Catherine had uttered such words.

The earl and his wife both nodded. "Yes, milady," Lady Rutland said. "Then she laid her head upon the block and that was it."

I had to ask the next question even though I was frightened at hearing the answer. "And did the axeman do his job well?"

"Yes, milady," Lady Rutland said, shuddering. "It took just one clean blow, and it was the same for Lady Rochford. Not like what happened to Thomas Cromwell." And then she shuddered again as she remembered the bloody scene that she had witnessed some two years earlier. And before she could continue with her report I also shuddered as I too recalled how the axeman had butchered Thomas Cromwell at his execution.

Catherine had been queen for less than two years and then to die like this. It was too much. And just as I was thinking of the past, the Earl of Rutland continued with his report.

"Then they brought Lady Rochford to the scaffold and…"

"But wait a minute, my lord," I said, holding up my hand. "Wasn't she declared mad and that mad people can't be executed?"

"She may have been declared mad," the earl said, "but that didn't stop His Majesty from wanting to get rid of her. At first the guards thought that she'd resist them, but she didn't. To everyone's surprise she was very calm, said a few words and then her head was chopped off quite cleanly, too."

There was nothing left to say. My friendly but misguided Catherine, who I'd always thought of as my young and chattering lady-in-waiting was now dead, cut down by an axeman by order of her husband, a disappointed and angry king. I knew that women, especially his wives had to be or to do two things for him. They had to be as perfect as possible, 'a rose without a thorn' as Henry had once called Catherine. They also had to give him sons, or at least one healthy son. Catherine Howard had been or done neither and so she'd paid the price for her double failure.

She'd been a very pretty and happy young lady who had played with her life and lost. She had hurt nobody except for one person, her husband who had also happened to be the king. And it was because of this that she'd paid this terrible price for her folly. I wondered as her last days closed in on her if she'd realised that she had been used by all who had surrounded her: her admirers and her lovers, her family but mostly by her over-reaching uncle, the Duke of Norfolk. I shook my head and Lady Rutland gave me her handkerchief. It was all so sad and now she was gone I wondered what would happen next. Would His Majesty wish to marry again? Had he set his eyes on anyone else in the meantime? Would he ask me to return to court and be his wife again? Would I want to? I shivered at the thought. He'd had five wives. He had executed two of them, divorced another two, including me, while his third wife had died only one week after giving birth to his son.

Was it worth considering whether I should return to his household as his wife again? I wasn't sure. I'd have to give this question a lot of serious thought but in the meanwhile I couldn't stop thinking about the young girl who had tried to please her royal master and had failed most fatally.

Chapter Twenty-One - Enter Catherine Parr

As I said earlier, I was in a strange mood following the death of Catherine Howard. Maybe this was due to the fact that I kept thinking that perhaps I should have been more assertive and pushed myself forward to become the king's wife once again. I spent much time during the spring of 1542 pondering this question and as the time passed I realized that despite all that had happened, yes, I had wanted to become the sixth wife of King Henry the Eighth. However, I arrived at this conclusion in a way that was entirely unexpected.

I found out that at the beginning of the year, that is, soon after Catherine Howard had departed this life, that John of Luxembourg, the son of the Count of Brienne, a person whom I had never met, had written a book called *The Remonstrance of Anne of Cleves*. In it he'd written that I'd become so sad over my divorce that I'd thought of committing suicide. He'd also written that I still loved the king and continued to honour and serve him. It seems that this book - which was written as though I had written it - had become very popular and had been read all over Europe.

I heard that His Majesty had ordered a copy and after he and his council had read it they realised that I had not written it. Nevertheless, for a while, it gave me some hope that the king would take me back as his wife, a position which I decided would be preferable to being merely his 'Sister' who spent most of her time entertaining at Richmond Palace.

It was during this period that I became seriously ill with a fever and the king sent his own physicians and servants to look after me. He himself did not come to visit me but I was flattered by his constant attention and saw this as a sign that he was still concerned about my health and general welfare. As I lay in my sick-bed looking out over the well-tended gardens I wondered whether his concern meant that he thought of me returning to him as his future wife.

"What do you think, Lady Browne? Am I to be called back to London to be his queen again?"

"I don't know, milady. All I know is that the palace gossip says that His Majesty is said to have a fancy for Lord Cobham's daughter, Elizabeth, as well as for my husband's niece and also for Mistress Anne Basset."

"Mistress Basset? Wasn't she one of Queen Jane's ladies-in-waiting?"

"Yes, milady, but from what I hear, the spark that'd been lit once doesn't seem to be burning so brightly now as it was then."

"*Ach so*, so he *is* still interested in marrying again?" I asked.

"Yes, milady. It would indeed appear so."

And so, despite His Majesty's past marital failures, Lady Browne's words gave me some hope about being recalled to London especially as one of my main reasons for wanting to return to Cleves, to be with my dear mother, was now no longer relevant. I heard that she had died and in addition, my brother had been forced to surrender much of his ducal territory to the Holy Roman Emperor, King Charles the Fifth.

It seems that my brother, William, had made a politically good but loveless marriage to Jeanne d' Albret, the daughter of the king and queen of Navarre and the Emperor's niece. Then, when the relations between France and the Emperor broke down, my brother decided to support the French. As a result, the Emperor declared war on Cleves and the Low Countries. Despite their early successes on the battlefield, the combined Clevian and French forces lost the war and had to sue for peace. This meant that my brother had to cede much of his land and wealth, a situation which caused my mother to die of grief at the end of August 1542. It was after hearing these reports that I decided that, whether I married the king again or not, I would end my days here in England either as the queen or the 'King's Sister.' There was nothing left in Cleves to call me back to the land where I had been brought up.

This last point was also brought home to me one day when I was at the palace where I'd had an interesting conversation with Archbishop Cranmer. I had asked him, as one who was in almost daily contact with the king if there was any chance that His Majesty would take me again to be his sixth wife. Although we were speaking very quietly, he looked around cautiously and then said quite definitely that His Majesty would never marry me again.

"How do you know? Did you ask him?"

"Yes, milady, but not in so many words," he replied. "It was like this. Your brother, Duke William, wrote to the king soon after Queen Catherine was executed and through his ambassadors asked whether he'd consider taking you back to be his wife. Naturally, as His Majesty's most trusted advisers, the ambassadors came to speak to me as well."

"And what did you say?"

"I said, milady, that I would petition the king about this matter."

"And did you?"

"I most certainly did, and…"

"And what did the king say?"

"He told me quite forcibly that I was to inform your brother that he would never marry you again and that that was the end of the matter."

So now I knew I would continue not as the queen but as the 'King's Sister' and that I would remain in England. It was now up to me to make the most of my life in this country. I was thirty-two years old and had no serious problems with my health. I could now speak English quite well and had good relations with many people at court. Now I knew that there was no point in hoping for any major change in my life. I should just be happy with my lot and enjoy what the Good Lord had granted me. I mean, how many other people receive four thousand pounds every year from their king? Who else had as much property and gowns and jewels as I had? Very few. So I thought, I should look forward to the future and be happy with what I'd been granted.

It was also during this period when I was enjoying one of my visits to the court that I heard some surprising news. I was sitting in a small chamber overlooking the river when there was an urgent knock on the door. I put my embroidery aside, opened the door and ushered in my chamberlain, the Earl of Rutland and his wife. It was clear that they had hurried over to tell me something and a few minutes passed before they could regain their breath and calm down. Over a goblet of hippocras and some sugared fruits they told me that the king was planning to marry again.

"Marry? Again?"

"Yes, milady," the earl replied. "To Lady Latimer."

"Lady Latimer?" I repeated. "Who is she? I've never heard of her."

"You probably know her as Lady Catherine Parr. She's the daughter of Sir Thomas Parr and Maud Green and has spent much of her life in the north of England," Lady Rutland explained. "And if she marries His Majesty, he will be her third husband."

"So she must be quite old," I remarked.

"Oh no, milady - she's about your age. You see, her first husband, Sir Edward Borough, died over ten years ago after only one year of marriage. He was quite old at the time and then she married John Neville, Lord Latimer, soon after."

"And did he die soon after as well?"

"No, milady," the earl smiled. "But he nearly did."

"What do you mean? In a battle or something like that?"

"No, no, milady. His Lordship became involved in the Pilgrimage of Grace, the northern rebellion against the king that broke out before you came to England. It looked as though the king was going to execute him for this but his wife, Lady Latimer, interceded and managed to save his life. But then he died a few years later."

"Yes," added Lady Rutland. "And he left her as a rich widow with lands and plate and everything."

I was curious to know all I could about this mysterious woman, this woman who may have prevented me from marrying the king again.

"So how did His Majesty become friendly with her if she spent most of her time in the north?"

"That's easy to explain, milady," my chamberlain said. "It seems that Catherine Parr's mother had been friendly with

Catherine of Aragon, the king's first wife. Then as a result Catherine Parr became friendly with her daughter, Princess Mary. So she used to come to court quite often and that is when His Majesty first noticed her."

"Ah, but there was a problem," Lady Rutland added, winking at her husband. "For in the meanwhile, she'd fallen in love with Thomas Seymour."

"Queen Jane's brother?"

"Yes, and they wanted to get married."

"But?"

"But the king heard about this and he - like King David in the Bible when he lusted after Batsheba - sent Thomas Seymour away to be an ambassador in Brussels so as to get him out of the way."

"Oh, I'm sure Catherine Parr was pleased about that," I said sarcastically, "Having her lover sent away and then being asked to marry the king."

"You're right, milady," Lady Rutland said. "I heard that when His Majesty proposed to her, she replied, 'I, your wife?' in quite a shocked tone."

"And there was another problem as well," the earl added. "A scandal in the Parr family. It was when…"

"Let *me* tell her, Edward," interrupted Lady Rutland. "I tell these stories much better than you do. You always leave out the best parts."

My chamberlain stepped aside and let his wife take over.

"So my milady," Lady Rutland began, smiling sweetly at her husband, "it was like this. It seems that Lady Latimer's brother, William Parr, wanted to divorce his wife, Anne Bourchier, because she'd been unfaithful to him. She'd taken a lover and had run away with him. So William applied to parliament for a divorce and he was so angry with her that he asked parliament to have his wife executed as a punishment."

"Executed?" I asked. "Is that allowed?"

"Yes, milady," the earl answered. "It's a somewhat rare and extreme punishment but it is allowed."

"And so," Lady Rutland continued, "when Lady Latimer heard about this, she went straight to His Majesty and from what I heard, she threw herself down at his feet and said that she would not rise until he promised to spare her sister-in-law's life. At first His Majesty refused by saying that no-one was above the law, but then Lady Latimer said that as he was the King of England, he *was* above the law and had the authority to spare her life."

"And did the king accept this? Did he agree?"

Lady Rutland, like all good storytellers waited for a few tension-filled seconds before answering. "Yes, milady," she smiled. "The king said that if Lord Parr agreed, then he, the king would agree to spare her life. But," and here Lady Rutland paused again, "William's divorced wife, Anne Bourchier, had to pay a price for her infidelity. Parliament ruled that the children she'd had through her lover would be bastards and, as such, they wouldn't be allowed to inherit the family wealth when the time came. In addition her own lands and titles were to be transferred to her husband and later he was created the Earl of Essex."

"Ah, Chancellor Cromwell's old title," I said.

"That's right, milady," the earl nodded. "But between you and me, I'm not sure it's such a blessèd title, but as they say, time will tell."

"So the real heroine of this story is Lady Latimer," I said. "The lady His Majesty wants to marry now."

"Yes, milady," Lady Rutland said, "and she..."

"And what is she like, this Lady Latimer, this Catherine Parr?" I asked, still unable to shake off the feeling that because of her, I would not be queen again. "Is she anything like Catherine Howard?"

"Oh, no, milady," said Lady Rutland and her husband together. "She's nothing like that."

"Why, is she fat and ugly?"

"No, milady," answered Lady Rutland, understanding the unsaid thought behind my question. "She's quite a comely young lady. She is a two or three years older than you I believe but, unlike you, she hates sewing and embroidery and all manner of things like that. In fact, one of the ladies at court said that Lady Latimer told her that when she was a young girl she said her hands were for holding crowns and sceptres and not spindles and needles."

"So what *does* she like doing?"

"She loves reading and learning languages and talking about ideas. She can speak French, Latin and Italian and I heard that she wants to start learning Spanish as well."

"Hmm," was my comment. "She doesn't sound as though she's going to be a very gay or exciting wife for His Majesty."

"I'm not sure that he's still looking for excitement milady, you know, another Catherine Howard," the earl said in reply. "I think that his 'rose without a thorn' pricked him too much. Now I think he's looking for a daisy or a violet - a quieter life and wife."

"Like with his third wife, Jane Seymour?"

"Yes, milady."

I pondered for a moment. A quieter life - that is exactly what I would have given him, but he had turned me down. I had realised, some time ago, that I was nothing like Catherine Howard but there was nothing that I could do about it now.

Once he had chosen her, the king wasted little time in marrying his new bride. Two days after Archbishop Cranmer had issued a special marriage licence, His Majesty married Catherine Parr on 12 July 1543. The wedding, a quiet event, took place in the queen's chambers at Hampton Court. Twenty people including myself were present as well as several members of Catherine's and the king's families and also a few members of the court. The Bishop of Winchester, Stephen Gardiner, conducted the service and I noticed that the king was in high spirits as he made his marriage vows. I also noticed that when his new wife made her vows, she sounded much less joyful than her new husband. I could only assume that she was thinking that she'd have preferred to have married her real love, Thomas Seymour, instead.

Afterwards we were invited to a modest wedding feast and then I returned to Richmond. I was asked to stay for a while but despite the fact I needed to reconcile myself to the fact that His Majesty had married Catherine Parr instead of me, I still found this a little difficult. So I excused myself and took my leave.

It did not take long for the new queen to make her influence felt at court. Gone were the days of the masques, balls and banquets that had taken place during my short reign or that of Catherine Howard. Instead, the king invited writers and other scholarly men to court, men such as the well-known teacher and academic, Dr. John Cheke from Cambridge, as well as Roger Ascham and the Bishop of Ely, Richard Cox. These men would sit with His Majesty and talk at length about religion and philosophy and I also heard that, occasionally, Her Majesty would join in these discussions with great enjoyment.

One of the results of this was that the court which had been a centre for dances and entertainments of all kinds now became a verbal battlefield where all sorts of religious views were advanced. Some were for the old-style Roman Catholic faith, others were based on the new reform ideas. At the same time, other people were putting forward ideas that were even more extreme and radical than we had heard about before. Of course each idea had its own defenders. Archbishop Cranmer and several academics were for the reformist school sometimes referred to as Protestant, while the Earl of Southampton and Bishop Gardiner were very strongly opposed to them in their fervent defence of the True Faith, the name they gave to the Roman Catholic religion.

Of course, the court not only provided a battleground for religious ideas, there were also battles for the king's ear and influence. But this was not all that the learned men were fighting about. The king had asked Dr. Cheke and Dr. Cox to provide instruction for the young Prince Edward, now a bonny but somewhat serious seven year-old boy. His studies were to include languages, philosophy and liberal sciences. However, the fact that the prince's new teachers tended towards the reformist school was too much for Bishop Gardiner and his supporters.

And in the middle of all of this stood the king's new wife. She was known to favour the more reformist views and was also engaged in writing a book to be called *Prayers or*

Meditations. At first I found this very difficult to believe - a woman, and a Queen of England, to boot - writing a serious book about religious philosophy. This really seemed too much but it was not for me to say anything. I just sat on the sidelines as it were and watched as the various members of the court and the chief clerics fought to gain the king's ear.

But soon after the battle of ideas started, another battle broke out, and this was a real one, with men, armies and weapons. In July 1544 His Majesty set out for France at the head of his army to fight in what would be his last military campaign. Before leaving, he appointed the queen to stand in for him as his regent and she was to be advised by Archbishop Cranmer, Chancellor Wriothesley, Lord Hertford and several others. By appointing his wife as regent was one way of showing how much His Majesty relied on her common sense and judgement.

Towards the end of September I asked my chamberlain how the campaign was progressing. His reply was to grimace.

"The reports that I've read, milady, say that His Majesty conquered the town of Boulogne after a siege but, on the same day, he learned that his ally, the Holy Roman Emperor, Charles the Fifth, had sued for a separate peace with the French."

"So what did the king do next? Continue fighting or come home?"

"He didn't come home, milady. He decided to march on to Montreuil, a small town several miles south of Boulogne and together with the Duke of Norfolk's men, take this town as well."

"Did he succeed?"

"No, not really, milady. The reports said that the weather was not in his favour. It was very wet and rainy and it was extremely difficult for His Majesty's army to move his heavy siege engines and his wagons full of equipment. Then he ran out of food so he had to burn all his engines and lift the siege. I hear he'll be returning to London in a week or two, but that of course depends on the weather and the state of the Channel, if it's stormy or not."

Of course, as soon as he'd said those words I couldn't help

but think of the storms that had delayed my own journey over to England some five years ago. That had been a journey full of expectation and speculation about what it would be like for me, a lady from a small Rhineland duchy to become the Queen of England.

As my chamberlain predicted, the king did return two weeks later, but instead of everyone at court being pleased to see him safely home again, they walked around and conducted their business in a very subdued manner. During his absence he had become more irritable and short-tempered than he'd ever been before. Perhaps this was due to his legs which were causing him great pain. In addition, he was becoming fatter, almost visibly, by the day. He was eating and drinking enormous quantities and his complexion which had never looked good - at least since I had known him - now looked even worse. It was redder and marked with more coloured blotches and his skin seemed to hang about his jowls even more heavily than before. He could hardly walk, even with the aid of his thick silver-knobbed stick and so he had to be carried around the court, either in a chair like a litter or moved about on a special wheeled chair. The fact that he was now dependent on his servants of course did nothing to help his temper. This meant that everyone was very wary of how they approached His Majesty about anything. However, none of this prepared me or anyone else for the next shock.

One day in the late autumn of 1545 after the queen had published her book, Lady Browne and Lady Edgecombe came to visit me at Richmond. When I asked them which wine they would like they told me that the news they had to tell me was far too important to worry about than deciding which wine to drink.

"First of all, milady, you mustn't come to court for the time being. It has become a very dangerous place. It has happened again," Lady Browne began.

"What has happened? Tell me. Does His Majesty wish to rid himself of this wife as well?" I asked, half in jest.

"Yes," Lady Edgecombe said, and I could see tears in her eyes.

The only thing I could do was to put my hands to my mouth. Again? I thought. How many wives will this man kill or have put away?

"Tell me what you know," I said at length, fearing the worst.

"Well, milady," Lady Browne continued. "You know that the queen enjoys talking about religious and philosophical matters and that she's in favour of the reformist ways?"

I nodded. Yes, I knew this.

"So the most important Catholics at court, those that believe in the pope and..."

"Who? The Earl of Southampton and Bishop Gardiner?"

"Yes. Well, they've been poisoning the king's ear about his wife," Lady Edgecombe said. "They kept telling him that it wasn't good for a woman to be so interested in books and religion and the king was heard to say, 'A good hearing it is when women become such clerks and to come into mine old days to be taught by my wife.'"

I sat there shocked. This sounded exactly like the time when Archbishop Cranmer and others had talked about Queen Catherine Howard to the king. However, this time it was the Catholic Bishop Gardiner who was doing the same about Queen Catherine Parr.

"And that's not all, milady," and Lady Edgecombe visibly shuddered as she continued. "Bishop Gardiner actually told His Majesty that it was a perilous matter to cherish a serpent within his own bosom."

I sat there, frozen like a block of ice. What was happening in the court? Was no woman safe there these days? I realised that I had best stay out of London if I did not wish to be involved in this terrible place. Catherine Parr had been good for His Majesty. She had calmed him down and had made life at court more tolerable for everyone there. He'd become more relaxed but now the Duke of Norfolk and Bishop Gardiner were trying to wreck all this for their own selfish needs. They wanted the Roman Catholic Church to return and if anyone were to suffer, they did not care.

"Yes," added Lady Browne. "There are also rumours flying around that His Majesty is thinking of taking another wife and annulling his present marriage. I heard from the imperial ambassador, François van der Delft, that the Earl of Suffolk's widow, Catherine Brandon, would be most suitable. These rumours have even been repeated in Antwerp and they say that Catherine Brandon would be more fertile than the queen. She'd be able to give him a son or two and that is what His Majesty wants more than anything else. Don't you agree?"

I nodded miserably. I wasn't very fond of the queen but I had no wish to see her harmed.

"And," added Lady Edgecombe, "people are saying, especially those who are friends of Bishop Gardiner, that the queen has been married twice before and not produced even one child, let alone a son."

"But that's not fair!" I protested. "Everybody at court knows that her first two husbands were old men. The first one died after only one year of marriage."

"We know that, milady, but that hasn't stopped the rumours," Lady Browne said, looking worried. "I wonder what's going to happen now. I must tell you, milady, I stay away from court now as much as I can. It's only because of my husband and his duties that I go there at all."

Soon after this frightening conversation, the two women left but returned two days later. Neither of them greeted me with a smile as they usually did. After a quick discussion and seeing that it was a sunny day, we agreed to have our conversation in a small arbour in the garden far away from anyone else's ears. I asked a servant to bring us some sweet wine and refreshments and then told him that we were not to be disturbed for the next hour. Then I settled down to hear my visitors' urgent and important news.

Lady Browne began. "You remember that we told you that the Duke of Norfolk and Bishop Gardiner want to get rid of the queen?" she asked.

I nodded. "And have they succeeded?"

"Let me tell you, milady, what happened before I tell you the end of the story," Lady Browne said. "I know everything that happened because I had to stay at court while Lady Edgecome here had to return to her country house on some domestic matter so I'll tell you everything that I heard and saw. Well, first of all, the council had the queen's ladies arrested."

"What! Lady Herbert, the queen's sister, and Lady Tyrwhitt and Lady Lane?"

"Yes, and then they were interrogated about which books they were reading and about which books Her Majesty was reading. Then the officers searched their rooms hoping to find some proof of the queen's heresy."

"And did they?"

"No, milady. Fortunately they found nothing that could even be thought of as heretical and so all the ladies were released."

"And did Her Majesty know about this?" I asked.

"No, milady. At least, if she did, she only learned about it later."

"Oh good," I breathed out in relief. "At least she is safe from the king's vultures."

Lady Edgecombe put a warning finger to her lips. "Just one minute. Lady Browne has not yet finished."

I sat there, as tense as a drawn bowstring. For one minute I had thought that the queen was safe and now I was to hear that this was not the case.

"Then," Lady Browne continued, wiping a few cake crumbs off her lips. "The queen heard about what'd happened and she became very nervous. She started crying and took to her room and there she started screaming hysterically."

"That's quite understandable" I said. "She was probably thinking of what'd happened to Anne Boleyn and Catherine Howard, and perhaps about Catherine of Aragon as well."

My two visitors nodded their heads. "I'm sure you're right, milady," Lady Edgecombe said grimly.

"In any event," continued Lady Browne, "The king, seeing her behaving like this, sent his new physician, Doctor Thomas Wendy, to see what was causing his normally calm and well-behaved wife to behave in such a manner."

"And did the queen tell the doctor?"

"Yes, milady. She sent the other physicians away and confided in him about what'd happened. But what the queen didn't know," Lady Browne added, "was that the king had already told Doctor Wendy about the whole situation, for he'd known about it all along. Then the doctor warned the queen that the duke and the bishop were plotting against her and that she should go and, to use the good doctor's words, 'conform herself to the king's mind.'"

"Did that help Her Majesty, to know what was being plotted behind her back?"

"I think so, milady," Lady Browne said. "But she still appeared to be very nervous and later, when the king came to see how she was, she told him everything."

"That's right," Lady Browne added. "And later Lady Lane, my friend who'd been waiting quietly at the back of the room behind some curtains, told me that the queen had told the king that he was her husband, lord and supreme head and governor here on earth and that he was next unto God to lean on."

The more I heard of all this plotting, the happier I was that I was now not a regular visitor at court. It sounded like a real snake-pit; a dangerous quicksand for the unwary.

Lady Browne continued. "Then His Majesty asked her why she'd tried to instruct him about religious matters."

"And what did she say to that?"

"Oh, milady, she gave him such a clever answer. She said that she'd engaged him on religious subjects only because she knew he was so interested in them. She said that while they were discussing these weighty matters he would not be thinking about the pains in his legs."

I clapped my hands. That was indeed a clever answer. But then I had to ask, "But did it save her?"

"Yes, milady," Lady Browne smiled. "He kissed her and called her his sweetheart and said they were perfect friends again, even more so than they had been in the past."

"So everything was settled," I concluded.

"Almost," Lady Brown said. "There is however one more chapter to this story, but I'll let Lady Edgecombe tell you."

Again my fears returned. "Tell me quickly," I said. "I must know."

"And so you shall, milady. The next day the king and queen were walking and talking in the gardens at Whitehall when suddenly the chancellor, the Earl of Southampton appeared, together with an escort of forty guards. When His Majesty asked him why he was there, Southampton told him that they had come to arrest the queen and escort her to the Tower. 'Come here, man,' the king called out to him and demanded an immediate explanation. After seeing that he'd made a terrible mistake, Southampton fell to his knees and started to beg for mercy and...."

"Yes," Lady Browne smiled and interrupted. "The king was so angry with his chancellor that he cut short his pleading, and in front of everyone - the queen, the guards, me and some other people who had appeared to see what was going on - he shouted at the chancellor that he was 'a knave, an arrant knave, a beast and a fool!' Lady Browne began to laugh. "It was so amusing to see that pompous ass get up off his knees trying to escape the king's hands as he tried to box his ears. And then he scrambled away like a rabbit and shouted to his men to follow him out of the garden."

"And so now Her Majesty is safe?" I asked.

"I think so, milady, I certainly hope so. But she told me that she won't be reading any more books that may be thought of as heretical. She said she had been concerned only with looking after His Majesty. I think the danger has passed."

"At least for the moment," I couldn't help adding.

"We hope for all time," Lady Edgecombe said. "And now that we've told you everything we must return to Whitehall. The tide will soon be ready for us to return."

"My ladies," I said as I escorted them to the small landing quay. "Why did you keep me in such tension if you knew this story had a happy ending?"

"Milady, we wanted you to feel what we've all been through these last few days at court," Lady Browne answered, perhaps a little sheepishly. "If we'd just told you the happy end, as you call it, you might not have listened to the whole story as carefully as you did. But fear not, we certainly had no intention in causing you to worry unduly. We love you too much for that."

And with those reassuring words, the three of us hugged one

another and then I bade them goodbye and returned to my chamber.

That night, as I watched the sun go down behind the clouds over the Thames, I thought how dangerous it was to be so near the king. On thinking back, I now realized that it had all been for the best – that is, the safest course for me - when I had learned that he did not wish to marry me again. It was safer that I spend most of my time here at Richmond Palace or at Bletchlingly. If I were to go to court, I'd make sure that my visits were short and I wouldn't allow myself to become involved in anything that could be interpreted by anyone as plotting or treasonous.

From now on, until the king's death at the end of January 1547, my life for the most part followed a very pleasant routine. My friendship with the king's daughter, Princess Mary, grew stronger and more intimate and we saw that we could talk about any subject that we wanted - apart from religion and politics. She had inherited her mother's strict and fervent belief in the old Roman Catholic Church while my beliefs tended to be more liberal. Nevertheless, a true friendship developed between us and on one occasion she made me a very generous gift of a long length of some beautiful Spanish silk.

Moreover, I saw that the princess, who was only one year older than me, felt so well staying with me at Richmond that she also gave presents to my officers and servants. They truly appreciated this gesture and tried even harder to serve the woman who perhaps one day would become the next Queen of England.

At the same time, when I wasn't entertaining the princess, I began to make more frequent but short visits to court. In fact, I became such a regular visitor that I heard a courtier say that the Lady Anne goes and comes at her pleasure. And a pleasure it was. I was on good terms with the queen, with His Majesty and with the two princesses. The king liked me to be in his presence so much that I was included in the list of courtiers who greeted the Admiral of France during the grand reception held in his honour in August 1546.

But while this was a very exciting celebration, it was also the last time I saw His Majesty, even though I didn't realize it at the time. I noticed how ill he looked and said as much to Lady Rutland.

"You must look at him," I indicated with my head towards where the king was speaking to the admiral and several of his men. "He looks so ill. It is as though he's in permanent pain."

Lady Rutland nodded. "He can hardly walk and he's carried around now almost all of the time. The wounds on his legs give him no rest and they are constantly leaking. Oh, my dear, I'm so glad it's not one of my duties to dress his legs, for they smell so foul that anyone who does dress them must be a saint or have no nose."

"And he is so fat," I whispered. "How can anybody be that size?"

"Well, you would also be like that if you ate and drank like he does. His doctors have warned him but he won't listen. And most of what he eats is far too rich for him. I'm sure it can't be doing him any good."

It wasn't. From that autumn on, His Majesy's health began to decline. He spent less time at court and had less to do with both his wife and with me. His only concern was about the affairs of state and about his son, Prince Edward. The little boy had grown up to be a bookish and precocious nine year old who apparently preferred discussing ideas to playing games or riding his horse in the palace grounds.

The end of the king's life came during the last days of January 1547. A month before, during the Christmas season, he had sent the queen to Greenwich Palace together with most of his household and courtiers. As no reason for this was officially given, it caused more rumours to circulate and, all the while, His Majesty's physician's worked on his bloated, ulcerous legs. I'm sure that they knew he was dying but as it was treason to predict the king's death they said nothing but did the best they could to alleviate the pain.

During this period His Majesty began to isolate himself from more and more people and, to my surprise, didn't even summon his son to come to his bedside from his country home at Ashridge. Instead, he held long conversations with William Paget, my past secretary and now his Privy Councillor and close adviser. Later I was told that they, together with Queen Jane's older brother and uncle to the young prince, Thomas Seymour, organized all the details for the new government. This would come into power when the prince became king but because of his young age he would have to be aided by an advisory council.

On a more personal level, the king decreed that he should be buried at Windsor, next to the body of Queen Jane, his beloved third wife. He also gave orders that the Duke of Norfolk, who had been imprisoned in the Tower in the meanwhile for treason two weeks before Christmas, was to be executed.

However, the duke's luck held. The king died before this grim sentence could be carried out and as the new council did not want to start the young King Edward's reign with a bloody execution, it was decided that the duke was to remain in prison for the time being.

I heard that the only official present when my one and only husband died on 28 January was Archbishop Cranmer. Because of all the plotting and planning that surrounded the setting up of a new government to be led by Edward Seymour, the news of the king's death was delayed for a while. Together with everyone else in the country, I learnt of this through hearsay but later several of my ladies came to confirm that what I had originally heard as gossip was in fact true.

I heard the news with mixed feelings. On one hand he had been my husband during a rather unpleasant six-month period. On the other, once we were divorced, he had treated me well even though that could not be said by many other people. They had suffered from his quick temper and unpredictable nature. I heard that the king regretted having had Cromwell executed and he complained that not one of his other officials had ever worked so well as his past chancellor.

Finally, his death meant, of course, that I was no longer the 'King's Sister.' Until Prince Edward came of age, the country would be run by Edward Seymour, the Lord Protector. What would become of me and how I would be treated was a question that only time would tell.

Chapter Twenty-Two - Matters Domestic and National

The ink had hardly dried on the official documents concerning my past husband's death when the Lord Protector conferred higher ranks upon himself and several of his favourite councillors. From being the Earl of Hertford, he now took the ancient and honourable rank of the Duke of Somerset, while at the same time he promoted his younger brother, Thomas, to be Baron Seymour of Sudeley Castle.

And although the queen had given the king much comfort and good advice during his last years, he did not see it fit to grant her a place on the Regency Council. Soon after the king's death, I suggested to Lady Browne that this was probably because she was a woman and we knew what the king and most of his councillors thought of women – their role was to be merely decorative and to provide sons.

Lady Browne shook her head. "I'm not sure I agree with you," she said. "I think that perhaps he thought that if a widow and a wealthy one at that, could have so much money and influence, she could find herself married off to any unsuitable man; one who was marrying her only for her wealth and her position. And perhaps," Lady Browne added, "His Majesty did her a favour by not appointing her to the council. Now she'll be able to live out her life as she pleases, either as a wealthy widow or marry again to someone who gains her heart."

And someone did gain her heart. Thomas Seymour himself. It was an open secret at court that Catherine Parr had been in love with the Lord Protector's brother four years before she had been forced into marrying the king. However, now that she was free, she could do what she wanted. And that is what she did. As usual I learned of this through a conversation I had with Lady Rutland.

"Have you heard, my dear, that the queen or, rather, the past queen has married Thomas Seymour?" she asked me one spring day about three months after Henry's death. "They were secretly married, I believe in Chelsea and my spies..."

"You mean your gossips," I laughed.

"Well, yes, my gossips told me that Lady Catherine's cousin, Sir Nicholas Throckmorton, conducted the service but that very few people attended it."

"Why? Wasn't she happy to marry her loved one at last?" I asked.

"Oh, I'm sure she was, my dear, but she didn't want to anger her brother-in-law or his proud wife. You know," she said leaning forward conspiratorially and obviously enjoying this conversation, "that the newly created duchess is such a proud and overbearing woman that I'm not surprised that Lady Catherine wanted to delay the news for as long as possible before that impossible tyrant found out."

I smiled. "And now that the king's widow has married him I don't suppose Lady Throckmorton can do much about it, can she?"

Now it was Lady Rutland's turn to smile. "No," she said. "All she can do, and probably will, is to shout at her husband who, knowing him, will run off to the council chamber where he knows no women are allowed."

Despite my earlier, mixed feelings about Lady Catherine, I was very pleased on her behalf. She had been married to three older men and for her, marriage often meant acting more as a nurse to them rather than being a lusty wife with her own feminine needs to fulfill. This time she was marrying for love. What could be better than that?

And in addition to running her new household, she took in her two cousins, Princess Elizabeth and Lady Jane Grey. These two lively girls were just the sort of daughters Lady Catherine would have wanted for herself. They were bright, loved to read and to learn and they both had sharp enquiring minds. They were just like younger versions of their aunt. They would provide her with all the warm and intellectual companionship that she needed when her husband was away from home.

And so 1547, a year which had started with my past husband's death turned into 1548 a year which started with the news of a birth.

One windy day at the end of March Lady Browne told me that Lady Catherine was with child.

"Are you sure?" I asked, for neither she nor her husband were very young. She was thirty-six and he was ten years older.

"Yes, I'm sure," she said. "The baby is due at the end of the summer - some time in August or September."

I clapped my hands. "That's such lovely news," I said. "And I suppose she'll be wanting a boy to carry on the good name of the family."

"Of course, my dear Anne. Oh, I'm so happy for her. I do hope everything works out well for her. She certainly deserves it."

But it was not to be. At the end of that summer, ten days into September, the Earl of Rutland and his wife sought me out while I was paying a brief visit to court. They beckoned me to follow them and led me to a small and little-used chamber at the back of the palace where we could talk in private. As my eyes grew accustomed to the dim room and the single flickering torch, I noticed that the eyes of my chamberlain's wife were wet. I put my hand on her shoulder and asked what was wrong.

"Has anything happened to you or your family?"

"No, my dear, but it has to Lady Catherine. She is dead."

I stood there in shock. It was not possible. I'd seen her only recently and she had been so happy at the thought of giving birth to her first child. She had said that she was sure it was a boy. 'Just feel him kicking inside me,' she had said and placed my hand on her round belly. 'I'm sure it's a boy,' she'd smiled, 'but whatever it is, I just want it to be healthy. Oh, my dear Anne, I cannot wait for the day. I've wanted to be a mother for so long.' And then she'd told me that her husband was so happy that he'd even put aside his quarrels with his brother.

But now their happiness had crashed into dust. The baby, a girl whom they'd called Mary in honour of Princess Mary, was born without too many problems. Everyone was so happy and

Lady Catherine lay back in her bed, radiant in her new-found motherhood. And then a week later she was dead. The dreaded childbirth fever had killed her.

"Just like with Queen Jane," Lady Rutland sobbed. "It's so unfair."

One hour later I ordered my carriage, and my guards and I left the palace. There was no point in staying there. My visit had turned to ashes. Anything I'd wanted to do that day could wait for happier times. I was in no mood to speak to the council or any of its officers about the state of my finances, one of the reasons I had come to London.

One of the first things I'd noticed after King Henry's death was that my financial situation had worsened and that the upkeep of my belovèd Richmond Palace had become a serious burden. As the time passed I found it harder and harder to pay for repairs to the luxurious apartments in its massive stone keep or to pay for the repairs to the wooden galleries which linked the apartments to the gardens. As the palace began to look more and more neglected, I began spending more time at my other residence at Bletchingly. Although it was not as grand as Richmond, it was, as the English say, more 'cosy.'

My keeper of the house and lands at Bletchingly was Sir Thomas Cawarden. He was a man of many parts. Although he'd been appointed for this rôle seven years earlier, in 1540, he'd also become the M.P. for Bletchingly two years later and then held this position for five years. He must have kept His Majesty happy for while he was fulfilling these two positions, the king appointed him to be his Master of Revels and Tents. I must admit that I found this a strange sounding title and so one day when she was on one of her visits to me I asked Lady Rutland what it meant.

"My dear Anne, it means that in addition to being responsible for the various entertainments we enjoy at court, Cawarden is also responsible for all the equipment that the players, musicians and others use as well as being in charge of the upkeep of all of His Majesty's tents."

"But why is that so important? Why cannot one of the stewards have this job?"

"Because, Sir Thomas not only has to look after the tents used for our entertainment, but he also has to look after those used in war – on the battlefield. That's why King Henry took him on his campaign to France a few years ago."

"And is that why the king granted him the right to keep forty liveried servants for his own use?"

"It is, indeed. It seems that Sir Thomas pleased His Majesty so much that he knighted him on the battlefield at Boulogne and that's why he has that expensive house now at Blackfriars in London."

"I see," I said slowly. "And I suppose that's why he keeps asking me if I'd be willing to sell Bletchingly to him."

"Why, my dear, does he like this place so much?"

"He certainly does. He just can't wait to get his hands on its sixty-three rooms and its deer parks."

Lady Rutland then muttered something about how some people were never satisfied with their lot and were always grasping for more.

"I suppose," she said, "it's because he was born the son of a trader – a cloth fuller – and now he sees it as his right to grab as much as he can, especially as he has found favour in the king's eyes."

I agreed with her and then asked if she could tell me something about the present financial situation and why although I was considered very wealthy, I was finding it very difficult to pay all my bills for Richmond Palace.

"I'm not quite sure, my dear," she answered as she sipped a glass of sweet red wine. "I usually leave such matters to my husband, but I heard him say that the price of food has risen so much recently and that, together with the king's debasement of the coinage, hasn't helped. You know that our English coins over the past few years have been minted using base metals? According to my husband, that means they aren't as in demand as other coins, say those from France or Spain."

I nodded my head as I absorbed Lady Rutland's explanations. So there were good reasons for my present financial problems. It was not just a case of me overspending.

"And Cawarden," I said, "has become so unpleasant

recently. In addition to criticizing me about the state of the house itself, he complained when I had some small buildings built, such as the inn, and also when my servants cut down some trees for firewood."

"He did that?" exclaimed a shocked Lady Rutland. "And to you, a past Queen of England? Me? I would chop off his head for impertinence."

I smiled. "I'm not sure I would go as far as that but he kept saying that those trees were very valuable and that it was a real waste of good wood to cut them down. I mean, what does the man want? That I should freeze to death during the winter months? But then I think he regretted being so forward because a short while after he'd complained to me, Sir William Goring…"

"Your new chamberlain?"

"Yes, and Goring told Sir Thomas to send me forty loads of charcoal so that I wouldn't need to cut down any more of his precious trees."

"Oh, how very generous of him," Lady Rutland said with a half-smile. "Or could it be that he still wants to buy Bletchingly complete with its own woodland?"

I nodded in agreement and it seemed that Lady Rutland's comment was well placed. In April that year, Sir Thomas Cawarden with help from King Edward was able to buy Bletchingly from under my feet, as it were, and add it to his own growing list of properties. As a result, I moved to my other manor at Hever Castle, Anne Boleyn's birthplace, some twelve miles to the east.

As you may imagine, forcing me to move my household - at the age of thirty-five - did nothing to endear Cawarden to me. Apart from his grasping nature, one of the reasons he acted thus was because of the religious differences between us. He was an ardent reformer, while I was more conservative. I heard that as soon as he was able to do so, he carried out some drastic changes in the church at Bletchingly. He whitewashed over the beautiful wall paintings and decorations, defaced the altar and removed the church's rood loft.

But to his surprise and annoyance, he discovered that he

couldn't ride rough shod over me all of the time. There were occasions on which I enjoyed some form of revenge. When I paid him visits at Bletchingly, as I had to from time to time, or to visit him at his fine Blackfriars house, I made sure that such visits cost him dearly. I would bring as many members of my household as I could. This meant that that our host had to pay for all our food, drink and other provisions such as fodder, clean floor rushes and candles. Naturally we would be wanting a very good meal after our journey and of course I insisted on being fed with nothing but the best! Naturally he had to supply us with everything we asked for as he had no wish to acquire the reputation of being a mean host. This meant that we dined well on spiced foods which included ginger, pepper and cloves, and that our meat dishes were garnished with prunes and raisins. And if that weren't enough, Sir Thomas had to pay for our firewood and torches.

It seems that my household's demands were so many and so expensive that after we returned to Hever Sir Thomas wrote to the king's council seeking financial compensation for our visit. I never found out if he received any but that was not my problem. He had treated me in such a high-handed way that he could not expect any sympathy. Usually I got on well with everyone I met, but I didn't want my usual undemanding nature to be taken for granted, especially by the likes of this grasping official.

Despite being relieved of maintaining Bletchingly, my financial situation worsened as the reign of King Edward progressed. I was forced to petition the council for funds but these took a long time in coming. His Majesty used his progress around the kingdom as an excuse for not replying promptly to my request and I looked back longingly to the days when his father would generously grant me extra funds and financial gifts whether I needed them or not.

The situation became so bad that I seriously began considering whether to return to Cleves after all. I wrote to my brother and his reply was to send several ambassadors to England to speak to Archbishop Cranmer. The archbishop promised to do what he could but unfortunately these were just empty words. I appealed to the council again and eventually they granted me some money but it was not enough.

If money was a problem then so too was religion. The new king had been brought up as a Protestant and so now that he was in power he surrounded himself with like-minded advisers. The most senior of these was Queen Jane's older brother, Edward Seymour, the Duke of Somerset. He called himself the Lord Protector and presided over a council of sixteen members. Their duty was to advise the young king until he reached his maturity at the age of eighteen. The idea of this council had been devised by King Henry and he'd hoped that it would ensure a smooth succession after his death. Unfortunately, this didn't happen. The Lord Protector faced much opposition from several of the council members including his younger brother, Thomas. Baron Sudeley.

On one of her visits to Hever, Lady Browne told me about the council's problems, especially those that existed between the two brothers, Edward and Thomas Seymour.

"My dear," she said as we sat in the gardens looking out over the rolling hills of the North Downs. "If you think you have had problems with your brother, they are nothing in comparison to what the Lord Protector is having with *his* brother. They're much more serious. My husband told me that Thomas raised so many objections to Edward's decisions that the Protector had to buy him off with a barony and a promotion."

"What sort of promotion? To be in charge of the army?"

"No, my dear, the navy. The Protector made his brother Lord Admiral."

"And was he satisfied with this?"

"No. Thomas Seymour insisted that as he was one of the king's uncles, he wanted more power."

"Did he get it?"

"No. So Thomas began plotting behind Edward's back and did things such as giving extra pocket money to the king and telling him that it was his older brother, the Protector, who was keeping him in such a beggarly state."

"Did the Protector find out about this?"

"Oh, he most certainly did. When he found out what was going on, he had his brother arrested on charges of treason and embezzlement. And not only that. There is to be a trial and the king is to testify against Sir Thomas."

This was terrible news. Whatever difficulties I'd had with my own somewhat stubborn brother I could not imagine him putting me on trial for treason. We had been brought up to keep our problems within the family and not let the whole world know of any disagreements we may have had. But clearly, the Lord Protector did not think like that. He arranged for the king to testify against Thomas Seymour and, as a result, an Act of Attainder was passed against him. Shortly afterwards, Lady Browne informed me that the younger Seymour was executed at the Tower and I felt very sad about this.

I had met him a few times when I had attended court at King Henry's palaces at Hampton Court or Whitehall and had found him to be a gentleman who was very courteous and pleasant to converse with. He never spoke about anything serious but I knew he had harboured great affection for Catherine Parr when she had been alive. Some people said that he loved her money and title more than the lady herself, but I am willing to give him the benefit of the doubt and say that he loved her for herself.

What I learned from the above was to make sure that I did not become involved in any politics or intrigues particularly those connected to the Regency Council. This meant that I visited the court only on rare occasions and that I spent most of my time entertaining my friends at Hever Castle. Perhaps I was somewhat too lavish in my entertaining for sometime in 1552, Jasper Brockehouse, my treasurer, told me that I was exceeding my annual budget by one thousand pounds every year. He tried to help me by trying to reduce my expenses and many in my household were very unhappy when he told them that they'd have to tighten their belts. One man who was greatly put out by the more economical way of life was my young cousin, Count von Waldeck. He had come to stay with me for a long visit and had brought eight servants with him.

Now that he was told that they could not eat and drink and spend money on their horses as freely as they had been doing he became very angry.

One day, while I was sitting in my chamber reading Sir Thomas Wyatt's poem, *I Find No Peace*, my cousin knocked on the door and without waiting for permission to enter, stormed in and started complaining.

"What's happening here?" he shouted, standing there facing me, arms akimbo. "Why can't I order that meat like we had last month and why can't we have another half dozen barrels of that sweet red wine as well? Who is this Brockehouse fellow to tell me how I should wine and dine?"

"My dear cousin," I replied as calmly as I can. "We've been living too extravagantly and now we have to limit ourselves for a while and..."

"Well," he continued belligerently. "I didn't come all this way to England to live like a peasant."

"I'm sorry, but you are going to have to, as you say, live like a peasant until our finances improve. Remember, this isn't like the old days when King Henry was alive."

"Why not?" he pouted.

"Because then he'd always give me extra money so that we'd not have to think about what we were ordering," I explained, "but now those days are over."

"Well, I'm not going to live like this. I'm going back to Cleves and after I return home I'll tell your brother what it's like here and how you treated me," and he turned around and stormed out in the same way he had stormed in.

He was as good as his word. A few days later he and his servants returned to Cleves and told my brother what he'd seen. Apparently he also told my brother that I should get rid of Brockehouse and his wife, Gertrude, and another servant called Otto Wyllik. All this I learned from a letter and after reading it I decided I wouldn't carry out my brother's 'requests' as he called them. What right had he to tell me how to run my life? He hadn't seen me for twelve years. But my stubborn brother wouldn't accept my decision and he wrote to the council and told them about my financial affairs and how I was living my life.

The result was that the council ordered four of my servants including Brockehouse and Wyllik to 'depart from the house and family of the Lady Anne of Cleves' and if they returned to England it was 'at their uttermost peril.'

This miserable affair made me very sad, for I'd grown very fond of my servants, especially Brockehouse's wife, Gertrude, but it paled in contrast to what was happening outside my private domain. However, this I will tell you about in the next chapter.

Chapter Twenty-Three - Power and Death

Edward Seymour, the Protector, was not having an easy time ruling the country in the king's name. Two rebellions had broken out: one in the south-west and another in East Anglia. The causes of the unrest were religion and land enclosures. I learned later that Seymour had become so unpopular in the council that Sir William Paget had written him a note saying, 'Every man of the council hath misliked your proceedings.' This and other remarks made the Protector feel so unsafe in London that he fled to Windsor castle. I also learned that this was not only a case of the Protector not succeeding as an efficient ruler but also that John Dudley, the Earl of Warwick, was trying to oust him at the same time. The earl planned to rule the council and, therefore, the country in his stead. He succeeded in doing this three months later.

For a short while it appeared that Seymour and Dudley had resolved their differences and were now working in harmony, but it soon became clear that Edward Seymour was not happy at having to share power with the equally ambitious Earl of Warwick. Then, as time passed, Dudley discovered that Seymour was plotting against him in order to regain his former and complete control of the council. Dudley wasted no time. He had Seymour arrested for felony - which I understood was a very serious crime - and soon after had him executed at the Tower in January 1552.

"He went the same way as his younger brother, Thomas," I commented to Lady Browne when I heard the news. "Killed by the axeman."

Lady Browne shrugged. "That's what power does to you, my dear. It raises you up and it brings you down."

"Yes," I said with a grimace. "As Saint Matthew says, 'The power and the glory.'"

"So let's see what the power and the glory do for the Earl of Warwick," Lady Browne said. "Now that he has risen, will he also be brought down?"

He was, but not in the way he imagined. Towards the end of the year rumours started circulating around the court that young King Edward was not well. Each time his coughing fits started, they took longer and longer to cease. My ladies told me that the poor lad was growing visibly weaker and paler and that the Earl of Warwick, who had promoted himself to be the Duke of Northumberland, was trying to cover this up by saying the king was merely suffering from a passing childish illness. At the same time, he arranged for his son, Guildford, a spoilt and callow youth, to marry the king's fifteen year old cousin, Lady Jane Grey. At first she would not consent but her parents - who were always looking for advancement - would not allow their daughter to refuse. In the end the poor girl was bullied into this unwanted marriage. The result was that the marriage of Lady Jane Grey and Guildford Dudley took place at the Duke of Northumberland's London home towards the end of May 1553.

At first I couldn't understand why the duke was so insistent that Lady Jane marry his son. After all, young Guildford loved hunting and the outdoor life while nothing kept his new wife happier than reading Latin and Hebrew texts or discussing religion and philosophy with grey-haired academics.

"Did the marriage take place just because the duke wishes his son to marry into the powerful Grey family, or is there more to it than meets the eye?" I asked Lady Rutland on one of her visits.

"That's part of the reason, my dear, but it's also because Lady Jane is a cousin of the king. And if," and here she looked around carefully before continuing, "and if anything should happen to His Majesty, then Lady Jane will be next in line to the throne…"

"And the duke's son, Guildford, will be the next king," I said, finishing off her explanation.

"Exactly."

"But what about the princesses, Mary and Elizabeth?" I asked. "I know that King Henry declared in an Act of Succession that they should succeed his son in that order, first

Mary and then Elizabeth if, God forbid, anything should happen to Edward."

"I know that," Lady Rutland said quietly, almost whispering, "but word has got out that Northumberland has persuaded, some say forced, the king to declare his sisters illegitimate. He said they are the daughters of the divorced Catherine of Aragon and the beheaded Anne Boleyn and so the next in line should be Lady Jane."

"And is the Duke of Northumberland in favour of Lady Jane because she is also a Protestant and because Princess Mary believes in the old faith?" I asked.

Lady Rutland nodded. "And although Princess Elizabeth is thought to be more in favour of the Protestant faith, her sister Mary is older. And as Northumberland cannot get rid of Mary unless he chops off her head or something like that, he will do his best to have Lady Jane on the throne if he wants the Protestant ways to become established in this country."

I listened to all this carefully and became further convinced to stay away from the devious Duke of Northumberland.

"Yes, my dear Anne," Lady Browne added, rising to leave. "It all depends on His Majesty's health. If he should die, poor lad, then this country will know no peace."

Lady Browne's predictions came true. The poor young king lay in his bed coughing and becoming more and more frail. His life ended on 6 July 1553. Four days later the Duke of Northumberland had Lady Jane crowned the Queen of England. It seemed that he had succeeded. His aim was to rule the country as the chief adviser hovering in the background behind his son, Guildford, and the new queen. But it was not to be.

Despite the threats made by the duke and her parents, Queen Jane refused to make her new husband king. In addition, the council which at first had supported the duke, now switched their allegiance and decided to support Princess Mary's claim to the throne. In the meanwhile, Mary had left London and was busy gathering her forces in East Anglia.

To forestall her plans, the duke took his own forces and planned to capture the princess before she could succeed in entering London as Queen Mary, the rightful queen as designated by her father, King Henry. However, Northumberland failed and was taken prisoner. The triumphant Princess Mary, together with Princess Elizabeth and eight hundred lords and nobles at the head of a large army, then entered the capital to claim her throne. The duke was thrown into the Tower, a prison he now shared with his son and his daughter-in-law, Lady Jane Grey. She had reigned for nine days and had not enjoyed one single moment of it. So much for the power and the glory, I thought.

I was present when Princess Mary was crowned shortly afterwards and this was the last time that I was to appear in public. The celebrations lasted for several days and they included a royal procession from the Tower through the City of London to Whitehall, where the coronation took place. The new Queen Mary made a speech and as she held the ceremonial ring she declared, "I am already married to this Common weal and the faithful members of the same, the spousal ring whereof I have on my finger."

Two weeks later, the Protestant Duke of Northumberland, the man who had condemned Seymour, King Edward the Sixth's Lord Protector to death and who had tried to prevent Queen Mary from succeeding to the throne met a similar fate. Queen Mary had her revenge and started on her campaign to bring the Roman Catholic faith back to England.

When I heard about this I repeated Lady Browne's words to her about power having a way of raising you and then bringing you crashing down.

"I wonder what'll happen to our new queen?" I asked. "I wonder how she'll survive in a man's world." Then I asked her if Queen Mary was the first queen who had reigned in England.

"No, my dear. Four hundred years ago there was a Queen Matilda who was also known as Queen Maud. She called herself 'Lady of the English' and she tried to take the crown away from her cousin King Stephen."

"Did she succeed?"

"Yes, but only for a very short time. She was very arrogant

and wouldn't reduce the taxes for the people of London. So they threw her out after a few months they took King Stephen back again."

"So Mary doesn't really have a good example to follow, does she?"

"No, my dear. I'm afraid she doesn't."

A few months later I decided to seek an audience with the queen as I had some ideas about whom I thought she should marry and I wanted to discuss them with her in private and not through any letters or messengers. I must admit I was thinking about a marriage not only for love but one that would also benefit Cleves.

The queen greeted me in her private chamber as graciously as she had done when she was a princess. We chatted about our friends and families and ate a few cakes and drank a little wine. Then feeling comfortable in her presence, I started to tell her about my ideas.

"Your Majesty," I began. "I've been thinking of this for some time now. I think the time has come for you to take a husband."

She smiled and her eyes twinkled. "I've also been thinking the same, and I've probably given this problem even more thought than you have - and for a longer time as well. So my dear Anne, who do you have in mind? Who will keep me and the country happy?"

"The Archduke Ferdinand."

"Your brother-in-law?"

"Yes, Your Majesty. After all, not only is he the King of Hungary, Bohemia and Croatia, but he is also an observant and God-fearing Roman Catholic like yourself. And of course, it goes without saying that he comes from good stock."

"Yes, my dear, I know that. And I also know that he is a very forthright soul as well. Did you know his motto is, *Fiat iustitia, et perea mundus* – Let justice be done though the world perish?"

I told her that I didn't know that particular fact but if she married him, there was a good chance that he would give her many healthy sons.

"Yes," she replied, her sharp eyes twinkling. "And if I married him it would be good for your duchy as well."

This queen was no fool and she promised that she would consider my suggestion.

Later I discovered that my brother and I had not been the only ones to suggest that she marry the archduke. The King of the Romans had also sent an ambassador to London with the same idea in mind but for some reason that I didn't understand at the time, the queen refused to meet him. Whenever an appointment was arranged, the queen suddenly felt ill and said that it was impossible for her to meet with him. At first when I asked one of my ladies for an explanation they couldn't give me a credible answer. But then Lady Rutland told me what she had heard.

"It's because of Philip of Spain," she said.

"The Emperor's son?"

"Yes, my dear. It seems that quite some time ago Her Majesty decided to marry him."

"But would such a marriage be accepted in England?" I asked, surprising myself somewhat as I found myself thinking about this problem from the English and not the Clevean point of view. "You know how much the English love the Spanish. You only have to say *Spanish* and the English say *Inquisition*.

"I know that, my dear Anne, but don't repeat what I am going to tell you now. Not to anyone. From what I've heard, the queen will not hear a single word spoken against him. She thinks he is a saint."

When I heard that the queen wished to marry King Philip I was very disappointed, especially as I couldn't think of how this marriage would bring any benefit to my native country. I also found out that I wasn't the only one who was disappointed. The newly appointed Lord Chancellor, together with the Duke of Norfolk, was also in favour of the queen marrying an English subject. He suggested that she should marry Edward Courtenay, a descendant of King Edward the Fourth. I knew the queen liked him for she had released him from prison where, in 1538, Henry the Eighth had sent him for alleged conspiracy. Since his release, she'd created him the

Earl of Devon and it was he who had carried the Sword of State at her coronation. However, we were soon to learn that once the queen had decided to marry the Spanish king, the newly-created earl stood no chance of becoming her husband.

What none of us realised at the time was that the queen's idea to marry Philip would start a rebellion which the rebel leaders hoped would lead to her overthrow and replacement by a Protestant monarch. The rebellion was to be led by several lords and knights who would bring their forces to London from the four corners of the country. This was not to be a minor one-day uprising but a well-organised national rebellion. Three of the ringleaders included Sir Thomas Wyatt, the son of the poet, Lady Jane Grey's father, the Duke of Suffolk, and Edward Courtenay.

The rebellion broke out in January 1554 but within a week the queen's troops had put it down and the ringleaders had been sent to the Tower. A few were released but several others including Sir Thomas Wyatt and Lady Jane's father were incarcerated in the Tower. Over eighty of the rebels were hanged.

"And that's not all," Lady Browne said when she came to visit me a few days later with Lady Edgecombe. We were sitting out in the garden enjoying the weak wintry sunshine. "Do you remember that I told you that Sir Thomas Wyatt and the Duke of Suffolk had been sent to the Tower?"

I nodded.

"Well, while they were there, the queen had Lady Jane and Guildford executed as well."

"Why?" I gasped in shock. "She was such a sweet and innocent creature. The only things that interested her were her books and learning foreign languages."

"I know that, my dear," Lady Edgecombe said, laying a supportive hand on my shoulder. "But the queen, aided by her Catholic advisers, decided that Lady Jane Grey was too near the throne and too Protestant to be allowed to live."

"That's right," added Lady Browne. "And they also claimed that the poor girl had been tainted by her father. They said that since he had supported Sir Thomas Wyatt, his daughter was also suspect of being part of the plot."

"But how can that be?" I asked, wiping my eyes. "She's been in prison for these past six months."

"I know that, and you know that, but these Catholic supporters of the queen aren't interested in any logical explanation like that. All they want to do is snuff out all reformist or any other plots before they start."

I sat there silently for a few minutes thinking of that young girl laying her sweet, clever head on the block. Oh, the waste of it all. Jane was the last person in the world who'd threaten the queen. In the past they'd got on so well when they had met each other at Catherine Parr's house but now Queen Mary had ordered this small scholarly girl to be hacked to death. It wasn't right. It just wasn't. And what had turned the gracious Mary I had known into such a ferocious killer? Was she the only one to make these cruel decisions or had she been pushed by her advisers who were interested only in bringing the Roman Catholic Church back to England? I thought back to my earlier conversation with the queen. Did she also believe in *Fiat iustitia, et perea mundus* – Let justice be done though the world perish?

And that wasn't the only grim news I heard that chilly February. Two weeks later I was told that Lady Jane's father and Sir Thomas Wyatt had also been executed.

If before I had gone to the court only on rare occasions, now I visited it even less. First of all, the extreme and suffocating atmosphere there did not appeal to me and secondly, I was beginning to suffer from longer and longer periods of ill-health. I was spending more of my time in bed and in order to be nearer London and my physicians I moved into my manor house in Chelsea.

In the spring of 1557 I could feel the end was coming and as I lay in my sickbed or sat in the peaceful gardens in what had been one of Catherine Parr's favourite houses, I started writing out my will. I bequeathed various sums of money and jewellery to my friends, ladies and servants and I also remembered to leave money for the poor folk of Richmond, Bletchingley, Hever and Dartford. I also left jewels for Queen

Mary and Princess Elizabeth and I knew that on my demise my lands would revert to the Crown.

The last thing I remember was that on 15 July 1557, I was smiling and holding the hands of one of my ladies and feeling particularly weak and sleepy. More than that, I cannot recall.

THE END

Epilogue

Anne of Cleves died on 18 July 1557, her final request being "that we may have the suffrages of holy church according to the Catholic faith, wherein we end our life in this transitory world."

Queen Mary, appointed as executor of the will, provided a splendid funeral for her. Of all of Henry VIII's six wives, Anne of Cleves was the only one to be buried in Westminster Abbey. Today it is difficult to locate her tomb due to all the other monuments that tend to hide it. Nevertheless, despite the fact that many of the ornaments that decorated the tomb were stolen soon after the ceremony, it is still possible to make out the letters A and C carved below a crown on two sides of her tomb.

One month after she was buried, according to tradition, Anne's household officers symbolically broke their white staves of office and threw them into the tomb. Their period of employment had come to an end.

Queen Mary wrote to Anne's brother to inform him of her death and he ordered memorial services to be held throughout the Duchy of Cleves for 'Princess Anna, Duchess of Julia, Cleves and Berg, Queen of England.'

To sum up the English half of Anne of Cleves' life, she was in many ways the most fortunate of all Henry VIII's wives. Despite her bewildering and unpleasant marriage and quick divorce from a man obsessed with having sons, she stepped down from the throne with much money and property in addition to all the jewels, plate and rich clothes she had acquired during her short six months as Queen of England. Her relationship with her past husband improved and with time they grew to be very friendly. However, her greatest achievement of all was to walk away from this bloated and demanding king with her head on her shoulders.

*   *   *   *   *   *   *   *   *

And what happened to those who played an important rôle at the end of Anne's life? **Queen Mary** threw away the popularity she had gained at the beginning of her reign when she married the Spanish king, Philip II, just eight months after her coronation in October 1553. In addition, she became increasingly fervent in her Roman Catholic beliefs. Nearly three hundred Protestants paid for this with their lives by being burnt at the stake. This grim statistic caused the once gentle queen to be known forever as Bloody Mary.

One of the most famous men she had executed was Henry VIII's Archbishop of Canterbury, **Thomas Cranmer**, the major compiler of the Book of Common Prayer. With Mary's rise to power, Cranmer was arrested and spent two years in prison before being burnt at the stake. During this period and under relentless pressure from the Roman Catholic authorities, he recanted his Protestant beliefs. However, on the day of his execution he publicly rejected his Catholicism and demonstrated this by placing his right hand in the flames; the hand that had signed his earlier recantation.

One of Cranmer's major opponents, the Catholic **Duke of Norfolk**, was released from the Tower, restored to his former position on the Privy Council by a grateful queen. The last service he rendered her was to command a force of men to put down a planned rebellion by some of the country's Protestant gentry. However, he did not enjoy his new-found power for long as he died aged 81 on 25 August 1554, just one year after Mary had come to power.

One of the chief clerics who had supported the Duke of Norfolk for many years was **Stephen Gardiner, the Bishop of Winchester.** Like Norfolk, he was also restored to power by a grateful queen and like Norfolk, did not live very long to enjoy his new-found power. Among his first official tasks was to crown the queen at her coronation and to open the first parliament as the new Lord Chancellor. In May 1555 he was sent to Calais to work out a peace agreement with the French but did not succeed. Five months later he died as one of the queen's chief judges whose task was to investigate and prosecute the country's Protestant clergy.

As for Queen Mary's younger sister, *Princess Elizabeth*, despite living through a dangerous period in which she was imprisoned in the Tower and accused of treason and heresy, she managed to survive. She inherited the reins of power five years after her sister's coronation and restored the country to the Protestant faith. Apart from this major feature of her reign, she encouraged a more liberal atmosphere in the country, an atmosphere that bred writers and poets such as Shakespeare, Ben Jonson, Sir Walter Raleigh and Edmund Spenser.

One of the chief players in this story was *Thomas Cromwell.* It is no co-incidence that his surname reappears in English history one hundred years later. Oliver Cromwell was the great-great-grandson of Thomas Cromwell's sister, Katherine. As the Lord Protector of England during the Civil War, Oliver Cromwell was the only man to rule England when the country was a republic. Although he died a natural death, Cromwell's body was exhumed, decapitated and hanged in chains by Charles II following the restoration of the monarchy in 1660.

Anne of Cleves' brother, *William, Duke of Cleves*, continued to rule his duchy until his death in Düsseldorf in January 1592. Having divorced Jeanne d'Albret in 1541, he married Maria of Austria five years later. They had seven children, most of whom made politically important marriages for themselves. William spent much of his reign building palaces and fortifications in Cleves, some of which may still be seen today.

Anne's older and more beautiful sister, *Sybille*, married the Elector of Saxony, John Frederick I, "The Magnanimous." She married him in 1527 and had four sons. She must have been a strong character as, during her husband's absence during the siege of Wittenberg, she was responsible for defending his city. She died in February 1554, and he died three weeks later, aged forty-two.

Like Anne, her younger sister, *Amalia*, also had her portrait painted by Holbein. She is depicted as a severe young woman looking directly at the painter. She died in 1586 aged sixty-nine and was thus the longest living of the three sisters.

According to an article by Retha M. Warnicke, and the book, *Anne of Cleves* by Mary Saaler, Amalia never married. Other sources disagree and say she may have married Herman op den Graeff van de Aldekerk. However, what we do know to be true is that she wrote a book of songs of which copies may be found in Berlin and Frankfurt. In her will, Anne of Cleves left Amelia a diamond ring.

And what of ***Hans Holbein the Younger***, the painter whose portrait of Anne of Cleves is at the heart of this story? He continued to paint 'likenesses' of the rich and famous for only four more years after his famous portrait of Anne had brought her into the Tudor spotlight. He died in November 1543, but his portraits live on today in museums and art and history books, one of the best-known ones being of Anna von Jülich-Kleve-Berg, better known to us as Anne of Cleves.

The famous and fateful oil and tempera portrait itself still exists and can be seen in the Louvre, Paris.

Bibliography

Although *Anne of Cleves: Henry's Luckiest Wife* is a novel, it is based on historical facts. To write this book, in addition to various Internet sites, I consulted the following sources:

Mike Ashley, *British Monarchs*, Robinson Publishing, London, 1998

Peter Brimacombe, *Life in Tudor England*, Pitkin/Jarrold Publishing, Andover,
Hants., 2006

J. Cannon & R.Griffiths, *Oxford Illustrated History of the British Monarchy*, Oxford
Univ. Press, 1988

Carolly Erickson, *Great Harry: The Extravagant Life of Henry VIII*, Robson Books,
London, 1998

Petronelle Cook, *Queen Consorts of England: The Power Behind the Throne*, Facts on
File Inc., New York, 1993

Antonia Fraser, *The Wives of Henry VIII*, Phoenix, London, 2002

Robert Hutchinson, *Thomas Cromwell: The Rise and Fall of Henry VIII's Most
Notorious Minister*, Phoenix, London, 2007

Andrew Langley, *History of Britain: The Tudors*, Heinemann, London, 1997

David Loades, (Gen. ed.) *Chronicles of the Tudor Kings*, Bramley Books, Godalming,
Surrey, 1996,

David Loades, *Henry VIII & His Queens*, Amberley, Stroud, Glosc., 2010.

Elizabeth Norton, *Anne of Cleves: Henry VIII's Discarded Bride*, Amberley, Stroud,
Glosc., 2010

Judith Richards, *Mary Tudor*, Taylor & Francis, London, 2008

Jasper Ridley, *The Tudor Age*, Constable & Robinson, London, 2002

Mary Saaler, *Anne of Cleves: Fourth Wife of Henry VIII*, Rubicon Press, London,
1997

Alison Sim, *Food and Feast in Tudor England*, Sutton Publishing, Stroud,
Glosc., 1997

David Starkey, *Six Wives: The Queens of Henry VIII*, Vintage, London, 2004

Retha M. Warnicke, *The Marrying of Anne of Cleves: Royal Protocol in Tudor*
England, Cambridge Univ. Press, Cambridge, 2000

Alison Weir, *The Six Wives of Henry VIII*, Arrow Books, London, 1995

Alison Weir, *The Children of Henry VIII*, Ballantine Books, New York, 1996

I would also like to take this opportunity to thank, Marion Lupu, my faithful editor.

She has worked with me on most of my novels and can spot a missing comma at fifty paces and an errant king at five hundred.

*

Printed in Great Britain
by Amazon

45601190R00168